BROTHERBAND
CHRONICLES
BOOK 2
THE INVADERS

PHILOMEL BOOKS
A division of Penguin Young Readers Group. Published by The Penguin Group.
Penguin Group (USA) Inc., 375 Hudson Street, New York, NY 10014, U.S.A.
Penguin Group (Canada), 90 Eglinton Avenue East, Suite 700, Toronto, Ontario M4P 2Y3,
Canada (a division of Pearson Penguin Canada Inc.). Penguin Books Ltd, 80 Strand, London
WC2R 0RL, England. Penguin Ireland, 25 St Stephen's Green, Dublin 2, Ireland (a division of
Penguin Books Ltd). Penguin Group (Australia), 250 Camberwell Road, Camberwell, Victoria 3124,
Australia (a division of Pearson Australia Group Pty Ltd). Penguin Books India Pvt Ltd,
11 Community Centre, Panchsheel Park, New Delhi—110 017, India. Penguin Group (NZ),
67 Apollo Drive, Rosedale, Auckland 0632, New Zealand (a division of Pearson New Zealand Ltd).
Penguin Books (South Africa) (Pty) Ltd, 24 Sturdee Avenue, Rosebank, Johannesburg 2196,
South Africa. Penguin Books Ltd, Registered Offices: 80 Strand, London WC2R 0RL, England.

Published simultaneously in Canada. Printed in the United States of America.
Edited by Michael Green. Design by Amy Wu. Text set in 13-point Centaur MT.

Library of Congress Cataloging-in-Publication Data is available upon request.

ISBN 978-0-399-25620-2
1   3   5   7   9   10   8   6   4   2

COMPANION TO THE BESTSELLING
RANGER'S APPRENTICE

BROTHERBAND
CHRONICLES

BOOK 2: THE INVADERS

JOHN FLANAGAN

PHILOMEL BOOKS - An Imprint of Penguin Group (USA) Inc.

ALSO BY JOHN FLANAGAN

The Ranger's Apprentice Epic

Book 1: The Ruins of Gorlan

Book 2: The Burning Bridge

Book 3: The Icebound Land

Book 4: The Battle for Skandia

Book 5: The Sorcerer of the North

Book 6: The Siege of Macindaw

Book 7: Erak's Ransom

Book 8: The Kings of Clonmel

Book 9: Halt's Peril

Book 10: The Emperor of Nihon-Ja

The Lost Stories

Brotherband Chronicles

Book 1: The Outcasts

*To my brother Pete, who made the
best wooden swords ever!*

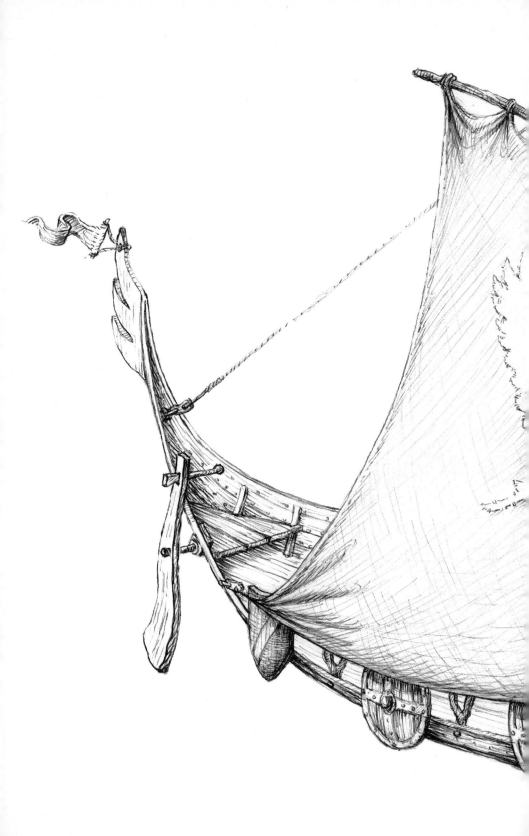

A Few Sailing Terms Explained

B ecause this book involves sailing ships, I thought it might be useful to explain a few of the nautical terms found in the story.

Be reassured that I haven't gone overboard (to keep up the nautical allusion) with technical details in the book, and even if you're not familiar with sailing, I'm sure you'll understand what's going on. But a certain amount of sailing terminology is necessary for the story to feel realistic.

So, here we go, in no particular order:

Bow: The front of the ship, also called the prow.

Stern: The rear of the ship.

Port and starboard: The left and the right side of the ship, as you're facing the bow. In fact, I'm probably incorrect in using the term *port*. The early term for port was *larboard*, but I thought we'd all get confused if I used that.

Starboard is a corruption of "steering board" (or steering side). The steering oar was always placed on the right-hand side of the ship at the stern.

Consequently, when a ship came into port it would moor with the left side against the jetty, to avoid damage to the steering oar.

One theory says the word derived from the ship's being in port—left side to the jetty. I suspect, however, that it might have come from the fact that the entry port, by which crew and passengers boarded, was also always on the left side.

How do you remember which side is which? Easy. *Port* and *left* both have four letters.

Forward: Toward the bow.

Aft: Toward the stern.

Fore-and-aft rig: A sail plan in which the sail is in line with the hull of the ship.

Hull: The body of the ship.

Keel: The spine of the ship.

Steering oar: The blade used to control the ship's direction, mounted on the starboard side of the ship, at the stern.

Tiller: The handle for the steering oar.

Yardarm, or yard: A spar (wooden pole) that is hoisted up the mast, carrying the sail.

Masthead: The top of the mast.

Bulwark: The part of the ship's side above the deck.

Belaying pins: Wooden pins used to fasten rope.

Oarlock, or rowlock: Pegs set on either side of an oar to keep it in place while rowing.

Telltale: A pennant that indicates the wind's direction.

Tacking: To tack is to change direction from one side to the other, passing through the eye of the wind.

If the wind is from the north and you want to sail northeast, you would perform one tack so that you are heading northeast, and you would continue to sail on that tack for as long as you need.

However, if the wind is from the north and you want to sail due north, you would have to do so in a series of short tacks, going back and forth on a zigzag course, crossing through the wind each time, and slowly making ground to the north. This is a process known as **beating** into the wind.

Wearing: When a ship tacks, it turns *into* the wind to change direction. When it wears, it turns *away* from the wind, traveling in a much larger arc, with the wind in the sail, driving the ship around throughout the maneuver. Wearing was a safer way of changing direction for wolfships than beating into the wind.

Reach, or reaching: When the wind is from the side of the ship, the ship is sailing on a reach, or reaching.

Running: When the wind is from the stern, the ship is running. (So would you if the wind was strong enough at your back.)

Reef: To gather in part of the sail and bundle it against the yardarm to reduce the sail area. This is done in high winds to protect the sail and the mast.

Trim: To adjust the sail to the most efficient angle.

Halyard: A rope used to haul the yard up the mast. (Haul-yard, get it?)

Stay: A heavy rope that supports the mast. The **backstay** and the **forestay** are heavy ropes running from the top of the mast to the stern and the bow (it's pretty obvious which is which).

Sheets and shrouds: Many people think these are sails, which is a logical assumption. But in fact, they're ropes. Shrouds are thick ropes that run from the top of the mast to the side of the ship, supporting the mast. Sheets are the ropes used to control, or trim, the sail—to haul it in and out according to the wind strength and direction. In an emergency, the order might be given to "let fly the sheets!" The sheets would be released, letting the sail loose and bringing the ship to a halt. (If *you* were to let fly the sheets, you'd probably fall out of bed.)

Way: The motion of the ship. If a ship is under way, it is moving according to its course. If it is making leeway, the ship is moving downwind so it loses ground or goes off course.

Back water: To row a reverse stroke.

So, now that you know all you need to know about sailing terms, welcome aboard the world of the Brotherband Chronicles!

John Flanagan

PART 1

SHELTER BAY

We can't keep this up," Stig said.

Hal looked at him, eyes red-rimmed from salt water and exhaustion. He'd been at the tiller of the *Heron* for the best part of ten days now. The storm winds had continued to sweep out of the southwest throughout that time, keeping them on a constant starboard tack—which was all to the good, as there had been no opportunity to repair the yardarm broken in the final brotherband race.

As first mate, Stig had tried to give Hal short breaks whenever he could. But the wind-driven waves had grown so high and steep that they were regularly breaking over the small ship and flooding her. Everyone on the crew was forced to bail continuously. They worked in teams of four, an hour on, an hour off. When a team's shift was over, the boys would fall, soaked and exhausted, to the deck, trying to snatch a few minutes' sleep, heedless of the freezing seawater constantly smashing over them. So Stig hadn't had much time to help Hal—not that Hal liked to hand over control. He felt the responsibility for the safety of his ship and crew deeply.

Stig glanced doubtfully back over the wake the *Heron* was carving. There was no pursuit in sight. But they'd be there somewhere.

"D'you think we're far enough away from Hallasholm now?" he asked.

In the hope of recovering the Andomal, Skandia's most sacred artifact, the boys had left the Skandian capital against the orders of the Oberjarl, Erak Starfollower. And they'd taken Hal's ship, *Heron*, which Erak had planned to confiscate. The boys were in no doubt that Erak would order a pursuit, and if they were caught, Stig didn't like to think what their punishment might be.

"I don't want to risk them catching us," Hal said.

Stig shrugged, and looked at the angry seas around them.

"They won't catch us if we sink," he said. "But that won't do us a lot of good."

"True," Hal said. "They may not have even left harbor yet. This storm's been blowing nonstop since we got away."

Whether they were being pursued or not, it was definitely time to look for a safe anchorage. Hal sensed that the wind had increased in force in the past half hour. White spray was being blown from the top of the waves. He gestured for the bigger boy to take the tiller, then ducked under the canvas screen into the small sheltered nook in the stern of the ship where he kept his navigation equipment and notes—notes he had assiduously collected during the brotherband training period.

He studied the chart for the eastern coast of the Stormwhite Sea for some minutes before he found what he wanted. The majority of bays and coves along this coast faced south—almost directly into the wind and sea. But then he spotted a small, almost insignificant gap that cut into the coastline, with its entrance facing north and with high ground on the southwestern side to provide shelter from the wind and sea. It looked an ideal place to set up a camp until the weather improved.

He carefully wrapped the notes in their waterproof oilcloth cover and ducked out into the open again. A breaking wave drenched him and set him spluttering. Then he grabbed hold of the backstay and climbed onto the stern bulwark, balancing easily against the ship's plunging motion, studying the coastline a few kilometers away.

There! He could make out one of the landmarks noted on the chart, a high headland, cliffs on either side, and denuded of trees. The dark granite rock was obvious against the gray-green of the pines that covered most of the coastline.

He dropped lightly to the deck and took the tiller once more. Thorn, sitting huddled in his soaked sheepskin jacket with his back to the mast, had noticed his movements. He came aft now to join the two boys.

"Thinking of putting in to shore?" he asked.

"There's a little sheltered bay about three kilometers southwest," Hal said. "I'm heading for that."

Thorn nodded. Not that Hal, as skirl of the *Heron*, needed his approval in any way. A skirl, even a young one, had absolute authority on his own ship. But Hal was glad that Thorn agreed. It would be foolish to ignore his opinion. The old sea wolf had seen a lot more storms at sea than either Hal or Stig.

In the event, they very nearly missed the entrance to the bay. Visibility was bad, with the air full of flying spray and rain, and the small gap between the headlands guarding the entrance had a high, timbered hill directly behind it, making it look as if the coastline was uninterrupted. At the last moment, Thorn's keen eyesight noticed a flash of sandy beach in the gap as *Heron* rose on a wave. He threw out his shortened right arm, pointing with the wooden hook Hal had fashioned for him.

"There it is!"

Stig and Hal exchanged a quick glance. There was no need to give Stig orders. He scrambled forward, beckoning Stefan and Jesper to join him at the ropes holding the reefed sail taut against the wind. As Hal brought the ship round to port, so that the wind was coming from astern, the three crew members eased the sail so that it stood out almost at right angles to the hull.

Heron, with the wind and sea now behind her, began to swoop over the rollers like a gull. It was an exhilarating sensation but Hal kept a watchful eye astern for rogue waves. If one came at them harder and faster than the others, the ship could easily be swamped from behind. There was no relaxing in this sort of weather.

After several minutes, he saw Thorn glance at him in an unspoken question and he nodded. They'd come close enough to the coast now to swing back to a course that would take them into the bay. As he heaved on the tiller and brought the bow round to starboard, Stig and the other two hauled in on the sail, setting it taut to the wind. The motion of the ship changed again, going from surging and swooping ahead of the wind back to the rolling, shuddering impacts of the waves coming from the beam. Hal glanced ahead and gauged his leeway—the amount the wind was setting the ship downwind and off course. He adjusted the ship's heading until he could see that he'd clear the entrance to the bay easily.

They glided into the bay. As the high surrounding cliffs masked the wind and waves, the *Heron* rode more upright, cutting smoothly through the calm waters. The boys relaxed as the motion eased. They sprawled on the rowing benches, setting aside the buckets they had been using to bail the water out. Only now, looking at them, did Hal realize how close they had been to utter exhaustion. He'd decided to look for shelter not a minute too soon, he reflected.

At the bottom of the bay was a strip of sandy beach, with wooded hills rising behind it. Hal pointed the bow toward it and the *Heron* responded, the bow wave chuckling down the hull, audible now that the noise of the storm had abated.

"Welcome to Shelter Bay," he said to Stig.

"Is that what it's called?"

Hal gave him a tired grin. "It is now."

Initially, they slept aboard the beached ship, with its heavy tarpaulin cover rigged as a tent to protect them from the weather. They had spent the previous ten days bracing themselves against the wild movements of the *Heron*, even when they slept. It was a welcome change to be able to relax completely, without having to subconsciously guard against a sudden lurch or roll that might pitch them against the hard timbers of the hull. But by the second morning, they set to work constructing a more permanent shelter, similar to the framed tent they had built for their brotherband training.

When they had retrieved their weapons and personal belongings from their brotherband campsite, Stig had experienced a flash of inspiration. He had stripped the canvas cover they had used as a roof and bundled it up, stowing it aboard the *Heron*.

"Never know when it might come in handy," he'd said.

Now Hal and the others appreciated his foresight. They cut and trimmed saplings from the forest to make wall and roof frames, then stretched the canvas tightly over the top to make a snug roof. The walls were lower than their original tent's but the pitched roof gave them ample headroom inside. Mud-daubed, woven sidewalls did a reasonable job keeping out the worst of the weather, although invariably there were chinks that let in the keening wind when it hit full power. But they were young and a few drafts weren't enough to dampen their spirits.

Thorn chose to sleep on the boat. With the others quartered in their tent, he had plenty of room to himself. The others respected his desire for privacy. He had spent many years alone and he had become accustomed to keeping his own company. Besides, even though he liked the *Heron* crew, they were teenage boys, with the usual tendencies of that breed to squabble, talk loudly and tell jokes they thought were brand-new, unaware that generations of boys before them had told the very same tales.

Once their sleeping quarters were organized, Hal, assisted by the ever-helpful Ingvar, built a small shelter to use as a workshop. Then he and Ingvar and Stig went into the forest to select a sapling to replace the broken yardarm. After several hours, Hal found one to his liking and gestured to Stig.

"Cut it down."

Ingvar carried the sapling back to the camp, where they stripped off the bark and left the sapling to dry for a few days, removing the surface sap. Then Hal cut and trimmed it to shape and they attached the port sail. Only then did Hal feel a sense of relief. Being ashore with a half-crippled ship had been preying on his mind, he realized. Now the *Heron* was fully ready for sea in case of any emergency.

He set up a roster for camp chores, with each boy taking a turn at cooking. This didn't last long. After successive meals prepared by Stig, Ulf and Wulf, Edvin had put his foot down.

"I didn't come on this quest to die of food poisoning," he said acerbically. "I'll do the cooking from now on."

And since he had already demonstrated some skill in this area, the others were glad to leave the task to him. In turn, Hal relieved him of other camp duties, such as wood and water gathering. After a few days, Edvin sought Hal out with a further request.

"We've got plenty of dried foods and provisions," he said. "But we could use fresh meat and fish."

The bay was teeming with fish, and Stig and Stefan were both keen anglers. They undertook to keep a steady supply of bream and flounder coming. Hal and Jesper went into the woods in search of small game. Once again, Ingvar went along as Hal's faithful shadow. Unfortunately, he was a good bit noisier than a shadow, blundering through and into the trees, stepping carelessly on deadfalls. So while the two hunters saw plenty of evidence of small game—rabbits, hares and game birds—they saw none of the actual creatures themselves. Eventually, Hal had to put his hand on the huge boy's arm and stop him.

"I'm sorry, Ingvar, but you're making too much noise."

"I'm not doing it on purpose," Ingvar said.

The young skirl nodded. "I know. But you're scaring all the game away. I want you to sit here and wait for us, all right?"

Ingvar was disappointed. Since he had joined Hal's crew, he had felt a new sense of worth and purpose. In his short life before this, nobody had ever looked to him to contribute, or expected much of him. But as a member of the Heron brotherband, he had participated in their success and their victory over the other teams. Hal had been the first person to expect anything of Ingvar and Ingvar hated to feel that he was letting his skirl down—although, deep down, he knew Hal was right. He was too clumsy and noisy to help with the hunting. But now that all the heavy work of building was finished, he had nothing to do.

"All right, Hal. If you say so." He lowered himself to the ground, leaning back against the bole of a tree. Hal saw the disappointment on his face.

"Ingvar, don't worry. I've got a job in mind for you. And you'll be the only one who can do it. Just be patient."

Leaving Ingvar a little mollified, Hal and Jesper continued farther into the woods. Almost immediately, Ingvar's absence bore fruit. They hadn't gone fifty meters before they saw a plump rabbit, nibbling at the moss on the base of a fallen log on the far side of a large clearing.

Jesper put his hand on Hal's arm and pointed. Carefully, Hal unslung his crossbow. Putting his foot in the stirrup, he drew the heavy cord back with both hands until the retaining latch clicked into place.

The rabbit looked up warily at the sound and both boys froze. The fat little animal's nose quivered as it tested the air, and its long ears swiveled back and forth, searching for any further foreign sound. By sheer chance, they had come upon it from a downwind direction. They waited, holding their breaths, until the animal satisfied itself that it was safe to continue grazing.

Hal slowly raised the crossbow to his shoulder. He flipped up the rear sight. They were less than twenty meters from the rabbit, so it would be a flat shot, with no elevation necessary. He set the bottom mark on the sight against the foresight pin, let out his breath, took in half a breath and held it.

Then squeezed the release.

There was the usual ugly *crack* as the bow's limbs snapped forward and the bolt streaked away across the clearing.

"I got him!" Hal said triumphantly. He dashed across the clearing, Jesper following a little more slowly.

"You certainly did," Jesper said dryly as he caught up with the triumphant shooter. "The question is, where is he?"

The heavy, iron-tipped crossbow bolt, designed to penetrate chain mail, had totally demolished the rabbit. The crossbow might be a useful weapon in a battle. But for hunting small game, it was sadly deficient.

"Maybe we should build some snares," Jesper said.

J esper and Stefan were arguing. Again. The weather was miserable, with the wind blowing constantly and regular showers of rain slanting in from the sea. There had even been occasional flurries of snow. As a result, the crew tended to stay inside their tent, lying on their bedrolls and staring at the canvas ceiling above them. It was inevitable that arguments would break out—simply as a way of passing the time. The twins, Ulf and Wulf, bickered as a matter of course, but now the malaise had spread to the others—and Jesper and Stefan seemed to find plenty of reasons to disagree.

Thorn and Stig could hear their raised voices as they trudged into the camp, back from a patrol of the woods behind the beach. As an old warrior, Thorn was never comfortable with his back to the sea and the ship beached unless he knew there was no potential enemy nearby. He looked around, searching for Hal. But he and Ingvar were busy in the tent workshop he had set up some distance away. They were building something, Thorn knew. But he had no idea what it was.

"I know you took it!" Stefan was saying. "Why don't you just admit it and give it back?"

"Oh, you know, do you? And how do you know that?" Jesper's voice challenged him.

"Because everyone knows you're a th—" Stefan stopped himself just in time.

"A 'th . . .'?" Jesper said, his voice even more furious. "What do you mean, a 'th . . .'? Were you perhaps going to say *thief*?"

"I didn't say that," Stefan said, now sullen and wary.

"Oh, for Gorlog's sake!" Stig muttered. He pushed the canvas screen aside and stepped into the tent.

Ulf, Wulf and Edvin were lying on their bedrolls. Stefan and Jesper faced each other in the center of the tent. Both were red faced and angry.

"Will you two shut it?" Stig said wearily. "You've been picking away at each other for days. What is it now?"

"Jesper stole my whetstone!" Stefan said.

Instantly, Jesper shot back. "You say!"

"Yes, I do! I know you took it. You . . . take things. Everyone knows that."

Too late, Stig realized that he hadn't stopped the argument. He'd merely taken it back to its starting point. "Look, let it—"

"Maybe I do take things sometimes," Jesper shouted over him, leaning closer to Stefan. "It's a challenge. But I always give them back!"

"Well, give back my whetstone!"

"I would, if I'd taken it. But I didn't! There's no challenge taking your things. You're always leaving them lying around."

"That's true," Ulf said, and instantly Wulf was into the argument as well.

"You should talk! Your kit is always scattered all over my sleeping space!" In fact, the previous day, he had found one of Ulf's socks lying beside his bedroll. Since it was an excellent sock, he had appropriated it but, in his eyes, that didn't alter the fact that it was infringing on his space.

"Maybe if you didn't take up more space than you should, that wouldn't happen!" Ulf cut back.

Then Stefan went back on the attack.

"Well, I didn't leave my whetstone 'lying around,' as you put it. So you must have taken it."

"Why me? Why not someone else?" Jesper shouted. "Why not Ulf, or Wulf?"

"Are you saying I took it?" Wulf said. He had a fleeting moment of guilt. Maybe Jesper had seen him slip Ulf's sock into his pack.

Jesper shook his head, exasperated. "No! I just was making a point that—"

"Well, I didn't!" Wulf said.

Of course, Ulf took that as his cue. "You probably did. It's just the sort of thing you'd do. Then you'd blame it on Jesper."

"Who blamed it on Jesper?" his twin yelled. "I never blamed it on Jesper!"

"No, but you stood by and let Stefan blame him, instead of owning up."

Stig looked around the tent at the angry faces. He met Edvin's steady gaze. Edvin leaned back on his pillow, closing his eyes.

"I give up," Stig said. "You're all barking mad."

Outside the tent, Thorn shook his head.

"I couldn't agree more," he said. He turned to trudge through the wet grass toward Hal's workshop. As he went, the angry voices from the tent followed him, accusation meeting counteraccusation.

"Boys," he muttered to himself. "Thank Lorgan I was never one!"

Hal and Ingvar were bent over a timber construction on the makeshift workbench Hal had built. It was a complex-looking arrangement, and Thorn, eyeing it, couldn't define any possible function for it. Hal looked up as he heard the old warrior approach.

"What are you making there?" Thorn asked.

Hal shrugged and flipped a length of canvas over the contraption to cover it from view.

"Just a couple of ideas," he said vaguely, gesturing round the inside of the shelter. Among the offcuts and stray lengths of timber was a strange open-topped box with a slot cut into its bottom and a flat-cut piece, rather like a broad, blunt blade, inserted into it. Once again, Thorn could divine no function for it and obviously Hal wasn't ready to discuss his ideas yet. Putting that aside, Thorn got back to the matter in hand.

"Well, while you're busy putting whatever that is together, you might be interested to know that your crew is falling apart."

"The crew?" Hal replied, frowning. "What's wrong with them?"

"They're bored. They've got nothing to occupy them. And they're starting to fight among themselves. Stefan has accused Jesper of taking his whetstone."

Hal shrugged. "Is that all? Well, that's not too serious. I suppose it's only natural that they're a bit bored. Once we get back to sea, things will be all right again," he said carelessly.

Thorn shook his head. "It *is* serious, Hal. Has it occurred to you that Zavac has a crew of over fifty men—all of them pirates and hardened fighters? While you've got a crew of boys who are spending their time squabbling over totally unimportant matters?"

Zavac was the pirate who had stolen the Andomal from under their noses. For a moment, Hal said nothing. Perhaps Thorn had a point, he thought. Thorn continued relentlessly.

"When you were doing your brotherband training, you built up a real spirit among this crew. You brought them all together into a disciplined force with a common purpose. They *were* a brotherband. Now they're deteriorating into a bunch of bored children. If you let that go any further, pity help you when you catch up with Zavac. If you don't whip them into shape, you'll get them all killed."

"Maybe so . . . ," Hal said, reluctantly facing the truth.

"That's if you ever catch up with Zavac! When you put to sea again, all that teamwork, all that sense of acting like a crew will have been eroded. You could well get them all killed in the first heavy seas you face. You know a wolfship is no place for petty jealousies or disputes. They've got to work together!"

"What do you want me to do?" Hal asked, and Thorn snorted.

"I want you to start acting like the skirl!" he said. "Take charge! That's what skirls do! Get your crew back into shape instead of wasting all your time here with these . . ." He gestured angrily at the unidentified items in the workshop. "Whatever they are!"

Hal colored slightly. "I'm not wasting my time. I'm working on a couple of ideas that will help us when we come up against the *Raven*," he said. The *Raven* was Zavac's ship.

Thorn rolled his eyes. "That's all very well. But they won't be much use to you without a crew! Get them off their backsides and get them doing something useful! Then you can come back to your contraptions."

"If you say so——" Hal began, but Thorn held up his wooden hook to stop him.

"Not if I say so. If *you* say so! It has to come from you. Let them know you're still the skirl."

"Are you sure it's as bad as you're making out?" Hal asked.

Thorn eyed him balefully for a few seconds before answering.

"Let me put it this way," he said. "Yesterday, Ulf and Wulf were arguing over their sleeping spaces."

Hal made a dismissive gesture. "Well, that's nothing. Ulf and Wulf are always arguing. It's what they do best."

"I'm not finished. The others have started taking sides in the argument," Thorn said. Hal's eyes opened wider at the words.

"That *is* a problem," he agreed. "We'd better go and sort this out. Come on, Ingvar."

Setting his tools back into their places in a rack behind the workbench, he strode out of the workshop, the immense Ingvar following behind him like a trained bear.

Thorn nodded in satisfaction. "And high time too," he said to himself.

Well, no wonder I couldn't see it!" Stefan was shouting as Hal entered the hut. "My space is too far from the entrance. It's dark and it's stuffy. It's all right for you! You get plenty of fresh air and light where you are!"

Jesper spread his hands, defeated by the lack of logic in Stefan's argument.

"Is that my fault?" he asked. Before Jesper could reply, Ulf interjected, taking a pace toward Stefan.

"You should complain! I'm right by the entrance. It's cold and it's drafty and last night someone trod on me when he went to the privy!"

"I suppose you think that was me," Wulf said, always ready to take offense when his brother spoke.

Ulf glared at him. "It probably was. It's the sort of thing you'd do."

"Except I didn't get up to go to the privy last night! So roll that up in your blanket and throw it in the creek!"

"Boys," Hal began, striving for a reasonable tone, "just calm down a . . ."

But his voice was drowned out by an outburst of squabbling from Ulf, Wulf, Stefan and Jesper. The twins continued to debate whether or not Wulf had gone to the privy; Ulf maintaining that, even if he hadn't, he wouldn't put it past his brother to get up simply to tread on him. Stefan and Jesper, meanwhile, had launched into a dispute over the inadequacies of Stefan's sleeping space, hard up against the rear wall of the hut. Hal, realizing that his voice would never carry over their heated words, turned to Ingvar and gestured for him to step forward.

"Shut them up, will you, Ingvar?"

The huge boy nodded. Hal knew from their brotherband training period that Ingvar's massive chest could produce a deafening volume of sound. He stepped away as he saw the large boy draw in a deep breath.

"QUIET!" Ingvar boomed. "QUIET, THE LOT OF YOU!"

Silence filled the hut as the four arguing boys were stunned by the sudden roar. They all turned and, for the first time, noticed Hal. Taking advantage of the sudden silence, he spoke before they could recover their wits and resume fighting.

"What in Gorlog's name is going on here? Are you all crazy? What are you arguing about?"

"My bed space is no good," Stefan said. "It's dark and it's too close to the back of the tent. It's stuffy. And the smell of everyone's dead socks gathers back there."

"You should try it by the entrance where I am!" Ulf said. "It's freezing!"

Hal looked at him, frowning. He had the space directly opposite Ulf's and he liked the fact that it provided plenty of fresh air. If it got a little drafty, it was a simple matter to pull the blankets up and huddle down under them. Hal quite enjoyed that, as a matter of fact.

"We drew lots for the sleeping spaces," he pointed out, striving to keep a reasonable tone.

Ulf shrugged petulantly. "Well, if I'd known I was going to be so close to the door, I would have drawn a different one."

Hal gave up trying to be reasonable. He glared at Ulf.

"Do you realize how abysmally stupid that statement is?" he demanded.

Ulf stepped back a half pace, disconcerted by the anger in Hal's voice. Hal was their skirl. The crew had elected him unanimously to that position and he had proved himself more than worthy of it. He had earned their respect and their loyalty. During brotherband training, he had shown an ability to outthink and outplan and outwit their opponents. He was an expert helmsman and navigator—qualities held in high esteem by all Skandians. Plus he had another indefinable quality—an air of natural authority and leadership. All of those things combined to earn Ulf's respect and deference. As a result, when Hal became angry, as he was now, Ulf tended to back down. If Hal was a natural leader, Ulf was a natural follower.

"Well, I . . . er . . ."

Hal stopped him with a dismissive gesture and turned to the others.

"Anyone else got a problem with his bed space?" he demanded.

The others exchanged looks. Stig was the first to speak.

"I'm fine," he said.

Edvin, Wulf and Jesper all mumbled agreement. From behind him, Hal heard Ingvar's deep rumble.

"I'm happy where I am."

"And so am I," Hal said, turning his gaze on Ulf and Stefan. "So that leaves just you two, correct?"

Both boys looked uncomfortable, realizing that they were very much in the minority. Stefan shrugged awkwardly.

"Well, as I said, my space is kind of dark and—"

"No need for a speech," Hal told him sharply. "Just yes or no will do fine. Do you have a problem with your bed space?"

Stefan looked around the tent, as did Ulf. Neither of them saw any support or sympathy from their companions.

"Um . . . yes. I guess so," Stefan said finally.

Hal switched his gaze to Ulf. "And you? You're not happy either, is that right?"

"Er . . . yes. I suppose so."

"Good," said Hal. "In that case, you two can swap."

There was a moment of silence. The other boys turned away to hide their smiles. Stefan and Ulf stared at Hal, not completely sure that they'd heard him.

"What?" Stefan said finally.

"Swap spaces. You take Ulf's. He takes yours. Do it now."

"But . . . ," Ulf began. In truth, he was relatively content with his space by the entrance. He had simply been complaining for the sake of having something to say. And Stefan felt much the same. His spot at the rear of the hut was warm and cozy. It might get stuffy occasionally, but that was a small matter in this cold weather.

Both boys realized how foolish they would appear if they changed their minds now. Still they hesitated.

"I can have Ingvar do it for you if you like," Hal prompted, and that was enough to stir them into activity. They knew that if Ingvar moved their belongings, he would drop and scatter things through the hut. They changed places, moving their bedrolls and small piles of possessions and spare clothes to their new positions.

As Stefan laid out his bedroll, a gust of icy wind shook the hut. The canvas flap by the entrance did little to stop it. He looked reluctantly back to his former cozy spot at the rear, where Ulf was now spreading his own bedroll. He sighed. He supposed he should feel resentment toward Hal but he was honest enough to admit that it was all his own fault. Like Ulf, he had only been complaining because it was one of the few activities available to them. Hal had done nothing more than call his bluff.

Hal watched, standing with his arms folded over his chest, as the two boys changed places. The others lay on their bedrolls, propped up on their elbows and watching with wide grins. They admired the way Hal had cut the ground from under the two complaining crew members. Their smiles faded when the changeover was complete and Hal's voice cracked out a new command.

"All right, everyone! Off your backsides and outside! Right away!"

They rose uncertainly. Jesper frowned as he looked out through the entry and turned back toward his bedroll.

"It's raining," he said. "Why do we have to go outside?"

He felt an iron grip on his left arm and looked round to see Stig's face a few centimeters from his own.

"Because your skirl says so!" Stig told him, grinning fiercely. "Now, move!"

Then Jesper was propelled through the canvas curtain and sent staggering on the wet grass outside. He stood disconsolately, waiting for the others to join him. One by one, they straggled out of the hut.

Stig was the last to leave. He paused by Hal's side as he went.

"Nice to have you back in charge," he said.

Hal nodded apologetically. "Sorry I've let things slip. Form them up out there, will you?"

Stig nodded, still grinning, and followed the others out into the open. Hal waited a few seconds, took a deep breath, then went out to join them.

He saw Thorn was off to one side, sitting on a log. The ragged old sea wolf nodded discreet approval. Obviously, he had heard everything that went on inside the hut.

The other members of the crew were lined up in a semicircle, waiting for him. Stig was at the right-hand end of the line. Hal stepped forward and looked keenly along the line of faces, taking particular note of Ulf and Stefan. He was pleased to see no trace of continuing resentment in their expressions. To be truthful, they both had a grudging admiration for the way Hal had handled their complaints. Jesper, he noted, looked a little sulky, possibly because of his rough handling from Stig. Hal shrugged mentally. Jesper often looked sulky. The other boys were waiting expectantly to hear what he had to say.

"We've lost our edge," Hal told them, and he saw a few of them look at him curiously. "We spent three months in brotherband training getting fit, learning weapon craft and seamanship. Best of all, we learned to function as a brotherband—to work together as a team and help one another. Now that seems to have evaporated. We've become strangers again."

The boys exchanged glances and he could see their reluctant agreement with what he had said. Edvin took a half pace forward.

"We're bored," he said. "It's as simple as that. There's nothing to do here but lie around all day."

Several of the others mumbled agreement. Hal hid his delighted smile. He could have cheerfully hugged Edvin for stating the problem for him.

"That's right," he said. "And that's going to change. Starting tomorrow, we're going back into training."

There was a mixed reaction to that. Stig, Edvin and Stefan nodded instant approval. The twins considered it for a few seconds and then nodded too. Jesper, predictably, was the one to raise an objection.

"Training? What sort of training?"

Hal met his gaze steadily until Jesper dropped his eyes. "The sort of training we did in brotherband. Weapon skills. Fitness training. Seamanship. Sail handling."

"But we've done that. Why do it again?"

Hal stepped closer to Jesper to make his point.

"We did it for three months. Three months! Do you think we know it all after such a short period? And we're looking to confront the *Raven* and its crew of fifty pirates. They're warriors who've spent all their lives fighting and killing. Do you think three months' training has prepared us to face them? Because I don't. And I want to get the Andomal back when we catch up with them, not get killed in the attempt." He turned toward Thorn, still sitting on the fallen log.

"Thorn!" he called. "Will you take on the position of trainer?"

The shaggy figure stood slowly from the log and walked across to join them.

"With pleasure," he said when he was closer.

Stig raised a hand to get Hal's attention. "Hal, you said we'd practice seamanship and sail handling. How can we do that while these storms keep blowing?"

Hal nodded his appreciation of the question. "We'll set up a mast onshore here and rig the sails and yardarms to it. We'll make it so that Ingvar can turn it according to the wind, and we'll work on our sail handling and trimming skills. If there's calm weather, we'll put to sea, or do training in the bay."

Stig thought about the answer, his head tilted to one side. "Good idea," he said.

Hal grinned. "I thought so." Then, as another hand was raised, he turned a little wearily back to Jesper. "Yes, Jesper. What is it now?"

"Well, no offense," he began, and Hal had a moment to reflect that whenever people began with "no offense" they invariably went on to be extremely offensive. "But what qualifies Thorn to train us? I mean . . . he's Thorn, after all. No offense," he repeated.

Thorn smiled at him but the smile never reached his eyes.

Hal turned to him. "Thorn, would you like to show Jesper how qualified you are?"

Thorn appeared to think about the question. Then he moved

with blinding speed, covering the ground between himself and Jesper.

Jesper, a former thief, was accustomed to moving quickly when threatened. But he never had time to register that Thorn was moving. The old sea wolf's left hand closed on Jesper's collar in an iron grip and he hoisted the boy off his feet, holding him suspended, his feet dangling clear of the ground.

Then he gathered himself and hurled Jesper away like a sack of potatoes. The boy flew several meters through the air, hit the ground and lost his footing, crashing over on his back. As he lay winded, he looked up into Thorn's bearded face, a face wreathed in a fierce smile.

"How's that for qualifications?"

Jesper nodded several times, and waved weakly in reply.

"Tha's pretty good," he gasped breathlessly. "Pretty good indeed."

There was only the faintest glow of light touching the tops of the trees on the eastern headland when Thorn woke the boys the following morning.

Perhaps *woke* is a little misleading. It implies a certain amount of care and consideration. The old sea wolf erupted into the hut, bellowing at the top of his voice and jerking blankets from cowering, whining forms. He carried a long baton made from a trimmed hickory branch and he beat noisily on the frames of the hut to punctuate his cries.

"Up! Up! Up!" he roared. "There's perfectly good daylight going to waste and we only get one chance at it before it's gone! On your feet and get dressed. Up! Up! Up!"

"What daylight?" Stig grumbled, bleary-eyed. "I don't see any daylight."

"There's plenty of it in the Eastern Steppes," Thorn told him. Of course, far to the east, the sun would have risen hours ago. Then he smiled evilly at Stig. "And if you don't get moving, I'll have you seeing stars."

He slammed the hickory baton down on the ground a few centimeters from Stig's head. Startled, the muscular boy sprang up from his bedroll and began fumbling for his breeches. Still half asleep, he managed to trip and fall as he pulled them on. Around him other members of the crew were having the same problem. Thorn surveyed them, shaking his head in disgust.

"What a bunch of doddering old biddies you are!" His eye fell on Hal, who was on hands and knees, searching for his clothes, unaware that they were hidden under the blankets that Thorn had dragged off him. He yawned, then the yawn turned into a yelp as Thorn gave him a none-too-gentle rap on the behind with the hickory baton.

"And you're the skirl!" Thorn said scornfully. "You should be leading the way, not blundering round on your hands and knees like a dozy old badger! Up! Up! Up!"

Within a few minutes, the Herons were standing in a ragged line outside the tent, some of them still fastening their pants and jackets, all of them tousle-haired and shivering in the cold, dim morning. The faint glow on the treetops was now a much more defined red. Stefan looked back enviously at his warm bed. In spite of Ulf's predictions that he'd freeze in his drafty new spot, he'd slept soundly and blissfully, until Thorn's insane yelling and banging had startled him awake.

Thorn, infuriatingly jovial and depressingly wide-awake, surveyed the sniffing, shuffling group.

"Gorlog's bleached and broken bones but you're a sorry lot!" he boomed. "You'd strike fear into any pirate's heart—once he stopped laughing. Now, let's get warmed up! Jump! Jump and clap your hands over your head. Come on!"

Reluctantly, they began to jump in place, slapping their hands together over their heads as they did so. Thorn strode down the line behind them, exhorting them to greater efforts with a stream of abuse and judicially placed whacks with the hickory baton.

Stig, next in line to Hal, muttered out of the corner of his mouth as he leapt in the air and clapped his hands.

"I think I preferred him when he was an old drunk. This rehabilitated Thorn is a bit hard to . . . OW!"

The exclamation was wrung out of him as Thorn, who had approached without Stig's being aware of it, put a little extra venom into a whack across his behind. Stung by the blow, Stig leapt somewhat higher than he had planned to, and Thorn chuckled.

"That's the way, Stiggy boy! Higher and harder! Show the others how to do it!"

Stig bit back an angry retort and continued to leap and clap. As he did so, he realized that already he was warming up. The blood was flowing freely through his legs and arms and warming his extremities. And, as he breathed deeply with the exercise, the oxygen he was dragging into his lungs was driving the sleepiness away.

Beside him, Hal grinned at him unsympathetically. People always find it amusing when they see a friend suffering, Stig thought.

"Serves you right for talking . . . OW! OW!"

Hal was sure that Thorn had moved away from behind them. Now he realized that the shabby old sea wolf had sneaked back, unnoticed. Not for the first time, he marveled at how quietly and quickly Thorn could move these days.

"Should be setting a better example, skirl!" Thorn guffawed.

Some of the other Herons laughed as well. Ruefully rubbing his stinging behind, Hal reflected on Thorn's tactics. By punishing the skirl, he made sure that there could be no charges of favoritism leveled at him. And it definitely raised the spirits of the others to see Hal leap in shock—just as it had cheered him when it happened to Stig.

Thorn moved down the line, pausing behind Ingvar. The huge boy was barely leaving the ground. His face was set in determined lines and he tried to hurl himself higher from the ground with each leap. It was his sheer size that was keeping him earthbound. But he was *trying*. Thorn watched him approvingly for several seconds, nodding to himself. There was a lot of value in Ingvar, he thought, shortsighted or not. Ingvar's sense of loyalty to Hal meant he was always first to volunteer when there was a task to be done.

"Don't hit me, Thorn," Ingvar said, some sixth sense warning him that Thorn was behind him. "I'm jumping as high as I can."

"I can see that, Ingvar," Thorn said softly. He moved on, casually flicking the hickory baton at Ulf's backside as he went.

"Ow!" Ulf cried. "What did you do that for?" He'd been jumping and clapping his hands as high and hard as he could.

"My mistake," Thorn said. "I thought you were your brother."

"Oh. That's all right then," Ulf replied.

Thorn frowned, wondering at the twisted logic in the statement. Finally, he rounded the end of the line of leaping, clapping boys and moved to stand before them.

"That's enough!" he yelled and, gratefully, they stopped their leaping and cavorting. A few of them leaned forward, resting their hands on their knees to breathe deeply. There were one or two coughs from the line of boys.

"You really have let yourselves go, haven't you?" Thorn chided them. There was no answer. The boys were embarrassed to realize that he was right. It had been several weeks now since they had been subjected to this sort of rigorous exercise, whereas during their brotherband training it had been a daily event. Even during the run down the coast in the *Heron*, they hadn't had to row. They'd had a constant wind on the beam the whole time.

"Very well," Thorn continued. He pointed down the long, curving beach that ran along the edge of the bay. "It's time for a run."

The boys looked in the direction he was pointing and groaned. The beach was almost two kilometers long.

"Down and back," he said. "Right to the far end. And you see that nice, firm sand along the water's edge?"

He waited until they looked and then nodded that yes, they could see it.

"Well, we're not going to run in that, are we? We're going to run in that nasty, soft, dry sand above the high watermark. Much better for us."

"Us?" Stefan queried. "Are you coming too?"

Thorn regarded him, a light of amusement in his eyes. "Well, now, what do you think?"

Stefan shrugged resignedly. "I think you're staying here."

"And who said you were slow on the uptake?" Thorn replied. Then he made a shooing gesture at them. "Off you go. And remember, no walking. I'll be watching you all the way."

The boys turned and set off in a ragged group, Jesper quickly moving to the lead. As they straggled away, Thorn barked out a command.

"Edvin! Not you! Back here!"

Edvin dropped out of the group and walked back to where Thorn stood, his head tilted curiously.

"Did I do something wrong?" he asked, eyeing Thorn's hickory baton warily.

Thorn shook his head. "Not at all. Get a fire started. Make tea and get some bacon and bread ready for them when they get back. They'll need a good breakfast."

There was a warmth and a level of concern in his voice that belied his previous uncaring manner as he'd stalked along the line of leaping, clapping boys. Edvin, placing dry kindling in a pyramid stack in the fireplace, watched the old warrior shrewdly.

"You're not really as mean as you make out, are you?"

Thorn eyed him coldly. "Oh yes, I am," he replied. "And you'll find out just how mean I can be if you tell anyone otherwise."

Sometime later, the Heron brotherband straggled back into the campsite. They had strung out during the run. Jesper was well in the lead when they returned and Thorn noticed that the boy was barely breathing hard. Ulf, Stefan and Wulf came in next, and finally Hal and Stig arrived, each one holding an arm of the lumbering Ingvar. Thorn pursed his lips. A shame, he thought. Ingvar was so big and powerful and he had enormous reserves of strength. It was his poor vision that was holding him back. It made him clumsy because he was constantly worried about losing his balance. He could see just enough to make him fearful.

Thorn rapped the baton on his leg. Maybe there was something he could do about that, he thought.

Then, absentmindedly, he rapped a little harder than he'd intended.

"Ow!" he muttered, making a mental note not to do that again. He glanced up and saw that several of the Herons, now tucking into hot bread and bacon, were grinning at him. He scowled and the grins disappeared.

But he knew those grins were still there, below the surface, and he was glad of the fact. He didn't want them cowed and resentful. He needed to build their spirits and help them regain the esprit de corps they had lost during the long, boring days in camp.

He beckoned Edvin over. "Have you eaten yet?" he asked.

Edvin shook his head. "I've been busy serving the food out. I was just about to."

"Then put it to one side to stay warm. It's your turn for a run now."

Edvin looked stricken. "But I'm the cook!" he protested.

"Yes, you are. And if you find yourself facing some blood-thirsty pirate intent on separating you from your head, I'm sure you can tell him that."

He paused while Edvin assessed that and slowly nodded grudging agreement.

"I see your point," he said.

Thorn patted him on the shoulder. "Besides, this way you can see that I *am* really as mean as I make out," he said. Then he ruined the effect of that statement by pointing to a small grove of trees halfway down the beach.

"No need to run the whole way. Just to those trees and back. Then you can have your breakfast."

Edvin turned away, then turned back again.

"Thorn," he said, "don't worry. I won't be telling anyone that you're not mean."

"Does my heart good to hear it," Thorn told him. Then he made that same shooing motion and Edvin set off down the beach, watched curiously by the other boys. They had finished eating and were leaning back, relaxing, as they drained the last of their hot tea. The relaxation didn't last long as Thorn chivvied them to their feet.

"All right! More work to do! Wash and clean up the camp. Someone take care of Edvin's gear, then be back here in fifteen minutes! Bring your saxe knives."

The boys quickly went to work, washing in the chilly waters of a stream that ran out of the woods and down to the bay, then setting the campsite to rights. By the time Edvin had returned and eaten his delayed breakfast, they were grouped around Thorn. He looked thoughtfully at Hal.

"This contraption you're working on," he said, nodding toward Hal's workshop tent. Hal nodded. "Is it important, or is it just some highfalutin idea—like that running water system you built in your mam's kitchen?"

Hal sighed. "Am I ever going to live that down?"

Thorn pushed out his bottom lip thoughtfully, then looked at Stig. "What do you think, Stig?"

The tall boy shook his head. "I shouldn't think so," he replied.

"Me either," Thorn said. He turned back to Hal. "Well, what do you say?"

Hal gave both his friends a resigned look before he answered. "This one is worthwhile," he said. "It could give us an edge over Zavac and his men when we catch up with them."

Thorn nodded, satisfied. "In that case, get on with it. I suppose you need Ingvar?"

"Yes. He's been helping me with it."

Thorn looked at Ingvar and gestured with his thumb. "All right, Ingvar, you stay and help Hal. The rest of you come with me."

"What are we doing?" Ulf asked.

"We're gathering vines and young beech saplings to make rope. Lots of rope."

"Why do we want lots of rope?" Wulf asked, and his brother scowled at him. He had been going to ask that question.

"Because when you make a net, you need lots of rope," Thorn replied. Then, seeing several mouths open, he forestalled the next question. "And don't anyone ask why we need a net."

Erak and Svengal watched the waves surging through Hallasholm's narrow harbor mouth. Where they smashed against the protective rock walls on either side, white spray exploded high in the air. The two sea wolves heard the deep boom of the waves as they broke, and felt the impact as a dull vibration underfoot. The unbroken section of each wave that passed through the entrance swept across the harbor until it hit the solid quay. For a second, that wave would seem to gather itself, then it would heave up and green water would surge over the quay, up to a meter deep, only smashing itself into spray when it hit the inland retaining wall.

The wind was remorseless, blowing in from the southwest and keening through the masts and rigging of the ships hauled up to safety on the beach, well above the high watermark. There was a constant rattle of loose halyards as they snapped back and forth against the masts.

Wolfwind, Erak's wolfship, was on the beach. Sensing that the weather was going to deteriorate further, Svengal had moved her from her customary position against the quay, opposite the harbor entrance. The surging waves there now made it too dangerous for the ship. No matter how many wicker fenders they might put along her sides to protect her from the quay wall, in this sort of weather, they'd soon be mashed and splintered, and then the hull itself would begin to take the damage.

In the event of a freak wave, there was even the chance that she might be swept bodily onto the quay.

Like the other ships on the beach, she had a long tarpaulin tented over the open hull to keep out the worst of the wind and spray. Erak inspected her thoughtfully.

"She's fitted out and provisioned?" he asked.

Svengal nodded patiently. It was only the tenth time Erak had asked him this question in the past week.

"As far as she can be. There are some perishables we'll take on board at the last minute: bread, meat and fresh water. And there's other equipment that I don't want soaked by the rain and spray. But once this storm dies down, we'll be ready to go in an hour."

Erak grunted moodily, looking at the sea once more and sniffing the air.

"Once this storm dies down," he repeated. "Whenever that might be."

"It can't last much longer," Svengal said optimistically. "It's been blowing now for ten days straight."

"Knew a storm when I was a boy that blew nonstop for over a month," Erak replied.

Svengal raised an eyebrow. "So you keep telling me, chief. But think about it. Storms like that don't happen very often. You were a boy, and that's a long time ago."

Erak glanced sidelong at his former first mate, bridling at what he saw was an implied insult.

"It's not that long," he said stiffly. "I'm not exactly on my last legs yet, you know."

Svengal rolled his eyes to the heavens. "You're not exactly in the first bloom of youth, either."

Erak squared his shoulders and turned to face Svengal directly.

"First bloom of youth?" he repeated incredulously. "*First bloom of youth*? That's a bit fancy, isn't it? When did you become a bard?"

"All right," Svengal replied. In fact, he'd heard the phrase in a love poem read to him by a strikingly attractive young lady a few nights ago and he'd been rather taken by it. Of course, it seemed more appropriate in her company than in Erak's. "If you prefer plain talk, let me put it this way. You're no spring chicken."

"Is that right?" Erak took a half pace closer to Svengal, his chest thrust out aggressively. Erak's chest was quite a substantial matter and there were men who might have quailed before such an obvious challenge. Svengal, however, wasn't one of them. He was every bit as bulky as Erak and he'd known the Oberjarl for many years. They'd sailed together, raided together, celebrated together and mourned lost shipmates together. He wasn't about to be intimidated by him now because he had a fancy title. He stood his ground and replied calmly.

"Chief, I'm not concerned with your advancing years," he said, and saw Erak's eyes narrow. "The point I'm making is that you *were* a boy when that storm lasted for a month. And that was many, many years ago. So it's not the sort of thing that happens frequently, is it?"

Erak's features softened a little. The glare died away from his eyes as he thought over Svengal's words. "I suppose not," he said reluctantly.

"So the odds are good that this storm won't last as long, aren't they?" Svengal persisted.

The Oberjarl nodded. "No. I suppose you're right."

"And in any event, whether it does or not, there's nothing you nor I nor my dear old aunt Bessie can do about it, is there?"

"I thought your dear old aunt was named Winfredia?" Erak challenged.

Svengal shrugged. "Aunt Bessie was her younger sister. A lovely woman, she was."

The Oberjarl shook his head. Svengal was fond of invoking his dear old aunts to make a point but their names seemed to change regularly. At last count, Erak could recall at least nine.

"In any event, what does she have to do with things?" he asked.

Svengal grinned at him. "She was fond of saying, *We can change our breeches. We can change our minds. But we can't change the weather.*"

"You just made that up," Erak said.

"Maybe, but that doesn't make it any less true. Or less wise. The fact remains, when the storm blows itself out, we'll be ready to go in an hour."

Erak harrumphed. The delay was chafing at him. He couldn't maintain Svengal's philosophical attitude to it. He wanted *Wolfwind* away and searching for the members of the Heron brotherband— and the pirate ship that had gotten away with the Andomal, the great treasure of the Skandian nation.

He glanced up at the wind-driven clouds racing across the sky. There was no sign of any abatement.

"It'll be just my luck if this is the first one since I was a boy that *does* last a month," he muttered.

Svengal considered the thought. "I suppose when you think about it, the fact that it hasn't happened in such a long time might make it more likely that it'll happen again now."

Erak frowned at him. "You're a great comfort," he said. Then he turned away toward the path leading back to the Great Hall. "No sense standing out here in the rain. Let's take a look at the charts and see if we can figure where they might have gotten to."

Svengal fell into step beside him. "Let's see if we can guess, you mean."

Erak grunted. "That too."

They strode into the Great Hall. The bad weather meant there were more men gathered there than usual, drinking and telling tall stories to pass the time. They glanced incuriously at Erak and his first mate and a few called greetings. Most of them could guess where the two men had been.

There was no standing to attention or any other signs of deference as Erak entered. Even though he was the Oberjarl, the supreme leader of all Skandia, Skandians didn't believe in bowing and scraping. They were a democratic lot and they liked to express their independence by a general show of indifference to their ruler—unless he was angry. Then they made sure they paid attention. Erak took no offense. He had behaved the same way to the previous Oberjarl.

Gort was one of a group of men sitting at a table to one side. Erak caught his eye and beckoned to him. Gort had been the instructor responsible for training the Heron brotherband. He probably knew more about their ship and its capabilities than anyone in

Hallasholm. Gort rose, carrying his ale cup, and crossed the Hall to join them.

"Need to pick your brain," Erak said, and led the way to his private rooms.

They seated themselves at a large wooden table. Most Skandian furniture was large, in keeping with the size of its owners. Erak spread a chart of the Stormwhite out before them and pondered it.

"We're trying to figure out how far Hal and his crew might have gone before they had to put in to shore," he explained.

Gort leaned forward, his eyes narrowing as he studied the chart. Truth be told, dead reckoning navigation wasn't one of his strong points. He'd instructed the boys in seamanship and weapon craft. But this was a relatively simple matter.

"One thing, chief," Svengal asked. "Why am I looking for the boys? Why not that thieving snake Zavac?"

Erak glanced up at him. "Obviously, if you can get a lead on Zavac, go after him. But there's a good chance the boys might have some idea where he's gone. They went after him almost immediately and the trail was still warm."

"So if I find them . . . ?" Svengal asked hesitantly. "Do you want me to bring them back?" He thought he knew what was in the Oberjarl's mind but he wanted it in black-and-white.

Erak shook his head. "Help them," he said. "There's only nine of them against Zavac's crew. They'll need you."

"They've got Thorn, of course," Svengal said.

Gort looked at him. "What is it about Thorn?" he asked. "He's just a broken-down old drunk, isn't he?" He recalled that Sigurd, the senior brotherband instructor, had once implied that there was more to Thorn than met the eye. But the conversation had been cut short.

Erak and Svengal exchanged a glance and Erak motioned for Svengal to explain.

"He used to sail with us," Svengal told the instructor. "And he was the best fighting man in our crew. Better than me. Better than Erak." He glanced at the Oberjarl for confirmation and Erak nodded briefly. "The only one who came close to him was his best friend, Mikkel—Hal's father."

Gort pursed his lips thoughtfully. "Still, what difference could one warrior make? Particularly a one-armed man?"

"He was more than just one warrior," Erak told him. "Thorn was the Maktig."

"Three years running," Svengal added, and that set Gort back in his seat.

"The Maktig?" he said. "Thorn?" The Maktig was the warrior acclaimed as the mightiest in all Skandia. Somehow, Gort couldn't equate that with the shabby, shambling figure that he knew. Then Svengal's words struck him and he stared in disbelief. "Did you say three years running?" he asked. He was twenty-nine years old, younger than Erak and Svengal, and he had no memory of the days before Thorn had lost his right hand. The other two nodded somberly.

"Nobody else has ever done that," Erak said. "So even with one hand gone, he's still a force to be reckoned with."

"Particularly since Hal made that false arm for him," Svengal said. "Did you see it? A big, studded club on the end of a false arm." He shook his head. "He's quite a boy, that one."

Erak nodded slowly. "That's why I want you to find them and help them."

"But you punished them," Gort said, frowning. "You disbanded them and told us to expunge all records of the Heron brotherband. And you told them to hand over that ship of Hal's."

"I know," Erak said. "I had to be seen to do that. They committed a terrible mistake letting the Andomal be stolen, so I had to punish them. But I also had to give them a chance to redeem themselves. Their only hope for any sort of future was if they could retrieve what they had lost."

"You knew they'd take off after Zavac?" Svengal asked. Erak had never admitted this to him before.

"I hoped they would. We can't afford to lose people like that. They have too much potential value. Hal is pretty much a genius when it comes to ship design, even if the *Heron's* spars are a little on the light side. And he's already an expert helmsman and navigator."

"He did lose a spar in that final race," Svengal protested.

Gort shook his head. "And he recovered from it. He handled the problem brilliantly by improvising. Anyone can make a mistake, Svengal. It's how they learn from it and recover from it that shows their true worth."

"I guess that's right," Svengal said. He leaned over the chart again. "Well, let's see where they might have gone, and where they could have taken shelter."

He made a circling gesture over a section of the coastline with his forefinger.

The others leaned closer. Svengal was pointing to the eastern coast of the Stormwhite, a politically unstable area where a number of small independent states, each more quarrelsome and vexatious than the other, had for years competed with one another to secure a section of coast for themselves. Some were barely larger than the cities or large towns that were their nominal capitals. Others might stretch for ten kilometers or more along the coast and into the hinterland behind—until a jealous neighbor annexed territory from them.

There were at least a dozen of these troublesome city-states and the situation between them was one of constant flux. The mapmakers of the time had long ago given up trying to keep track of them, and had arbitrarily marked the territory as belonging to Teutlandt. The rulers of Teutlandt blandly accepted this. But since their country was itself constantly racked with internal disputes and power struggles, they had no opportunity to actually claim the land granted them by mapmakers.

But then, Erak thought, mapmakers were notoriously lazy and they rarely traveled to this section of the world.

"They'd been gone about ten days before that storm really turned nasty," Svengal said. "I figure they would have gotten about this far."

But Gort was shaking his head once more. "In a normal wolf-ship, maybe. But the *Heron* is fast. She's a real flyer. And with the wind on her beam like that, she would have been pretty much on her fastest point of sailing—even with the sail reefed."

He paused, screwing his lips up in concentration as he moved his finger farther down the coast from the point Svengal had indicated.

"They could well have gotten this far," he said, and all three men leaned closer, studying the chart.

"Hal had a copy of this chart, of course?" Erak asked.

"It was issued to all the brotherbands in their navigation classes. Knowing Hal, he will have kept it."

"There," said Svengal suddenly. He was pointing to a small inlet, almost unnoticeable, on the coast. The entrance faced north and the bay inside was shielded by hills on the southwestern side. "That looks like the best shelter for kilometers along the coast. It faces away from the wind and it's shielded by this high headland. If you think they could have gone that far, I'll wager that's where I'll find them."

"If they haven't been sunk by the storm," Erak said, but Gort made a negative gesture.

"They won't. Hal's too good a seaman. And the Herons are a good crew." He glanced apologetically at the Oberjarl. Erak had commanded that no reference ever be made to the Heron brotherband. "Sorry."

Erak waved the apology aside.

"Then that's where I'll look for them," Svengal said, studying the chart intently and imprinting its details on his memory.

"If this storm ever stops," Erak said despondently, leaning back from the table.

Svengal grinned at him. "My dear old aunt Tabitha knows a bit about the weather," he said. "I'll see what she thinks."

Gort frowned at the two of them. "Your dear old aunt Tabitha?" He wasn't aware of any old lady in Hallasholm by that name. "Who the blazes is she?"

Erak turned a long-suffering look on him. "Don't ask," he said. "Just don't ask."

The Heron brotherband spent the rest of the day making meters of strong rope by twisting young, thin birch saplings and creepers together, then coiling it. At the end of the day, their fingers and wrists ached with the effort of twisting and weaving the tough strands. Hal and Ingvar continued to work in the small tent. The sound of cutting, sawing and hammering reached the others clearly. A few of them wondered what the two boys were up to.

"When Hal's ready, he'll tell us," Stig said. "He never likes to show his work too soon."

Just before sunset, Thorn called a stop to the rope making and sent them on another run down the beach while Edvin prepared dinner.

That night, after the meal, there was little talk and certainly no bickering. The exhausted boys were glad to crawl into their bedrolls. A few hours after dark, the camp was silent, with only the dark silhouette of Thorn hunched before the remains of the fire. When the coals finally died down, he walked quietly down the beach to the ship, climbed aboard and settled down for the night.

The following morning the routine started again before first light. Thorn's hickory stick beat a rattling tattoo on the hut frames, and on the backsides of any boys who were tardy in rolling out of their blankets.

He put them through their paces, flapping arms and leaping high into the air until they were thoroughly warmed up, then sent them off down the beach once more, while Edvin prepared a meal.

Wrapping a chunk of bacon in a slice of bread, Thorn busied himself laying the rope out in a grid pattern, some eight meters square. He adjusted the cross pieces so that the sides of the grid squares were about forty-five centimeters long. The crew arrived back, ravenous for breakfast. They grabbed their bread and bacon and hot tea and crowded round to study Thorn's handiwork.

"It's a net," Stig said. "Why do we need a net?"

Thorn said nothing. Boys and their questions, he thought to himself.

"Pretty big mesh," Stefan commented. "What are we going to catch in that? Bears?"

Thorn studied him for a moment, straight-faced.

"No. We're after an even more horrible prey," he said. Then, as Stefan cocked his head in a question, he added, "Teenage boys. They're not as fierce as bears, but they smell a whole lot worse."

"You're a fine one to talk about that," Hal told him.

Thorn raised his eyebrows. "I smell all right," he said.

"You smell, all right," Hal agreed.

Thorn looked at him suspiciously. "I had a bath only five weeks ago," he said, then decided there was no point bandying words with the young skirl.

"Tidy the camp. Then get back here," he said gruffly, and the boys, grinning, hurried to their chores.

The previous day, while they'd been cutting creepers and young birch strands, Thorn had collected a supply of tough vines, the thickness of thin cord. He tossed them on the ground when the boys returned.

"Tie the intersections of the net together," he said. Then he gestured to Ulf and Wulf. "You two, cut a bundle of stakes about half a meter long. Trim them and sharpen the ends."

"How many do you need?" Ulf asked.

Thorn thought for a few seconds. "Sixteen should be enough."

They set off into the forest. By the time they returned with the supply of stakes, the others had finished fastening the net together. Thorn inspected it, tugging at a few of the knots. But the boys had all been working with boats and ropes and knots since they were tiny and all of them were tight.

"Very well," he said. "I want this net suspended thirty centimeters above the ground on those stakes. Put a stake at each corner, then another halfway along each side. Pull the net so it's good and tight. I don't want it sagging."

"What's it for?" Stefan asked.

"Drop Bears," Thorn told him. He seemed to be completely serious and Stefan frowned. He seemed to recall he'd heard of Drop Bears somewhere before.

"Drop Bears?" he said doubtfully.

"Small bears with a light membrane between their front and

back legs that lets them glide for miles through the air. When they get tired, they fall out of the sky," Thorn told him. "This way, we'll be ready to catch one."

"As long as he's considerate enough to fall on this particular spot," Hal said.

Stefan sensed the smile in his voice and turned quickly. He saw the other Herons were all trying to hide grins and realized that he was the butt of a joke.

"Oh," he said. He considered taking offense, then realized there was no point in it. Thorn's joke wasn't malicious. He smiled in his turn, then challenged the others.

"But if you're all so smart, maybe one of you can tell me what this horizontal net is for?"

Thorn chuckled then. "Good point, Stefan." He looked at the others. "Well, do any of you superior geniuses have any idea what this is for?" They all looked suitably chastened. "Then let's find out. Weapons and shields and report back here. On the double!"

As they raced away to the tent to collect their weapons, Thorn smiled to himself. The little interplay between Stefan and the others was a good sign. A day ago, the exchange would have tended to be sarcastic and a fight may well have started. Today, after a day of physical exercise and hard work, followed by a good night's sleep and more exercise on top of it all, the atmosphere in the camp was already improving. The boredom had been relieved and the boys were eager to see what the net was for. There was a sense of purpose about the group once more. Thorn felt a small flush of pleasure to know that he'd helped create it.

The boys lined up expectantly with their weapons. Thorn

studied them thoughtfully. Stig would be the best to start with, he thought. He was athletic and well coordinated and balanced. He gestured to the tall boy.

"Stig. Over here. Put your two feet into the net. Leave one square gap between them."

Puzzled, Stig did as he was told, stepping into two of the gaps along the side of the net. He looked at Thorn.

"Now," said the old warrior, "I'm going to call directions and you follow them. You go forward, back, left or right as I tell you. I'll tell you how many steps to take each time. Do you follow?"

Stig nodded, frowning in concentration. He was beginning to see what this was about.

"All right. Shield up. Ax ready. Eyes up—there's a savage Magyaran facing you. Now start to move. Forward three . . . right two . . . back one . . . left two . . ."

As he called the moves, Stig performed the actions, lifting his feet high to clear the net and stepping lightly. At first, the instructions were slow and steady, but as Stig gained confidence, Thorn increased the pace, adding in *half left* and *half right* so the boy moved diagonally. As Stig moved, his face a study in concentration, Thorn would issue other commands, reminding Stig to keep his shield high or his eyes up.

After a minute or so, the inevitable happened. Stig caught his right foot in the net as he attempted to follow a command to move to the left and was sent sprawling. The others laughed, but each of them knew their shipmate had performed very well. Most of them doubted they could match his sure-footed movements for so long.

Crestfallen, Stig climbed to his feet. But he was rewarded by a nod of approval from Thorn, who then turned to survey the rest of the group.

"Nothing to laugh at. I doubt anyone else will do better."

The group nodded good-naturedly. But Jesper—why was it always Jesper, Hal thought—had to query Thorn.

"How about you, Thorn? Can you do it that well?"

Thorn considered the question, and the boy who had asked it, for several seconds.

"Hmmm. Good point. Can I do it? It's been a long time. I may have forgotten. But let's see." He held his wooden hook out to Stig. "Shield," he said, and Stig helped him slip the strap over his right arm, watching with interest as Thorn fastened the ingenious clamp onto the shield handle and tightened it.

"Ax," he said, when the shield was secure. He took it in his left hand and hefted it onto his shoulder.

He walked toward the net, pausing to look at the boys uncertainly.

"I wonder if this is such a good idea?" he said. Then he shrugged and sighed deeply as he stepped into the net. "Hal, you call the steps."

Hal hesitated a second, then began to call instructions, setting the same pace Thorn had begun with for Stig.

"Forward two . . . left three . . . right one . . ."

"Faster!" Thorn snapped, and Hal upped the pace.

"Left four, forward three, back two . . ."

"Faster!" Thorn called. "What's all the delay?"

"Right three forward one left two . . ."

"Faster! Come on! Faster!"

"Back-one-left-two-right-three-half-left-forward-one . . ."

And as Hal began to issue the orders in a seemingly nonstop volley, Thorn matched them easily, stepping high and confidently with each one, never missing a beat until he seemed to be dancing in the net, moving lightly on the balls of his feet, always in balance, always in motion. Then he began adding extra movements, lunging to the side with his ax as he stepped left, or raising the shield high over his head as he moved back. Once, he performed a complete turn, high stepping around through a full circle, as Hal hesitated in the call. A murmur of admiration and surprise was torn from the boys as they watched, their eyes riveted on the cavorting figure.

Then, ignoring the next set of orders, Thorn spun so he was facing them and they could see he had his eyes shut tight. Hal's voice fell silent as Thorn carried out an intricate pattern of steps, his feet never touching the ropes as he moved. Then, his eyes snapped open and he charged forward at the watching group of boys, moving at a full run and finally leaping off the ground with both feet to clear the net and land crouching before them, the shield up and the ax drawn back behind his head.

"YAAAAH!" he yelled at them, and startled, they drew back involuntarily.

Thorn straightened from his crouch, lowered the ax to the ground and smiled at Jesper.

"Well, what do you know?" he said. "I've still got it."

Jesper nodded several times. He was impressed—very impressed. And he made a mental note not to challenge Thorn quite so often in the future.

"Yes," he said. "I'd say you've still got it, all right."

"Thorn," Hal said, "can you tell us the point of this exercise?"

Thorn looked at him and nodded. Hal had a good grasp of the principles of commanding a crew, he thought. Sometimes, when you were first imposing discipline, it could be necessary to demand blind obedience. But there were other occasions when there was real value in an explanation. Men—and he thought of the crew now as men—performed better when they understood why they were being asked to carry out a task. With this exercise, he wanted more than blind obedience. He wanted that understanding, knowing it would lead to greater commitment and, in the long run, abilities that might save their lives.

"It's all about speed and agility," he said. "They'll be your biggest assets when we fight the *Raven*'s crew. They have experience on their side of the ledger. They've been raiding and fighting for years. You don't have that. But you're young. Your main assets will be your speed and agility when you fight. That's what we're going to be working on while we're here. Speed and agility. We'll work on them until we get them to the highest possible pitch for each of you. And if we do work on them, they may well save your lives."

He paused and looked around their faces, suddenly grim as they thought about what he had said. They could see beyond a bizarre exercise with a net between their feet. They were looking forward to a time when the sort of agility and speed of movement that Thorn had just displayed might well be the difference between winning and losing. Living and dying.

"Now," he said, nodding toward the net, "who's next?"

The morning wore on, and the rest of the crew took their turns in the net, with varying degrees of success. As Thorn had expected, Stig was the best at this drill, and he improved each time he stepped into the mesh and took a turn. But the old warrior was pleasantly surprised to see that Hal was not far behind him, and Jesper was pretty much equal to Hal. Of course, Jesper was a thief and thieves tend to be nimble and light-footed—as well as light-fingered. And Hal had always had a fine sense of spatial awareness. It was one of the qualities that made him such an outstanding helmsman.

Ulf and Wulf were both good, although each tended to sneer at the other's performance—ridiculous when you saw that one was the equal of the other. Stefan was capable but Edvin had problems with the drill, often snagging his foot and falling before he had gone three or four paces. He would set his face in a frown and try again—invariably trying to move too quickly and coming to grief again.

"Slow down," Thorn told him. "You have to work at it to let it become instinctive. Walk before you can run." Edvin glared at him, red faced and angry at what he saw as his own failure.

"Any other clichés you'd like to share with me?" he said.

Thorn took a deep breath before replying. His first instinct was to wallop Edvin over the back of the head for being so insolent. But he realized that the boy was trying. In fact, he was trying too hard. He could see the others performing the movements with comparative ease and he wanted desperately to match them. He didn't have the same coordination as the others and he was trying to compensate for the fact by going too fast.

"Listen to my count and slow down," Thorn told him. "I promise you, you will get it. But it's something you have to build up to. You can't just step into the net and do it perfectly each time."

"Stig did," Edvin replied.

Thorn shook his head. "Stig didn't," he said. "He did it better than you because he's a little bit better coordinated and balanced than you are. But you can make up for that. You simply have to practice. And build up your speed. Don't try to match him each time. Work at your own pace and let it build. All right?"

"All right," Edvin agreed reluctantly, and Thorn waved him forward into the net once more.

"Now, listen to my count. Don't try to get ahead of me. As I see you're improving, I'll speed it up. Understood?"

Edvin's face was set in determined lines. He nodded, his lips moving wordlessly as he waited for Thorn's command.

This time, Edvin stayed with the count. Thorn called the steps more slowly than he had before and the other boys lounged on the grass and watched Edvin as he moved, stepping high and with exaggerated care in time with the rhythm Thorn was setting. As he saw the boy was managing the slower pace, Thorn imperceptibly increased the rate of his call.

"Keep your eyes up!" he shouted suddenly. Edvin was letting his gaze drop to the net at his feet and that was an almost certain precursor to a fall. The boy had to sense the rhythm and the proximity of the cords around his feet. If he tried to look at them, he would never keep up with the call, even at the slow speed Thorn was currently setting.

Thorn increased the pace a little further and still Edvin kept his feet. Finally, Thorn called a halt, and Edvin stood, resting his sword on his shoulder, letting his shield arm fall. Thorn patted him on the shoulder.

"Much better," he said.

Edvin shook his head. "Stig went a lot faster than that," he said. "So did Hal and Jesper."

"And so will you," Thorn told him. "The more you work at it, the faster you'll get. Trust me."

"As fast as Stig?" Edvin asked. Thorn opened his mouth to reply, then decided honesty would be the best course.

"Probably not," he said, and saw an angry light begin to smolder in Edvin's eyes. "But you will get fast enough to save your life in battle, and that's not too bad. Face it, Edvin, we all have differing levels of ability. What we must do is make the most of what we've got."

"I suppose so," Edvin said. But his voice lacked conviction.

Thorn eyed him carefully for a few seconds, then said, "I know what you're thinking. You're thinking that if you practice long and hard enough, you'll show me that I'm wrong—that you can be as fast as Stig. Correct?"

Edvin's chin went up and he colored slightly. Then he answered, defiantly, "Yes. That's exactly what I'm thinking."

"Then good for you!" Thorn said, and slapped him heartily on the back. The impact was such that Edvin nearly went tumbling over in the net. He staggered, and as he did so, he took several high steps to recover.

"Nice save," Thorn said. "Now take a break. You can practice again later."

He watched as the boy walked a few paces away from the net, let the heavy shield slip from his arm and slumped to the grass. Edvin would take up the challenge, he knew. The boy had something to prove—to himself as much as to anyone else. If that gave him the incentive he needed to improve his performance, all the better. As Thorn had pointed out, it might save his life one day.

Finally, he turned toward Ingvar and nodded.

"Okay," he said. "Let's have you."

There was a murmur of expectation from the rest of the group. So far, Ingvar hadn't attempted the net. Nobody had expected Thorn to order him to.

Ingvar rose, peered in Thorn's direction and hesitated.

"Are you sure, Thorn?"

"Yes, I'm sure," Thorn said testily. "I don't say things unless I'm sure. Step forward into the net."

Ingvar moved awkwardly forward to the edge of the net. As he went to step into it, his left toe caught on one of the strands and he lurched uncertainly, waving his arms for balance and dropping his massive club in the process.

Someone sniggered. Thorn turned quickly and caught sight of Stefan hiding a smile behind his hand. Thorn's eyes narrowed.

"Laughing at a shipmate, Stefan?" he said, his tone deceptively mild. Stefan hurriedly assumed a more serious expression.

"It's all right, Thorn," Ingvar said. "I'm sort of used to it."

"Well, I'm not." Thorn addressed his words to the watching group. "In my book, we never laugh or make fun of a shipmate who's trying his best."

"Yeah. Don't be an ass, Stefan," Ulf said, and to everyone's surprise, Wulf reiterated his brother's thought.

"That's right. Shut up."

Thorn's eyebrows went up in surprise. May the Great Blue Whale fly up to the sun, he thought.

"Sorry," said Stefan. It wasn't so much the warning note in Thorn's voice that did it. It was the fact that Ulf and Wulf, for the first time in living memory, agreed on something. And that something was the fact that he, Stefan, was an ass. It was a sobering thought.

"Thanks, fellows," Ingvar said.

"Think nothing of it," Wulf said.

And Ulf chorused, "Nothing at all."

Then Wulf turned to Thorn. "Carry on, Thorn," he said magnanimously, gesturing with his right hand.

Thorn shook his head. "Oh, thank you very much," he said, and the other boys all smothered their laughter while Wulf grinned at them.

"That was well said," Ulf leaned over and told him.

Wulf nodded smugly. "I know."

"In fact, it was so well said, I'm surprised *I* didn't say it," Ulf continued.

Wulf, who had been leaning back on one elbow on the grass, now straightened abruptly and glared at his brother.

"Are you now?" he said. "Well, I'd—"

"Drop it!" Hal's voice cut like a whip and Wulf turned toward him.

"Drop what?" he asked.

Hal shook his head in annoyance. "Whatever you planned to say. Just drop it. You've got a laugh out of everyone, so quit while you're ahead."

"Quit while you're behind, more like," Ulf sniggered, and Hal turned his glare on him.

"You drop it too," he snapped and was surprised when Ulf looked considerably chastened.

"Yes, Hal," he said meekly.

Hal turned back to Thorn and repeated Wulf's earlier gesture. "Carry on, Thorn."

"You're sure?" Thorn replied, his voice dripping with sarcasm. "Nobody else has anything to say? You're all happy for me to *carry on*, are you?" He let his gaze travel around them. Nobody spoke. "Well, in that case, I think I will. Ingvar, are you ready?"

"I'm not sure, Thorn," Ingvar said truthfully. He certainly didn't feel too ready.

"All right then. Now, you saw what Edvin was doing, correct?"

"Ummm . . . not too clearly. There was a bit of jumping and arm waving going on, is that right?"

Thorn suppressed a smile. "Yes, jumping and arm waving is a

pretty good description of what everyone's been doing," he said. Edvin looked suitably insulted by the description, but he said nothing. He suspected that it *was* a fairly accurate description of what he'd been doing.

"Very well, let's try it slowly, Ingvar. Ready?"

"I think so."

"I'd like you to *know* so," Thorn told him.

The big boy nodded several times, licking his lips nervously. "All right. I know so." But he didn't sound convinced.

"Then here we go. One forward . . . two to the right . . . careful!"

This last comment came as Ingvar caught his left toe in the net and swayed precariously. With a great deal of difficulty, he recovered his balance and turned, peering in Thorn's direction. Thorn waited until he was standing evenly again and continued.

"Good. Now, two forward . . . one left . . . three right . . . one . . . help him up, will you, Stig?"

Ingvar had snagged his foot again and fell awkwardly. At Thorn's order, Stig leapt to his feet and heaved Ingvar upright.

"Thanks, Stig," Ingvar said. Then he turned to Thorn. "I think we're wasting time here, Thorn. I'm just no good at this."

Thorn rubbed his chin thoughtfully. He'd noticed that as Ingvar moved, he was peering down at the net and at his feet. It was a natural reaction. In fact, he'd had to tell a couple of the boys not to do it, but instead to keep their eyes up and sense where their feet were going. He strode toward Ingvar now.

"Ingvar, can you see the net?" he asked.

Ingvar shrugged unhappily. "It's pretty blurry."

"I think that might be the problem. You can see it. But you

don't see it well enough, and that's causing your loss of balance. You're tensing up because you're uncertain. Let's try something. Close your eyes for me."

Ingvar complied.

"Now breathe very steadily," Thorn said. "In and out. In and out." He watched the boy's shoulders rising and falling. "Now relax . . . Now imagine you can see the net. See it in your mind's eye."

"His mind's eye?" Jesper commented quietly to the others. "What's that?"

"In your case," Hal replied dryly, "it's a *very* small eye."

Jesper went to reply, realized he had nothing to top that comment and shut his mouth.

"Can you see the net now, Ingvar?" Thorn asked.

Ingvar, eyes shut tight, nodded.

"All right. Then, with your eyes shut and seeing the net in your mind, let's begin again. One back . . . two left . . . three forward . . . two right . . ."

The other boys watched in amazement as Ingvar began to follow Thorn's directions confidently and carefully. The pace was slow, of course. But he was stepping cleanly and the tendency to wave his arms wildly and teeter off balance was almost gone. Once, his right foot caught on a strand of the net and Thorn, watching like a hawk, immediately called on him to stop.

"Stand up straight!" he ordered. Ingvar did so and breathed deeply as he recovered his balance. Then Thorn began again and Ingvar continued his slow, careful movements.

Careful, Hal noticed, but no longer cautious and lacking in

confidence. He shook his head and murmured quietly to Stig. "He's amazing, isn't he?"

Stig grinned. "Who would have thought Ingvar could do that—even as slowly as he's moving?"

Finally, Thorn called for Ingvar to stop and open his eyes. The big boy stood in the middle of the net, face flushed with pleasure.

"Well done, Ingvar. We'll have you running through that net before you know it."

Ingvar shook his head, but his wide grin showed how pleased he was with his progress.

"Maybe not in no time, Thorn. But give me four or five years and I could work up to walking pace."

The assembled group laughed. But this time they were laughing with their crewmate, and not at him.

"Good lad," Thorn told him. "Now step out of the net. No!" he cried quickly as Ingvar looked cautiously down to see where to place his feet. "Keep your eyes up! See the net in your mind."

And to the amazement of those watching, Ingvar, head up and eyes straight ahead, walked clear of the net, stepping high and cleanly, without so much as a stumble.

Then, unfortunately, as he stepped onto the clear ground, he caught his toe against a grass tussock and fell flat on his face. This time, he laughed with the others as he clambered to his feet. But nothing could detract from his feeling of accomplishment.

"I guess I didn't see that in my mind," he said, and they all laughed again. Thorn nodded, smiling at the boy.

"Just keep practicing," he said. "Practice and practice and practice. The more you practice, the better you'll get."

• • • • •

Late that night, long after the camp had gone to sleep, Hal woke, as a strange sound impinged on his subconscious. He lay frowning for a few minutes. It was a rhythmic trudging sound and he strove unsuccessfully to identify it. By now, he was accustomed to the usual night sounds of the sea and the wind and the rain around the campsite in Shelter Bay. But this was something new.

He rolled out of his blankets and, seizing his belt with the saxe knife in its scabbard, he stood and stepped quietly out of the tent.

He followed the sound to the area where they trained each day. Trudge . . . slide . . . slide . . . trudge . . . scrape. He became aware that he could hear a voice, pitched low and muttering. The words were indistinct. Then he relaxed, slinging the belt and scabbard over his shoulder as he realized there was no danger.

Ingvar was in the center of the net. He was facing Hal, and in the moonlight, the skirl could see that Ingvar's eyes were shut as he moved deliberately in a complex pattern of steps. Right, forward, left, back, left, right, his feet slid and trudged on the dew-damp grass. His lips moved as he called the steps to himself in an undertone.

"Right two . . . back three . . . left one . . . forward two . . ."

Hal smiled to himself and turned away, heading back to the warmth of his bed and leaving Ingvar to his private practice.

The training continued each day and all the members of the crew improved their performance in the net, even Ingvar—although he was a long way behind the others. After several days, he could even move in the net with his eyes open.

And even though he couldn't equal the others' performance, he was moving far more surely than he had ever done in his life. He would never be called nimble, but his sense of balance and movement had improved remarkably.

Which would stand him in good stead when they went back to sea, Hal thought, and he had to move around the rolling, pitching deck of the *Heron*. He was going to need Ingvar for the idea he was working on, and he welcomed the improvement that Thorn's training had brought about.

After working the boys in the net for a week, Thorn introduced a change to their training. He set them to practicing mock combat, with wooden weapons, one against the other. When he did so, he quickly noticed a fault in their technique.

"It's not surprising," he told Hal. The crew had spent the morning hard at work, and Hal and Thorn were sitting discussing their progress. "After all, their instructors in brotherband aren't experts themselves. They're all reasonably competent, but they're just teaching the basics, not the finer points."

Hal smiled at him. "I guess none of them were *Maktigs*," he said.

Thorn nodded, shrugging. "I suppose not. But I find it frustrating when I see the boys practicing bad technique. That just tends to entrench bad habits, and they're that much harder to break."

"Then show them where they're going wrong," Hal told him.

Thorn pursed his lips. "Are you sure? You're the skirl, not me. I don't want to undermine your authority."

Hal laughed. "I'm the skirl and when we're at sea, they'll obey me. I'll see to that. But as skirl, I've appointed you as our battle trainer. You're the most qualified for that job. I certainly can't teach them. I'm learning myself."

"I'm glad to hear you say it," Thorn said. "I just needed to check it with you."

"One thing," Hal said, then hesitated. He wasn't quite sure how to broach the subject. Then he decided the best way was to simply go ahead with it. "Quite a few of them are wondering about you. That demonstration in the net caught them by surprise. They're wondering where all that skill and knowledge came from."

Thorn was shaking his head before he finished the sentence. "I don't want people to know about—"

But Hal interrupted him. "These aren't people. These are your crew. Thorn, I can understand that when you were in Hallasholm, you didn't want people looking and saying, *See how far Thorn has fallen? He used to be the Maktig.* But the boys won't think that way. They look up to you already. They're not comparing you with the way you once were. They see you as you are and they admire you."

"They look up to me?" Thorn said, disbelief in his voice.

Hal nodded emphatically. "Of course they do. What's more, I think it might do their confidence a lot of good if they knew they were being taught by a real expert. And confidence is going to be important if we have to fight the crew of the *Raven*."

Thorn shrugged reluctantly. "Perhaps you're right," he said. "Let me think about it."

"I know I'm right," Hal said. Then he smiled. "After all, I'm the skirl. Now, what have you got in mind to improve their technique?"

"I'll show you this afternoon," Thorn said.

After the lunch break, Thorn called the boys to order and told them to gather round him. He motioned for them to sit in a semicircle, and strode back and forth in front of them, slapping the hickory baton against his boot as he searched for the words he wanted to say.

Finally, he decided that a demonstration would be the best way to broach the subject. He harrumphed once or twice, trying to ignore the semicircle of curious faces, then pointed the baton at Stig.

"Stig, on your feet and fetch your practice weapon and shield. Bring me a shield too."

Stig hesitated. "Just a shield? Don't you want a practice ax?"

Thorn shook his head and swished the hickory baton through the air. "This'll be enough. Hop to it now."

As the tall boy ran to fetch two shields and a practice ax from the training area, Thorn turned back to the waiting boys.

"We've been working on agility and balance," he began, "and you've all improved remarkably. Even Ingvar." He smiled at the big boy. "Problem is, it all goes off to visit your grandma when you start weapon practice."

He looked up as Stig returned with the practice equipment. He took the shield and slipped it over his right arm, then watched as Stig settled his own shield on his left, and hefted the wooden practice ax. Thorn retained the hickory baton in his left hand.

"All right, Stig," he said. "Let's see your style."

They faced each other, and each of them dropped into a crouch. Stig's eyes were slitted and he concentrated fiercely on the shabby figure in front of him. In spite of the matted beard and gray hair, and the tattered, patched clothes, Thorn with a weapon in his hand was a different matter altogether from Thorn, the disheveled old derelict. The years seemed to fall away and he moved lightly and confidently as they circled each other. The shield was up and ready while the hickory stick described a small circle in the air. Except for Hal, Stig was the only member of the crew who was aware of Thorn's past. He knew he was facing an expert warrior and he was in no hurry to rush in. Thorn's easy, confident manner made him even more reluctant to do so.

"Hyaaah!" Thorn shouted, leaping forward and raising the stick for an overhead blow. Stig leapt back with an involuntary shout of surprise. His foot caught on a tussock and he stumbled, barely managing to retain his feet.

A ripple of laughter ran round the watching boys and Stig flushed as he realized Thorn's move had been a feint. The old sea wolf was grinning at him now, and rolling his eyes. Throwing caution to the winds, Stig attacked.

He hammered at Thorn's shield with the wooden ax, raining blow after blow down on it, hitting with every ounce of his strength. The wooden practice weapon cracked against the shield, which always seemed to be in position just in time to prevent Stig's weapon knocking Thorn's head clean off his shoulders. The boys shouted encouragement as Thorn began to back away and Stig went after him, redoubling his efforts.

Then, in the blink of an eye, it was over.

Stig launched one last, massive blow at Thorn. This time, instead of blocking the attack, Thorn caught it on the slanting face of his shield and deflected it. Meeting no real resistance to his attack, Stig lurched forward, off balance, exposing his right side as he followed through.

And as he did so, Thorn jabbed the baton painfully into his ribs, like a snake striking.

"Owww!" Stig yelped, recoiling from the bruising impact.

Instantly, Thorn leapt back a pace. "That's it. It's over!"

As Stig, now thoroughly angry, gathered himself to launch another attack, Thorn brought the stick up to face level and pointed it warningly at him.

"That's it, Stig!" he said crisply. "Finished!" He kept his eyes fixed on Stig's. Gradually, he saw the anger fading away and the boy let his shield and ax drop to the ground. There was a time when Stig's temper would have flared beyond control, but brotherband training had helped him to manage it. He rubbed his ribs gingerly.

"That hurt, Thorn," he complained. Thorn nodded, loosening his clamped hook from the shield's handle and letting it slip off his arm.

"It would have hurt a lot more if this had been a sword," he said, brandishing the hickory baton. He saw realization dawning in Stig's eyes then and the boy managed an abashed grin.

"I hadn't thought of it that way," he said.

"Think of it now," Thorn told him. Then he turned to include the other members of the brotherband, who were watching in silence. Thorn's speed of hand, and the ease with which he had met and countered Stig's attack, had overawed them.

"All of you think about it," he repeated, letting his gaze travel over the suddenly very serious faces before him. "Imagine that had been a sword driving into Stig's ribs. We'd be busy telling tales of what a good fellow he'd been during his short and colorful life, and how much we all miss him." He paused. "Or maybe not."

That drew a small ripple of amusement from them and he continued.

"Stig is probably the best of all of you with an ax," he said. He looked for any sign of disagreement, but all he saw were slight nods, confirming his statement. "But his training has been sadly lacking."

"His brotherband training, you mean?" Edvin asked.

Thorn nodded. "Your instructors taught you the very basic strokes. And they encouraged you to whack and bash at the practice pads, and at each other, as hard as you could go. Am I right?"

Again he paused and again he was greeted by nods.

"The point is, most Skandian warriors are capable axmen. Competent, let's say. But only a few are better than that. And only a very small number are experts. Your instructors were all pretty average warriors."

He paused, seeing a few frowns. "I'm not saying that with any disrespect. It's a fact. They're only supposed to teach you the basics.

And they only have a few months to work with you, in which time they have to teach you a whole lot of other basic skills. Brotherband training is just the beginning. It doesn't teach you everything. It can't. The instructors simply have no time for showing you the finer points. When you were practicing weapon skills, the command I heard most often was, *Hit harder! Give it all you've got! Call that hitting?* That sort of thing. Am I right?"

A few murmured yeses answered him.

"Now that's fine if you're looking to build up muscles and tire yourself out so you sleep nights. But it's not good enough in a fight.

"Think of it this way. You're in a battle. You swing your ax at someone as hard as you can. If you hit him, you split him open maybe down to here." He indicated a point in the middle of his chest. "Now, if you don't hit him quite so hard, you might only go this far."

He pointed to a spot between his eyebrows. Again, nods greeted the demonstration. Slightly puzzled nods, but nods nonetheless.

"Is he any less dead?" he asked them, and saw a few faces showing understanding. "You've got to learn to control your power," he continued. "Keep in balance when you strike. Don't overswing. You just saw how easy it was for me to deflect Stig's stroke and send him off balance. And that opened him up to a counterstroke.

"Tomorrow, we're going to start a new exercise that'll help you learn to hit so you stay in balance."

The boys exchanged glances and he could see he'd caught their imagination. They were wondering what this new form of training was going to be.

Good, he thought. If they're wondering, that means they're interested.

"That's it for today. You can head back to your tent and take it easy. Tomorrow is going to be a tough day."

It was Jesper who asked the question. Hal could have guessed it would be him.

The boys were relaxing on their bedrolls, mending clothes or equipment, sharpening weapons or talking quietly among themselves, when the former thief voiced the thought that had been in many of their minds.

"How come Thorn knows so much about fighting?" he said. "After all, for as long as I can remember, he was the town drunk." A few of the others nodded and he continued, his gaze seeking out Hal.

"I mean, we all saw him today, when he took on Stig. He made it look so easy." Stig glanced up quickly at that, and Jesper hastily made an apologetic gesture. "No offense, Stig. We know you're not an easy opponent to beat. So how did Thorn manage it? And you've got to admit, he did make it *look* easy, even if it wasn't."

Hal and Stig exchanged a meaningful look, with Stig asking an unspoken question. Hal finally nodded.

"It's time they were told," he said. "Go and ask Thorn to come in here, will you?"

Stig nodded and rose to his feet. As he left the tent, he heard a storm of questions break out from his shipmates. He smiled to himself. They were in for a surprise.

Thorn pulled back the canvas flap that covered the tent doorway and stepped inside into the light. As he did so, the babble of voices that had been coming from the tent cut off abruptly, and every eye turned on him. Stig slipped through the opening behind him and took his place on his own bedroll, grinning expectantly.

Thorn scanned the ring of incredulous faces and settled on Hal.

"I take it you told them?"

Hal nodded. "It's time they knew," he replied.

Thorn chewed the ends of his mustache for several seconds, not sure what to say next. Finally, he began to turn away toward the door.

"All right," he said. "So now you know."

There was a storm of protest as the boys realized he was about to leave.

"Just a moment!" That was Jesper, of course. "You can't go now! Tell us about it!"

"About what?" Thorn replied.

This time, it was Stefan who answered. "About being the Maktig," he said.

And Edvin added, "Three times!"

"Well, it was a lot of hard work," Thorn said uncertainly. Talking about himself was never his strong point.

"What events did you compete in?" Hal prompted him. He could see Thorn needed a little help to get going. The old warrior looked away, thinking back to the days of the Maktig contests.

"Oh . . . wrestling matches. Mock combats with sword and ax. Spear throwing. Footraces. Endurance tests . . ."

"Like what?" Ingvar asked, and a thoughtful look touched Thorn's leathery features.

"Like spending the night out in the mountains in winter wearing nothing but my drawers."

"What was that like?" Ulf asked.

Thorn allowed himself a faint smile as he answered.

"Cold," he said sincerely. "Very cold. Nearly froze my backside off, as a matter of fact." A ripple of laughter ran round the boys. They were sitting watching him, hanging on his every word. He looked sidelong at Hal.

"I'm not getting out of here any time soon, am I?" he said, and Hal shook his head slowly.

Thorn sighed and lowered himself to sit cross-legged on the floor of the tent. Strangely, after all these years of trying to bury his past, he found it was vaguely pleasant to talk about it with these wide-eyed boys, and to see the nonjudgmental admiration on their faces.

"Might as well make myself comfortable then," he said, then he made an encouraging gesture. "All right, let's have it."

"Were people surprised when you won the second and third times?" Stefan asked.

Thorn looked at him with a grin. "Well, *I* certainly was."

Again, the boys laughed and he settled himself, feeling more at home, more at ease.

"Who was your toughest opponent?" Stig asked.

Thorn didn't even have to think about that one.

"Hal's father," he said, and every eye turned on Hal, who flushed with pleasure. Then Thorn added, "Your dad was good too, Stig. He made it to the semifinals in my second year."

"My dad?" Stig said, surprised.

"He was a pretty handy warrior. Very good with an ax. You've got a lot of his talent."

Stig looked down, trying to hide the sudden tears that sprang to his eyes. In all his young life, he couldn't remember anyone saying anything positive about his father, who had disappeared after stealing from his shipmates. He was glad when Jesper claimed the attention of the others.

"How many mock combats did you have to fight?"

Thorn drew a deep breath as he calculated the answer to that question.

And so it went on for another forty minutes, with the boys eagerly asking questions and Thorn answering them—hesitantly at first, but gradually gaining in fluency as he realized that none of his young shipmates were looking to criticize him or belittle him. Quite the opposite, in fact. They were glad to have him as a member of their crew, glad to have him training them. Proud to be his shipmates and students. Hal had been right, he thought; knowing of his achievements might make them more inclined to pay attention and work on their skills.

Best of all, he realized, they weren't comparing him as he was now with how he had been when he was the Maktig. That was before their memory. They were comparing him with the way he had been when he was a shambling, forlorn drunkard, and the admiration in their eyes as they looked at him now was all too obvious.

When Hal finally called a halt to the discussion, pointing out that the Herons' personal Maktig had a big day planned for them the following morning, Thorn felt as if a great weight had been lifted from his shoulders—a weight that had been balanced there for too many years. He was aware that these boys respected and admired him, and aware that for the first time in too long a time, he had reason to feel proud of himself.

He nodded good night and rose to go. As he stepped to the doorway, there was a momentary silence, then Jesper broke it.

"Thanks, Thorn," he said simply, and the others immediately chorused their thanks as well.

He stepped out into the night and looked up at the stars in the frosty sky above. He took a deep breath. He felt better than he had done for a long, long time.

"Who would have thought it?" he said softly to himself. "Who would have thought it?"

trike! Parry! Strike! Deflect! Pick yourself up, Ulf!"

"I'm Wulf," said the red-faced twin.

"Whatever," Thorn told him. "Just don't swing so hard. Control it! Stay in balance! You too, Wulf!" he added as the other twin went crashing to the ground as well.

"I'm Ulf!" the second twin protested as he scrambled to his feet, rubbing his bruised backside.

"Tell someone who cares," Thorn said, looking away at the sound of another yelp and seeing Stefan fall flat on his back as his feet shot out from under him. "I've told you!" he bellowed to the group in general. "Don't swing so hard that you lose balance. Start small and gradually extend your swing. Take it slowly!"

The eight Herons were attempting to master Thorn's new practice technique. While they had been on their morning run down the beach, he had set up eight low hurdles. On each, a sturdy round branch was supported about twenty centimeters from the ground by a forked stick at either end. The forks were greased so that the branch would roll and turn easily in them. The result was a highly unstable platform on which to practice basic combat moves. Each of the boys took a stance on one of the hurdles and tried to maintain his balance while practicing ax strokes and shield parries.

As Ulf, Wulf and now Stefan had already discovered, if they swung so hard that they went out of balance, the round branch would roll under their feet and they would fall to the ground.

In Ingvar's case, Thorn had decided to let the big boy simply practice balancing on the branch, without attempting any mock blows with his club.

"It's so heavy you'd never manage to keep your footing if you swung it," he told Ingvar. Now Ingvar, the tip of his tongue showing through his teeth, stood swaying precariously on his perch, arms spread as he beat at the air to keep his balance.

"Relax," Thorn said as he walked past. "If you tense up, you'll never recover your balance. Loosen your muscles and keep your movements small."

As he spoke, Ingvar teetered backward, the branch turned and he fell, just managing not to measure his length upon the ground.

"Smaller than that," Thorn told him. Ingvar shook his head and gingerly climbed back onto the hurdle, swaying and waving arms to get himself set. He forced his tense muscles to relax and beamed at Thorn as he felt his footing steady.

"That's a lot better," he said, and promptly fell forward, hitting the ground with a thud that made Thorn wince. The old warrior moved on as Ingvar picked himself up again.

The boys were having varying degrees of success with this drill. Hal and Stig had mastered the technique relatively quickly. Even if they did fall, they could control the movement so they landed on their feet. Jesper had the knack as well. Thorn frowned slightly as he watched him. Jesper was a smart aleck and tended to be lazy—which was a pity when he had so much natural athletic talent.

Ulf and Wulf were letting their customary ill temper cause them problems. With each fall, they would scramble angrily back onto the crossbars and begin again. But their frustration was making them move too fast, and within a few seconds they would lose their footing and fall to the ground again. It was almost as if they felt that, by moving quickly back onto the perch, they would erase the fact they had fallen off in the first place. They'd be better to wait a few seconds, settle themselves, then step up carefully.

At least they had learned not to try to regain their balance at all costs. That merely led to a more severe fall as the crosspiece would spin suddenly and throw its occupant off. Now, once the twins felt their balance going, they would accept the inevitable and step down. Then, they would snort and begin again—usually hurling an insult at each other as they did.

"Take it slowly," Thorn exhorted them yet again. But he had little hope that they'd pay attention to him. He shrugged. Eventually they would learn the hard way to be more circumspect in their movements.

He let the practice session continue for a few more minutes, then called a halt. Wearily, the Herons stepped down or, in some cases, stumbled down from their perches and sat on the grass. Some of them rubbed cramped calf muscles and sore ankles and heel tendons. Trying to stay balanced on such an uncertain perch put great strain on those muscles and joints, Thorn knew.

He grinned at them. "Hard, isn't it?" There were nods all around. "You'll get the hang of it before too long."

"What happens when we do?" Edvin asked. He and Stefan had performed reasonably on the hurdles. They weren't outstandingly good, nor were they outstandingly bad. That pretty much summed up the two of them in physical workouts. They were average performers. Still, Thorn thought to himself, he'd work to make them above average.

He looked now at Edvin as he answered. "When you can stand on the crossbars without falling off for a couple of minutes, we'll match you up in practice fights."

"On those glorified bird perches?" Edvin said incredulously. And when Thorn nodded, he shook his head. "We'll never manage it."

"You might surprise yourself," Thorn told him. "Now, when you've had a few minutes' rest, how about getting the lunch started?"

"Ulf and Wulf," Hal said, "you can help Edvin. Get the fire started for him, Ulf. Wulf, you can fetch fresh water and peel some vegetables. Anything else you need done, Edvin?"

Edvin shook his head. "That should see to it. We've got some cold venison left, and I baked a loaf of bread last night."

Thorn listened to the exchange. It was interesting, he thought, how Hal quickly reassumed authority when the practice sessions were over. While they were working on their combat skills, Thorn was in undisputed charge. And he'd noticed that, since their conversation the previous evening, the boys seemed to pay closer attention to his instructions than they had before. But the moment they reverted to normal camp discipline and chores, Hal took over again without seeming to think about it. Not for the first time, Thorn reflected that the boy was a natural leader.

Hal rose now from where he had sprawled on the grass, rubbing sore calf muscles, and walked across to Thorn. He was limping slightly as the muscles cramped and knotted.

"What have you got in mind for this afternoon?" he asked. Thorn nodded toward the net, where it was suspended above the ground nearby.

"I'll give them another session in the net," he said. "They'll find it a lot easier after those greased rollers."

"Can you spare Ingvar and me?" Hal asked.

Thorn nodded. "Why not? If you feel you're falling behind, you can always join him on one of his midnight practice sessions."

Hal raised his eyebrows at that. "Oh, you've seen him too, have you?"

Thorn glanced across at Ingvar, who was smiling and talking to Stig and Stefan. "He wants so much to be a valuable crew member."

Hal followed his gaze. "He will be," he said. "When you see what we've been working on, you'll see what I mean. He'll be doing a job none of the others could manage."

"Good. Everybody needs to feel he's contributing in a crew and it's easy for someone like Ingvar to become the target of jokes. So when do we get to see this wonderful new contraption of yours?" Thorn asked.

Hal considered the question. "If all goes well, later this afternoon. We have some final adjustments to make."

"No small details overlooked?" Thorn said, just managing to stop the grin that wanted to break out across his face.

Hal sighed. "I wish you and Stig would get over that."

Thorn assumed a look of concern. "You'd like us to stop saying that?"

Hal gave him a hard look. "Yes. As a matter of fact, I would."

Thorn finally let the grin off the leash.

"Isn't going to happen," he said happily.

"Didn't think so."

After forty minutes' hard work in the net, Thorn called a rest break and the boys ambled back to their tent to sprawl on their bedrolls and relax. Thorn took a seat on a tree stump close to the fireplace and made himself a mug of coffee. Their supply of coffee beans was limited and he decided to wait until the boys weren't around before making himself another pot.

"No sense in wasting it on them," he told himself, replacing the sack of beans in the hiding place that Edvin had no idea he knew about.

He was satisfied with the boys' progress in the agility exercises he'd devised for them. In a few days, he'd start working on the finer points of combat techniques. He was also pleased with the change of atmosphere in the camp. There was nothing like hard work and sore muscles at the end of the day to keep boys occupied, he thought. But even as he had that thought, he realized that he and Hal would have to keep ringing the changes and creating new ways to stretch the crew's abilities.

"If the weather would ease, we could take the ship to sea," he said to himself. "A spell of rowing and sail handling would do wonders for them."

But even though there had been a few calm breaks in the past few days, none of them lasted for long and there was always the risk of being caught on the open sea when the storms resumed. They could always practice rowing in the calmer waters of Shelter Bay. But such an exercise would be rather pointless. They had been around boats and ships all their lives and their rowing technique was sound. To simply row up and down the bay would not hold their attention for very long.

While he was musing about this, he became conscious of a very faint sound. A voice? No, two voices.

He stood up and gazed down the beach. Sure enough, the distant figures of Hal and Ingvar were looking back toward the camp. He could see the pale ovals of their faces. Then they raised their hands to cup them around their mouths, and a few seconds later, he heard the faint sound again, carried on the wind.

"Tho-o-orn!"

"About time too," he muttered. He waved to them, letting them know he had heard them, then tossed the dregs of his coffee into the fire. He was setting the mug down when a thought occurred to him. Edvin might spot the remnants of his coffee in the pot. He tipped water from the pail of fresh water standing by the fireplace, swirled it around until there was no trace or smell of coffee left, and threw it out.

Then he walked briskly to the tent where the boys were relaxing—some talking quietly, several snoozing and others working on repairing torn or damaged clothing and equipment. Those who were awake looked up as he approached. He jerked a thumb toward the beach.

"If any of you are interested," he said, "the great inventor is ready to show us his latest work."

That definitely got their interest. Since they had seen the success of Hal's revolutionary sail design, the Herons tended to treat Hal's inventive skills with great respect. Thorn and Stig, who had seen one or two of his brainstorms go disastrously wrong over the years, were a little more cynical.

But now, as the boys tumbled eagerly out of the tent, heading for the beach in a ragged group, Thorn felt a small tingle of anticipation. Most of the time, Hal's ideas worked, and worked well. Without realizing it, he found himself quickening his pace to catch up with the boys.

Whatever Hal had to show them, he didn't want to be the last to see it.

It's a crossbow," said Stig, shaking his head in wonder as he stared at the device.

"Biggest crossbow I've ever seen," Edvin commented.

The massive crossbow crouched on a wooden carriage before them. It was a meter and a half in length and the limbs of the bow were almost a meter from tip to tip. They were made from several layers of wood, laminated together, glued and bound with deer sinew. Thorn nodded thoughtfully as he noted them. In the past week, Hal had been successful in shooting several deer for food. Obviously, he'd wasted nothing from the carcasses. He must have boiled the hooves down to make glue—Thorn recalled a dreadful smell emanating from the workshop a few days ago.

Hal indicated the limbs of the bow. "I've used different types of wood for these," he said. "Sapwood on the outer side of the curve for flexibility and heartwood on the inside for strength and rigidity."

"How will you shoot it?" Ulf asked. "You could never lift it."

"I'll shoot it from the carriage," Hal said. He indicated a

wooden ratchet gear on one side. "I can elevate it with this." As he spoke, he turned the ratchet and the crossbow angled up on its carriage.

"Ingenious," Stig said, and he grinned at his friend in admiration. "You've tested it? It does actually shoot?"

Hal regarded his friend with an icy smile. He'd been waiting for the inevitable question about small details and suspected this might be a prelude to it.

"It shoots all right," he said. "We've been testing it this morning. It'll throw one of these for almost four hundred meters."

He held up a heavy hardwood projectile, half a meter in length. The point had been sharpened and hardened in a fire, and it was reinforced with four iron strips, fastened around its edges and tapering to a point. At the far end, three thin wooden vanes, triangular in shape, were set around the shaft like the fletching on an arrow.

"Although for practical purposes, we're saying the range is three hundred meters. We've been graduating the sights while you lot have been snoozing," he added.

Stefan stepped forward to study the huge weapon more closely. "It's magnificent," he said. He seized hold of the heavy cord that stretched between the two bow limbs. It was made from plaited birch creepers. He tried in vain to haul it back. He could manage to move it no more than a few centimeters.

"The question is, how do you load it?" he said, frustrated.

"I don't," Hal said. "And I doubt any of you could. But Ingvar can."

He gestured for Ingvar to demonstrate. The big boy stepped

forward, smiling, and a little pleased to be the center of attention. There were two levers, one set on either side, angled forward and coming up just below the string. They were joined by a rod running through the carriage, under the body of the bow.

He pulled the levers up and back, and as they swiveled, the levers caught the bowstring and began to draw it back.

"Hold it a moment, Ingvar," Hal ordered, and the young giant let the levers back down to their original position. Hal glanced at Stig.

"Why don't you try it?" he suggested.

Stig shrugged and stepped forward.

"If you say so," he said, smiling. Ingvar moved to one side to give him access to the bow and he took hold of the levers and heaved on them.

And stopped.

The smile faded from his face as he realized he had moved the string only halfway back before he could move it no farther. He strained mightily and the string moved another centimeter. Then, shaking his head, he let the levers back down again and gestured to Ingvar.

"Show us how it's done," he said. He suspected that Hal had arranged the demonstration not to make fun of him, but to indicate Ingvar's unique ability to his shipmates. Ingvar stepped in again, seized the levers and hauled them all the way back in one smooth movement, until the string engaged a latch set in the body of the bow and was held tight, fully cocked. He replaced the levers in their original position, below the main body of the bow.

There was a mutter of appreciation from the assembled Herons.

Stig was stronger than any of them—aside from Ingvar. If he couldn't manage to cock the huge crossbow, they knew that none of them would be capable of doing so. Hal caught Stig's eye and nodded at him, confirming Stig's earlier suspicion.

"I just wanted you all to see that," Hal said. "Without Ingvar, this bow would be useless. He'll load the bow for me when I'm shooting."

Thorn moved closer, studying the massive weapon. There was a definite air of menace about it, he thought. The effort required to cock it indicated that it would fire its projectiles with enormous power and speed. But he wasn't sure how Hal intended to deploy such a heavy piece of equipment in a battle.

"Just how do you plan to use it?" he asked. Hal's proud smile widened.

"I'm going to mount it in the bow of the *Heron*," he said, "on a swiveling platform. Then, when we catch up with the *Raven*, we can stand off a hundred meters or so and knock great big holes in her. I doubt that they'll enjoy being peppered with these beauties." He held up one of the heavy projectiles and they all looked at it, imagining it slamming into the relatively light timbers of a ship's hull.

There was a general chorus of approval and enthusiasm from his crew. It was a truly radical idea—but they had come to expect radical ideas from their skirl. Even Thorn looked impressed.

"You plan to arm the ship," he said. It was something that Skandians had never done. They used their ships as a way to reach a battle, not a way to fight it.

"That's right. The ship becomes our weapon. If we get too close to the *Raven*, she'll ram us. This way, we can keep our distance and pound her." He looked at Stig. "You'll have to take the helm when we're fighting her," he added.

Stig grinned and nodded. "My pleasure."

Hal looked at the others. "Stefan, Jesper, you'll take charge of raising and lowering sails. Ingvar can help you if necessary. We won't be shooting if we're tacking or wearing the ship. Ulf and Wulf, you'll be on sail trimming and sheet handling. Edvin, you'll stand ready to assist Stig, and to pass on my signals. Once we can put to sea again, we're going to have to drill constantly to coordinate all our actions—steering, sail handling and shooting—if this is going to work."

He turned his gaze on Ulf and Wulf. "And that means you two are going to have to work together without your usual bickering," he said firmly. "Our lives are going to depend on cooperation. If you two can't get on, I'll have Ingvar throw you overboard."

"And I'll do it too," Ingvar said very seriously. The crew sensed that Ingvar would do anything that Hal asked of him. And, having seen the recent display of his amazing strength, nobody doubted his ability to carry out such an order.

Ulf and Wulf exchanged a look and came to an understanding.

"We won't let you down, Hal. You have my word on it," Ulf said.

"The same goes for me," Wulf added. "And it's not just because of Ingvar's threat—although we know he *could* do it."

"And we know he *would* do it," Ulf agreed. "But we also know you're right. All of our lives will depend on quick sail handling and teamwork."

Hal looked from one to the other, looking deep into their eyes.

He could see that his message had gotten through. There was a new look of determination about the twins.

"Good," he said. "I'm glad to hear it." Then, as Ulf raised a tentative hand, he went on, "Yes, Ulf, what is it?"

"I'm Wulf," the twin said, frowning.

Hal made a how-am-I-to-know gesture. "If you say so. What is it?"

"Do we have to stop bickering when we're not fighting the *Raven*? I mean, at normal times like this? Do we have to stop bickering now?"

"We're not bickering now," his brother pointed out.

"I know that! But we could be, any minute now!" Wulf replied.

"Maybe, but—" Ulf began, but Hal cut him off.

"It would be nice if you didn't bicker," he said. "But I suspect that might be a bit too much to ask."

"I think so," said Ulf, who Hal had formerly assumed to be Wulf. "We're kind of . . . used to it, I suppose."

"Just wouldn't seem the same without it," Wulf agreed.

Hal sighed deeply. "Then you're exonerated from your promise during normal times. Sorry about that," he added, casting an apologetic glance in the direction of the other crew members.

"I must say, I'm relieved," Stig said. "It wouldn't be the same if they weren't constantly sniping at each other."

"Yes, it wouldn't be the same," Edvin agreed, "but it would make a pleasant change." He said it in a mock-weary tone, but there was an underlying sense of good humor and the others chuckled quietly at his words.

Hal looked keenly around the ring of young faces. The expressions were serious as they all realized that they would eventually be facing a very dangerous enemy and fighting for their lives. But there was no fear there. There was a sense of confidence, and a growing sense of trust in their shipmates.

Thorn coughed expectantly and they looked at him.

"Which is all very well and good," he said. "But none of it will matter if this monstrous mangler of a machine doesn't work." He jerked a thumb at the huge crossbow, crouched on its carriage like a bird of prey with its wings spread. "Do you think you might be able to show us what it can do?"

Hal nodded and moved to stand behind the huge weapon. He crouched and sighted quickly down its length, then glanced up at Ingvar.

"It moved offline after the last shot," he said. "Get the lever, would you?"

There was a long trimmed branch lying a few meters away. Ingvar moved round the crossbow to fetch it. It was about three centimeters across and two meters long, but he hefted it as easily as if it had been a broomstick. He stepped back to stand beside the crossbow while Hal peered down the length of it.

"Move it a little left," Hal said.

Ingvar dug the end of the wooden pole into the sand beside the right-hand side of the crossbow's carriage. Then he heaved slowly against it to swing the weapon to the left.

"A little more," Hal said, still intent on the line of sight.

Ingvar began to tap the end of the lever with the heel of his right hand—short, sharp blows that moved the crossbow a few centimeters at a time. Finally, Hal raised his arm and Ingvar stopped.

"That's it," Hal said. He stood back and turned to the others. "When I have it on a swiveling mount, it'll be a lot easier to move it from side to side," he told them. "For the moment, we're making do with Ingvar's muscle power." He smiled at the big boy, who grinned back.

He's enjoying having a purpose in life, Thorn thought. Then his eyebrows raised in surprise as another thought struck him. Just as I am. Hal was still speaking and the old sea wolf brought his attention back to what he was saying.

". . . graduated the sights to those targets down the beach this morning. We paced out the distance and set them up at fifty-pace intervals. The nearest is one hundred paces away."

Now, as the others looked in the direction he was pointing, they could make out a series of five wooden targets set up on poles hammered into the sand. Thorn squinted at the nearest. It was a square shape, made up of thick branches nailed onto a wooden frame. The sides of the frame looked to be about a meter in length.

"I figure the branches will offer about the same resistance as the planks of a ship," Hal said. He took his position behind the bow again, peering at the target. Then he flipped up a flat piece of wood on the side of the weapon, marked with a distance scale. He pointed to the first mark and turned to the watching Herons.

"This indicates a range of one hundred meters," he said. "When I line this mark up with the bead of the foresight, I have the right elevation for the shot."

The boys leaned forward to peer at the weapon and they saw a wooden pin, surmounted by a small white bead, set ahead of the limbs, just clear of the line of flight that the projectile would follow.

"That's like the sight on your small crossbow," Stig said, recognizing the system.

"That's right. I figured if it worked there, it'd work here. And it does."

He crouched and concentrated once more on the sighting picture. He saw the bead of the foresight was in line with the target, but a little below the graduated mark on the rear sight. His hand went to the wooden cogwheel the boys had noticed earlier and he wound it slowly. The front of the crossbow began to rise as he did so. Then he stopped, checked once more and nodded to himself.

He picked up the heavy projectile that was lying on the ground beside him and set it in the shallow trough cut into the top of the bow, fitting a notch at its end into the thick cord.

"Stand clear," he warned them, and pulled the trigger lanyard. It tripped the latch holding the string, and a fraction of a second later, there was a massive crash as the limbs released. The entire bow bucked with the recoil and the heavy projectile shot away on its shallow, curving trajectory.

Initially startled by the noise when the bow released, the crew followed the bolt's flight with their eyes. A second later, they saw the target shudder under a massive impact. A cloud of wood splinters were hurled into the air and they heard the cracking sound of breaking timber. The pole holding the target lurched drunkenly to one side and the target itself hung loose on an angle, swinging back and forth from the force of the impact.

"No wonder it goes off line when you shoot it," Stig muttered.

Hal didn't reply. "Ingvar!" he called, and the giant boy stepped forward, seized the two cocking levers and heaved the string back onto its retaining latch. Hal placed another bolt onto the string, then crouched behind the sights. Ingvar had already retrieved his lever and he began to traverse the bow in accordance with Hal's orders.

"Right!" Hal commanded and, as Ingvar began to heave the crossbow round to the right to line up with the second target, he continued in a singsong tone.

"Right . . . right . . . right . . . easy now. A little right. A little more. A little more. Stop!"

His arm flew up in a signal to stop. Ingvar laid the pole aside and stood by as Hal wound the elevation wheel and the front of the bow came farther and farther up. Hal peered at the sights, made another small upward adjustment.

"Stand clear!" he called. He pulled the trigger again.

Once more, there was the massive crash of wood on wood, and once more, the crossbow bucked with the recoil. This time, the watchers could follow the flight of the projectile more easily, as it flew through a greater distance and with a slightly higher arc of flight.

The second target lurched under the impact and there was a splintering sound as more wood fragments flew. This time, however, the impact was slightly off center and the target was wrenched bodily from the support pole.

The watching crew members cheered at the sight. Nothing like a little wanton destruction to get boys excited, Thorn thought, smiling to himself. But, at the same time, he felt like joining them. Hal had come up with a fearsome weapon in this giant crossbow.

If they caught up with Zavac and the *Raven*, the pirates were in for a very nasty surprise.

Hal was smiling, relieved that the demonstration had gone so well. Stig stepped forward and slapped him on the shoulder.

"You've done it again!" he said. "This is brilliant—and no small details forgotten." He added the last with a giant grin and another hearty slap on the back. Hal accepted both philosophically.

Stig ran his hand along the smoothed timber of the huge crossbow, admiring the workmanship that had gone into it. There was nothing ornate about it. It was simply a well-crafted piece of machinery.

"I can't wait to see Zavac's face when you start shooting big holes in his ship!" he said.

"And his crew!" Wulf added enthusiastically as he pictured the panic on board the pirate ship.

"They'll be jumping overboard!" Ulf agreed, and they all laughed as they gathered round the crossbow to admire it.

"We should call it something," Jesper suggested. They all muttered agreement, then there was a pause as each tried to come up with a name before the others could think of one.

"Big Bessie!" Ulf suggested impulsively.

Wulf snorted derisively. "You want to give it a girl's name?" he jeered.

Ulf went red. Sometimes he wished he could remember to think twice before he spoke. Or even once.

"How about Gorlog's Hammer?" Edvin suggested. The others looked at him, frowning.

"Bit classical, isn't it?" Stefan said. Edvin shrugged diffidently, then Jesper pointed out a fault in the name.

"Gorlog doesn't have a hammer," he said. "Tharon has a hammer." Tharon was the god of thunder.

"Well, Tharon's Hammer then," Edvin suggested, trying to salvage his idea. But he was greeted by headshakes all round.

"Naaah. Still too classical," Stig said. "We want a good blood-and-guts name for it."

There was another silence. Hal eventually broke it.

"I like what Thorn called it," he said. They looked at him curiously, so he reminded them. "The Mangler."

They considered it. Gradually, smiles began to break out.

"The Mangler," Stefan said, approval obvious in his tone.

"That's what it'll do, all right," Ulf put in, and even his brother had to agree with that.

Hal grinned at Stig. "Well, what do you think? Is it blood-and-gutsy enough for you?"

Stig nodded, grinning broadly in his turn.

And so the Mangler it became.

The *Heron* was cruising in Shelter Bay.

It was the day after Hal had demonstrated the Mangler to his crew. Outside, on the open seas, the wind still howled out of the south, whipping the ocean into steep, fast-breaking whitecaps. It was no place for a small open ship like the *Heron*. But the tall headlands broke the force of the wind so that inside the bay there was nothing more than a stiff breeze.

The crew were made aware of the wild conditions outside when they looked at the trees on top of the headlands, and high on the inland ridge. They were bending and swaying madly, tossing their heads in the savage gusts that hit them.

The *Heron* was sailing parallel to the beach, about three hundred meters offshore. The wind was coming over their port side and the sail was trimmed in tight.

"Stig," Hal called, and gestured to the tiller.

His friend leapt eagerly up to the steering platform and took control of the ship. He twitched the tiller from side to side, testing the ship's instant reaction to the helm, and smiled at Hal.

"I love this," he said. "She's so light and responsive."

"I never get tired of it myself," Hal agreed. Then, in a more businesslike tone, he continued. "We're coming up on the first target. When I signal, head her in toward the beach. I'll shoot when we're a hundred meters out."

They'd discussed the plan the night before and the details were clear in Stig's mind. But it didn't hurt to run through them one more time. Hal hesitated. It seemed strange to leave the *Heron* in someone else's hands. Stig shoved him playfully.

"Get for'ard to the Mangler!" he said.

Hal laughed, turned away and made his way to the bow. He passed Ulf and Wulf, who were crouched by the sheets that trimmed the big sail. They nodded to him with serious faces, and he nodded back, knowing they were obeying his rule about not arguing on board ship. He ducked under the port-side shrouds supporting the mast and joined Ingvar beside the Mangler.

The huge crossbow was now mounted on a wooden platform that swiveled through a forty-five-degree arc, either side of the bow. Hal had added a small bench seat to the carriage so he could look over the sights as Ingvar traversed the weapon to either side. He crouched on it now, watching the target onshore. Then he turned to Edvin, who was waiting to relay his instructions to Stig, and pointed to starboard.

"Come to starboard!" Edvin called, and as Stig hauled in on the tiller and the bow started to swing, and the wind came from astern, Ulf and Wulf let the sail out so that it stood out from the hull. It was a prearranged maneuver that they had discussed the previous night and everyone knew his part. Thorn moved forward from the waist of the ship and stood with his back to the mast to observe the shot.

Hal crouched and peered down the sights, setting the hundred-meter mark against the front bead.

He was slightly to the right of the target. He held up his left hand.

"Left . . . left . . . left," he called as Ingvar traversed the Mangler, heaving on a long lever inserted into a socket at the rear of the carriage. The big crossbow moved smoothly on its platform.

"Stop," he called as the sights lined up with the target. Ingvar had already cocked and loaded the weapon while Hal was making his way forward.

The bead sight was still below the target, but as the *Heron* moved closer inshore, it was gradually coming up. The ship was pitching with the waves, so that the sights now started to move slightly above the target, then drop below it again. He'd have to compensate for that, Hal thought.

He waited until the sight was on target in the middle of the upward pitch, and pulled the trigger lanyard.

SLAM!

The limbs of the bow banged forward, the carriage bucked and the bolt went streaking away. He sat upright to watch it, eyes riveted on the target.

There was an explosion of sand five meters behind it.

"Missed," Thorn said. He might be the oldest member of the crew, but his eyes were still sharper than anyone else's.

There was a groan of disappointment from the crew and Thorn turned to speak to them.

"Early days yet," he said. "It's not easy shooting from a moving platform."

"Bear away," Hal said to Edvin, who repeated the order to Stig. They were getting too close to the beach. Hal couldn't hide the disappointment in his voice. He'd been hoping for a perfect shot first time. He'd underestimated the difficulty of dealing with the movement of the ship, and the slight delay between pulling the trigger and the bow's release.

Stig shouted sail trimming orders and the *Heron* spun neatly to port, angling out away from the beach. Ulf and Wulf hauled the sail in to match the new course.

"Was it close?" Ingvar asked. Of course, Hal thought, he hadn't been able to see the result.

"Five meters long," he said.

"But on line," Thorn reminded him.

Hal shrugged. At least that was something, he thought. He glanced at Thorn.

"This is going to be harder than I thought," he said.

The ragged sea wolf inclined his head. "Keep practicing. You'll get it."

But success continued to elude Hal. They tried four more times. On the third, the bolt clipped the right-hand side of the target. On all the others, it sailed clear—either over or under or to the side. Hal was left with only one bolt for the crossbow.

They stood off the beach and Hal called a council of war with Stig and Thorn.

"We're going to have to get closer," he said. "We're pitching and rolling—and the *Raven* will be doing the same. A hundred meters is too far for accuracy. Let's take her in to fifty meters for the last shot."

Thorn screwed his mouth up. Stig looked doubtful as well.

"Fifty meters?" Thorn said. "That'll be getting awfully close if we're fighting the *Raven.*"

Hal spread his hands in a helpless gesture. "It's no good staying away from her if I can't hit her."

Thorn nodded reluctant agreement. "You'll be well in range if any of them are archers," he pointed out.

Hal's brows came together in frustration. "We'll deal with that later," he said. "Let's see if we can hit the target from fifty meters."

He made a quick mental calculation as he returned to the bow. The minimum setting on the sight was one hundred meters, and the bolt flew virtually flat for that distance. If he set his aiming point slightly below the target, that should be enough.

"Load her up," he told Ingvar. As the big boy heaved the cord back and placed the last bolt in its groove, he told him what they were planning. Ingvar's mouth twisted into a thoughtful expression.

"Fifty meters? Isn't that getting a little close?"

Hal raised one eyebrow. "So everyone tells me," he said as he took his seat behind the bow.

The crew held their collective breath as the *Heron* swept in toward the beach. Ingvar eased the crossbow around until it was on line and Hal crouched over the sights, concentrating fiercely. The bead foresight rose and fell above and below the target.

"Any time now," Thorn called. He was estimating the range. They'd agreed he would give Hal five seconds' notice when they were coming up to fifty meters.

Hal watched the rise and fall of the foresight. Allowing for the slight delay between pulling the trigger and the crossbow's release, he'd need to be a little below his selected aiming point.

Almost . . . almost . . . now!

SLAM!

He sat up in time to see the target explode in a hail of splintered wood. They were close enough to hear the smashing sound as the bolt crashed into it. As the thought hit him, he realized they were also coming perilously close to the beach.

"Bear away!" he called, and Stig brought the bow round once more. Hal slumped on his seat. The tension of the last few minutes had exhausted him. The other boys were cheering. Jesper and Stefan were dancing a jig on the deck between the rowing benches. Even Ulf and Wulf were pounding each other on the back.

Thorn slapped him on the shoulder. "Good work!" he said, a wide smile on his face. Hal rolled his eyes.

"Maybe. But you were right. We'll be getting awfully close to them. I'm going to have to figure how we'll handle that."

Several days passed, and the Herons continued in their new schedule: physical drills and workouts in the morning and shooting practice with the Mangler in the afternoon.

The results of the shooting were improving. Now Hal could hit the target at least one time in four from one hundred meters. From fifty meters, the results were much better, with target after target being smashed to splinters.

But fifty meters was a dangerous distance, as Thorn had pointed out. In addition to the risk of arrows or other missiles being shot from the *Raven*, it left no margin for any errors in ship handling.

The Magyaran ship was fast and, under oars, highly maneuverable. Any slight mistake or delay could leave *Heron* vulnerable to that cruel ram *Raven* carried in her bow. In his mind's eye, late at night, Hal had visions of that dreadful iron-shod beam smashing its way through *Heron*'s fragile timbers and the cold water pouring through a huge rent in the hull.

He discussed the problem with Stig and Thorn late one night when the others had taken to their bunks.

"It's not as bad as you think," Stig said. "After all, the *Raven* is a lot bigger than a one-meter target. It's not as if you'd miss her entirely if we shot from one hundred meters."

Hal shook his head. "I want to be able to hit specific targets," he said. "The rudder, for example, or the hull at the waterline. Or the bulwarks where the shrouds supporting the mast are attached. Or Zavac himself and whoever's on the tiller. We won't have enough bolts to just shoot away at the entire ship and hope we hit something important."

"So we need to get close," Thorn said and, when Hal glanced at him, he continued. "We can always mount our shields higher on the bulwarks to protect the crew. And Edvin could cover you and Ingvar with a shield."

"Ingvar particularly," Hal said. "If he's injured, we can't load the Mangler. But it's not just that. If we get in as close as fifty meters, and any one of us makes a mistake—Stig on the tiller, me with my timing, Ulf and Wulf on the sheets—we could find ourselves at the *Raven*'s mercy."

"And that's not a quality she's renowned for," Thorn said. Although there was no proof, he was convinced that the *Raven* was behind the disappearance of a small Skandian trading fleet many weeks ago.

"Can we trust Ulf and Wulf on the sail trimming?" he continued. "Should we switch them with Jesper and Stefan?"

Hal pursed his lips thoughtfully. "We'll still need to use them somewhere," he said. "And they have a good feeling for the trim of the sail, don't you think, Stig?"

"Yes," Stig agreed. "It's a bit of an instinctive thing to get it exactly right so we get the best performance out of the ship. They have the right feel for it. I don't have to keep telling them to adjust it. They get it right first time."

Hal nodded. He'd noticed the same quality in the twins.

"But if they start arguing—"

Hal cut Thorn off. "I don't think we need to worry about that. They know their lives will depend on it."

"It's not their lives I'm worried about," Thorn replied. "Mine will be depending on it as well."

There was a short silence while they considered that. Then Hal came to a decision.

"We'll leave them as they are for the moment and keep drilling. If there's any sign of an argument during the drills, I'll switch one of them to raising the yardarm with Jesper and switch Stefan to sail trimming."

Thorn looked at him keenly for a few seconds. There was no trace of doubt in Hal's voice, or in his eyes. Finally, the shabby warrior nodded assent.

"You're the skirl," he said.

"There's something else I wanted to bring up," Hal said. "You've said the key to our winning a fight is speed and agility."

Thorn nodded, waiting to hear what was coming next.

"I think it's going to be the same in a ship-to-ship fight. Particularly if we're getting in close. We need to get maximum speed out of the *Heron*. And we need to make her turn and change course as quickly as she can."

"She's pretty responsive to the helm now," Thorn said. "And she's fast."

"I think we can make her faster," Hal said. He glanced at Thorn. "What do you think, Thorn? Do you think she's faster than *Raven*?"

Thorn rubbed his bristled chin before answering.

"Most of the time, yes," he said. "If there's a good wind. But if the wind drops and *Raven*'s under oars, she'll be faster. And she'll turn more quickly. All Zavac has to do is back oars on one side and row forward on the other and she'll turn in her own length. What's your idea?"

Hal paused, ordering his thoughts. "Two years ago, I went on a trading voyage with Anders," he said. "He was buying hemp and timber and we went into several Sonderland ports. I saw some of their big trading vessels there. They had huge wooden boards on either side of the ship that they could raise or lower as they wished." He looked questioningly at Thorn, who nodded.

"They call them leeboards," Thorn said. "They extend below the hull when they're lowered. They give the ship a greater resistance against the water, so they make less leeway. That's important for them because they spend a lot of time in shallow coastal waters, with the wind blowing toward the shore. When they get into really shallow water, they can raise them again so they don't run aground."

"I was thinking of trying something similar on *Heron*," Hal said.

The others looked at him doubtfully.

"You can hardly mount big, heavy boards along *Heron*'s sides," Stig said.

Thorn agreed with him. "Those Sonderland barges are massive slab-sided craft," he said. "The *Heron*'s built much lighter and the hull is curved. There'd be no place to put leeboards—no structure to support them."

"I wasn't thinking of putting them on the sides. I thought I'd use one in the middle. Beside the keel."

"And how would you mount it there?" Thorn was still trying to get his mind around this idea.

"I thought I'd cut away a section of the planking next to the keel and—"

"Just a moment!" Stig protested. "You're planning to cut through a plank *next to the keel*?"

Hal nodded. "That's right. Then I could—"

"You *do* know what happens when you cut a hole in the bottom of a ship, don't you? The ship tends to sink." He looked to Thorn for corroboration. "You tell him, Thorn."

Thorn raised his eyebrows. As a rule, he trusted Hal's ideas, but this did seem extreme.

"It's not usually considered a good idea to cut holes in the bottom of a ship," he said. Stig threw his hands in the air in a see-what-I-mean gesture.

"I'm not *cutting holes in the bottom of the ship*, as you put it. It's only one hole." But Hal got no further before Stig erupted again.

"It's only one ship! How many holes do you want? One will definitely be enough to do the job! You cut. We sink. Not a good idea, Hal!" He shook his head violently. "Or is this just another one of those small details you tend to forget?"

Hal's head snapped up angrily at those words. "I wondered when we'd get to that," he said.

Stig threw his hands up again. "Well, it's a pretty obvious question, isn't it? You do have something of a track record with water going where it shouldn't."

They all paused for a second, remembering the disastrous scene in Karina's kitchen when Hal's running water system had gone disastrously wrong, flooding the kitchen and nearly landing a large cask on Stig's head.

"This is different," Hal said.

Stig nodded vigorously. "It's different, all right. That time we just got wet. This time we could drown!"

Thorn decided it might be time to intervene. At least, he thought, Hal should be given a chance to explain his idea.

"Let's hear what Hal has to say without interrupting all the—"

"Who's interrupting?" Stig said. Then, catching Thorn's steely gaze, he subsided. "Oh . . . well, yes. I suppose I am."

"I suppose you are," Thorn agreed. Stig shrugged several times, then made a rolling gesture with his hand.

"Well, sorry. Carry on, Hal. I'll try not to interrupt."

"That would be nice," Hal said. He paused, to see if his friend had anything further to say. When he didn't, Hal continued. "You see, water seeks its own level—"

But Stig couldn't help himself.

"That's what I'm saying! You cut a hole and it will seek its own level. It will come into the boat and sink it and we'll all drown." He paused and shook his head at Hal. "But your way of putting it is much more scientific."

"Stig," said Thorn, "if you don't shut up for five minutes, I'll take you down to the beach and drown you right now. You won't have to wait for the boat to sink."

Stig met Thorn's eyes and saw a nasty glint there. He sensed that the old sea wolf wasn't making an idle threat.

"All right," he said, with very bad grace. "I'll shut up."

"If I could believe it—" Hal began. But Thorn cut in testily.

"Don't you start or I'll drown the two of you! Get on with this crazy scheme of yours."

"Hah!" said Stig, feeling he was vindicated by Thorn's words. Thorn swung a furious glance at him.

"You're trembling on the brink, boy. On the brink! Hal, go on."

"All right. Stig, you're right, if I was just cutting a hole in the bottom of the boat, we would be in trouble." He raised a hand to stop the words springing to Stig's lips. "But I'm not doing that. I'm going to remove a section of plank next to the keel, and then I'm going to build a cofferdam around it."

Stig frowned. "A coffledam? What's a coffledam?"

"Cofferdam," Hal corrected him. "It's like a barrier against the water—a reinforced box structure around the gap in the planks, which extends up past the waterline. The water will come up into it as far as the waterline of the ship, then it'll stop."

Stig frowned, not quite understanding. Thorn looked a little more convinced, but he wasn't one hundred percent sure.

"Why does the water stop?" Stig asked.

"Because it's reached its own level. It reaches the level of the water outside the hull and it doesn't go any farther."

"Are you sure?" Thorn asked. It all sounded very theoretical. But in his experience, theories didn't always work out in practice.

"I'm sure," Hal said, his entire manner positive. But they'd seen him be positive about things in the past and they both eyed him with some skepticism. He shrugged.

"All right," he said. "I've built a model to test it. I'll show you tomorrow morning."

Thorn rose, groaning slightly as his knees creaked with the movement.

"We'll look in the morning then," he agreed. "For now, let's get to sleep."

The boys rose as well and he watched them balefully, seeing how easily they accomplished the movement.

"One day your knees will creak," he told them. Stig looked up at him and rolled his eyes.

"If I don't get drowned by my best friend in the meantime."

The model was a simple rectangular box, one and a half meters long, half a meter wide and open at the top.

In the center of the bottom, Hal had cut a narrow rectangular hole. He had inserted another four-sided box into this, open at top and bottom, positioning it so that it rose up almost half as high as the larger box's sides. Ingvar carried the wooden structure to the water's edge. They had selected a sheltered rock pool for the experiment. At Hal's gesture, Ingvar placed the large box into the water.

Stig craned forward quickly, expecting to see water pouring up through the smaller box and flowing out into the larger one. He frowned in disappointment when he saw that nothing of the kind was happening. The large box floated serenely on the water's surface. The water rose a centimeter or two inside the smaller box, then stopped.

"The big box is drawing about two centimeters of water," Hal told them. "And that's as far as the water will come up through the smaller box. Load in some rocks, Ingvar."

There were plenty of large rocks on hand and Ingvar began loading them carefully into the box. It sank lower in the water as the extra weight was added, until the water had reached a mark Hal had made on the side.

"Check it now," he said.

Thorn and Stig both waded forward in the knee-high water and peered into the narrow central box. The water had risen to a second mark Hal had made on the inside.

"That mark corresponds to the mark on the outside of the hull," Hal explained. "As the boat sinks lower, the water will rise inside—but only as far as it does on the outside."

"Fascinating," Thorn said, shaking his head as he peered into the box. "I suppose it's logical when you see it. But you knew this would happen, did you?"

Hal hesitated, then decided truth was the best option.

"I thought it might work like this but I couldn't be sure." He grinned at Stig. "After all, it does seem to be tempting fate to put a hole in the bottom of a boat. That's why I thought I should test it."

"I didn't think it'd work either," Ingvar said. "But Hal seems to know about these things."

"Your faith in me is touching, Ingvar," Hal said, and looked meaningfully at Stig.

His friend shrugged, unabashed. "That's because he never saw what happened to that cask on the kitchen wall," he said. "But I have to admit you're right this time. Now, tell me, what's the point of doing this, clever as it may be?"

"All right," Hal said, suddenly all brisk and businesslike again.

"Let's assume we're sailing, and the wind is coming from the side. We trim the sail in hard, and the boat tilts under the wind's pressure, right?"

Thorn and Stig nodded. Hal gestured to Ingvar and he pushed down on one side of the box, tilting it to represent a boat under sail.

"Now, the harder we haul the sail in, the faster we go. But . . . the harder we haul in, the more the boat leans."

Ingvar pushed farther until the water was lapping the side of the box. A liter or two spilled into the box.

"Eventually, we start taking water over the side, so we have to let the sail out. The boat comes more upright . . ." Ingvar allowed the box to resume a more upright position. "And we lose speed."

Hal looked at them for confirmation and they both nodded their understanding.

"But, if we could keep the sail hauled in tight without having the boat lean so far, we'd get more speed."

As he spoke, he waded back to the edge of the rock pool and picked up a small plank that Ingvar had left there. He inserted the plank straight down into the narrow central box. It fitted snugly and he pushed it all the way down until the plank protruded below the bottom of the box.

"Now as the wind tries to tilt the boat, there's extra resistance from the board below the waterline. That extra resistance will stop the boat leaning so far. The end result is, we can keep the sail trimmed tighter and we'll go faster."

"It's like a big fin below the water," Stig said. Initially skeptical, he had been won over by the demonstration. He looked up at his best friend, admiration in his eyes.

"You've done it again," he said. "First the sail, now this big, retractable fin. What do you think, Thorn?"

"It certainly looks logical to me," he said. "Sometimes when *Wolfwind* was leaning too far, Erak would make the crew sit on the windward rail to help keep it upright. This would have a similar effect. Just don't make me watch when you cut a hole in the bottom of the *Heron*."

They began work on the modification that afternoon. Stig supervised the rest of the crew as they emptied the ship of stores and the ballast rocks that lay below the deck. He grinned apologetically at Thorn.

"I'm afraid you'll have to find another place to sleep for a few nights," he said.

Thorn grunted. "I'll pitch a tent under the trees. Anything to avoid bunking in with you lot. I can't abide boy-smell."

Stig raised an eyebrow at that. "You're not exactly a nosegay yourself, you know," he said, but Thorn snorted derisively.

"Here we go again . . . There's nothing wrong with the way I smell," he said. "I've got a mature smell, I have."

"So has cheese," Stig told him.

As Thorn couldn't think of a crushing reply, he stalked off, leaving Stig grinning behind him.

While the rest of the crew were emptying the ship, Hal took Ulf with him into the forest to select a suitable tree for the fin. They found a young fir tree with a trunk about fifty centimeters across. They cut it down, trimmed it, and set themselves to sawing off a section a meter and a half in length. When they had dragged that back to the camp, Hal would use his splitting wedges to progressively pare away the outer, curved edges, leaving a flat-sided rectangle of heartwood, fifteen centimeters thick. He would do the final trimming and shaping with an adze.

By the time he and Ulf returned to the camp, dragging the heavy log behind them, the ship had been emptied. A rope was attached to the top of the mast. Ingvar and Wulf hauled on it while the others assisted by pushing to roll the hull over on its side, then propping it in that position, so that Hal had access to the bottom of the ship.

Hal marked a section of plank alongside the keel and between two of the ship's rib-like frames and, working quickly with his hand drill and saw, cut it out.

"It'll be a little off center," he said. "But we can't cut through the keel itself—it's the backbone of the ship. Besides, this way I can fasten the inner box firmly to the keel to give it extra strength."

Thorn and Stig nodded wisely, as if they understood everything he was saying. Then he added extra nails to the cut ends of the plank, fastening them more securely to the two hull frames. The light had almost gone by the time he was finished and he rose from his crouched position and gestured for the props to be removed.

"You can let her sit upright for now," he said. "I'll be working inside the hull for the next few days."

Gingerly, the crew loosened the rope and removed the props,

allowing the *Heron* to roll upright once more. Hal dusted off his hands, satisfied with a good day's work.

"Now let's see what Edvin has got ready for supper," he said.

Over the next few days, the rest of the crew returned to their combat training under Thorn's direction, while Hal attended to the detail work of fitting the new fin. He split and shaped the fin itself, then constructed the waterproof box that it would slide up and down in. He assembled the box in place, fitting it into the hole he had cut and fastening it firmly to the keel on one side, and to the frames at its front and back. Its interior was lined with leather and sheepskin to hold the sliding fin tight, and to waterproof the box itself.

Hal cast a critical eye over his dwindling supply of materials. When they had left Bearclaw Creek, he had taken all his tools, plus his supplies of timber, cordage, nails, canvas and iron from his workshop. Now he was running short.

"I'm going to need to restock soon," he muttered. He'd checked his maps and knew there was a trading port a day's sail to the south. Once the weather moderated, they could take the *Heron* out to test the new fin, and he could pick up supplies. He was particularly short of the iron strips he needed to reinforce the points of the Mangler's bolts and he needed to prepare a good supply of those. He'd already lost a third of his current supply during the practice sessions.

He sighed. He could face that problem when the wind slackened, he thought.

He straightened momentarily, easing the aching muscles in his back. Then he returned to his gluing and nailing, and caulking the new joins with scraps of oiled rope and wool. Finally, as the last light faded, he tapped one final piece of oiled wool caulking into place and sat back.

"That should do it," he said. "Tomorrow, we'll see if it works."

Hal woke suddenly, later that night. He lay for a moment, wondering what had woken him, hearing the faint sounds of the other boys sleeping. Someone was snoring softly—probably Ingvar, he thought. Another of the boys was muttering incomprehensibly every so often. But it wasn't these noises that had awoken him. He lifted the canvas flap at the entrance of the tent and looked out. The moon had set, so he knew it must be after midnight. Quietly, he rolled out of his blankets, pulled on his sheepskin vest and went outside.

The wind had dropped.

That was what had woken him. The wind, howling in from the southwest, had been a constant factor in their lives all the time they had been here in Shelter Bay. It tossed the treetops high on the headlands surrounding the bay, setting up a sound like surf on a beach.

As he moved away from the tent, he realized that he could still hear the waves outside the bay, breaking on the protective headlands. It would take a while for the waves to dissipate, he knew, but the trees were still and, as he glanced up, he could see stars without the usual racing cloud wrack covering them. The sky was clear.

"I think the worst of it is over."

Hal started at the sound. He turned to find Thorn a few meters behind him.

"Why don't you make a noise when you walk up behind someone?" he asked a little petulantly.

"Just habit," Thorn said, grinning. Then he looked up at the stars, brilliant in the blackness of the sky. "We could probably put to sea tomorrow," he said. "I think the storm has blown itself out—at least for a few days."

Hal sniffed the air. He had no idea why. He'd seen older sailors do it, but he had no idea what they were smelling that would help them determine what the weather was going to do.

"I think you may be right," he said. He had no basis for knowing whether Thorn was right or not, except that he trusted the older man's instincts. Thorn had spent many years at sea and he understood weather patterns. "I need some supplies. We'll take *Heron* out tomorrow and head down the coast. I saw a town on the map, about a day's sail to the south. Called Skegall."

Thorn nodded, then flapped his arms, slapping them against his body. He was wearing trousers and a woolen shirt, with no outer covering. Now that the cloud cover had gone, the temperature had dropped considerably.

"It's cold," he muttered. "Couldn't find my sheepskin vest. Have you seen it?"

Hal hesitated. "When?" he asked.

Thorn regarded him with an annoyed look. "When do you think? Today!"

Hal shook his head. "No. I haven't seen it today." He looked away, avoiding Thorn's eyes. Thorn shivered again.

"Blasted nuisance. I'm freezing."

"Maybe you can buy a new one in Skegall," Hal suggested, but Thorn snorted irritably.

"I don't want a new one. I like my old one."

"It was pretty beaten up and raggedy," Hal said.

"That's why I like it. It suits me," Thorn replied. Then, after a pause, he asked, "Why did you say it *was* old and raggedy?"

"Well . . . it was. And it is. Wherever it's gotten to. I'm going back to bed."

And he hurried back to his blankets, with Thorn watching suspiciously after him.

The *Raven* was at sea.

South of Shelter Bay, the weather had cleared several days earlier and Zavac had put to sea immediately. The *Raven* was a bigger ship than the *Heron*, with a much larger crew to handle her, and to bail her out if necessary. So Zavac had no fears about her ability to handle the waves.

And Zavac's hunting instincts were aroused.

After a lengthy storm like the one that had finally passed, he knew that traders would be eager to get to sea as soon as possible. The first ships to reach trading ports in the weeks to come could demand a premium for their cargoes, since goods would be scarce due to the storm's delays. Once more and more ships were at sea, however, the prices would come back to normal.

That meant there would be lone ships on the ocean, laden with valuables and trade goods. Their captains would be after those initial high profits. They wouldn't wait to travel in company with other ships—even though such a course might be safer—their speed would be restricted to that of the slowest ship in the fleet.

And they would be competing with the other captains to sell their cargoes.

Greed and an appetite for gold were wonderful motivators, Zavac thought. And he should know. They were what motivated him. He'd taken the *Raven* to sea the previous day, standing by the tiller until a few hours before dawn. Then, deciding that the weather held no unpleasant surprises in the near future, he'd turned in, leaving the helm to his second in command.

He woke hours later, sensing movement in the ship as the rowing crew changed. He rolled out of his sleeping furs and sat upright. Unlike the *Heron*, the *Raven* had a decked-in section running the full length of the ship. Zavac had a small sleeping cabin at the stern, accessed by a sliding hatch close to the steering platform. The headroom was minimal—barely a meter and a half. But it was sheltered and dry and it gave him privacy when he wanted it.

It also gave him an excellent place to store his personal treasures. He sat on the deck and pulled on his sealskin boots and a fur-trimmed leather jacket. His sword lay to one side in its scabbard and he picked it up, preparatory to going on deck. He half stood, crouching in the low headroom, then paused. There was a shelf to one side of the cabin, set on an upward angle to prevent its contents spilling out as the ship rolled. He reached toward it and stroked a chamois sack nestled on it, as he did every time he left the cabin. He felt the hard round shape inside the sack and smiled to himself.

"Oh, Oberjarl Erak, wouldn't you love to have this back?" he said softly. Then, still smiling, he slid back the hatch and clambered out onto the deck. Andras, his first mate, greeted him with a nod as he scanned the horizon.

"Any change?" Zavac asked, and his henchman shook his head.

"Wind may have moderated a little," he said.

Zavac nodded thoughtfully. "That'll suit us."

Andras, one hand on the tiller, pointed forward with his free hand.

"*Viper's* still on station," he said. Zavac had seen the smaller ship when he first scanned the horizon. It had been the first thing he looked for, in fact. She was half a kilometer away, rising and falling on the waves that continued to sweep in toward them. Like *Raven*, she was under oars, with her sail lowered to the deck, so that she would be less visible to other ships.

Originally named the *Sea Lion*, she had been one of the small Skandian trading fleet that he had captured some months previously. Zavac had ordered his men to burn her with the other trading ships. But a few minutes later, he had rescinded the order. The *Sea Lion*, or *Viper*, as he had renamed her, was a seaworthy ship, with plenty of cargo space for trade goods, and he thought he could put her to good use.

Not that Zavac intended her to carry trade goods. But that cargo space could also be used to conceal fifteen to twenty men, and unlike the *Raven*, the *Viper* looked relatively harmless. Most trading skippers, if they were sensible, would turn and run at the sight of the long, low *Raven*. But the *Viper* was a different matter.

If she appeared to be disabled or sinking, the chances were good that a ship would come to her aid. Once they were alongside, the concealed pirates would pour out of their hiding places and overwhelm their would-be rescuers. Traders carried relatively small crews, as Zavac knew only too well. And of course the *Raven*, hovering just over the horizon, could swoop in and finish the job.

"No signal from her?" Zavac asked.

Andras shook his head. "Nothing so far. But it's early yet."

Zavac grunted. His first mate was right. They had been at sea for less than half a day. Still, he was impatient. They had spent weeks moored in a sheltered creek on the Stormwhite coast—a spot known only to himself and several other Magyaran pirate skippers—and he resented the unproductive time. His men were loyal to him—but only so long as he could provide them with gold and silver and other booty. He knew he had a reputation as a lucky skipper but that could change after a few weeks of cruising without finding any victims. Zavac was superstitious and he half believed that if they didn't find a ship to prey on today, they would have lean pickings over the next few months.

He glanced down the double line of rowers, watching them lean forward, brace their feet, then heave back. The oars rose and fell on either side of the ship like a bird's wings, each one leaving a circle of white foam on the water as the ship swept past.

"Do you want to take her?" Andras asked, indicating the tiller. But Zavac shook his head. Most skippers felt an affinity for their ships and enjoyed the sensation of command. But Zavac took no great pleasure in steering his ship. She was a means to an end, a way of getting from point A to point B, nothing more.

Andras scowled. He'd been on the tiller for nearly six hours while Zavac had slept, and the strong current and steep waves of the cross-sea made it hard work to keep the ship on course. The rowing crew had changed ten minutes ago. They changed every two hours. But he'd had no respite. Andras resented Zavac and he was looking forward to the day when he'd saved enough of his plunder to buy his own ship.

He also felt that Zavac's disinterest in the *Raven* made him a less-than-expert ship handler. In Andras's opinion, a captain had to be thoroughly attuned to his ship, to understand her nuances and idiosyncrasies. That way, he would be equipped to get the very best performance out of her. Zavac's lack of instinctive feel for the ship might cost them dearly one day. So far, he'd been successful because she was very fast, even if she wasn't handled as well as she might be. But she'd never really been challenged by a ship that might match her speed, Andras knew.

"*Viper's* signaling!"

The lookout's call snapped Andras's mind back to the matter at hand. Both he and Zavac craned to see along the length of *Raven's* hull. The view forward was relatively unrestricted with the sail stowed. They saw a flash of light from the stern of the *Viper* as one of the crew there used a mirror to flash the sun's rays toward the *Raven*.

"Answer them," Zavac snapped.

The lookout at the bow took a polished piece of metal and, angling it to the sun, sent a series of random flashes back to the *Viper*. There was no need for a message at this stage. The simple act of flashing the light at the other ship would let the *Viper's* skipper know they were watching, waiting for the other ship to communicate using the simple code Zavac had devised.

There was a solitary flash from the other ship's stern. Then a long pause, then another single flash.

One. One ship. It could only be a ship. There was nothing else out here for the *Viper* to signal about.

"Answer!" Zavac ordered again. The lookout sent another random series of flashes across the intervening ocean, telling the signaler that *Raven* had understood the message so far and he could now move onto the next part, which would be to indicate the course of their intended target.

The light flickered rapidly from the other ship. Zavac and Andras both counted under their breaths.

"Eight," they said simultaneously as the light stopped flashing. There was a pause, then it started again. Again, they both counted eight flashes. Zavac glanced at his first mate for confirmation.

"It's heading northwest," Andras confirmed.

In their simple code, the major points of the compass were indicated by numbers, with one being north, two being northeast, three being east and so on. Eight flashes meant northwest. As they considered this, the light began its rapid flashing again. The sender would continue until they acknowledged that they had received his message.

"Answer, blast you!" Zavac snapped irritably at the lookout. The sailor rolled his eyes. It wasn't up to him to acknowledge any of *Viper*'s signals until he was told to do so. Zavac had no call to vent his anger at him. Now he angled his steel plate across the sun in a back-and-forth movement to send a return series of flashes.

Zavac thought for a moment. The wind was out of the south, veering occasionally to the southwest. To be heading northwest, the unknown ship would be under sail, with the wind coming from her port beam.

"Signal three," he called to the lookout. The man nodded and began to send a slow-paced series of flashes, three at a time. He continued until the *Viper* replied with a rapid flashing signal indicating that they'd received the message.

Zavac, his eyes fixed on the *Viper*, spoke out of the corner of his mouth to Andras. "Stop rowing."

As the first mate relayed the order, the men raised their oars parallel to the surface of the ocean and rested their elbows on them. Gradually, the way ran off the low black ship and she rocked and pitched on the waves.

On board *Viper*, the crew were hurriedly shoving a tangled mass of sail, rope and a broken spar over the starboard side, so the hull listed heavily. Then, as one of the crew at the stern lit a small iron pot filled with oily rags, a column of dark smoke began to drift upward. Within a few minutes, the trim little ship had taken on the appearance of a cripple—and one in desperate straits.

"Take her away to port," Zavac said, and Andras ordered the crew to start rowing again, heaving on the tiller so that the *Raven* began a long turn back to the northeast. Gradually, the *Viper* dropped below the horizon, until all they could see of her was the column of smoke, drifting on the moderate breeze.

"Hold her here," Zavac said.

Andras issued orders for the rowers to alternately row and back water so that the *Raven* held her position.

"Raise the bow whip!" Zavac called, and several crewmen got busy, raising a slender mast and attaching it to the bow post. The lookout quickly climbed the narrow pole. It swayed beneath his weight but held firm. There was a crosspiece near the top and he settled onto it, wrapping arms and legs around the vertical spar.

"I've got *Viper* in sight," he called.

Zavac nodded, satisfied. The slim spar the lookout was resting on would be far less visible than the *Raven*'s thick mast and crossyard. Chances were their victim would never see the figure of the lookout, suspended just above the horizon.

They waited. Minutes passed with no further report from the lookout. Finally, Zavac called out in exasperation.

"Do you see anything?"

"Just the *Viper*," came the reply.

Andras eyed his skipper with mild scorn. "He'd say if he had," he muttered.

Zavac swung on him. "Don't tell me my job!" he snarled. "Just make sure you're doing yours!"

Yours and mine both, Andras thought. But he wisely said no more.

More waiting. Zavac's hand clenched and unclenched on the hilt of his sword, its scabbard thrust through the heavy belt at his waist. He cursed under his breath, wondering what was happening beyond the immediate horizon. The unknown ship may have smelled a rat and turned away. His hastily devised signal code wasn't sufficiently sophisticated for the *Viper* to send him a minute-by-minute account of proceedings. She could tell him how many ships there were and which way they were heading, little more.

"Lookout!" he snapped. "Do you see anything?"

There was a pause while the lookout considered shouting back

If I did, I'd tell you, wouldn't I? But he discarded the notion. Zavac had an uncertain temper and the lookout had seen men killed for insubordination far milder than that. Instead, he replied as before.

"Just the *Viper*."

There was another pause, while Zavac stalked the deck, back and forth, scowling in fury. Andras was tempted to point out that, if their quarry had sailed away, *Viper* would not be keeping up the appearance of a ship in distress. The fact that the smoke still drifted above the horizon indicated that she was doing so.

"Captain!" yelled the lookout.

Zavac's head snapped up.

"There's another ship in sight! A nice, fat trader by the look of her. And she's heading for the *Viper!*"

R eady oars!" Zavac shouted, not bothering to relay the
order through Andras. The rowers settled themselves
more firmly on the benches, rolling their shoulders
and stretching their muscles prior to beginning to
row again.

The rest of the crew were busy arming themselves, and making
jokes about the fate of their intended victim.

"Lookout!" snarled Zavac.

"She's coming alongside *Viper* . . . almost there. Now she's alongside . . . Hah! There go *Viper*'s boarders!"

The last report was delivered with a triumphant shout. The
lookout craned round on his perch to see what Zavac's reaction
would be. He didn't have long to wait.

"Oars!" Zavac shouted.

The oars dipped into the water, paused, then sent the pirate
ship surging forward with a sudden burst of energy. The lead rower,
seated halfway along the port side where he could be heard by all
his companions, called the stroke for a few beats, then they settled
into their rhythm and he needed all his breath for rowing.

Gradually, the other two ships climbed over the horizon as *Raven* swept toward the battle. In a few minutes, Zavac could make out details—his own men swarming over the bulwarks onto the trading ship, hemming her crew into the bow as they forced them backward along the deck. The dark figures of the pirates seemed to cover the deck of the other ship. Zavac could make out no more than eight in the trader's crew. Possibly less.

He turned to Andras.

"Bring us along her port side," he ordered. The *Viper* was already grappled to the trader's starboard side, clinging like a leech.

Andras nodded and leaned into the tiller. The *Raven* swung until she was on course, then steadied.

"Faster!" Zavac shouted, and the lead rower called a new cadence, increasing the pace of the oars. The *Raven* seemed to leap forward.

They were close enough now to hear the cries of wounded men and the clash of sword against sword, punctuated by the dull, heavy thuds of axes striking wooden shields. Occasionally, as a blow went home, they could hear splintering sounds.

They were almost up to the two ships now and Zavac called a warning.

"In oars!"

The port-side rowers instantly hefted their oars up out of harm's way, holding them vertically as the ship slid alongside the trader, then grated against her with a drawn-out, shuddering crash.

Other crew members were standing by with grapnels and they hurled them now and hauled in tight on the ropes, locking *Raven* to the trader. As the two bulwarks ground together, Zavac drew his sword and led the way onto the other ship.

"Come on!" he shouted, and a score of battle-ready pirates followed him.

There were only four of the trader's crew left alive by now. At the sight of the overwhelming numbers facing them, they let out cries of despair and then, in response to one who was obviously their captain, they let their weapons fall to the deck with a clatter.

The gesture of surrender was too late for one of them, as a pirate's spear was already thrusting forward. It took him in the middle of the body and drove him back. He screamed and fell to the deck, the spear still transfixing him as the pirate struggled to free it.

"Enough!" roared Zavac. "Lower your weapons!"

A few of the men from the *Viper* seemed reluctant to obey. Their fighting blood was up and they had no wish to stop. Zavac had expected as much and he'd prepared three of his own boarding party, all big men armed with clubs, to take charge. He gestured them forward now.

"Stop them," he said.

It wasn't done out of any sense of mercy. He'd noted the captain, who had given the order to surrender, was one of the survivors. Zavac wanted time to question him. Sometimes, trading captains could provide very valuable information.

The three big men barged through the *Viper*'s crew, shoving them out of the way. They reached the spearman just as he freed his weapon from the sailor's body. His eyes were still wild and he was looking for another victim. One of the big men stunned him with a blow to the head. It was so offhand, so casually brutal, almost an afterthought. The spearman crumpled and fell to the deck.

Zavac then shoved forward through the group who surrounded the remaining three sailors. He grabbed the captain's collar in his left hand. His right held his long, curving sword.

"You!" he shouted. "You captain, yes?"

The man looked at him, contempt in his eyes. Then he spat on the deck.

"*Oui,*" he replied. "*Je suis le capitaine.*"

"Gallican?" Zavac demanded, and the man nodded. Zavac glanced quickly at the other survivors. They were both common sailors. Their plain, rough clothes, weathered faces and hands and tarred pigtails made that obvious. They'd have little useful information. Zavac gestured at them with his sword.

"Kill those two."

As the captain, realizing what was about to happen, tried to shout a protest, two of the *Raven* crew stepped forward and cut the sailors down. One died in silence. The other gave a brief cry of pain and despair, then fell to the bloodstained deck.

"Search the ship," Zavac ordered. He re-sheathed his sword, then jerked a thumb at the Gallican captain. "Bring him aft," he ordered.

Two of the big men who had followed him aboard grabbed the captain by an arm on either side and marched him to the stern of the ship. At Zavac's signal, they threw the captain onto the deck. Zavac leaned against the bulwark close to the tiller, looking down curiously at the captain.

"Now, let's see what your ship is carrying," he said mildly.

It turned out that the trader was lightly laden, which indicated that she'd already sold most of her cargo farther to the south.

"You were quick off the mark," Zavac said cheerfully as he inspected the small pile of remaining trade goods dragged up from the cargo space. There were a few barrels of wine and ale, some clay jars of oil and several bales of wool.

Andras inspected the latter. "Pretty poor quality," he called.

Zavac nodded. They must have been unable to find a buyer for the wool, he thought.

"So, you've traded all your goods," he said to the captain. The man glared at him, seeming to not understand, until Zavac's thin veneer of good humor was cast aside.

"Don't playact with me!" Zavac shouted, drawing a long dagger from a sheath on his belt. "You speak the common tongue! You're a trader!"

Quick as a striking snake, he slashed the thin blade of the dagger across the Gallican's face, laying open a long cut. The man's hands flew to his face, then he stared, uncomprehending, at the blood staining them. Zavac's attack had been so fast, and his blade was so sharp, that the captain had barely felt the cut. Now the pain registered with him, a burning sensation across his face, accompanied by the rush of blood dripping down onto his clothes.

He huddled away from the Magyaran, hunching his shoulder in a futile attempt to avoid further punishment.

"Speak to me," Zavac demanded, his voice quiet once more.

The captain, one hand still pressed to the cut on his face, answered slowly. "What should I tell you?"

Zavac smiled, and pointed the tip of the dagger at the man's face, holding it loosely on the palm of his hand and letting the blade bounce up and down on his fingers.

"You've sold your cargo. That means your cash chest will be full of gold. Where is it?"

A lifetime of preying on other ships told him that somewhere there would be a concealed strongbox, where the gold they had earned would be kept. Of course, his men could find it eventually, if they tore the ship apart. But gold was relatively easy to conceal and it was generally simpler to have his victims tell him where the strongbox was.

The Gallican, however, shook his head. "There's no gold," he said. "Trading has been bad. The ship was damaged in the storms and I had to pay for repairs. There's nothing left, I swear."

Zavac looked at the dagger in his hand, seemed to come to a decision and re-sheathed it. He sighed deeply, looking up at the sky, rather than at the surly figure of the captain on the deck in front of him.

"You know," he said in a musing tone, "I wonder how many ships I've taken and sunk over the years. One hundred? Two hundred? Probably two hundred is closer to the mark. And I have to wonder why, in just about every one of those cases, the captain told me that there's no gold. There's no strongbox. There's no hidden compartment on his ship. They say the same thing every time. And do you know what?"

Now he let his gaze fall on the captain. The man was still nursing his injured cheek, although the blood was starting to congeal and wasn't flowing as freely. The captain looked up at the pirate with fear in his eyes. Zavac prompted him to answer his question.

"What?" said the captain.

"They were all lying. Every one of them. So, why should I think you're any different?"

"I . . . ," the captain began. Then he fell silent. He sensed it was useless talking to this man. He knew his life was forfeit and the only possible revenge he could have was to deny Zavac the knowledge he was seeking. Zavac looked at him with mock pity. Then he made a dismissive gesture.

"I can see you're not going to tell me," he said. He turned and walked away, heading back toward the bow. He hadn't gone more than three paces before he turned back to his two big henchmen.

"Torture him," he said briefly. "Call me when he's ready to talk." He considered his statement, then he amended it. "On second thought, when he's ready to talk, keep torturing him for another five minutes. Then call me."

It took fifteen minutes for the Gallican skipper to give in. Then, as instructed, the torturers continued their ghastly work for another five, before Zavac called a halt.

The captain was barely recognizable now. His face was a mask of blood and more blood stained his shirt. Two of the fingers on his right hand were missing, as was his left ear. There was a deep cut under one eye. It was this that had finally convinced him to give in. Even though, logically, he knew he was going to die, the thought of losing that eye had been too horrible.

Zavac surveyed him with professional interest, then smiled at his two heavily muscled assistants.

"Amazing what you can achieve in a few minutes with just a couple of sharp blades," he said. Then he dropped to one knee beside the captain, who was lying facedown in a pool of his own blood, breathing noisily past a broken nose.

"Now," said Zavac. "The strongbox."

He had to bend closer to hear the reply, slurred and breathless with pain as it was.

"False panel . . . behind anchor cable . . ."

Zavac slapped the man heartily on the shoulder.

"That's better!" he said. "I'm sure the truth has purged your soul of wickedness." He rose and started toward the bow. One of the torturers stopped him.

"Will we finish him off?" he asked, but Zavac shook his head.

"Wait till we see if he's telling the truth," he said. "I may have to ask him more questions."

But the strongbox was where the captain had said, concealed behind a false panel. There was no lock. The hiding place was considered security enough. But when Zavac pried the lid open, his eyes grew wider with avarice.

There was gold there, of course. And plenty of it. But nestling in a small compartment of their own were nine magnificent emeralds—the biggest and finest that Zavac had ever seen.

"Hello," he said quizzically. "Where do you suppose these came from?"

He repeated the question to the captain, who shook his head wearily, unable to summon the strength to answer. Zavac was tempted for a moment to hit him, to shake him and force the answer from him. But he sensed this would be the wrong approach. Instead, he dropped to one knee, leaned close and whispered to him.

"Tell me where the emeralds came from. And I'll make the pain stop."

The blood-rimmed eyes rose to meet his and he nodded encouragingly. Finally, the Gallican summoned his strength.

"Limmat. They came from Limmat."

Limmat was a trading port to the south of where they now were. Zavac frowned. He'd never heard of emeralds in that part of the coast.

"Don't lie to me," he warned, the smile fading from his face. But the Gallican shook his head doggedly.

"True. There's a mine in the hills behind the town. Hidden. Secret."

"Hidden? How is it hidden?"

"A barn. Built at the base of a hill. It hides the mine entrance."

Zavac rubbed his chin thoughtfully. "They've gone to a lot of trouble to hide it," he mused. The captain drew in another shuddering breath before replying.

"They don't want word to get out."

Zavac's smile returned. "I don't blame them," he said. "If it was well-known, it might attract the wrong sort of people."

He rose, a thoughtful expression on his face. He'd need more men if he was going to take Limmat. It was quite a large town and its inhabitants would presumably be ready to fight to save their emerald mine.

But Zavac knew where he could find reinforcements. There was a bay a few leagues away on the coast that served as an assembly point for Magyaran ships. It was standard practice for pirates to call there on their outward journeys, checking for word of a plum target like this one. Any captain who had come across such an opportunity and needed more men could find willing reinforcements there.

He'd go there, he thought, and see if any of his countrymen were there. If not, he'd wait a few days. At this time of year, with the hunting season starting, a ship would almost certainly call there in the near future. He began to pace away, deep in thought, when the captain called after him.

"You promised . . ."

Zavac turned, frowning. "I promised? Promised what?"

"Stop the pain . . ." The man held out a beseeching hand. With two fingers missing and caked in rapidly drying blood, it reminded Zavac of a bird's claw more than a human hand.

"Did I?" he said, then he smiled as he seemed to remember. "So I did."

He turned back to the captain and, drawing his curved sword, ran the man through.

"And I'm a man of my word."

Then he turned to his accomplices and jerked a thumb at the dead captain.

"Throw that overboard."

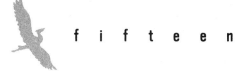

I n oars," Hal said. The Herons hurried to comply with the order. Then, anticipating the next command, Jesper and Stefan moved to the halyards, preparing to raise the yardarm and sail. As they did so, Ulf and Wulf moved to the sail trimming sheets.

The ship was riding the waters of Shelter Bay like a gull, some fifteen meters offshore. Soon, they would see if Hal's new fin worked or not.

The fin itself was poised at the top of the keel box. Thorn stood by, ready to push it down so that it extended below the hull.

"Starboard sail," Hal ordered, and Jesper and Stefan sent the starboard yardarm and sail soaring up the mast. The wind in the bay was moderate, but still strong enough to set the sail billowing out to starboard. Without needing to be told, Ulf and Wulf hauled in on the sheets and tightened the sail to the wind. As the ship heeled, with the starboard gunwale coming close to the water, they eased off and she came more upright.

Hal felt the accustomed moment of excitement as the ship

came to life, surging across the bay, the tiller vibrating slightly against his hand. The water slapped against the hull, and he could feel the small impacts through the soles of his feet. As the *Heron* gathered speed, he nodded to Thorn.

"Let it down."

Thorn leaned his weight on the fin and pushed it down through the keel box and into the water below. The padding and baffles that Hal had added to the inside of the box made it a snug fit. A few splashes of water came up through the box, displaced by the fin as it went down.

Instantly, Hal felt the difference as the fin began to bite. A shallow-keeled boat like the *Heron* tended to drift downwind, and the hull would skid slightly as she turned. Now the extra resistance of the fin took effect, so that as he pushed the tiller to starboard, the boat responded instantly, pivoting round the resistance of the fin with virtually no sideways skidding motion.

He glanced at Stig, who was watching him anxiously from the port-side rear-rowing bench.

"How is it?" Stig asked. Hal's huge grin told him the answer. But the young skirl beckoned him to the steering platform.

"See for yourself."

As Stig bounded up to join him, Hal called to Thorn.

"Raise the fin, Thorn." He wanted Stig to feel the difference as the fin was lowered and took effect.

Thorn grunted with effort as he raised the fin. Hal felt the downwind drift begin again almost immediately.

"That's a snug fit," Thorn said. "What did you line it with?"

"Oh, leather and some sheepskin," Hal said distractedly. He failed to notice Thorn's sharp look as he said *sheepskin*. Stig was standing beside him, eager to take the tiller. Hal handed it over and called to Thorn again.

"Down fin, Thorn."

Thorn glared at him, then shoved the fin down savagely. Water splashed up out of the keel box.

"Down through all that sheepskin, you mean?" he muttered darkly.

But Hal was watching Stig's face as he felt the fin take effect. A grin to match his own spread over his friend's features.

"That's amazing!" Stig said. "She tracks much more truly! There's hardly any drift!"

"Try a turn," Hal suggested. Once again, the new fin showed its value as Stig pulled the tiller toward him and the ship pivoted neatly and immediately, without skidding.

"She was good before," he said, his eyes wide with amazement. "But now she's perfect."

They were farther out in the bay now and the wind was blowing more strongly. Hal took the tiller and called to the twins.

"Bring the sail in hard."

They heaved on the trimming sheets. As the sail hardened and flattened, the *Heron* began to heel under the increased pressure. But it was balanced by the resistance of the fin below the surface. Ulf and Wulf were able to trim the sail in farther and farther. The *Heron* moved faster and faster through the water. Eventually, they reached a point where the water was only inches from the starboard gunwale, racing past the ship's side in a froth of white foam. They eased the sail a little to prevent the boat from being swamped. Astern of the ship, the white wake showed the speed of her passage.

Stig and Hal both shouted triumphantly.

"Incredible!" Stig said. Hal was too delighted to say anything. His enormous smile said it all for him. Ulf and Wulf looked up at the steering platform. Ulf shook his head in disbelief.

"Amazing!" he said. "We could never haul in this far before!"

"Look at how fast she's going!" Wulf said.

Hal beckoned to Thorn.

"Come and try it, Thorn!" he said. "Ease the sail, boys, and Stig, you bring the fin up!"

Thorn and Stig changed places. Stig waited until Ulf and Wulf had eased the sail considerably, then heaved the fin up once more.

As he did so, Thorn said meaningfully, "Careful. It's quite a tight fit. Apparently somebody lined it with *sheepskin*."

Suddenly, Thorn's preoccupation with the lining of the keel box registered with Hal and he looked guiltily at the old sea wolf.

"Oh . . . ," he said awkwardly. "Sorry, Thorn. I didn't know it was your sheepskin vest . . . I sort of found it . . . and I . . ."

"You assumed a sheep had died and left you its coat?" Thorn said with heavy sarcasm. "Just slipped out of it and left it lying around for you to find?"

"Well, no. Not really. I just didn't think . . ."

"And we're all used to that, aren't we?" Thorn replied. He held Hal's gaze until the young skirl dropped his eyes.

Point made, Thorn thought. Then he reached for the tiller.

"Right. Let's see how this fin of yours works."

Once again, they went through the sequence of actions to test the fin's effect, and like Stig and Hal before him, Thorn was amazed at the difference it made to the ship's performance.

"Well, you've done it," he told Hal. "Speed and agility. You've got them both now, in large amounts." Keeping tension on the tiller with his hook, he clapped his young friend on the shoulder with his left hand. "I suppose next you'll be putting wings on her so she can fly?"

Hal laughed. "I've been thinking about that. Not sure if I can get it to work . . . yet."

While testing the fin, they had been running back and forth inside Shelter Bay. Now they were heading for the entrance again. Hal studied the sea outside the bay. The waves were bigger, but nothing that *Heron* couldn't handle. He glanced at Thorn.

"Do you think this weather will hold?" he asked. Thorn glanced up at the sky, his eyes narrowed in concentration.

"I'd say it's cleared now. We should be all right for a couple of days, at least."

"Then let's head down the coast to that trading village," Hal said. "I've got supplies I have to buy."

"Including a nice, expensive new sheepskin vest," Thorn told him.

Hal nodded several times. "Well, of course. That's first on the list."

"Really? I'd like to see that list," Thorn said.

Hal tapped his forehead with one finger. "It's all up here in my head," he said. "But *sheepskin vest* is the first item there. Trust me."

"I did that once," Thorn replied. "Look where it got me."

PART 2

THE INVADERS

The town of Limmat was on the eastern side of a small
harbor, situated on the western shore of a wide, deep
bay. A wooden palisade surrounded the town.

The harbor entrance was narrow and guarded by
wooden watchtowers on either side. A heavy log boom ran across
the harbor mouth, barring entry to strange ships. Any ship that
tried to force its way through the boom could be raked by arrows
and lead shot from archers and slingers in the towers. Inside, the
harbor widened out to provide a sheltered anchorage. Any invading
force approaching from the wide, open bay to the northeast would
have to break through this palisade. A heavy gate was set into the
palisade on the northeastern side, where a small stretch of beach
ran from the gate to the waters of the bay.

On the southwest shore of the bay, the ground consisted of
low-lying, impenetrable swampland. The water was shallow, around
waist deep, and the bottom was treacherous with shifting mud.
Any attack from this side would quickly bog down in the marshes.
It might be navigable by small skiffs or coracles, but it would take

too many of them to carry a large force through the swamp. And even if attackers did manage to get through, they would be scattered during the approach and the town's defenders would have ample warning of their coming.

In addition, any attacking party that did manage to thread their way through the swamp and regroup would still find themselves on the wrong side of the harbor and the palisade that enclosed the inland side of the town.

It was a well-situated, eminently defensible position, Zavac thought as he surveyed it from the steering platform of the *Raven*. The long, low ship cruised past under oars, four hundred meters offshore. He could see movement on the watchtowers as the defenders caught sight of her. She was obviously a warship, not a trader, and the alarm would have gone up.

Looking to the narrow harbor entrance, he could make out a line of white water. He pointed it out to Andras.

"The boom is closed," he said.

His second in command nodded. "They probably have it in place all the time," he replied. He shaded his eyes and peered at the headlands on either side of the entrance. There would be winching devices somewhere that would allow the Limmatans to move the log boom back and forth, opening it to admit those ships they wanted to give entry to and closing it again to bar other, less welcome visitors.

"They've seen us," Andras said to Zavac. "We've lost the element of surprise."

Andras was puzzled. If they planned to attack and overrun Limmat, it would be better if the defenders had no idea they were in the area. A night attack would be the best, he thought, slipping in under cover of darkness and assaulting one of the two watchtowers with scaling ladders. But now that *Raven* had been seen, there would be little chance of pulling that off. The defenders would be alert. Chances were they'd double the watch during the dark hours, expecting just such an attack.

And a forewarned, nervous garrison was a much harder nut to crack than a complacent, sleepy garrison, feeling safe and secure inside their stronghold.

Zavac smiled at him. "I want them to see us," he said. "I want them to know we're in the area. I have a different kind of surprise in store for them. Now, let's give them a show."

He nudged the tiller and swung the *Raven* toward the shore. The rowers maintained their easy rhythm and the black ship glided through the water. As they came closer, he could make out the shouted cries of defiance from the men on duty in the watchtowers. Sunlight flashed on the blades of weapons as the garrison members brandished them.

He aimed the *Raven* for the gap between the harbor promontories.

"Faster," he ordered, and the rowers increased their pace. *Raven* began to surge forward, her speed building. A white bow wave formed at her prow as she arrowed for the boom—four massive hardwood logs, linked together by short lengths of chain, floating just below the surface of the water. If it wasn't for the small waves breaking across it, the boom would be all but invisible.

He measured the distance. They were one hundred and fifty meters out now and the sound of shouting and clashing of weapons was louder with each stroke of the oars. Suddenly he threw up his arm.

"Back water!" he shouted. The oarsmen strained against their oars as they reversed their thrust. He felt the *Raven* check suddenly and he stumbled a pace forward before regaining his balance.

"Back port! Forward starboard!" he ordered and, as the two banks of rowers pulled and pushed frantically in opposing directions, the *Raven* lurched in a hard turn to port, heeling steeply as she did so, so that water ran in over the port gunwales.

From the shore, he hoped, it would appear that he had noticed the log boom at the last moment and thrown the ship into an emergency stop.

"Slow forward," he ordered, and the rowers settled into a smooth rhythm once more.

The shouts and jeers from the watchtowers redoubled as the *Raven*, seemingly thwarted, began to move away.

"What was that all about?" Andras asked.

Zavac smiled. "We'll come back tomorrow."

His second in command shook his head, perplexed. "Do you expect them to do anything different tomorrow?"

"Oh yes. Tomorrow, they'll welcome us with open arms," Zavac said, then added, with a shrug, "Well, with an open boom, at least."

"Ship coming! To the south!"

The lookout in the eastern watchtower bellowed the report. Instantly, there was a stir among the men around him as they leapt to their feet to join him at the wooden balustrade. He heard movement inside the small hut that provided shelter for those who weren't on duty, then the watch commander emerged, hastily buckling on his sword belt. Done with that, he brushed crumbs from his tunic as he joined the lookout at the balustrade. He'd obviously had his lunch interrupted.

Tension among the guards was high. Their numbers had been doubled since the pirate ship had been sighted the day before and they were ready for an attack.

"Is it that black ship we saw yesterday?" the commander asked.

The lookout shook his head, pointing. "No. Much smaller. A trader, I'd say. And she's in a hurry."

The commander followed the pointing arm and frowned. She was a small, neat trading ship and she was definitely in a hurry. Her eight oars beat the water rapidly. Even from this distance, he thought he could sense a feeling of panic in their movements. They weren't rowing smoothly in a coordinated rhythm. Rather, it looked as if each oarsman was simply thrashing his oar at the water as fast as he could manage.

"She's in a hurry, all right," he muttered, squinting his eyes in an attempt to make out more detail. But the distance was still too great.

In addition to her eight oars, the little ship had her square sail set and it billowed out with the following wind. As they came closer, the commander could see that the sail was an old one, stretched out of shape by years of use. Sails were expensive and most trading skippers would choose to save money by not replacing them, or having them re-cut, as they lost their efficient shape. They'd save money right up till a day like today, when the ship had to race for its life from danger.

And there was the danger now. Two kilometers behind the trading ship, a dark, sinister shape eased over the horizon.

"That's what's got her panicked!" the commander said, pointing.

"It's that pirate!" someone shouted. "The black ship that tried to attack us yesterday!"

"Pity he saw the boom at the last minute," the lookout muttered. He'd been on duty the day before when the black ship had headed at full speed for the harbor mouth, only just managing to halt her headlong progress when she sighted the boom. The garrison had watched eagerly as she approached, hoping to see her shatter her bow against the huge logs that barred the harbor entrance. There had been cries of disappointment when she managed to stop, just in time, then slink away with her tail between her legs.

Obviously, she had gone in search of easier prey, quartering the ocean over the horizon for a ship heading for Limmat to trade.

"She's gaining!" a soldier shouted. No need to say which ship he meant. In contrast to the jerky, spasmodic actions of the trader's oarsmen, the black ship's twin banks of oars moved down, back, up, forward and down again in perfect time. She was streaking across the water, rapidly closing the distance to the trading ship.

"There's another!" the shout went up as a third ship slipped into view over the horizon. Her hull was dark green and she was nearly as long as the black ship.

"Another pirate, I'll be bound," said the watch commander. But the new arrival was too far astern to affect the outcome of the desperate race before them. He looked back to the trader. He could see more detail now. The sides of her hull were festooned with arrows and there were several bodies sprawled unmoving on the deck.

The sail, old and misshapen as it was, was further affected by a large split that ran down one side, allowing the wind to spill out.

He glanced back to the black pirate ship. She was definitely gaining, but the trader was getting closer and closer to the harbor mouth. It was going to be a near-run thing, but after a few more minutes, he could see that the trader would just make it to safety in time.

He turned to the men leaning on the balustrade beside him. Some of them had begun shouting encouragement to the small, stricken ship limping toward them.

"Get down to the mole!" he shouted. "Get the boom open and let her in!"

The tower vibrated from the rush of feet as the men poured down the ladders to obey him. He followed, lingering a few minutes to measure the relative speeds and distance of the two ships engaged in the life-or-death race.

The trader would make it, he saw. But they'd have to move smartly and close the boom again before the pirate reached them. He ran out onto the quay and seized the signal horn from its bracket, blowing a long blast to alert the guards on the opposite mole. His own men were already unfastening the huge shackle that held the eastern end of the boom in place. As they did so, he waved frantically to the men across the harbor.

The incoming tide began to swing the log barrier away from the mole. Then the soldiers on the far side manned the massive windlass set there and began to drag the boom open even faster. As it went, his men paid out the heavy cable that they would use to haul the logs back into place again. As they let it out, it sank below the harbor surface, where it wouldn't impede the approaching ship.

The watch commander looked up from the opening boom to see the trader was only twenty or thirty meters away and now rowing with far more purpose and coordination. But instead of heading straight into the harbor, she was angling for the mole where he was standing.

And suddenly, a terrible doubt assailed him. The trader had been under attack by the black pirate and its consort. That much was obvious from the dead bodies on deck and the arrows that bristled along the hull. They must have been fighting at close quarters—perhaps a hundred meters or less. So how had she managed to escape? And how had she built up such a lead over the black ship?

He dashed forward as he realized what was happening, gesturing to his troops to man the windlass on this side of the harbor mouth that would bring the boom shut again.

"Close the boom! Close the boom! It's a trick!" the watch commander shouted, his voice cracking with the tension of the moment. But it was too late.

The trading ship was already nosing into the gap, angling toward the harbor mole. She ran alongside the stone wall with a splintering crash and suddenly men were swarming up from her decks and onto the jetty—more men than she could possibly have in her crew. He also noted that the sprawled, seemingly dead sailors on board had come to life as if by some dark magic and, weapons in hand, were clambering up onto the mole, screaming threats and battle cries.

He drew his sword and ran to try to drive them back. Already his men, caught by surprise, were falling. A few managed to rally together and mount a defense. But they were pitifully few.

He saw a tall, swarthy man hanging back and shouting orders

to the pirates and changed direction toward him. If he could kill their leader, the town might have a chance. From the corner of his eye, he could see the black ship looming closer to the open harbor mouth. He'd have to act quickly, he realized.

The pirate leader was facing away from him and he drew back his sword to strike.

A few seconds before the *Viper* crashed alongside the harbor wall, Zavac threw open the cargo hatch and yelled to the men crouching below.

"Come on!"

There was an answering roar from the twenty men concealed belowdecks and they poured out of their hiding place, following him as he ran to the bow to scramble ashore. Two of his men, detailed for the job, were lashing the ship to a mooring ring set in the harbor wall.

As he made it to the jetty, Zavac stood aside and let the first rush of men behind him go past. Shouting and screaming, they fell on the disorganized garrison members, some of whom had begun to try to operate the giant windlass and bring the boom closed again. Zavac drew his long, curved sword and waved it at them.

"Stop them!" he shouted, and half a dozen of his own men angled off toward the windlass, cutting the garrison members down before they had a chance to defend themselves. He waved the rest forward to where a small knot of defenders were standing together, desperately trying to stem the tide of pirates as they swarmed along the jetty.

"Kill them!" he shouted. "Kill them all!"

He glanced over his shoulder. The *Raven* was almost at the harbor mouth. As he had been instructed, Andras would secure her alongside the jetty farther inside the harbor and send the rest of *Raven's* men ashore in a rush. Once the tower garrison had been disposed of, Zavac and his men would head down the mole to join up with them.

Stingray, the dark green ship he had recruited at the Magyaran meeting point up the coast, would land her men in a few minutes and any further resistance from the Limmatans would be futile.

He drew breath to call another order, then sensed movement behind him. Instinctively, he dropped to a crouch and felt a sword blade whistle close, just above his head. Without looking, he pivoted on his right foot and thrust viciously with the long curved blade in his hand. He felt it strike a momentary resistance, pause, then penetrate.

Only now, he looked, and saw his sword deep in the belly of one of the garrison—an officer, judging by his clothes and armor. Zavac's thrust had gone just below the highly polished breastplate that the man wore. The officer's eyes were wide-open with shock. His mouth gaped, moving soundlessly. Then his legs collapsed under him and he fell sideways, supported for a moment by Zavac's blade, deep in his body, then falling as the pirate jerked it free.

"Bad luck." Zavac smiled at him. "Nearly had me there."

Then the smile faded and a black rage came over him, directed at this small-town nobody who had so nearly ended Zavac's life with a lucky swipe of his blade.

He put his foot against the fallen soldier and rolled him to the edge of the pier and into the harbor.

The deer stepped daintily into the clearing, paused, then advanced a few paces to a clump of thick, lush grass. It paused, head turning, ears pricked for the slightest sound, nostrils twitching to detect any foreign scent borne to it on the light breeze.

But Lydia was downwind and no trace of her scent reached the animal. It lowered its head to the grass, began to graze, then suddenly jerked upright again, searching the trees lining the clearing to the right of the spot where Lydia stood, motionless, in the shadow of a tree.

The deer was in excellent condition, plump and fit looking. It had obviously fed well since the weather had improved over the past few weeks. It was half grown and Lydia guessed that this was its first season away from its mother. Its meat would be tender and delicious, she thought, not tough and stringy like that of a full-grown adult. And she knew her grandfather would welcome the addition of twenty kilograms of prime venison to their larder. Things had been difficult for him since he had lost his small ship to pirates two seasons past—and with it his son and daughter-in-law.

He relied now on his meager savings, and whatever he could manage to earn doing odd jobs at the boatyard in Limmat. His wife was dead many years now and the one bright spot in his life was Lydia. Although, paradoxically, while he treasured her company, he felt the responsibility for her well-being as a burden.

In the last few seasons, Lydia had contributed to the household larder and income with the fresh meat she brought in. She was an expert hunter and she was able to provide meat for their own table as well as extra to sell to the vendors in the market. Rabbit, hare and game birds all sold well. But the most popular of all among the citizens of Limmat was venison—particularly tender meat from a young deer like the one that stood twenty-five meters away. She'd keep the choice cuts and sell the rest, she decided.

She smiled wryly. First kill your deer, she thought, then you can count the money you'll make selling it.

Lydia was sixteen. She was slightly taller than other girls her age, possibly because of years of activity and exercise in the woods. She could outrun most of the boys in town and she was a far better stalker than any of them. She was slender, with long, well-muscled legs and slightly broader shoulders than most girls—again, probably the result of a lifetime of exercise.

Sixteen-year-old girls in Limmat tended to primp and preen and protect the softness of their delicate hands and features, shielding them from the sun and from the rigors of hard work. Lydia had little time for that. She reveled in the freedom of the timbered hills and cleared fields. She was tan and fit, and moved with the same grace and economy of motion as the animals she hunted.

Her hair and features were the despair of other girls. While they spent hours before their looking glasses, combing, teasing and applying lotions and scented oils, she simply brushed her lustrous black hair and tied it back with a black ribbon. And where they felt the need to apply shading and coloring around their eyes, hers were clear hazel and slightly uptilted. Her grandfather often mused that somewhere in her distant ancestry, a Temujai raider had bequeathed her those eyes. Her cheekbones were high—further indication of that long-ago Temujai—and her skin was unblemished.

In all, she was a strikingly beautiful girl, although she was totally unaware of the fact. Her grandfather, Tomas, often told her so, of course. But she shrugged that aside. All grandfathers thought their granddaughters were beautiful. Or at least, they told them so.

The deer, its fears allayed for the moment, lowered its head to the grass and began to graze in earnest. Moving with infinite care, Lydia fitted the dart she had been carrying into her atlatl, the throwing stick that gave extra force and speed to her casts.

She had chosen the atlatl and its long, arrowlike darts as her hunting weapon after long consideration. Most of the boys in Limmat used bows. But boys tended to be heavier built and more heavily muscled, and Lydia couldn't match their sheer strength. So a bow with a heavy draw weight was beyond her capabilities. She could, of course, have opted for a lower-powered bow, but somehow the idea of using an inferior weapon didn't appeal. Instead, she had chosen the atlatl, a weapon that would reinforce her own natural ability to throw a projectile.

Once she had selected the weapon, she had set about mastering it with her usual single-mindedness of purpose, practicing for hour after hour until she could hurl a dart with either hand and with surprising force and accuracy. The throwing stick was some forty centimeters long. A small, hook-shaped spur at one end fitted into a corresponding notch in the rear of the darts. When she cast the dart, the atlatl acted as a lever, multiplying the force of the throw many times over.

The darts were sixty centimeters in length, with feathered flights at the end like an arrow's, but slightly offset to make them spin in flight. The tips were razor-sharp iron, again like an arrow's. She had ten such darts in the quiver on her back, which was padded with sheepskin to hold the darts firmly in place so they wouldn't rattle and signal her position to her quarry. When hunting, she always carried an eleventh dart in her left hand, avoiding the need for unnecessary movement, with its potential for noise, in drawing a dart from the quiver.

She stepped smoothly out from behind the tree. Speed was essential now, as the deer would probably sense any movement. Sure enough, as her right arm went back, the deer raised its head.

She saw the muscles in its haunches tighten as it prepared to bound away, then she brought the atlatl forward, accelerating smoothly as she threw, and stepping into the cast to put her body weight behind it.

She could hit a rabbit at sixty meters. A half-grown deer at twenty-five was child's play. The dart flashed across the clearing and, even as the deer began to turn and flee, the projectile thudded into its left-hand side, behind and above the foreleg, and penetrated to its heart, killing it instantly.

The deer's legs folded up and it collapsed to the grass.

Lydia was already a few paces across the clearing as it fell. She had known when she had cast the dart that it was a good throw.

The deer lay on its side, eyes open but unseeing. One leg trembled violently in a nervous reaction, but she knew it was already dead as she knelt beside it.

"I'm sorry," she said. It was the automatic reaction of the true hunter. She had killed the deer for its meat, not for so-called sport, and not out of any form of sadistic pleasure. She regretted that the deer had to die but, at the same time, recognized the necessity.

She carefully withdrew the dart from the deer's side. The small amount of blood that flowed from the wound showed the heart had stopped pumping. She wiped the shaft clean with a handful of grass, then placed the dart in her quiver. Laying the atlatl to one side, she reached for the small skinning knife that hung from the right-hand side of her belt. It was balanced on the left side by a long, heavy-bladed dirk. If the animal had not been dead, she would have used this for a swift, merciful slash across the throat.

She rolled the deer onto its back and prepared to make the first careful incision, prior to gutting it.

Then she stopped, sniffing the air.

She could smell smoke. That was never a welcome sensation when one was deep in the forest, among thousands of resin-laden pines that would flare up like so many torches if a fire swept through. Nervously, she scanned the trees around her. She could see no sign of a fire, but the smell was stronger now and the wind was blowing from the direction of Limmat town itself. Frowning, she rose to her feet, slipping the atlatl into its sheath beside the skinning knife, and left the deer carcass where it lay, taking long strides up a small incline to her left, to a ridge that she knew led to clear ground, overlooking the town below.

Now she could see a column of smoke rising beyond the trees.

The fire was definitely coming from the town. And now there was something else. Faint, almost inaudible, but carried to her on the breeze. Voices. Shouting voices.

Well, shouting was logical if there were a fire, she thought. And from the growing density of that smoke column, there was definitely a fire. Then she heard voices raised in a higher note. There were people screaming. Women screaming.

She topped the ridge and looked down. Below the steep drop, the town of Limmat, with its harbor and its palisade, spread out below her. The fire drew her attention first. It focused on the garrison building on the inner end of the quay. The building was burning fiercely, and several smaller buildings close by—houses and shops—had caught fire as well. Smoke and flames poured from them.

But nobody seemed to be trying to bring the fires under control. As she looked, she saw men running along the quay, spreading out into the streets that led to the inner town. She saw sunlight flashing on weapons and her heart jolted with fear. The people of Limmat lived with the worry that the secret of the emerald mine, just outside the palisade, in the face of the ridge that rose steeply behind the town, would one day be discovered. When that day came, invaders and pirates would not be far behind it.

And it seemed that the day had indeed arrived.

Casting her glance wider, she saw a foreign ship in the harbor—a long, lean black ship that was tied to the inner wharf. Looking back to the watchtowers and the boom, she made out a smaller ship, moored at the point where the boom should close. And another warship, this one dark green, was beached at the inland end of the harbor.

"Pirates," she muttered to herself. Then, suddenly fearful, she looked toward the section of town where her grandfather's house stood. For a moment, she could see nothing. The narrow streets restricted her view of what was going on. Then she made out figures running and saw weapons rising and falling. The invaders had reached the part of town where she lived. Several smaller fires began to spring up. One of them looked to be ominously close to the street where Tomas's house stood. But she couldn't be sure. From this angle, the streets were too narrow and too jumbled together.

One thing she did know. If the attackers had penetrated that far into the town, her grandfather would be one of the first to run into the street to try to drive them back. But he was an older man now, and the speed and power that he'd enjoyed years ago had left him. He'd be no match for a young, fit, blood-crazed pirate.

She had to get down the ridge and help him.

She hesitated. The drop directly before her was too steep to negotiate. There was a path running down to the town, winding back and forth down the steep hill. But it was several hundred meters away, to the east.

There was no time to lose. She set out, running smoothly along the ridge, her long, even strides eating up the distance to the point where the path began its downward route. The beginning of the path was a shadowy entryway between the trees and she barely checked her pace as she plunged into it and began the long, twisting way down.

She stumbled once, barely managing to stop from falling and ending up hard against a pine. She realized that too much speed was counterproductive. If she fell and injured herself on the path, she'd be no use to her grandfather. She slowed her pace to a jog, chafing at the necessity to do so, but knowing that it must be done.

Branches whipped at her face as she continued down. In places, the path was barely wider than her shoulders and secondary growth and creepers grew across it, clutching at her and trying to slow her descent. But she forced her way through, her mind's eye picturing the horrifying sight of her grandfather slowly sinking to his knees beneath a pirate's sword, blood welling from between his fingers as he tried to close a massive wound in his body.

Stop, she said to herself. That kind of thinking won't help Tomas. She sped up again. Fell, rolled, picked herself up, continued, the image still horribly clear in her mind.

At last, the path was widening and the slope was decreasing. She burst into the clear at the foot of the hill and paused to gain her bearings.

The palisade was directly ahead of her. To her right, about three hundred meters away, was a secondary gate. The main gate, which led out onto the beach, was farther away. But it was in the direction of Tomas's house. So, after a moment's hesitation she turned left and began to run again.

The noise of fighting inside the town was much louder now, interspersed with screams that could only have come from women. She lengthened her stride.

Then, behind her, she heard a shout.

She turned. There was a group of half a dozen men running toward her. She had time to register the bandannas around their heads, the heavy boots and the curved swords and small, round metal shields.

Magyarans, she thought. Pirates. And they'd seen her. She started running again, blindly, with no idea where she might go to escape. The pirates were behind her. And there were more of them in the town ahead.

Something hit the ground to one side and she started violently. It was a spear, thrown by one of the men chasing her. They had obviously gained on her when she looked back, slowing her pace. For a moment, she toyed with the idea of stopping and sending three or four atlatl shafts hurtling at them. But three or four darts wouldn't stop them all. And she'd be overwhelmed and taken.

The shouting redoubled and she increased her pace, trying to draw away from her pursuers. But a quick glance to her right told her they weren't shouting at her, but to their comrades, on the palisade surrounding the town. She could see heads and shoulders there, and weapons being brandished.

Then something snaked over the wall and dropped to the ground. A rope.

Almost immediately, one of the pirates on the palisade walkway heaved himself over the edge and began to scramble down the rope to the ground outside. A second followed, and a third. They were trained seamen and they moved down the rope skillfully, running toward her to cut her off as soon as their feet touched the ground.

She angled away to the left, her heart pounding, her mind racing. She had no idea where to go, how to escape. All thought of reaching her grandfather's house had gone now. She was hopelessly cut off from that direction.

She plunged into the trees again and, forcing her mind to function, realized that she was heading for a narrow creek some fifty meters ahead of her. It would effectively bar her way, leaving her as easy prey for the men pursuing her.

Unless!

She remembered that Benji, a boy with whom she had a nodding acquaintance, sometimes left his fishing skiff drawn upon a tiny beach somewhere along this creek.

But where? Where was she now, and where did the small sandy beach lie in relation to her current position? She wasn't sure, but her innate sense of direction and hunter's instinct told her to the right. She angled that way, hoping beyond all hope that the skiff would be there. The creek was suddenly ahead of her, and she went right again, paralleling its banks. Behind her, she heard shouts and the sound of heavy bodies crashing through the undergrowth. Sobbing now with exertion, and doubled over with an agonizing stitch in her side, she blundered along the creek bank, her eyes searching the bushes and trees ahead of her.

There it was!

A small skiff, barely three and a half meters long. But heavily built of pine planking. It was drawn up well clear of the water, above the point where the high tide would reach. Her heart sank as she saw the distance she would have to move it to get it into the water.

She staggered breathlessly onto the beach and hurled herself at the boat, shoving and heaving with all her strength to move it. She might as well have tried to move a tree. The boat remained still.

Then she realized that she should pull it to the water, lifting the blunt stern to clear the sand so that it would move. She ran to the other end, seized hold, lifted and pulled. The boat slid half a meter before she was forced to let it drop.

Again, she lifted and heaved, this time maintaining the effort until the boat had moved a full meter and a half before she had to drop it once more.

The voices and the sound of running feet were closer now. Terror gave her extra strength. Sobbing with effort and fear, she lifted and heaved, staggering four paces, five, six, with the boat sliding behind her, moving more easily as she reached the firm sand below the tidemark.

Perspiration flowed into her eyes, stinging them and blinding her. She set the boat down. Lifted and heaved again, felt water around her ankles and realized she'd reached the creek. Now the boat began to slide more easily as the water took the weight from her. She slid it out into the creek, into knee-deep water, as the first of the pirates came blundering through the trees, barely ten meters away. He saw her and stopped, turning to shout to his companions.

"This way! This way! I've got him!"

It registered dully with her that, dressed as she was in a deer-skin jerkin, tights and cross-bound leggings, they had taken her for a boy. Not that it mattered. What mattered was getting away. The pirate's action, pausing to call his comrades, was what saved her. If he'd simply run after her, he would have caught her before she reached deeper water. But now the skiff was well and truly afloat and she vaulted into it.

There were two oars lying in the bottom of the boat. She fumbled to set them in the oarlocks and get the boat moving. But she was exhausted and they were heavy and unwieldy. And now the pirate realized his mistake. He plunged down the bank onto the sand and ran after her. She heaved on the oars, missing her stroke with one and crabbing the boat sideways. Then he was waist deep and almost up to her. The deeper water slowed him, and for a moment, she thought she had escaped. Then he grabbed hold of the stern, stopping the boat from moving.

She unshipped one of the oars and jabbed it at him, aiming at the hand that clutched the stern. He yelled in pain, releasing the boat. But then he grabbed the oar and began to haul her in, like an angler reeling in a fish. She heaved back on the oar, trying to wrench it from his grasp.

For a second or two, they struggled for possession. He was stronger than she was and he hadn't run down the mountain before they'd begun their deadly race.

Gradually, he was winning the contest, hauling the skiff back to shallower water. In desperation she released her hold on the paddle, giving one last push against it, and him, as she did.

Surprised, he staggered back and fell, going completely under. Under the impetus of that final push, the skiff glided away into deep water. The pirate floundered to the surface, cursing and spluttering, and saw that the little boat was now a dozen meters away. His companions emerged from the trees now and shouted threats after her, waving weapons in the air. She was relieved to see they had no projectile weapons. No bows, or throwing spears.

But she did.

Quickly, she drew a dart from the quiver, took the atlatl from its sheath on her belt, and fitted the two together.

She took quick aim at the man who had nearly caught her,

then cast. His comrades were startled as he screamed and threw his arms up, then fell backward again into the water, going beneath the surface once more. When he resurfaced, they saw the dart buried deep in his chest, and the banner of red blood drifting away on the water.

In a panic, they turned and blundered out of the water, shoving one another aside as they strove to put distance between themselves and the figure on the skiff.

But Lydia wasn't interested in sending more darts after them. She collapsed into the bottom of the boat. Belatedly, she realized that she had only one oar. She pushed it clumsily over the side of the boat, using it like a paddle. It was heavy and unwieldy and the boat responded slowly to her efforts. But it began to crab slowly downstream. The tide was ebbing, and after a minute or so, the skiff was caught up by it, moving with increasing speed toward the bay, as Lydia continued her awkward, ineffectual paddling. She was exhausted, mentally and physically, but the men who had been pursuing her were now out of sight as the skiff went around a bend. Dully, she realized that the tide would take her out of the creek into the bay, and then out of the bay into the ocean.

What would become of her then, she had no idea. But she brought the oar inboard and dropped it, rattling, on the floorboards of the skiff.

She'd worry about getting back later. For now, she had to get away.

kegall was a small fishing village, half a day's sail south of Shelter Bay. With the wind on their port beam, Hal set the *Heron* skimming down the coast. As they had found when they tested it, the new fin allowed them to brace the sail in harder, with considerably less lean, and the boat moved appreciably faster.

Stig had been studying the chart for several minutes. He emerged from under the small canvas shelter and moved to stand beside Hal. For a few minutes, he took in the motion of the ship, sweeping up the face of the waves that rolled in constantly from the west, then sliding down the far side, to slice into the green water and send spray flying high, either side of the bow. The crew, with nothing to attend to for the moment, lolled on the rowing benches, enjoying the sunshine. Only Ulf and Wulf remained alert, in case there was an unexpected need to adjust the sail. Stig inclined his head to them.

"Those two are behaving themselves," he said.

Hal nodded. "They still fight like cat and dog when we're

ashore," he said. "But neither of them wants to lose his position as a sail trimmer."

After the helmsman, sail trimmers enjoyed considerable prestige aboard a wolfship and neither of the twins was willing to forego it. They were proud of their instinctive ability, and they were aware from past experience that Hal followed through if he made a threat. So if they bickered while the *Heron* was under way, they knew that at least one of them would be instantly demoted and assigned to other duties.

"I was looking at the chart," Stig said. "Limmat is only another day down the coast, and it's a much bigger town than Skegall. According to the sailing notes, Skegall is little more than a village."

"That's why I chose it," Hal said. "I don't want to advertise our presence in case the *Raven* is somewhere in the area. The more people who see us, the more tongues will wag about it."

Stig considered the point, his face thoughtful. "True. But there'll be a bigger market at Limmat."

"A small market will serve our needs," Hal said. "We don't want anything exotic. Edvin wants a few staples like flour, salt and coffee. And I need rope, iron, nails and lumber."

"And a nice new sheepskin vest for Thorn," said a voice from beside the keel box, where the one-armed sea wolf appeared to be dozing, his eyes shut. Hal rolled his eyes at Stig.

"And a nice new sheepskin vest for Thorn," he repeated.

Thorn's eyes remained shut. "Just making sure you don't forget it."

"How could I?" Hal said, under his breath.

"Heard that," Thorn called.

As Skegall came into sight, Hal had the crew lower the distinctive triangular sail.

"We'll row in," he said. "I don't know if Zavac ever saw *Heron* under sail. But if he did, there's no sense in letting him know we're here."

With the same thought in mind, Hal had Ingvar cover the giant crossbow with a tarpaulin, and lash it down tight.

They brought the little ship into harbor, the oars rising and falling smoothly. The fact that the wind was coming from onshore helped their subterfuge. *Heron* could have zigzagged her way in, but a normal square-rigged ship would row. As they came in through the harbor mouth, Thorn hauled the fin up and stowed it behind the mast. Then he dropped a corner of one of the sails over the keel box.

"No sense in everyone knowing everything about us," he commented to Hal, who nodded his agreement.

A few onlookers watched with mild interest as they beached the little ship. But the *Heron*, without its distinctive triangular sail visible, was nothing out of the ordinary. The crew gathered in the bow while Hal gave them their assignments.

"Ingvar, you come with me. I noticed a boatyard on the edge of the harbor as we came in. They should have everything we need. Ulf, you stay here and keep an eye on the boat. Wulf, give Edvin a hand buying the supplies. Stig, you and Thorn wander around the market. See what you can find out. Jesper, you and Stefan do the same. Keep your ears open for any news of the *Raven*. But don't make it too obvious we're interested in her. And Jesper, try not to steal anything, all right?"

"I just borrow things. I always give them back," Jesper protested.

Hal wondered for a moment if he really wanted to be skirl of this group. Sometimes, he thought, handling them was like herding cats.

"Then this will save you the trouble," he said. "No borrowing." A thought struck him and he looked at Thorn.

"Thorn, it might be better if we all pretended that you're the skirl. If Zavac is in the area and word gets back to him about a ship captained and crewed by boys, he might just put two and two together."

Thorn nodded. "Good thinking," he said. "I'll also keep an eye out in the marketplace for a nice expensive sheepskin."

Hal rolled his eyes. "You do that," he said. He realized Ulf was frowning at him.

"How come Wulf gets to go with Edvin and I have to stay here?" Ulf complained.

Hal eyed him steadily for a few seconds, knowing Ulf already knew the answer. Then he replied, "Because we're not at sea and if I leave you and Wulf together, you'll fight."

"No, we won't," said Ulf.

"Yes, we will," Wulf responded instantly. As his brother drew breath to answer, Hal held up a hand.

"See? It's starting already."

Ulf pouted, then tried once more. "I want to buy something in the market. I'm hungry."

Hal sighed. He looked from one twin to the other. They really were impossible to tell apart, he thought.

"Look, I don't care which one of you stays and which one goes. Toss a coin to decide."

"I haven't got a coin," Ulf replied.

Hal spread his hands. "Then how were you going to buy anything in the market? Problem solved."

In fact, Thorn was the only one among them to have money. He quickly doled out a few kroner to each of the boys, giving extra to Edvin and Hal, who had to buy supplies.

"Jesper," Hal said, "find a food stall and get a pie or a sausage for Ulf. Buy it. Don't steal it," he added. Jesper looked offended, but said nothing. In fact, he had been planning to "liberate" a pie for Ulf and save some money. He didn't consider taking food to be stealing. Everybody did that, he thought. He just did it better than most.

"All right," Hal said. "Let's split up and meet back here in an hour."

As it turned out, he and Ingvar took a little longer than an hour to get what he needed. The boatyard was able to supply them with timber, nails and cordage. But they didn't have the small ingots of iron that Hal wanted. They directed him to a blacksmith's forge on the far side of the village, where he bought a good supply.

The others were all waiting when they returned, Ingvar carrying the heavier items. The crew were sitting in a circle on the beach, eating. Ingvar's eyes lit up when he saw a wrapped parcel in front of Thorn.

"Got you a pie," Thorn told Hal, gesturing to the parcel. Hal nodded his thanks and sank to the sand, reaching for the still-warm pie. He realized he was famished.

"Did you get me one?" Ingvar asked. His face fell when Thorn shook his head.

"I got you three," Thorn said.

Ingvar's face brightened. "Well, that'll do for a snack before dinner," he said, adding, without any appreciable pause, "When is dinner?"

Stig looked sidelong at him.

"You haven't even had lunch," he said, "and you're already thinking of dinner?"

Ingvar shrugged. "I'm a growing boy," he replied.

Stig eyed his already massive frame with some misgivings. "Perish the thought," he said.

Hal finished the first huge mouthful of pie that he had taken and brushed crumbs away from his mouth.

"Anyone find out anything?" he said, looking around as Edvin handed him a mug of hot coffee. He took it and had a swig.

"There's a big ship in the area," Jesper replied. "A warship, people think. Some of the fishing boats spotted her in the distance."

"We heard the same thing," Thorn put in. "Apparently she cruised over the horizon a couple of days ago, then turned and put back out to sea."

"Is it the *Raven*?" Hal asked eagerly. The thought that they might be within reach of their prey set his pulse racing with excitement—and apprehension. Thorn and Jesper exchanged a glance, each looking to see if the other had more information. They both shrugged.

"Nobody could tell us," Thorn said. "She was too far away to make out details. They said she had a dark-colored hull, but any ship in the distance looks to have a dark hull."

"The fishing boats didn't stay around to get a closer look," Jesper said. "Once they spotted her, they took off back to harbor."

"Makes sense, I suppose," Hal said thoughtfully, his previous excitement a little blunted. "But it *could* be the *Raven*. What other large ship would be in this area?"

"Well, that's the problem," Thorn replied. "We simply don't know. From the description, such as it was, it could have been the *Raven*. Or it could have been any large ship—even a wolfship."

"What would a wolfship be doing this far south?" Hal asked, frowning.

Thorn shrugged. "Probably nothing. I'm just saying, it might be the *Raven*. Or it might not. It could be anything."

"I suppose so," Hal said, reluctantly facing the facts. It was frustrating to have so little information. In a way, he wished they hadn't heard anything about the strange ship. He glanced at Edvin.

"Did you get everything you need?" he asked.

The other boy nodded. "Even managed to get extra coffee. We seem to be going through it at a prodigious rate." He looked accusingly at Thorn as he said this, and the old sea wolf assumed a look of utter innocence.

"I don't know what *prodigious* means," he said, and Edvin snorted in disbelief.

"All right then," Hal said, coming to a decision. "There's no reason to stay here any longer. Let's head back to Shelter Bay."

"There is one thing," Thorn said, holding up a finger. Hal looked at him curiously and he continued.

"While I was finding out all about this strange ship, I happened to see this rather nice, rather expensive sheepskin vest in the market."

He held up a new sheepskin. Hal had to admit that it was excellent quality, and well made.

"I decided I should let you buy it for me. It was ten kroner."

He held out his left hand, palm uppermost. Hal shook his head, perplexed.

"I don't have ten kroner," he protested. "I only have two and some change. And that came from the money you gave me earlier." He reached into the side pocket of his jerkin and produced the few coins he had left.

Thorn pursed his lips thoughtfully. "I see. Well then, give me those."

Hal did so.

"Now you owe me eight kroner." Thorn delved into the small sack purse he kept on his belt and rummaged around, producing a handful of coins. "So I will lend you eight kroner. Here, take them."

Hal did so, mystified by all this high finance. He realized Thorn was clicking his fingers impatiently.

"You want them back now?" he said.

Thorn nodded. "You owe me for the vest. Hand them over."

Puzzled, Hal did so, dropping the coins into Thorn's open palm. Thorn nodded in satisfaction and stowed them away in his purse.

"Now we're even," he said. "Except you owe me ten kroner."

"I what?"

Thorn held up his hook to stop further discussion. "Remember? I lent you eight kroner, and I also lent you the other two. Gorlog's reeking breath, boy, it was only a few minutes ago! So you owe me the ten kroner that I lent you to buy the vest for me."

"But . . ." Hal looked at the others. Stig was similarly confused, he could see. Ulf and Wulf seemed to think it was all perfectly logical, which proved it was anything but. "Wouldn't it have been simpler to just say I owe you ten kroner for the vest?"

Thorn shook his head. "No. You've paid me for the vest. Remember? I just lent you the money to do it. Now you owe me the money I just lent you so you could pay me."

"But it would have been the same result!" Hal protested.

Thorn smiled beatifically at him. "Maybe. But I just wanted to have you hand over some money."

Hal scratched his head, trying to fathom Thorn's thinking. He decided that was an impossible task.

"Is it all right by you if we leave now?" he said, giving in, and Thorn made a magnanimous gesture, sweeping his left hand toward the open sea.

"By all means. Just don't forget you owe me ten kroner."

They launched the *Heron* and rowed out of the harbor. A few of the townsfolk waved as they rowed out through the breakwater. Once they were far enough offshore, Hal ordered the oars in and Jesper and Stefan raised the sail. The wind was constant and soon the little ship was swooping over the incoming rollers. Hal reveled in the feeling as she would lift over each crest, then fly down into the trough behind it, and the sudden feeling of drag as the bow bit into the water at the base of the wave, slowing the boat momentarily until the wind sent her soaring up the face of the next wave.

The sun was very low to the horizon in the west and they wouldn't reach Shelter Bay before dark. He made a mental note to go in under oars. The entrance to the bay was narrow and he didn't plan on flying through there under sail in the dark. But for the moment, the crew could relax.

He beckoned Stig to the steering platform and gestured to the tiller.

"You might as well take her," he said, and Stig complied enthusiastically. Truth be told, Hal was reluctant to hand over control of the ship. She was his and he loved steering her, loved the feeling of control and response she gave him. But Stig would be at the helm when they went into battle, so it made sense for him to be thoroughly familiar with the feel of the ship.

And Stig was a good helmsman, he had to admit.

His friend seemed to sense his mood and smiled reassuringly at him. "Don't worry. I'll look after her. But she knows who her real master is."

Hal nodded and sat on a small stool close to the steering position. They continued in companionable silence for some minutes. The rest of the crew were relaxing on the rowing benches. Thorn was in his usual position, leaning his back against the keel box.

"Sail! Sail to the northwest!"

It was Jesper who was on watch, in the bow. He ran nimbly back now and swarmed up the shrouds to the lookout position at the top of the mast.

"She's a big ship. Square rigged. Coming this way."

As soon as he heard the first call, Thorn leapt to his feet and joined Stig and Hal at the steering platform. Without any need to discuss it, Stig turned the tiller over to Hal.

"Has she seen us?" Hal called. Even though Jesper was high on the mast, they could recognize his uncertain body language as he shaded his eyes and tried to see more clearly.

"No way of telling," he called, after a brief pause. "But she's not heading directly toward us and she hasn't altered course. So probably not."

"She's got the setting sun behind her," Thorn said thoughtfully. "We're against the dark mass of the land. She probably hasn't seen us yet."

Hal nodded and came to a decision. "Get the sail down!" he ordered. "Jump to it! Stig, give them a hand!"

Stig ran forward as Jesper slid down the shrouds. The twins let the sail fly loose and Stig, Jesper and Stefan brought the mast and sail down. Without its big, light-colored shape to catch the slanting rays of the sun, they would be almost invisible to the other ship.

"Out oars!" Hal ordered. "Don't bother stowing the sail. Do it later!"

The crew rushed to the rowing benches and ran the oars out. Stig took over control of the rowers.

"Give way all," he ordered, and they lowered their oars, set their feet and heaved. The *Heron* had come to a stop after the sail was lowered. Now she began to glide through the water once more.

"There she is!" Thorn said, shading his eyes as he peered over the starboard bow. Hal followed the line of his gaze and saw a small, light-colored rectangle just rising above the horizon—the other ship's sail, catching the last rays of the sun.

"Is it the *Raven*?" he asked, but Thorn was shaking his head.

"I'd know that ship anywhere," he said. "It's *Wolfwind*."

"*Wolfwind*? Erak's ship?" Hal said, a hand of panic clutching his heart. "Are you sure?"

"I sailed on her for twenty years," Thorn said. "It's her, all right. I wonder what she's doing in these parts?"

Hal's expression was grim as he answered his friend. "It's obvious, isn't it? She's come to take us back."

"So what do we do?" Stig asked.

Hal hesitated, thinking. If he continued to head north, back to their camp at Shelter Bay, he increased the chance that *Wolfwind* might see them. There was really only one choice. He had to get as far away from the other ship as possible. He leaned on the tiller, setting the *Heron* on a long, curving course until she was heading away from *Wolfwind*.

"We're going south," he said.

The sun set and the Herons raised the sail again, speeding due south, away from the course *Wolfwind* had been following. Thorn, Stig and Hal stood in a small group by the tiller, casting anxious glances astern. After an hour, the moon rose, casting a brilliant silver path down the sea. There was no sign of a ship following them.

"They mustn't have seen us," Stig said hopefully. The others were not quite so certain, but they didn't say anything. Hal had learned over the years that voicing your hopes like that often led to having them dashed. After several more minutes, Thorn replied.

"You could be right. We were in relative darkness when we sighted her. And even if she had seen us, and turned after us, there's no way she could hold to this course. She'd lose far too much distance downwind. We're heading south and she'd be blown onto a southwest course."

The thought was a comforting one. If the two ships sailed on those diverging courses for the eight hours of darkness that remained, dawn should find the *Heron* alone on the ocean, with no sign of *Wolfwind*.

"Unless they're rowing, of course," Thorn added, and burst that bubble of hope for them.

Hal fidgeted for a few seconds, his fingers opening and closing on the tiller. Finally, he reached his decision—the only logical one in the circumstances.

"We'll keep going," he said. "And we'll see how things are at first light."

They sailed on through the night, staying on the same tack. After several hours, the tense feeling in Hal's stomach eased. He passed the tiller to Stig, and lay down in his bedroll to rest. Stefan took over from Jesper as lookout and the rest of the crew dozed at their stations. But none of them slept soundly. They were all too aware of the presence of *Wolfwind*, somewhere out there in the darkness.

Ingvar was awake, seated with his back to the mast, legs sprawled out in front of him. A little after midnight, he saw Edvin shrug off his blankets, move to the rail and peer astern.

"See anything?" he asked quietly.

Edvin turned to him. "Nothing. Too dark out there. Can't see beyond the stern of the ship."

"Welcome to my world," Ingvar replied with a smile.

Sleep eluded Hal. He lay on the hard deck, feeling the movement of the *Heron* through his entire body. It was a soothing sensation, and the creaks and groans of the mast and the rigging were familiar friends. But the thought of *Wolfwind* behind them, and the devastating sense of despair he would feel if she were to find them and force them to return to Hallasholm, weighed on his mind.

This desperate voyage was their sole chance to redeem themselves. They had embarked on it on a wild impulse because, truly, it was their only hope for any sort of future life. If they could catch up with the *Raven*, and somehow retrieve the stolen Andomal, they would be able to return to Hallasholm with their heads high. They would have atoned for the terrible crime they had committed, in allowing Zavac to steal Skandia's most precious artifact in the first place.

But if *Wolfwind* caught them now and forced them back to Hallasholm in disgrace, they would simply have piled one failure on top of another. And they would never have another chance to set things right.

Zavac was somewhere close by. Hal could sense it. And this would be their best opportunity to find him and take back the Andomal.

What would he do if *Wolfwind* caught up with them? They couldn't fight Erak's crew. He knew that. They were Skandians. They were fellow countrymen.

Although, he thought bitterly, not *his* countrymen. Skandians had made that clear all his life. He was an Araluen in their eyes. And in the one brief, wonderful moment when they had accepted him as one of their own, the wonderful sense of belonging that he had always sought had been shattered by Zavac—and his own carelessness. If only he hadn't left his post, none of this would have ever happened. The Andomal would still be safe back in Skandia.

Their only course was to elude *Wolfwind*—to use *Heron's*

superior sailing qualities to escape from her. But the time they spent doing that was time when Zavac could be slipping farther and farther away from them. Up until now, the prevailing bad weather had kept the *Raven* confined to a relatively predictable area, somewhere on the Stormwhite's southeast coast. But now the weather was improving and she could head off in any direction, leaving no clue behind her, no trace of her whereabouts.

He rolled over and tried to relax his tensed muscles, hoping that the constant rising and falling rhythm of the ship would lull him. But the bitter thought of failure gnawed at his mind and dispelled the soothing oblivion of sleep, hour after hour.

"Dawn's coming up."

Stig's soft call intruded into his consciousness. At some stage, he must have finally managed to doze off. Although as he sat up, bleary-eyed and foggy-minded, it seemed that it must have been mere minutes ago.

He rose, stretched his stiff and aching limbs and moved to stand beside Stig. He saw that his friend's eyes were red-rimmed with fatigue.

"You stayed on watch all night?"

Stig shrugged. "You needed to sleep."

Hal touched his friend's shoulder in gratitude. "Didn't do much of that," he admitted.

He looked astern. Stig followed his gaze. "Still too dark to see anything," he said. "But I've got a crick in my neck from looking all night."

Thorn was huddled by the keel box, wrapped in his brand-new sheepskin. The rest of the crew were asleep at their sailing stations, with only Wulf awake. He had taken over as lookout some hours previously.

Hal called to him now.

"Wake them up, Wulf," he said, and the sail trimmer began moving among his shipmates, shaking them and rousing them from sleep. They stretched and yawned, as Hal had done, shivering slightly as they threw off their blankets and peered around to see if there was any sign of pursuit.

Wulf approached the huddled form by the keel box last of all. But as he stretched out his hand, he was greeted by a low, growling voice.

"You shake me, boy, and I'll throw you overboard."

Wulf snatched his hand back just in time and moved away. Thorn was obviously awake, he thought.

To the east, a narrow band of gray light was showing above the horizon. There was no sign of land, but the light was reflecting red off a bank of low clouds. The sea hissed past them, the white water of their wake showing up against the darkness. Gradually, the light began to grow and they could make out more detail. The dim shapes moving around the forward part of the ship became recognizable as individual crew members.

Handing the tiller to Stig, Hal climbed onto the rail by the stern post and balanced himself with one hand on the backstay. He scanned the sea behind them under the growing light. The knot of anxiety that had been in his gut throughout the night eased as he saw an empty horizon. Stig was watching him, waiting for his report. He smiled down at the anxious face.

"Nothing in sight," he said, and he saw Stig's shoulders relax.

He dropped lightly to the deck, feeling better than he had for some hours. The two friends exchanged relieved smiles.

Edvin had begun preparing a cold breakfast for the crew. He moved aft now, balancing three plates and mugs, and placed them on the deck beside Hal and Stig. He glanced at Thorn's huddled shape.

"Is Thorn awake yet?" he asked, indicating the third platter.

"Try shaking me and find out," came a low growl.

Edvin raised his eyebrows. "Sounds like a bear at the end of winter."

Stig grinned at him. "Compared to him, a bear would be a pussycat."

Edvin glanced at the heavyset figure again.

"I'll leave his here," he said, and made his way forward again. Edvin was no fool.

The meal was hard bread, cold, cooked bacon and a piece of spiced sausage. It wasn't the most appetizing fare, Hal thought. But he was ravenous after the long night and he wolfed it down gratefully. Stig made short work of his too, licking his fingers to make sure he had every last bit of the tasty bacon fat.

They washed it down with cold water. Hal yearned for a hot drink. A mug of coffee would be like heaven, he thought. Even an herbal tea would have been acceptable. Or just hot water, he thought moodily. But of course, there was no way of lighting a cook stove on board ship, so they had to be content with cold water.

"Breakfast's up, Thorn," Stig called. "Get a move on or I'll eat yours."

Thorn finally stirred. He rose and stretched both his arms over his head. Hal noted idly that Thorn had removed his false arm when he slept.

"This is a sea wolf's breakfast," he said to his two young friends. "A stretch, a scratch and a good look round."

He had already stretched. Now he applied himself to the second part of the formula, scratching himself liberally and enthusiastically.

"Careful you don't tear that lovely new sheepskin to shreds," Hal said dryly. "I'm not buying you another one."

"You haven't bought me this one yet," Thorn grunted. Finally, finished with scratching, he peered around the horizon, shading his eyes with his left hand. He'd heard Hal's report to Stig but it was ingrained in him from years of sailing and raiding to check for possible trouble in every direction. As he scanned in a circle and his view passed the bow and moved toward port, he stopped, hesitated, then went back.

"What's that?" he said urgently.

Hal's heart leapt into his mouth. Had *Wolfwind* somehow managed to slip past them in the night? Thorn was pointing to something just off the port bow and Hal followed the direction with his eyes.

His first sensation was one of relief. Whatever Thorn had seen, it wasn't *Wolfwind*. It was a small, dark shape several kilometers away. As he peered more closely, he thought he could discern movement. Instinctively, he went to swing the bow toward the object, then stopped as he realized the mast and sail would block his line of sight if he did so. Besides, it wasn't always wise to run down directly toward an unknown object at sea, he thought. He held his course, aiming at a point some twenty degrees to the right of the object. The dark shape appeared and disappeared regularly as *Heron* rose and fell on the waves.

The rest of the crew had heard Thorn's exclamation and were staring at it as well.

"Jesper!" Hal called. "Up the mast and report!"

Jesper waved acknowledgment and leapt to the shrouds, swarming up them until he reached the lookout position. There was a pause as he peered forward, during which time the distance diminished, making it easier for him to make out details.

"It's a boat!" he called. "A small boat. And there's someone in it! He's waving."

That was enough for Hal. One man in a small boat wouldn't present any danger to *Heron* and her well-armed crew. He swung the ship to port so she was heading for the boat. Ulf and Wulf automatically trimmed the sail to the new course.

Hal's mind raced with possibilities. One man in a small boat. A shipwreck survivor, perhaps? Then his imagination jumped to a whole new track. Maybe it was more than a simple shipwreck. This could be the lone survivor of a ship attacked and sunk by pirates. More specifically, by one pirate! This could be proof of the *Raven's* presence in these waters!

He sensed that Stig and Thorn were thinking the same thing. They exchanged glances, none of them wanting to voice the idea. Hal hit the heel of his left hand against the tiller, as if urging the boat to greater speed.

"Come on!" he muttered.

He eased the bow to starboard, clearing his line of vision again.

Except for Ulf and Wulf, who remained by the sheets, the crew were clustered in the bow as they ran down on the small boat. Edvin was keeping up a running commentary on events to Ingvar, who couldn't make out the boat.

As they drew closer, Hal could see that the boat was a one-man skiff. Its occupant was standing, waving a piece of cloth on the end of a pole—possibly an oar.

"Jesper! Come down. Get ready to lower the sail with Stefan," he called. The figure perched on the lookout post waved a hand, then slid down one of the shrouds to the deck.

"Edvin! Get the boat hook!" Hal called. The man in the skiff was barely fifty meters away. Now that it was obvious he had been sighted, he sat down wearily, laying aside the oar he had been waving.

Hal's eyes narrowed as he measured speed, angles and distance.

"Loose sheets. Down sail!" he ordered. Ulf and Wulf let the sail go free, and Jesper and Stefan hauled it quickly down, gathering its folds and stowing them loosely as they did so. Gradually, the speed began to run off the ship and Hal saw that he had timed it almost perfectly. *Heron* was barely moving as the skiff went out of his sight under the port bow and Edvin leaned over to hook onto her with the boat hook. Hal felt a slight thump as the skiff was drawn alongside the *Heron* and the two hulls came together.

"Careful," he muttered irritably. Stig, beside him, glanced at him and grinned. He knew that Hal hated anything bumping against his ship, even a harmless small boat like this.

"You're as bad as Erak," he said quietly. Hal ignored him.

"Get a line on that skiff," he called. "We'll tow it behind us."

In the bow, Edvin waved acknowledgment. He tossed a length of hemp over to the boat and made it fast. Then he helped the skiff's lone occupant over the rail. The others moved to help him as he did. Then there was a buzz of surprise from the *Heron*'s crew and Edvin turned to shout back to Hal.

"He's a girl!"

"He" was a girl indeed, Hal thought. And as she made her way aft, followed by the curious members of the crew, he realized she was a remarkably beautiful girl. She was slender and fit, with tanned skin and long black hair tied back with a simple ribbon.

She was dressed in hunting clothes—a deerskin jerkin over a woolen shirt and cross-bound leggings. She had a quiver of what appeared to be arrows slung over her back—although she had no bow. A long dirk and a strange carved wooden handle hung from her broad leather belt. She was taller than average, which placed her eyes on a level with his own. Behind her, Ingvar was whispering, in a completely audible voice, to Edvin.

"Who is she? What's she like?"

Edvin replied, equally audibly, "I don't know. But she's a real looker."

A smile touched the corner of the girl's mouth, then almost immediately disappeared. She looked around the crew, puzzled by their young faces and the almost total absence of adults. Then her gaze settled on Thorn, as she took in the wooden hook and the grizzled appearance.

"Are you the captain?" she asked.

Thorn threw back his head and laughed. "Not me, my dear! I'm more like the ship's cat." She frowned, and he elaborated. "I'm a bit of a pet for the skipper. He keeps me around for his own amusement. This is him. His name is Hal."

Her eyebrows rose as she studied Hal, seeing he was fresh faced, barely older than she was.

"Really?" she said a trifle skeptically. Hal was on the brink of taking offense, then realized that her reaction was a natural one.

"Really," he replied. "This is the *Heron*. She's my ship."

"And I'm Stig, first mate," Stig said hastily, pushing past Hal to offer her his hand. "Delighted to meet you. Welcome aboard."

As he spoke, he flushed bright red. Hal smiled to himself. Stig, tall and handsome as he might be, tended to be somewhat awkward around good-looking girls. He would either become absolutely tongue-tied or babble self-consciously. Obviously, this was a day for babbling.

She shook his hand and the smile touched her features again, but only briefly.

"Thank you. Pleased to meet you."

Stig, still flushing scarlet, swallowed several times, then realized he was still holding her hand and released it abruptly, almost shoving her away in his haste to do so.

"Ummm . . . er . . . Let me know if I can do anything to make you more comfortable. You know . . . anything at all. I'll be delighted . . . just, you know . . . let me know . . ." He realized that was the second time he'd said *delighted* and his voice trailed away uncertainly. The girl pretended not to notice his awkwardness.

"I certainly will," she said gravely.

Stig nodded several times to himself, cleared his throat again for good measure, then stepped back, stumbling over a coil of rope and just managing not to fall.

Hal stepped forward. "I didn't catch your name," he said, and she swung her gaze back to him. Hazel eyes, slightly uptilted. Flawless complexion. He realized that she had answered his question and he hadn't heard a word.

"I'm sorry? What was that?" he said, a little flustered.

Behind the girl, Thorn rolled his eyes skyward.

"Oh Bungall's braided beard," he muttered. Bungall was a minor deity, generally referred to as the god of acting in an embarrassing manner. His name wasn't often invoked and Hal wished Thorn had chosen not to do so this time. Hastily, he drew his attention back to the girl, before he had to ask her to repeat her name yet again.

"I'm Lydia," she said. "Lydia Demarek." She pronounced the surname with the accent on the middle syllable. Hal nodded several times, as if the name were no surprise to him. He realized that his crew were looking at him curiously, waiting for him to say something meaningful—or even mildly intelligent—and not stand here gaping like a peasant at this beautiful girl.

"So, Lydia Demarek, what brings you to be drifting out here at sea? Were you shipwrecked?"

She shook her head. "No. I came from Limmat. The town has been taken by pirates. I managed to escape. But I lost one of my oars and I've been drifting."

That sent a buzz of excited comment through the crew. Hal took a half pace toward her at the news.

"Pirates?" he said. "Are they led by a man called Zavac?"

But she shook her head once more. "I have no idea. I was in the hills, hunting, when they attacked. I saw them and managed to get away. Some of them chased me but I managed to reach the skiff and drifted out into the bay. The tide took me out. Then the current took me farther."

"When was this?" Thorn asked.

She glanced at him. "Yesterday, around midday." Her voice cracked and a frown touched her features as she looked back to Hal. "Could I have some water?" she said, a little reproachfully. "I'm absolutely parched."

"Of course!" Hal said apologetically, realizing that they hadn't shown her the normal basic courtesy a castaway might expect. They'd all been distracted by her beauty, and then by her reference to pirates. He indicated the small stool by the steering platform. "Sit down, please. Edvin, fetch something to drink, would you?" He looked back at the girl. "Are you hungry?"

She smiled gratefully at his sudden concern and made a negative gesture. "Not right now. But I really need some water. I didn't have any in the skiff."

Edvin returned with a large beaker of cold water. She took it from him, smiling her thanks, and drank deeply, finally lowering the beaker with a sigh.

"Oh, that's a lot better!" she said, and sank gratefully onto the stool, still holding the half-full beaker. She sipped again, more slowly now that her initial thirst had been slaked.

"Now, where was I?" she said.

"Limmat," Hal prompted her. "You said it was attacked by pirates."

And she nodded, her eyes clouding as she remembered the scene, the smoke pouring from the burning buildings, the screams of the townspeople. For the hundredth time, she wondered if her grandfather was all right.

"They must have forced their way through the boom," she said. "There was a small ship moored against the quay, so the boom couldn't close. Two others had got inside the harbor. A dark green ship and the biggest of the three—a black ship."

There was a stir of interest among the crew.

"Black, you say?" Hal said. "Are you sure of that?"

She nodded emphatically. "I'm sure. It was sighted the day before, cruising past. For a while we thought she was going to try to break through the boom. Then she turned and sailed away. Rowed away, actually," she corrected herself. Again, the Herons exchanged glances.

"We're hunting a black ship," Stig said. "She has fifteen oars a side. Did you notice how many oars this one had?"

But Lydia shook her head. "I didn't see her then. I heard people talking about her. When I saw her, she was moored alongside the quay, so I had no way of seeing how many oars she had. But she was big. She could easily have that many oars." She looked at the faces surrounding her, saw the level of interest, saw how her mention of a black ship had aroused it, and realized this might be her chance to return to Limmat.

"My grandfather is still there," she said. "I have to get back and make sure he's all right. Can you take me?"

"Of course we can!" Stig said impulsively. But Lydia looked at Hal. He was the skipper, young as he might appear. The decision would be his. Stig, too, turned to look at his friend. Hal was rubbing his chin thoughtfully.

"I think we have to see if this is the ship we're looking for," he said. "We'll take you back there. But you might not like what you find. And it will be dangerous."

She shrugged aside the mention of danger. "I can look after myself," she said. "As to what I might find, I have to know, one way or the other."

"If these pirates are still there," Thorn put in, "we can hardly sail into the harbor and wave hello."

Lydia thought for a moment. "There's swampland to the southwest of the town. We could go ashore there out of sight and take the skiff to get closer."

Thorn, Hal and Stig exchanged a look and came to a decision.

"Can you draw us a chart of this swampland?" Hal asked, and she nodded eagerly.

"Of course."

"Then let's get to it," Hal said.

They made good time back to the coast, then swung south toward Limmat. Long before the town itself came in sight, they could see the heavy pall of smoke that still hung over it.

Lydia's eyes filled with tears as she saw it. Her grandfather's chances, she knew, were getting slimmer and slimmer. He likely would have resisted the pirates, even though such resistance would have been futile. She moved to the bow and stared at the smoke on the horizon. The crew left her to her thoughts.

Finally, she came aft again. Her face was composed and her manner was calm. She indicated the low-lying shoreline.

"We should beach your ship here and go on in the skiff," she said. "Once we round that next point, we'll be in sight of the town."

Hal angled the ship into the shoreline. Lydia watched with interest as Thorn withdrew the fin, allowing the ship to run through the shallow water and gently onto the beach. Stefan and Jesper jumped ashore and made the ship fast with the beach anchor. They had been towing Lydia's skiff astern. Hal unfastened the line that attached it and dragged it along the side of the ship to the beach.

Lydia indicated the low headland to the east of their position.

"If we row round that headland, we can head into the marshes. A small boat like this will be pretty well invisible among the reeds and grass islands."

Hal nodded. "You, me and Stig," he said to her. "The boat won't take any more."

He looked at Thorn. "You stay in charge here, Thorn," he said, and the older man nodded.

"We'll be here," he said. "If you get into any trouble, just come running."

Hal smiled at him, grateful that Thorn hadn't remonstrated over being left behind.

"Get the ship turned round, facing out to sea," he said. "Just in case we have to leave in a hurry."

They boarded the skiff. As they had sailed toward Limmat,

Hal had quickly fashioned another oar for the skiff from a small spar. It was rough but it would serve, he thought. Stig set the oars in the oarlocks, testing their relative balance, and nodded that he was satisfied. Then he began to stroke smoothly, moving the skiff easily toward the promontory.

As the skiff gradually pulled away, the rest of the crew busied themselves shoving the *Heron* off the beach once more and turning her, dragging her stern first onto the beach. Hal looked back after a hundred meters and saw Thorn's heavyset figure a little away from the ship. Thorn raised his left arm and waved. Hal waved in return.

Once round the point, there was nothing but low-lying ground for several kilometers. Beyond, they could see the two watchtowers and the higher buildings of the town, rising above the marsh grasses and low bushes. A small creek ran into the marsh and Stig sculled them into it. Once they were among the drifting grass islands and tall reeds, they were virtually out of sight from the town. They had only occasional glimpses of the towers.

They followed winding, erratic channels through the marsh, diverging at times but always managing to return to their basic course. After an hour's rowing, Lydia indicated to Stig to head for a low spit of sand, covered in stunted trees and marsh grass.

"We'd better leave the skiff here," she said. "We're getting close and the odds are that it might be seen if we take it any farther."

They beached the boat and, at her suggestion, stood one of the oars upright in the sand.

"They won't see it from the town," Lydia said. "But it'll mark the spot where the boat is for us."

They crossed the sand spit and waded into the marsh water on the other side. It was waist deep, although Lydia warned them that there were occasional deeper pools. She led the way, probing ahead with a long branch Hal had cut for her.

They forged on, and gradually they could see more and more of the town. Aside from Lydia's occasional curt directions, they didn't speak. The effort of pushing through the water and the soft, oozing mud bottom of the marsh precluded idle chatter. Finally, Lydia signaled a halt and indicated a humpbacked island, covered in low vegetation and rising higher than the surrounding marshes.

"We'll be able to see the harbor from there," she said.

Hal shook his head admiringly. Even with his instinctive sense of direction, he knew he would have become hopelessly lost in this featureless tangle and the myriad twisting waterways.

"You certainly know your way around here," he said, and she flashed him a quick smile.

"I've been hunting and fishing in these marshes since I was nine years old," she said briefly.

They waded ashore, their clothes clinging soggily to them, and climbed to the low summit of the island, dropping to hands and knees as they approached the top. Before them, they could see the harbor of Limmat. Smoke still rose in several parts of the town, although the larger fires seemed to have been brought under control. The smell of burned wood was thick in their nostrils.

Hal scanned the harbor, noticing the smaller ship moored just inside the boom. He frowned. There was something familiar about her. Then he had it. She was the *Sea Lion*, one of Arndak's small trading fleet that had gone missing from Hallasholm some months before. He had worked on her in the shipyard the previous year, when she had needed several planks replaced after an unfortunate encounter with a whale. He indicated the little ship to Stig and saw a look of recognition on the other boy's face.

"So now we know what happened to the trading fleet," Hal said, pointing farther down the harbor.

There, moored against the inner jetty, was a long, black shape that both of them recognized.

"The *Raven*," Stig said.

Hal said nothing, staring at the evil-looking ship with a sudden hatred in his heart. After weeks of searching and hoping, here was their quarry, less than a kilometer away. Almost reluctantly, he dragged his eyes off her and studied the rest of the town.

The watchtowers on either side of the harbor entrance were the principal points of interest. They were simple timber platforms, each with a chest-high wooden balustrade on all four sides— probably pine planking, he thought—and a flat roof on top. A small enclosed room was in the center of the platform—the guard-room, he assumed. The towers were obviously designed as observation posts and as defensive sites from which arrows could be rained down on an attacker. Each of the platforms stood on a timber framework—four large uprights tied together by a latticework of smaller diagonal pieces. In the center of the support structure, a ladder ran from the platform to the ground.

He'd seen what he'd come for. Now he had to come up with a way for his small crew to take on and defeat the fifty-odd pirates who manned the black ship. Up until now, he'd avoided making any concrete plans. There didn't seem to be any point until they found the *Raven*. But now the problem had to be addressed. And quickly. There was no telling how long she'd stay in the harbor. He edged back from the low crest on his elbows.

"Let's get back," he said. "We've got some thinking to do."

They splashed their way back through the muddy water, Lydia leading the way once more. After half an hour, Hal saw the blade of the oar standing above the reeds on a nearby island and headed toward it. He glanced at Lydia approvingly. She was a handy person to have around, he thought. He never would have recognized that particular island again. They waded ashore, and while Stig heaved the skiff into the water, Hal retrieved the oar.

"Want me to row for a while?" he offered. But Stig shook his head.

"I'm fine. And I'm a faster rower than you. We'll get back to the ship sooner."

"You might," said a voice behind them and they swung round, startled, as a dozen men rose from the rushes and reeds, moving quickly to surround them. "But right now, nobody's going anywhere."

H al and Stig had left their weapons at the ship, knowing they would be wading through the marshes. But they both wore saxe knives and as they whirled to face the speaker, their hands dropped instinctively to the hilts of the heavy knives.

"I wouldn't do that," the man warned, and his followers brandished weapons of their own. Some of them had swords. The others had a random collection of clubs, maces and short spears.

"Forget it, Stig," Hal said softly. There was no point in fighting. They were too badly outnumbered. He rose from the crouch that he had fallen into, and moved his hand away from the saxe. Stig, looking angrily round the circle of men who faced them, came to the same decision a few seconds after his friend.

Hal studied the man who had spoken. He was a few years older than the two *Heron* shipmates, possibly twenty or twenty-one. He was average height but stocky, with shoulder-length dark hair and a broad face. He was clean shaven and at some stage his nose had been broken and badly reset, so that it was slightly offline, with a small bump in the middle. He was armed with a short-bladed sword and a small, round metal shield. He held the weapons easily, obviously accustomed to using them.

Most pirates were, Hal thought bitterly.

Which made the man's next words a little confusing.

"Well, men," he said, smiling briefly at his followers, "looks as if we've caught ourselves some pirates."

Puzzled, Hal opened his mouth to reply. But Lydia beat him to it. She had been standing behind Hal and Stig when the men sprang their ambush. Now she shoved between the two friends and stepped forward to face their captor belligerently.

"Pirates my foot, Barat!" she snapped. "You always get the wrong end of the stick, don't you? Now put your weapons away. All of you!" she added, glaring round the half circle of men facing them.

A few of them muttered expressions of surprise and amusement. The leader, the man she had called Barat, peered at her more closely. Like Stig and Hal, she was smeared with mud and dirty water from their passage through the marsh, and the late afternoon light was uncertain. Now his face lit up in recognition.

"Lydia? Is that you? It is! All covered in mud and muck, but it's you sure enough!"

He sheathed his sword and leapt forward, laughing delightedly, to sweep her up in an embrace, holding her close. Stig's lips narrowed. The two must be friends, maybe more than friends, he thought, with a twinge of resentment. But then Lydia wriggled uncomfortably and finally broke free. The other men gathered round, smiling and calling greetings to her. Several clapped her on the shoulder.

After a few moments, Barat glanced keenly at Hal and Stig.

"And who are these two?" he said. "I've never seen them before."

"They're Skandians—friends of mine," Lydia said.

"Skandians?" Barat's face clouded with suspicion. In his eyes, Skandians were little better than pirates.

Stig sensed the change in attitude and flushed angrily. He took half a pace forward, his hand dropping involuntarily to his saxe knife again.

Hal laid a restraining hand on his forearm. "Take it easy, Stig," he said quietly. After a second or two, he was relieved to see his friend's shoulders slowly relax, and Stig's hand moved away from the saxe knife's hilt.

Barat had noticed the impulsive movement and he locked eyes with Stig. The dislike between the two was almost palpable.

"Yes. Take it easy, Stig," he repeated.

Hal tightened his grip on his friend's forearm. This time, Stig didn't rise to the bait. He's changed, Hal thought. The old Stig would have given in to his fiery temper and done something rash.

"Stop it, Barat," Lydia said angrily. "They're friends of mine and they rescued me. They probably saved my life, if the truth be told. Then they went out of their way to bring me back here."

"Probably looking to see what they can get their hands on," Barat said scornfully.

"We're only looking for one thing," Hal said evenly. "That's the black pirate ship in your harbor. We've been after her for weeks. When Lydia told us she was here, we came to see for ourselves."

"So I suppose you have no interest in the em—"

"Shut up, Barat!" one of his men shouted, cutting him off before he could say more. Barat flushed and turned to the man who had interrupted him.

"I just thought—"

"You didn't think!" the man said. He was a little older than Barat, tall and heavily built. "You're a good battle commander, but you're always letting your tongue run away. It's time you learned to shut up. If Lydia says these boys are friends, that's good enough for me!"

A few of the others growled agreement and Barat subsided, but with bad grace.

"All right then. I was just saying . . ."

Lydia looked around the group and tried to relieve the tension in the air.

"So, Jonas, what are you all doing in the marshes?" She addressed the question to the man who had silenced Barat. He shrugged.

"Some of us got away when the pirates attacked. They caught us by surprise. You saw that smaller ship in the harbor?" He paused and when they nodded confirmation, he went on to describe the pirates' stratagem of faking a pursuit so that the Limmatans would open the boom.

"Then the other two ships joined in and they overran the town. They killed most of the garrison in the watchtowers. Some of us managed to band together and fight our way out. But we were disorganized and fighting in ones and twos. We didn't have a chance against them."

"We were lucky to get away," another man put in.

Hal looked at him. "How many of you got out?"

"Thirty-eight," Jonas said. "We've made a camp in the marshes. The pirates can't get to us here. We know the ground too well. Barat here got us organized after we got out, but there's not enough of us to attack the pirates—particularly when they're inside the palisade—so it's a stalemate."

Hal decided it was time to mend a few fences, so he addressed his next question to Barat.

"So you think they're here to stay?" he asked. "How many of them are there?"

Barat nodded, sensing Hal's peaceful overture, and responded in kind. "They'll be here for a while, I'd say," he said. "As to numbers, I'm not sure. Certainly more than us."

"There's at least fifty on the *Raven*," Stig said thoughtfully. "Maybe a few less on the other big ship. And *Sea Lion* could carry fifteen to twenty."

"*Sea Lion*?" Barat asked.

Hal gestured vaguely in the direction of the harbor. "The small ship. She was taken by the *Raven* sometime back. She's a Skandian trader."

"Not anymore," Barat said heavily. "She's a pirate now."

"True," Hal said. "So the question is, what do we do next? There's thirty-eight of you and nine of us. They outnumber us, so we'll have to surprise them somehow."

"How?" Stig asked, and his friend grinned at him.

"That's the big question," he said. "When I figure it out, you'll be the first to know."

Barat looked at the two young sailors. He had the grace to look a little shamefaced.

"You mean, you're planning to throw in with us?"

"We've got a common enemy," Hal said. "Zavac stole some-thing from us and I want it back. You want him out of your town. If we work together, we might both get what we want."

Barat considered this statement for a few seconds. Then he nodded agreement. He held out his hand to Hal.

"That sounds good to me," he said. They shook hands, then Barat offered his hand to Stig and the two of them shook as well, although there was still a noticeable reserve between them. Maybe it had something to do with the girl, Hal thought.

"We should get back to our ship while there's still light," he said, glancing to the west, where the sun was slipping ever closer to the ocean. "How are you placed for food in your camp?"

Barat pursed his lips. "We're on pretty short commons," he said. "There are fish and a few wild fowl in the marshes, but not enough to feed a large number. And we brought nothing with us. I'm afraid I can't offer you anything."

Hal shook his head. "That wasn't what I was asking. We've got supplies on the ship. And more at our camp farther up the coast. If a couple of you come back to the ship with us, we'll give you what we can spare. Then we'll head back up the coast, collect the rest of our gear, and more food, and come back here. By then, I may have figured out a plan of action."

Barat nodded gratefully. "I certainly won't refuse."

Quickly, he passed his orders to the rest of his men. He and two others would come back to the *Heron* and collect the supplies Hal had offered, while the rest returned to their camp in the marshes. Stig launched the skiff and set the oars in the oarlocks, and Barat and his two companions retrieved a similar craft from a hiding place in the reeds.

Hal looked at it, raising an eyebrow. "Where did that come from?"

The picture that Barat's men had painted of their retreat from the town didn't seem to include any time to stop and retrieve boats.

"A lot of our people leave skiffs moored in the marshes," Lydia said. "They use them for fishing and wildfowling." As Barat rowed the boat level with their own, she moved down the beach toward him. She went to speak, hesitated, then gathered her resolve and continued.

"I didn't have a chance to ask you," she said, her voice fearful. "Do you have any idea what happened to my grandfather? Did he get away?"

Barat's face told them the answer, even before he spoke.

"He was killed, Lydia. I'm sorry. He tried to fight the pirates—you know what he was like."

She nodded sadly. "I knew he would."

"There were too many of them," Barat continued. "And he was an old man, Lydia." His face darkened with anger as he recalled the scene. "An old man. They didn't have to kill him. They could have disarmed him. But they didn't. They killed him." He paused, looking at her. Her face was blank, showing no emotion.

"I couldn't do anything to help him, Lyd. I tried, but I couldn't get to him in time. Then more pirates arrived and I had to get away. There was nothing I could do, really."

She touched his arm and gave him a wan smile. "I know," she

said. "He would never have surrendered to them. He didn't realize he was old."

Abruptly, she turned away, hiding the tears that sprang to her eyes as she remembered the old man who had looked after her for so long. When she turned back, she had regained control of herself. She walked to where Hal was holding their skiff steady against the slight flow of the current through the marshes and stepped aboard, settling onto the seat at the bow.

"Let's get back to the ship," she said.

As Stig rowed the little boat around the headland, they could just make out the dark shape of the *Heron* on the beach. Hal nodded approvingly. Thorn hadn't allowed the boys to light any fires. Stig's smooth, powerful rowing took them across the bay in a few minutes. When they were fifty meters from the beached ship, Hal heard a soft challenge and answered.

"It's Stig and Hal. We've got some people with us. Friends."

They pulled into the shallows and he stepped out to guide the boat ashore. Barat and the other two Limmatans followed close behind them. As he hauled the skiff up the beach, Hal glanced around. To his surprise, he saw that the Herons were all fully armed. Their shields had been removed from the bulwarks of the ship and they were all wearing them. The starlight gleamed off ax heads and sword blades.

Thorn, he noticed, was wearing his battered old horned helmet, and had changed his day-to-day false arm, with the clamping hook, for the war club Hal had fashioned for him. He stepped forward now.

"You're all right?" he said suspiciously.

Hal smiled at him. "We're fine. These men are friends. Lydia knows them. They're going to help us take the *Raven.*"

Thorn studied the three Limmatans intently. Very sensibly, they showed no sign of hostility. Finally, he grunted, reassured that Hal wasn't speaking under duress.

"All right. Stand down, Herons."

There was a slight clatter of weapons as the boys laid them down. Hal introduced Barat and his companions and explained where they had come from and their need for supplies. Edvin nodded and moved quickly to the ship to pack up the food. Barat's two friends followed him. A few minutes later, they returned, carrying two heavy sacks.

"Thanks for this," Barat said, and Hal nodded.

"We'll bring more when we come back. Look for us in two days' time."

Barat shook his hand, then turned away, calling over his shoulder.

"Come on, lads. You too, Lydia. Let's get back to camp."

But Lydia hesitated awkwardly, not moving toward the skiffs. Barat turned, puzzled and a little annoyed.

"Lydia?" he said. "Come on."

Lydia looked down, one foot tracing small circles in the sand of the beach.

"I think . . . I'll stay with the *Heron,*" she said, then looked quickly at Hal. "If that's all right with you?"

Hal spread his hands in a surprised gesture. "That's fine as far as I'm concerned."

Stig grinned widely. "Me too."

Barat gave him a sour look, then gestured peremptorily toward the two skiffs.

"Don't be silly, Lydia. These aren't your people. Come with us. Now."

She raised her eyes. There was a determined light in them and she shook her head once.

"No," she said. "I'll stay with the Skandians."

Barat let out a snort that was half anger, half frustration.

"Fine," he said. "Forget your friends if that's what you choose. Stay with these foreigners."

"Yes. I think I will," Lydia told him, with growing conviction in her voice, and he turned away, unwilling to argue the point further. He stalked down the beach to the two skiffs, his back straight, never looking at her as he launched one of the boats and began rowing away. His two companions hastily piled into the second boat and followed.

Stig grinned at Lydia. "Good choice," he said.

But she turned away and said nothing further.

L ydia maintained her silence for most of the trip north to
Shelter Bay.

She stood alone behind the ship's figurehead, staring
out at the water as it rushed past, never flinching at the
continual sheets of spray that flew up from the bow.

"She'll be drenched," Stig said as he stood by Hal on the steering platform. "I'll fetch her a blanket." He started to move away
but Hal stopped him.

"Leave her be," Hal said quietly.

Stig hesitated. He wanted to talk to her. But Hal shook his
head and Stig finally decided his skirl was right.

Unlike their smooth run down the coast, it wasn't an easy
night. The wind veered into the northwest and varied in intensity,
so that the crew were at work continually, tacking and adjusting the
sails. Lydia, seeing she would be in the way if she remained in the
bow, moved to a spot on the port rowing benches, near the stern.
She watched as the *Heron* went from one tack to another, noticing
how much closer to the wind she could sail than the square-rigged

ships that were the norm in this part of the world. But, after a few changes in tack, she lost interest and resumed staring out to sea.

After four hours, the wind decided to settle on one direction and strength, and the boys took the opportunity to rest on the rowing benches. Several of them went to sleep immediately. Hal smiled to himself. They were seasoned sailors now, he thought, ready to snatch a few minutes' sleep whenever the opportunity arose. He turned the tiller over to Stig and looked around for a spot to rest. Lydia was sitting in his usual place. Shrugging, he stepped down and sat beside her.

She glanced up and nodded.

"Sorry about your grandfather," he said awkwardly. He'd cautioned Stig against bothering her earlier. He sensed that she wasn't in any mood for Stig's inevitably unsubtle attempts to win her favor. But he felt pity for her, alone among strangers, and grieving for the loss of her grandfather.

She gave him a wan smile.

"Thanks," she said. "He was a good man. But he should never have tried to fight them. He was too old."

Hal considered this for a few moments. "Maybe he wouldn't have been happy to simply let them walk all over him. Maybe he knew he was too old to fight them, but wasn't willing to simply stand aside and let them have their way."

"Probably. That'd be just like him," she said. There was a note of subdued pride and amusement in her voice as she thought of the old man. Then she glanced up at the big, triangular sail, swelling in a hard curve on the port tack. "This is an unusual ship."

He smiled, unable to resist the temptation to brag. "I designed and built her," he said. "She's my pride and joy."

Lydia looked at him with new respect. The sight of such a young ship's captain had initially surprised her. Now she began to understand how he had reached that position at such an early age.

"What's that big contraption in the bow?" she asked. "The one covered in canvas? Is it a hoist of some sort?"

He shook his head. "It's a weapon. We call it the Mangler," he said. "And it might just be the key to an attack on the pirates."

She looked up at that, expecting him to say more. But he shook his head. While he had been steering, an idea had been slowly forming in his mind. It came a piece at a time and, at the moment, was a set of unrelated concepts. He needed time to sit down and put them into order to turn them into a cohesive plan.

"I'll tell you later," he said. Then, to change the subject, he added, "Tell me about Barat. He seems a little prickly."

She snorted derisively. "That's an understatement. Barat is too full of himself for my taste. He's a good warrior—a very good warrior, as Jonas said. And he's a good battle commander. But that's where it ends. As a day-to-day leader, he's too impulsive and too disinclined to look after details." She paused. "And he takes too much for granted."

Hal sensed from the tone of her voice that this last statement was more personal than a general assessment of Barat.

"By which I assume you mean he takes *you* for granted?" he asked.

"He thinks he owns me," she said. "And he tells everyone that we're going to be married when we're older." She made an angry gesture. "It never occurs to him that I might like to have a say in that! That's why I didn't want to go back to the camp with him. I hope you didn't mind."

Hal shook his head. "You're welcome to stay with us as long as you choose," he said. "The boys like you."

"That's nice to know," she said. She was a little embarrassed by his statement and not sure how to respond. She searched for something to say and, looking up, noticed Stig's tall figure at the tiller.

"How long have you known Stig?" she asked, looking to change the subject.

Oho! So that's the way the wind is blowing, Hal thought. He looked at Stig in his turn. Outlined against the night sky, the first mate cut quite a heroic figure.

"Oh, we've been friends for years." There was another pause, then he said, "Now if you'll excuse me, I might get some rest."

He moved away a few meters and settled down, pulling a blanket round him. He wondered why her question had caused him a vague sense of disappointment.

Dawn was breaking by the time they reached Shelter Bay. The dazzling sun was low to the hills and right in their eyes. That, and the fact that there was a steep sea running and a tricky crosswind, convinced Hal that they should row the *Heron* into the bay. They dropped the sail a hundred meters offshore. The boys manned their oars as he guided her through the narrow entrance into the calmer waters inside. Closer in, the tall surrounding hills blocked the first light of the sun and the bay was still in semi-darkness.

There is an inevitable relaxation that comes at the end of any trip, when home, even a temporary one like their camp, comes into sight. Now they were in safe and familiar waters, Hal and the other boys relaxed, thinking of the warm and comfortable beds that awaited them in the tent. As a result, their vigilance was reduced, and none of them noticed the dark shape moored inside the southern headland of the bay as they passed it. It was only when the shape began to move that Hal sensed its presence.

He swung round. There was a large ship fifty meters astern of them, moving out from its place of concealment to block any possible escape from the bay. He heard the cries of alarm from the other boys as they noticed the ship. Caught by surprise, the Herons stopped rowing. Now Hal could hear the faint splashes of the oars from the ship behind them as she began to overtake them.

"It's *Wolfwind*," Thorn said quietly.

Hal's shoulders slumped in despair. After all they had gone through, after finding the *Raven* and having a chance to recapture the Andomal, it was over. They'd be taken back to Hallasholm in disgrace. And their reception would be even more icy than before, as they'd defied the Oberjarl and disobeyed his orders.

And I'll lose the *Heron*, he thought bitterly. Erak had already said he planned to confiscate the ship. Now, after Hal had absconded with it, he was sure to carry out his threat. Once the *Heron* was gone, the Heron brotherband was finished, he knew. While they had the ship, they had hope. Now that was gone.

Wolfwind moved up to within ten meters of their stern, then her oarsmen backed water, holding station on the drifting *Heron*. This close, Hal could recognize Svengal in the bow of the ship, standing on the railing, holding on to the forestay for balance.

"Hal!" he called across the intervening distance. "Keep rowing. Take her in to the beach near your camp."

Hal felt movement beside him. Stig had leapt up from his rowing bench.

"We can outrun them!" he said. But Hal shook his head bitterly.

"Not under oars. They're faster than us. And the minute we try to raise the sail, they'll be alongside us."

"Then we'll fight them!" Stig said angrily.

Thorn rumbled a warning. The Herons were badly outnumbered, and *Wolfwind*'s crew were seasoned warriors. But again, Hal refused.

"I'm not fighting my countrymen," he said simply. "Let's face it. It's over."

He looked down at the crew, waiting on their rowing benches for his orders. At the sternmost bench, Lydia watched him, a confused expression on her face. The Herons were Skandians, she knew. And the ship behind them was a Skandian wolfship. She wondered what the problem could be.

Before she could approach him, Hal gestured to the boys on the rowing benches.

"Oars," he ordered quietly. "Let's take her in and face the music."

Stig looked at him, hesitated, then shook his head in frustration. He leapt down and took his place on the rowing bench.

"Oars!" he repeated the order. "Give way!"

The oars dipped into the calm water of the bay, creating two lines of rippling circles as they broke the surface.

"Stroke," Stig ordered, and the *Heron* began to glide through the water, her bow wave chuckling along the side of the hull. At least you can chuckle, Hal thought miserably. A few meters from the sand, he ordered the rowers to cease and guided the ship in toward the beach. Distracted and dejected as he was, he nearly forgot to raise the fin. Fortunately, Thorn remembered it in time and heaved it up out of the keel box. The bow grated on the sand and *Heron* rode a few meters up onto dry land.

Stefan tossed the beach anchor over the bow, then dropped over the side after it. As he jogged up the beach to set it in the sand, there was a grinding noise as *Wolfwind* ran her prow aground alongside them. One of her crew mirrored Stefan's actions.

Hal looked sadly round his little ship. This would be the last time he commanded her, he knew, and he couldn't bring himself to leave her. He was aware that the other boys were waiting on his lead and he gestured toward the bow.

"All ashore," he said. They turned and made their way forward, a disconsolate group. Lydia, still puzzled, fell into step beside Stig.

"What's happening?" she asked him. He glanced at her.

"We're runaways," he said. "They've come to take us back."

She looked at him, her eyes wide. There was nothing she could say to that. Although as she thought about it, she realized that this would mean that her countrymen were now on their own against the pirates. There were only nine in the *Heron*'s crew, and eight of them were boys. But somehow, they had given her hope. Their optimism, their confidence in Hal and his ability to come up with a plan of action had given her belief. Now that was gone. Dejected, she followed the others to the bow.

Hal remained on the steering platform. He looped the restraining cord round the tiller, to stop it banging back and forth with the movement of the water. Then he remained, one hand on the smooth wood, now inanimate as the ship was beached and still.

Thorn dropped a hand on his shoulder.

"Come on," he said gently. "We might as well find out the worst."

They walked the length of the ship, then climbed over the bow. The other members of the crew were waiting in a dejected group. A dozen of *Wolfwind's* crew stood in a semicircle around them. As Hal dropped to the wet sand of the beach, Svengal strode forward, a huge grin on his face.

"At last!" he said. "Gorlog's bad breath, Hal, you've led us on a merry chase. Found your camp here a couple of days ago, but there was no sign of *Heron,* so we went looking for you. I thought we sighted you south of here the other evening, but you slipped away. So we came back here to wait. And here you are!"

He stepped forward and engulfed the surprised boy in a huge bear hug, then held him at arm's length, studying him.

"Thank the gods you're all safe. We've been worried sick about you. Erak would have skinned me alive if you'd come to any harm."

"I suppose he wants us in one piece when you take us back," Stefan said bitterly.

"Take you back? We're not here to take you back. Erak sent us to help you!" he said.

Slowly, Hal felt hope dawning in his heart. "You want to help us?"

Svengal turned to his crew. "They thought we'd come all this way to drag them back to Hallasholm!" He roared with laughter. His men joined in and he looked back at Hal.

"Who'd want a scruffy lot like you back again? No, Erak figured you had a head start on us, so you'd have a better chance of finding that murdering swine Zavac. So he sent us after you to give you a hand. After all, those Magyarans have you seriously outnumbered."

Svengal seemed to notice Thorn for the first time and grinned cheerfully at him. "Hello, Thorn. Nice sheepskin. What happened to the old one? Did it finally fall apart? It was more holes than sheepskin anyway."

"I see you still talk too much, Svengal," Thorn replied. A few of the *Wolfwind* crew murmured agreement. Svengal was unabashed, however.

"I never was the strong, silent type."

Hal shook his head as he considered this unexpected turn of events. He wondered if he would ever understand the workings of the Oberjarl's mind. When they had sighted *Wolfwind* the previous night, he had instantly assumed that the ship had been sent to capture them and take them back to Hallasholm in disgrace. Now Svengal was telling him that he and his crew were here to help. Things were moving too fast, he thought.

"As a matter of fact," Thorn was saying, "we have found Zavac. He's a day's sail down the coast, holed up in a fortified town." A murmur of interest ran through *Wolfwind*'s crew, and a satisfied smile spread across Svengal's face when he heard the news.

"Wonderful," he said quietly. "Simply wonderful. So what's our plan of action?"

"We're still working on that," Thorn told him. "But Hal will come up with something suitably brilliant. He usually does. Then we can go and winkle Zavac out of his rat hole."

"What fun," Svengal said. His men gave an assenting growl.

Zavac had murdered two of their friends when he stole the *Andomal*. *Wolfwind*'s crew were eager to avenge them.

Svengal clapped Thorn on the shoulder. "Nice to be working with you again, Thorn," he said. "It'll be just like old times."

Lydia looked at the fierce northmen and felt her spirits rising. Skandians were renowned fighters, she knew. They were still outnumbered by the Magyarans, but the odds were getting better all the time. And since everyone seemed convinced that Hal would come up with a plan to balance them even further, who was she to disagree?

The following morning, they broke camp and the two ships set out in company to sail down the coast to Limmat.

It was mid-afternoon when they reached their destination. There was no longer a plume of smoke rising above the town. Apparently, the pirates had gotten the fires under control. Or perhaps they had left the townspeople to look after them.

As *Heron* and *Wolfwind* headed for the beach, they saw two men waving. Barat had detailed them to wait for the *Heron*'s return and guide them through the swamps to his camp. Svengal left ten of his men behind on the beach to keep watch on the two ships. The rest of *Wolfwind*'s crew and the Herons loaded up with sacks of supplies and trudged through thigh-deep mud and water behind their guides, grumbling and complaining about the sand flies and mosquitoes, which seemed to swarm in the marshes by the thousands.

They followed a seemingly aimless path until they came to a larger-than-usual sand island. The sun was almost setting and they could see the glow of several fires as they approached.

Barat had watched them threading their way through the marsh for the last fifty meters or so and he made his way down to the beach to greet them as they squelched their way out of the muddy water. He gave a start as he saw how their numbers had increased. Eight boys and an older man had left two days before. Now they were back, with a further twenty Skandians.

"Who are these?" he asked Hal.

"Reinforcements. They're going to help us with the attack. And those sacks they're carrying are all full of food."

Barat's suspicious expression lightened considerably.

"Glad to see you," he said. But the direction of his gaze left them in no doubt that it was the food he was most glad to see. He noticed Lydia, who was standing close by Hal and Stig, and his expression grew cool.

"Hullo, Lydia."

She nodded a greeting. "Hi, Barat. Nice place you've got here."

She looked around the island. The men who had escaped from the town had no time to gather tents or tarpaulins when they retreated. Instead, they had constructed rough thatched shelters from tree branches and bushes. A burly figure was approaching them and Hal recognized Jonas, who had been Barat's second in command when they had first met several days before. The older Limmatan smiled a welcome now.

"You're back!" He too noticed the sacks. "And you didn't come empty-handed! Welcome to our lovely seaside holiday home, Lydia. How do you like it?"

He swept an arm around, in a gesture that encompassed the low-lying, scrubby island.

Lydia returned his grin. "It's just lovely, Jonas. Everything a girl could want."

"Well, come on into the camp and meet the rest of us," Jonas said, addressing Hal. He frowned and stepped closer, then spoke in a mock whisper, "If you don't mind my saying, you seem to have increased and multiplied since you've been gone."

Hal nodded. He liked Jonas. He had an easy, cheerful manner about him—in contrast to Barat's awkward, suspicious approach. Hal also sensed that Jonas's friendly greeting was intended to compensate for Barat's lack of welcome.

"Let's get to your camp," Hal said. "I'll introduce you all then."

They made their way into the camp proper. Jonas directed them to the cooking fire and the sacks of food were dumped there for the cooks to sort through and prepare a meal. Hal wasn't worried about handing over the food. They'd only be here for a few days if everything went to plan. Once they'd defeated the pirates, they could reprovision in Limmat.

And if they didn't defeat them, he thought grimly, they'd have no need of food.

They grouped around several fires while the meal was prepared and served. Spirits in the camp were high. Most of the men who had escaped from the town were only too glad to see their numbers increased by a body of trained warriors like the Skandians. Unlike their suspicious battle leader, they welcomed the newcomers heartily. Truth be told, a feeling of dejection had started to permeate the camp. The Limmatans knew only too well that forty of them had little hope of dislodging more than a hundred pirates from a well-fortified position like the town. The arrival of the nine members of the *Heron* crew, and now twenty additional Skandians, seemed to be a good omen. Accordingly, the meal was a cheerful one, with a lot of laughter and good fellowship.

When they were finished eating, the more senior members of the Limmatan party gathered round a smaller fire with Hal, Stig, Lydia, Thorn and Svengal. Ingvar, who had eaten at one of the other fires, moved over and sat a few paces behind Hal, in case he was needed. Svengal's second in command, Lars Bentknuckle, joined them as they waited for Hal to lay out the details of his plan.

Svengal and Lars, like most Skandians, claimed no ability to plan and no affinity for tactics. They were fighting men and they left such details to other people. All they asked was to be given a clear target and purpose and they'd happily go into battle.

Barat made some pretense at being a leader and a tactician. But in fact, he had been trying to think of a way to attack and defeat the pirates for some days now, to no avail. While he maintained the fiction that he had the authority to approve or reject Hal's plans, the truth was, he was hoping that the young Skandian would come up with a battle plan that would bring them a victory—although he had not the slightest inkling of what that plan might entail. At the same time, he was slightly jealous of the young Skandian skirl, possibly due to what he saw as Lydia's defection. So even though part of him hoped for a viable plan, another part was all too ready to criticize whatever Hal came up with.

"Surprise," said Hal, when they had all gathered close around the fire. "That's going to be the key to success for us. If we can take them by surprise, we can negate their advantage in numbers."

He spoke confidently. But the idea, once he had it, seemed so obvious that he was inclined to mistrust it. He couldn't help feeling that he must have left something out of his calculations. He shrugged mentally. If he had, both Thorn and Svengal were experienced campaigners. They might not be able to put a plan together themselves. But they would recognize any weaknesses if they saw them.

At least, he hoped they would.

"They know we're here," Barat sneered. "Little hard to surprise them, isn't it?"

"They don't know I'm here," Svengal pointed out. He was already becoming tired of this self-important Limmatan, who seemed always ready to criticize, but never put forward an idea of his own. "And that's come as a surprise to a good many enemies in the past."

"True," Thorn put in. "Svengal can be a nasty surprise."

Lars and a few of the Limmatans chuckled at that. Barat raised his eyebrows. He was annoyed by the prompt response to his criticism and annoyed that his fellow townsmen had laughed. But he refused to let this Skandian roughneck see it.

Hal pushed on, ignoring the exchange, seeking to smooth things over.

"You're right, Barat," he said. "The pirates know you're here. And they'll expect any attack to come from this side of the town."

"Naturally," Barat said. "If we tried to go round the palisade, they'd see us and they could simply move their forces to counter us."

"But they don't know that you have ships now. If we move under the cover of darkness, we can ferry your men to the far side of the town—to the east. We'll take a wide loop out into the bay to stay out of sight, then swing back in, hugging the northern shore. I figure we can do it over two nights. There's a promontory about four hundred meters from the town where you can stay out of sight until all your men are in position."

During the trip down the coast, he had asked Lydia to draw him a map of the town and its surroundings. He had studied it closely and now sketched a rough version of this in the sand, pointing to the spot where the land jutted out into the bay.

"On the third night, under cover of darkness, move your men up closer to the town so you're in position to attack at first light.

"Zavac will be watching the western side, where the marshes are—and where he thinks you are. And he'll have his men concentrated on that side, while you'll be attacking from a completely unexpected direction. That should give you a good chance of getting over the palisade—particularly if we mount a diversion at the watchtowers and tie up more of their men."

"Most of them are in the watchtowers," Jonas put in thoughtfully. "It's the logical spot for them, after all. They can watch the marshes and the entrance to the harbor."

"What puzzles me," Svengal mused, "is why they're still in the town. Surely by now, they've had time to load up with anything they want and be on their way."

Hal happened to be watching Barat and Jonas when Svengal made the point. He saw the quick glance between them.

They're hiding something from us, he thought. Neither he nor Svengal were aware that the pirates were still in Limmat because of the emerald mine. Zavac had the miners working double-time to extract the maximum possible number of precious stones from the rich seam behind the town. And, feeling no immediate threat from the relatively small party who had escaped into the marshes, he was in no particular hurry to leave.

After a moment's hesitation, Jonas spoke.

"There are a lot of wealthy merchants in the town," he said. "And they keep their money well hidden. My guess is it's taking the pirates longer than they planned to find it."

"Regardless of why they're here," Barat said, "your plan isn't going to work. I would have thought a sailor like you could see the obvious flaw."

There was a note of something like triumph in his voice. Hal cocked his head to one side.

"Oh? And what detail have I missed?" Had the objection come from Svengal, Lars or even Jonas, he might have given it some credence. But Barat seemed almost eager to find fault.

"The wind," Barat answered in a condescending tone. "I thought sailors knew all about that. At this time of year, the prevailing wind at night will be coming from the shore and it'll be dead against you. It'll take you most of the night to beat into the bay against it—particularly if you plan to take a wide loop on the way in and out. You'll just never manage it in time and the odds are high that the invaders will see you and guess what we're up to."

Hal smiled, relieved that Barat hadn't seen a real problem with the idea. Mind you, his point did have a certain validity. If *Wolfwind*, for example, tried to ferry the men into the bay, she would take too long beating into the headwind and daylight would expose her. But *Heron* was a different matter altogether.

"It won't be a problem," he said confidently. "My ship can sail upwind a lot faster than normal. Eight hours of darkness will be plenty of time for us to get there and back."

Barat opened his mouth to argue but Svengal forestalled him.

"Hal's right. That little ship of his sails upwind like a dream. She'll be able to nip in and out with time to spare."

Barat subsided, a scowl on his face. Jonas leaned forward to keep the discussion moving.

"You mentioned a diversion," he said. "What did you have in mind?"

"I noticed the watchtowers have a wooden balustrade," Hal said.

Jonas nodded. "It's pinewood."

Hal nodded. He had assumed as much. Pine was the most readily available timber in this part of the world.

"The planks are thick enough to stop an arrow or a crossbow bolt," Jonas went on.

"Not the kind I've got in mind," Hal said, smiling. He turned to Ingvar, sitting quietly behind him, paying close attention to the conversation. "Ingvar, can I have the bolt, please?"

Ingvar reached under his jacket and produced one of the bolts from the Mangler. He handed it to Hal. Hal tossed the heavy projectile onto the sand in the middle of the circle.

"I've mounted an oversize crossbow in the bow of my ship," he said. "It'll shoot one of these at three hundred meters."

Jonas came to his knees and retrieved the bolt. He weighed it, studied the iron-reinforced point and emitted a low whistle.

"This could make a real mess of things," he said, and passed the bolt to Barat, who raised his eyebrows as he examined it closely.

In spite of his antipathy to the Skandians, and their young skirl in particular, he couldn't help but be impressed by the deadly-looking projectile. He could imagine the havoc it could wreak in the wooden towers.

"I plan to cruise past the harbor mouth, attacking the two watchtowers with the Mangler," Hal said. He saw the puzzled expressions and smiled. "That's what we call the big crossbow. If these bolts start hitting the balustrade, they'll smash it to pieces. Pinewood splinters easily, so they'll send splinters flying in all directions as well."

His listeners nodded as they pictured the scene. The splinters of pine would become like so many small, deadly projectiles themselves, scything down the defenders.

"Once we've got their attention concentrated on the harbor mouth, your men can break cover and attack the rear palisade. With any luck, you'll be over it and into the town before they wake up to what's happening."

"What about us?" Svengal interrupted. "Do you expect us to sit quietly by while you're having all the fun?"

Hal smiled at him. "Well, if you really want to," he said. "After all, you've had a tiring time looking for us and you might want to put your feet up and rest . . ." He let the sentence hang and Svengal snorted dismissively. Then Hal continued.

"But I rather thought you might launch an attack from the marshes. If you take the western tower after we've softened it up, you can secure the boom. Then you can use the boom to get across the harbor to the second tower."

He paused, looking questioningly at Svengal. The massive log boom would be almost submerged, but the crew of *Wolfwind*, used to keeping their balance on a heaving deck in a storm, should be able to use it as a makeshift bridge to cross to the eastern tower, and the harbor mole. Svengal considered the idea, then nodded.

"Shouldn't be a problem," he said. "We did a similar thing some years ago, at a port in Teutlandt. And once we're across, we'll be hitting them on two sides."

"Three," Hal said. "When we've neutralized the towers, I plan to beach *Heron* on the far side, where the beach gate is." He had noticed on Lydia's sketch that there was a heavy timber gate on the eastern side of the town where the palisade ran down to the water's edge.

"We'll break that down while you and Barat are attacking and come in from a third direction." He looked at Barat. "What about the townsfolk? Once we're inside, will they join in?"

Barat nodded immediately. "I can guarantee it," he said. "Once they see they're not alone, they'll grab anything they can to fight the pirates."

"How do you plan to breach the beach gate?" Thorn asked. He'd been silent as Hal outlined his plan. But now he could see an area where he'd be involved and he was interested to know what his young friend had in mind. Hal grinned at him.

"I have a rough idea about that. I'll tell you when I've worked it out." He looked around the circle of faces, searching for disagreement or criticism. He saw only enthusiasm. Even Barat, after his earlier snide comments, seemed ready to embrace the idea.

"Well," Hal said, "are you with me?" He addressed the question to Barat. He wanted him to commit to the plan before anyone else.

Slowly, the leader of the Limmatans nodded. "When do we do it?"

There was a general growl of assent from those around him. Hal smiled.

"The dark of the moon is two days away," he said. "We'll ferry your men round to the east side then. That'll take two nights. Give me another day to arrange something for that gate on the beach side."

Barat looked upward, calculating. "So, we attack in five days?"

"That's how I see it," Hal said. "How does that suit you, Svengal?"

Svengal's mouth curled in a wolfish grin. "That suits me down to the ground. But how do you propose we get through the swamps to attack that tower? I don't fancy wading all that way carrying weapons and armor, and I don't see more than half a dozen skiffs here."

Hal nodded. He'd been anticipating the question.

"Use *Wolfwind*," he said. "Unstep the mast and take out all the ballast stones below the deck planks. Without all that weight, she'll only need about twenty centimeters of water beneath her. You can pole her through the swamp without too much trouble. And you won't even get your tootsies wet," he added, with a mischievous grin.

Svengal eyed him for a long moment. He was used to making mocking comments to Erak. It seemed strange to have the boot on the other foot.

"You've thought of everything, haven't you?"

The grin faded slowly from Hal's face.

"I hope so," he said. "But I'm sure there'll be something I haven't."

The two ships' companies made their way back to the beach where *Heron* and *Wolfwind* were moored. The camp on the sand island was in the heart of the swamp and the mosquitoes and sand flies were a constant annoyance. On the beach, a brisk sea breeze kept most of them at bay.

They posted sentries and settled down for the night, bedding down on the soft sand and rolling themselves in their blankets. Hal lay, listening to the regular breathing of his friends as they fell asleep. His mind was in turmoil as he thought about the next few days and all that had to be done.

Svengal's closing comment reverberated through his brain. The Skandian had meant it as a compliment, but Hal was only too aware that once the battle started, all the planning in the world couldn't foresee the unexpected. Had he thought of everything? What if Zavac decided to leave Limmat in the next two days? What if *Raven* quietly slipped out of the harbor under cover of night and headed off over the horizon? The thought that Zavac might escape after all they had been through to find him burned in Hal's mind like a hot iron.

What if Hal's accuracy with the Mangler wasn't up to the task he had set himself? What if something broke on the Mangler at a critical moment? He made a mental note to prepare a spare bow-string and to inspect the leather thongs that absorbed the massive recoil of the bow when he released the trigger. What if a chance shot from the towers hit Ingvar? He needed the massive boy's strength to cock and load the Mangler. Without him, their rate of shooting would be seriously diminished.

What if, what if, what if? The questions and doubts whirled around in his brain until he couldn't stand it any longer. He tossed his blankets aside and rose to his feet, then walked slowly down to the water's edge. With the dark of the moon only two days away, it was a thin sliver of yellow light, low on the horizon. He glanced at the dark shapes of the two ships. Tomorrow, Svengal and his men would start lightening *Wolfwind*. It occurred to him that he should do the same with *Heron*. She'd be carrying twenty men on each trip into the bay, along with her regular crew. Plus he should set about making a further supply of bolts for the Mangler. He'd need as many as he could make when they attacked the towers.

Then there was the beach gate. How was he going to make sure they could burn that? He'd blithely told the council of war that he had a plan for that, but he was still working on the details. It wouldn't be enough to simply shoot fire arrows at it from his cross-bow or the Mangler. The wood of the gate would be dry from years of exposure to wind and salt air. But it was hardwood and a single flame wouldn't be enough to make it catch. They'd need a solid source of fire to get it burning. Maybe a pile of kindling and fire-wood at the base of the gate? But they'd have no way of assembling such a pile without being seen and shot at from the palisade above them.

Oil, he thought. If they could drench the timber in oil, then hit it with a fire arrow, the whole thing would flare up. But how could he manage that? If they tried to land on the beach and run to the gate with containers of oil, they'd be cut down by the defenders before they went more than ten meters.

Unless he could place the oil there without being seen . . .

The germ of an idea began to form in his brain. But at that point, he heard a light footstep squeaking in the sand. He turned quickly and saw Lydia's slender form a few meters away.

"Can't sleep?" she said sympathetically.

He nodded. "I'm trying to work out all the things that can go wrong," he said. "So far, I've come up with about a dozen."

"Only a dozen?" she said, and he could sense the smile in her voice. He glanced at her, but her face was in shadow.

"Well," he said, trying to match her light mood, "that's just for starters. I haven't really hit my stride yet."

"Let's isolate your biggest concern," she said, her voice more serious, "and see what we can do about it."

He paused, thinking. What was his biggest worry? What was the one link that, if it broke, would be hardest to replace? It didn't take him too long to realize what it was.

"Ingvar," he said quietly. "I'm worried about him."

"Ingvar?" she said, surprised. "How could you doubt him? I've been watching him and he absolutely worships you. There's no way he'd ever let you down."

Hal was shaking his head before she had finished.

"I'm not worried he'll let me down. I know he never would," he said. "Quite the opposite. I'm worried that I'll be putting him in such a position of danger. I feel as if I'm letting *him* down." He could sense that she didn't understand, and realized that, of course, she'd never seen them shooting the Mangler.

"He's the only one strong enough to load the crossbow easily," he explained. "That means he'll be exposed in the bow of the ship when he's doing it."

"How close do you have to get to the target?" Lydia asked.

Hal took a deep breath and stared out to sea for a few seconds before answering. He wanted to increase the distance but he knew that he would be compromising the accuracy and power of the massive bow if he did.

"About a hundred meters. Maybe less," he said finally. Even in the darkness, he saw the whites of her eyes as they widened.

"That is pretty close," she said. "I thought you said this bow of yours had a range of three hundred meters?"

"The bow does. I don't. If I'm going to hit what I aim at, I need to be about a hundred meters away. That means Ingvar will be exposed when he's loading. He'll be the most prominent target on the ship. And he's pretty hard to miss. I'm wondering if I have the right to put him in such danger—particularly because I know he will never refuse me if I ask him."

"Of course," she said, "you're forgetting that you'll be exposed as well. The pirates may well see you as a more important target. After all, you'll be the one shooting at them."

"I'll be behind the Mangler," he pointed out. "It'd take a very good shot to hit me. But Ingvar . . ." He paused. "Well, aside from anything else, if he's hit, we're in big trouble. He's the only one strong enough to load the bow."

"What about Thorn?" she asked. "He's not exactly a weakling."

"It's a two-handed job," he said. "Even for Ingvar. Thorn may well be strong enough, but I doubt that his hook would take the strain. It'd probably pull off the end of his arm."

She turned and paced away a few steps, thinking. Then she returned.

"Maybe I can help," she said. "If I was up in the bow with you . . ." She saw him start to open his mouth to protest and she forestalled him quickly. "Don't worry, I won't be standing out in the open. I'll stay under cover." She paused and Hal nodded cautious agreement. "Anyway, if I keep watch, I could cover both of you. I could pick off any bowman who starts to take too much interest in you."

"With those darts of yours?"

She nodded.

"Are you that good?" Hal's question wasn't at all skeptical. It was a case of genuine interest. He was unfamiliar with the atlatl as a weapon. He had never seen one in use and had no idea of its range or accuracy.

"I can hit a man-size target at one hundred meters," she said confidently. Then she paused and qualified the statement. "Probably three times out of four."

Hal whistled softly. "That's pretty good," he said. "I'm not sure I could do better with my crossbow." He thought about it. "And of course, if you pick off one or two of them, the others will be less keen to be heroes."

She smiled at him and he saw her teeth gleam in the darkness. "It's good to think I'll be serving a useful purpose," she said. Then the smile faded. "That's another reason I wanted to stay with you and the boys. Barat would never let me get close to the action."

"Perhaps we won't mention it to him."

She sighed. "I'm sorry about the way he behaved. He just can't help himself. He's very possessive about me."

"I can see why." The words were out of Hal's mouth before he could stop them and he hesitated awkwardly, realizing they sounded like the clumsiest of heavy-handed compliments. But Lydia touched his arm gratefully.

"Thank you," she said simply.

He was glad the darkness meant she couldn't see how his face had reddened. He cleared his throat awkwardly and changed the subject.

"Well, now that we've solved the problem of Ingvar, I think I might be able to sleep."

"Me too," she said. "Good night, Hal. And thanks again."

"Good night," he said, and they turned and made their separate ways back to their bedrolls.

A little way up the beach, Stig had been awakened by the low murmur of their muted voices. For a few seconds, he lay frowning, trying to identify the sound. Then he raised himself on one elbow and looked down to the water's edge. He could recognize the two silhouetted forms in the dim moonlight. Hal and Lydia, he thought. He saw her lean forward and touch Hal's arm in a familiar gesture and felt a sudden stab of jealousy.

Then he flushed, angry with himself. Hal was his best friend, after all, and he hardly knew Lydia. It was foolish to let jealousy come between them, he told himself. But no matter how many times he repeated the sentiment in his mind, he couldn't get rid of that small niggle.

"I'm as bad as Barat," he said to himself. He rolled over and pulled his blankets up to his chin. But sleep eluded him for some time.

In spite of what he'd said to Lydia, Hal remained sleepless as well, staring wide-eyed at the dark sky and the brilliant stars above him, turning over the problem of the beach gate.

Oil, he thought once more. That was the answer. If he could drench the wood in oil, and then set fire to it, the burning oil would eventually cause the dried timbers to catch as well. Once they had burned, it would be relatively simple to break down the gate.

It would also be simple to set the oil on fire. He could do that with a fire arrow from his crossbow, or from the Mangler. But first, the oil would have to be put in place on the gate. And that brought him back full circle. Anyone trying to throw oil on the gate during the battle would be shot down by the defenders before he could reach it.

He shifted his position. There was a ridge of packed sand under his shoulder blade. He'd been trying to ignore it for the past few minutes but now it had become a real frustration—probably because of his inability to think of a way around the problem of the gate.

Angrily, he threw his blankets off and sat up. He folded back the waterproof canvas he was using as a groundsheet and smoothed the offending ridge flat. Then he replaced the groundsheet and, while he was about it, plumped up the roll of sheepskin he was using for a pillow.

Sighing with satisfaction, he turned and studied the beach once more before lying down. *Heron* and *Wolfwind* were canted over at an angle now, he saw. As the tide had receded, the ships had been left standing on the wet sand and had gently toppled over to their present position.

The tide had run out quite a long way. There was a strip of glistening sand on the beach between the ships and the sea some twenty meters wide. Just as well they didn't have to launch in a hurry, he thought. Of course, by morning, the tide would come in again and the boats would gradually rise from the sand and float upright once more.

The tide fascinated him, as it did most sailors. A great deal of his life was governed by it and the strong currents that it created. There was a fascinating inevitability about the tide, about the way it rose and fell twice each day.

He knew that some of the older Skandians believed that it was caused by a mythical Great Blue Whale as it breathed water in and out. He glanced around the dark huddled forms on the beach. He wondered how many of the *Wolfwind*'s crew still secretly believed that fable.

Not Svengal, he thought. Svengal was too practical. Thorn? Almost instantly, he dismissed the idea. Thorn was too skeptical to believe such a fairy story. But then, if it wasn't the Great Blue Whale that caused the tides, what did cause them?

He sighed. The inventor in him wanted to understand how it happened. But so far, nobody seemed to have a logical explanation. Perhaps the answer was simply to accept the fact that the tide came in and the tide went out, and that was that.

And as he had that thought, he realized how he was going to get the oil onto the beach gate.

Hal, Stig and Jesper were in a skiff borrowed from Barat's people, two hundred meters offshore from Limmat's eastern watchtower.

"Aren't you worried that they've seen us?" Stig asked. The pirates manning the tower were shouting insults at them as they rowed past, but although they had sent arrows toward the skiff, none had come close.

Hal shook his head. "They know that Barat and his men have small boats, so we're not giving anything away. And from this distance, they can't recognize us as Skandians."

Stig nodded uncertainly. But, as ever, he deferred to Hal's reasoning. "If you say so."

"They can't even see you're an Araluen," Jesper put in, grinning.

Hal rolled his eyes, realizing Jesper's comment was meant as a joke.

"Too true," he said. "Ironic, isn't it? These pirates may well be the first people to think of me as a Skandian. Ah, there's the gate."

A hundred meters beyond the watchtower, the palisade turned at right angles and headed inland, to the north. There was a small stretch of beach just beyond this turning point, and a heavy wooden gate was set into the palisade, giving access to the beach.

"It's closed," Jesper said. He was mystified about this reconnaissance trip. Hal hadn't told him anything about his plans; he'd just said that he wanted Jesper to see it—so he'd understand what Hal had in mind—and point out any possible problems.

"Lydia says it's always closed, unless there are ships drawn up on the beach," Hal said. "They're an untrusting lot and they don't let strange ships into the harbor."

"With good reason," Stig said, resting on the oars. "Look what happened last time they did."

"Exactly," Hal agreed. "So if a ship arrives that they haven't seen before, that's where they tell it to land. The strangers can unload their cargo on the beach and the townspeople use the gate to bring the goods inside the palisade."

"Very well," Jesper said slowly. "So here we are, after a pleasant boat ride, and we're looking at a gate that's kept locked. I assume they won't be opening it for us?"

"No. We're going to burn it," Hal said. "Then Ingvar is going to hit it with a battering ram to break it down."

"Well, if anyone can do it, Ingvar can. But how are we going to burn it?"

"We'll drench it with oil, then light the oil with a fire arrow from the Mangler."

"So far," Jesper replied, "I can't fault your logic. Except for one small, and I have to say potentially vital, point—"

"How do we get the oil on the gate in the first place?" Hal said. The ex-thief nodded.

"We're going to put it there the night before. We'll hang a full oil bladder on the gate. If we place it high enough, it won't be visible from the palisade. Then, on the morning of the attack, we puncture the skin with an arrow or a bolt. Oil flows out down the gate and we set fire to it with another arrow. Simple."

Jesper turned from his study of the gate and cocked his head at Hal.

"You have an interesting concept of the word *simple*," he said. "And you said *we'll* hang an oil bladder. How will *we* manage that exactly?"

"Well, actually, *we* won't," Hal admitted. "I'm hoping *you'll* do that part. Could you get from the water's edge to the gate without being seen?"

Jesper studied the ground between the gate and the water's edge. He stuck out his bottom lip.

"At night? I should think so. There's plenty of undulating ground to give me cover. Might take me ten or fifteen minutes, but I can do it."

"How does he get to the beach?" Stig asked. "Even at night, they'll see us if we try to take a boat in that close. And if they know someone's landed there, they may well check the gate and find your oil bladder."

"We're not taking a boat in that close," Hal told him. "We'll get to within three hundred meters. A small boat should be pretty hard to see at that distance and at night. Then Jesper and I will float in—on the last of the tide."

"Ah . . . there's another problem," Jesper said, holding up a hand. "I don't float. I sink."

Hal was an excellent swimmer. Jesper, like most Skandians, couldn't swim a stroke. But Hal had anticipated that problem.

"I can swim," he said. "And I'll be coming with you."

"Excellent," Jesper replied sarcastically. "You can watch me drown."

"You can't drown. I need you. We'll build a raft. Or better still, we'll find a log that's washed up as driftwood. We'll tow it behind the skiff till we're a few hundred meters off the beach, then slip overboard. I'll tie you on, Jesper. You won't sink."

"So you say," Jesper said doubtfully.

"If we stay in the water behind the log, we won't be seen. The pirates, if they notice anything, will see a piece of driftwood wash ashore. We'll give them ten or twenty minutes to get used to it, then you slip up the beach with the oil bladder."

"And how do you get out?" Stig asked. The workings of Hal's mind fascinated him. The idea seemed quite feasible now that he heard it.

"Same way we came in. We'll let the tide take us out again and you can pick us up out of sight of the towers."

"Me?" Stig said, surprised.

"You'll have to take the second group of Barat's men down the bay while we're attending to the gate. On your way back, wait offshore, out of sight, and we'll drift out to you."

"Just like that?"

"Just like that."

"What if we miss you?" There was genuine concern in Stig's voice.

"That would be embarrassing," Hal admitted.

Jesper eyed him with some alarm. "I'll be more than embarrassed," he said. "I'll be downright disappointed. We could drift halfway to Teutlandt if Stig doesn't spot us."

"Could this possibly be one of those small details that you so very occasionally overlook?" Stig asked innocently.

Hal frowned as he considered the problem.

"It should be all right. We should be able to predict where we'll drift to. And once we're off the beach, we can raise a flag on the log, so you should be able to see us."

"You know, I'm not fond of *should*," Jesper said, with some spirit. "I think I prefer *will*. Forgive me if I'm lacking enthusiasm for this scheme."

Hal pursed his lips, deep in thought, then he gestured back the way they had come.

"No need to keep hanging around here," he said, changing the subject. "I'll think of a way round this on the way back."

"I'd appreciate that," Jesper said.

Stig hid a grin. Jesper, a non-swimmer, was being asked to float into the beach, holding on to a log, make his way to the gate, avoiding being seen by any sentries patrolling the palisade, hang a bladder of oil on it, then drift out to sea again on the vague assurance that Stig and the other Herons would be able to find them. Welcome to Hal's world, he thought.

Stig set the oars in the water and began rowing back. He had been planning on suggesting that Jesper might spell him on the way home, but he decided that he had enough on his mind already. But he couldn't resist one final sally.

"You know, I've heard Teutlandt is very nice at this time of year," he said. "They do have very nice sausage there."

Both Hal and Jesper glared at him. He chuckled to himself. Hal will come up with something, he thought.

But by the time they arrived back at the camp, Hal still hadn't found a way to solve the problem.

"It should be all right," he said to himself as he trudged up the beach, deep in thought. "I should be able to calculate where we'll drift to and Stig can be waiting for us there."

The problem with that, he realized, was that, while Stig was an excellent helmsman, he wasn't a very talented navigator. He was competent, of course. He'd been through the brotherband training course and navigation was an important part of that. But Hal had done the advanced navigation classes, and knowing what a superb navigator Hal was, Stig had tended to skim through the theory work, assuming that his friend would be around to do the difficult part.

I'll work out reference points for him, Hal thought. That way, he could give Stig two points on the land on which he could take bearings, and that would set him in the correct position. But even that wasn't totally satisfactory. A lot of the finer detail of navigation came down to instinct and judgment. If the wind grew stronger or changed direction, for example, it would take their makeshift raft off the predicted course. Hal would be able to sense that and allow for it.

Would Stig? If Hal was completely honest with himself, he had to admit that he doubted it.

While he pondered the problem, he strode along the water's edge, looking for a piece of driftwood that he and Jesper could use as a raft. There was one large tree trunk that looked suitable. It was gray and dried with salt and still had a tangle of dead, bare branches at one end. Where three of them grew close together, they had collected a mass of lighter branches and dried weed among them. It looked like an outlandish bird's nest, Hal thought.

Or a bundle of kindling, he thought idly, as he walked back to fetch Ingvar and some of the others to help him drag the log into the water so they could float it to where the skiff would be launched. The log was half buried in the sand and it would be beyond even Ingvar's strength to move it on his own.

Hal stopped in mid-stride. The log *did* look like kindling, he thought. He headed back down the beach with a new spring in his step.

He found Jesper and Stig by the cook fire, drinking coffee with Thorn. The old warrior looked up as he approached.

"How did the reconnaissance go?"

Hal eyed him dubiously, wondering if Stig and Jesper had outlined the problem with his plan. He decided that they hadn't. Thorn's expression was ingenuous.

"Fine," he said. "Jesper's confident he can pull it off. We had one small problem, but I've got it solved."

Stig and Jesper both pricked up their ears at that, looking at him curiously.

"There's a big log down the beach that will suit us," he said.

"And it has a whole lot of lighter material tangled up in its branches. I'm thinking that if I take another small jar of oil, and a flint and steel, wrapped in a watertight pack, I could set fire to it once we're offshore. You'll see the smoke, Stig. Then you can come and collect us."

Stig nodded at the idea. He was impressed. "Sounds like it will work," he said. "I knew you'd come up with something."

Thorn nodded as well. "Good idea," he said. "If you mix a little damp seaweed in once it gets burning, you'll send up plenty of smoke. Should be visible for miles."

They all looked at Jesper, to see if he agreed. The former thief was shaking his head as he looked at Hal.

"I thought it was bad enough when you wanted to go drifting off to Teutlandt," he said. "Now you want to burn our raft out from under us."

Hal opened his mouth to protest, then realized that it was a fair assessment of the situation.

"Stig will find us before it gets to that," he said reassuringly and Stig made suitably concurring noises. Jesper glared at Hal, then at Stig.

"You'd better," he said. "Or I'm coming back from my watery grave to haunt you."

I'll be glad to be rid of the pair of you," said Thorn. "And that blasted log."

He and Hal were sitting side by side in the middle seat of the skiff, each taking an oar. With the added drag of the large log behind the little boat, Hal had decided to help his friend with the rowing on the outward journey.

The previous night, Hal had transported the first group of Barat's men to a point on the bay's shore well to the east of Limmat. Tonight, while he and Jesper were setting the oil bladder in place, Stig would take the second group on the same trip. Then he would pick up Hal and Jesper on the return trip.

Hopefully.

Thorn was rowing easily and Hal glanced down with a certain proprietorial interest at Thorn's right arm.

"How's the hook performing?" he asked. "Is it taking the strain all right?"

Thorn held up the device and studied it.

"It's fine," he said. "Mind you, I had to tighten the restraining straps as far as I could so it wouldn't pull off of my arm. I'll need to loosen them once you're gone."

Hal nodded. On the return journey, with only Thorn in the boat, and without the extra drag of the log towing behind, the rowing would be a lot easier. He glanced toward the shore, some three hundred meters away. The lights that marked the towers at the harbor mouth were slowly creeping past.

"Sure you don't want me to wait out here and pick you up?" Thorn asked. He was worried about the plan that had Hal and Jesper drifting out to sea for a rendezvous with Stig in the *Heron*. There were too many things that could go wrong. But Hal shook his head, smiling at the older man's concern. They'd already discussed this several times.

"It'll be getting light by the time we're done," he said. "There's too much risk you'll be spotted. Lookouts tend to be on their toes at first light."

Thorn shrugged. "I'll take my chances."

"I know you will. And thank you. But if they see you, they might look more carefully and see us. Then they'll start wondering what we've been up to and they might check the beach outside the gate. If they do that, they'll spot the oil bladder and the game's up."

"I'm just not happy with the idea of you just drifting away on the tide," Thorn said.

Jesper, sitting in the stern, leaned forward. "I'm with you there, Thorn. But nobody listens to me."

"We'll be fine," Hal said, with more conviction than he felt.

"If you say so," Thorn said.

Hal nodded. "I do."

Jesper rolled his eyes. "I don't."

Hal decided to ignore him. He glanced over the side of the boat and saw a few small branches drifting past on the ingoing tide. He glanced to shore again and saw that they had come past the harbor mouth.

"This should do it," he said. "Let's get the log alongside."

The driftwood log had been towing five meters behind the boat on the end of a stout hemp line. He and Jesper hauled it in now until it was floating beside the skiff, bumping occasionally against the hull.

"Take it easy," Thorn warned them. "If we wreck the boat, I'll have to join you on the log."

Hal grinned at him. "And we'd love to have you along."

Thorn gestured over the side. "Get a move on. Jesper, have you reversed your vest?"

Both the boys wore sheepskin vests, as did most of the *Heron's* crew. Jesper usually wore his with the fleece side outermost, as the oily wool provided a good waterproof shield against spray and rain. Hal wore his with the fleece inside, for the extra warmth it gave.

Jesper took his off now, turned it inside out and re-donned it. "What's the point of this again?"

"The air pockets in the fleece will trap water, and your body heat will gradually warm it," Thorn explained. "It'll keep you more comfortable in the sea, which is going to be cold."

"How kind of you to point that out," Jesper muttered.

Thorn shrugged. "Every little bit helps."

Hal turned so that his legs were over the side. Then, as Thorn leaned to balance his weight, he slipped over into the dark water.

The shock of the cold sea hitting him nearly took his breath away. He refrained from any exclamation, however, as he sensed that Jesper was probably on the edge of refusing to leave the boat. He took hold of the log and pulled himself to it. He carried a length of rope, which he tied to a protruding branch, passing the free end back to Jesper.

"Tie yourself on," he said. "Then get in the water."

Dubiously, Jesper fastened the rope around his upper body, under his armpits. Then he reached over and dipped a hand in the water.

"It's cold," he complained to Thorn.

The old sea wolf grinned. "What a surprise. Now, get going."

With one last, reluctant look at the seat in the stern of the boat, Jesper allowed himself to slip over the side into the water. His head went under and he splashed back to the surface, gasping with the sudden cold and floundering wildly in the water.

"Shut up!" Hal whispered fiercely, grabbing him by the collar and dragging him to the log. "They'll hear you ashore!"

Jesper gripped the log with the fierceness of utter terror. The idea of being afloat in deep water was completely alien. Normally, that would have been enough to terrify him. But the unexpected cold added to the fear. He looked back at Thorn.

"How long before the water in the fleece gets warm?" he asked pitifully.

"*Warm* is a relative term," Thorn said with a shrug. "It'll actually just be *less* cold. Should take a few minutes."

"I'll be dead by then!" Jesper complained.

"Shut up," Hal said unsympathetically. He reached back to the boat and Thorn passed him the waterproof package containing a small jar of oil and a flint and steel. The pig's bladder, filled with oil, was already tied securely to the log. Hal fastened the smaller bundle to a branch, tested the knot, then turned and nodded to Thorn.

"Shove us off," he said. "Time we were on our way."

Thorn untied the line that held the log alongside the boat, placed an oar against it and shoved. The log moved slowly away from the boat. Then, as the tide took hold of the log, it began to drift sluggishly toward the shore.

"Good luck," Thorn called softly. "See you tomorrow."

"Shut up," Hal called back. His voice sounded strained, as if talking was an effort. Chattering teeth would do that to a voice, Thorn thought. Then he heard Hal call again. "Thanks."

He nodded toward the dim shape, already five meters away, set his oars and turned the boat for home. Without the weight of the two extra passengers, and the drag of the log behind it, the boat felt light and easy to row. But somehow, he found he preferred the way it had felt when Hal and Jesper were safely on board with him.

As the tide took them toward the shore, Hal heaved himself up to get his bearings. They were drifting slightly to the left, he thought.

Instinctively, Jesper tried to haul himself up onto the log, to be clear of the water. Hal put a hand on his shoulder to restrain him.

"Stay down out of the wind," he said. "You'll be warmer that way."

"Perlins and Gertz!" Jesper replied, invoking the Skandian demigods of snow and ice. "It's freezing." But he lowered himself back into the water so that only his head was above the surface and he found that Hal was right. After a few minutes, he realized that Thorn had been right too. The water trapped close to his body was slowly becoming warmer, forming a barrier between him and the icy seawater.

That was fine as far as his upper body was concerned. But his legs, clad only in thick woolen leggings, were painfully cold.

"My legs are numb," he complained.

Hal checked his bearings again. "Then let's warm them up. We're going to have to swim the log a little to the right. The tide is setting us toward the harbor, not the beach. Grab hold of the log and we'll swim her right."

"I've already got hold of it," Jesper told him. "What makes you think I'd be letting go?"

Hal grinned at him. His own teeth were chattering and he knew the exercise of guiding the log would do them both good.

"All right. You've seen how a frog kicks? Do the same thing. Don't let your feet break the surface or we'll make too much noise. But kick like a frog and let's warm up a little."

Together, they began to scissor-kick their legs. At first, Jesper was awkward and uncoordinated with the unfamiliar action. But he gradually found his rhythm and they kicked constantly, forcing the log to the right. They made slow progress, but when Hal checked again after ten minutes, they had moved a considerable distance across the tide. He estimated distances and angles.

"A few more minutes' kicking," he said, "and we're there."

He was exhausted and freezing, but he could feel the blood flowing through his legs, fighting against the cold embrace of the sea. He realized he hadn't allowed for the debilitating effect of the cold. Another small detail forgotten, he thought wryly.

"Whatever you say," Jesper replied. His voice was tight. The cold had stiffened his lips and mouth.

"Come on!" Hal urged him. "Double time!"

They kicked harder than ever, all the time ensuring that they didn't break the surface and make noise, or a giveaway splash of white water. After a few minutes, they became aware of the sound of the gentle ripple of waves on the beach, only a few meters away. Then the log was bumping and dragging over the sandy bottom, eventually coming to rest in the shallows.

They lay for a few moments, resting. Both their hearts were racing as they waited for a cry of alarm from the palisade, indicating that their presence had been discovered. If that happened, Hal thought, they were finished. They had no way of escape, other than to drift out with the log on the outgoing tide.

Maybe I should have thought of that too, he told himself. But as more minutes passed and there was no sign that they had been discovered, he began to relax. Jesper stirred beside him. Hal noticed with interest that his friend didn't heave himself up to look over the top of the log. He slid sideways so that he could peer through the tangle of branches at one end, avoiding exposing his face to any possible watchers on the palisade.

He stayed watching for some time, then wriggled back to place his mouth close to Hal's ear.

"There's a guard on patrol. Passes every three minutes or so. He looks totally bored with what he's doing, hardly ever bothers to look out to sea."

"Do you think he's noticed the log?" Hal asked.

Jesper shrugged. "Hard to say. If he has, he doesn't seem too concerned. I'll wait till he passes again and get moving."

Hal nodded. He reached up and untied the cord securing the oil bladder, lifting it carefully down, avoiding snagging it on any of the sharp, broken-off stumps of branches. As he did so, Jesper reached inside his sodden vest to an inner pocket. He produced a small jar and began to rub a dark-colored substance on his face, forming an irregular pattern of stripes and swirls.

"What's that?" Hal asked curiously.

"Grease and ash. It breaks up the shape of the face so nobody sees a regular, white oval shape. Big giveaway if you're sneaking up on someone in the dark," Jesper told him.

Hal nodded, impressed by this piece of information about the thief's trade, noting it for future reference. You never knew when you might want to sneak up on someone in the dark, he thought.

"You really do know what you're doing, don't you?"

Jesper, finished with his face painting, grinned at him. His teeth were remarkably white in the dark mask.

"I'd better," he said, taking hold of the oil bladder. "Otherwise we'll both be in the soup."

He paused, then said with some feeling, "Mind you, right now, being in the soup might be quite a pleasant experience."

He slid to the end of the log, staying prone as he waited for the patrolling sentry to pass. Then he raised a hand to Hal and slid away from the log, staying low to the ground on his elbows and knees, dragging the oil bladder behind him.

Hal, having learned from Jesper's example, resisted the temptation to look over the top of the log. Instead, he slid belly down to the end, where the branches would screen him, and peered out after the former thief.

There was no sign of him.

"He really does know what he's doing," Hal said to himself.

Stig counted silently as the Limmatan fighters filed past him to board the *Heron*. As the last one climbed over the gunwale, he turned to Jonas.

"I counted twenty-four," Stig said, a note of accusation in his voice. They had expected to carry twenty men on each trip. With any more, the *Heron* would be seriously overloaded. But Jonas nodded.

"We've had four more men make their way out of the town over the past few days. Barat wanted them along. He said the more men we had, the better chance we'd stand."

Stig grunted a grudging acknowledgment. It made sense. But if he'd known about it sooner, he might have been able to compensate by unloading some of the ballast stones the *Heron* carried below her decks. Now there wasn't time to do that.

"I don't suppose anybody thought it might be a good idea to let us know?"

Jonas spread his hands apologetically. "I'm sorry, Stig. It didn't occur to me that it'd make any difference."

Stig pursed his lips. There was no sense in being annoyed with

Jonas. He was a farmer and he had no knowledge of ships. Barat, of course, was another matter entirely. He was a trader and had been around ships all his life. His family even owned several.

"Well, I'll have to lighten the ship as much as possible," Stig said. "And there's only one way I can think of doing it." He called up to the ship, floating a few meters off the beach. "Stefan! Edvin! Come ashore!"

The two crew members' faces appeared over the ship's side, peering down at him curiously.

"What's the problem?" Stefan asked, and Stig made a peremptory gesture with his thumb for them to climb down.

"We're overloaded. You'll have to stay behind."

"But who's going to lower and raise the sail?" Edvin asked. As he said it, Ulf and Wulf joined their shipmates at the railing.

"The twins will have to do it," Stig replied. He'd decided on this because the twins were the stronger of the four crew on board. One of them alone should be able to raise and lower the sail—or he could get help from the passengers if necessary. After all, it was only a matter of hauling on a rope.

"Ulf, you take over raising the sail."

"I'm Wulf," said the twin he'd indicated.

Stig set his jaw angrily. Then he said, very deliberately, "Then Wulf, you look after raising the sail. Ulf can take care of trimming."

"I'm happy to raise the sail if you want me to," said the twin he now knew as Ulf. Stig took a deep breath. He was beginning to wonder how Hal managed to keep his temper with these two. Then he realized that, quite often, he didn't.

"I don't care who does what, so long as both jobs get done. All right?"

The twins shrugged. "All right," they chorused. Then Ulf added, "So you do want me to raise the sail?"

"YES!" Stig exploded. "You raise the sail. And you, the other one, whoever the blazes you are, you trim the sail."

"I'm Wulf," Wulf said.

"And I don't care!" Stig told him. "Just do as I ask!"

"All right," Wulf said, rolling his eyes to indicate how contrary Stig was being. He and his twin withdrew and moved to their stations. Stefan and Edvin, who had watched the exchange with some amusement, climbed over the rail and dropped to the shallow water.

"You're leaving yourself short-handed," Edvin said to Stig.

The tall boy nodded grimly. "I know it. I have no other choice, do I?"

Edvin considered the point, then shrugged. "I suppose not. But if the wind dies, you'll only have two people to man the oars."

"The wind has blown steadily offshore every night for weeks," Stig told him. "Why should it drop tonight?"

"I don't know," Edvin admitted. "Maybe because you'll need it tonight."

Stig glared at him for several seconds. Edvin met his gaze, but he had the grace to look apologetic for raising the matter.

Finally, Stig said firmly, "The wind is not going to drop tonight. All right?"

"Fine," Edvin agreed. "Whatever you say."

"Good." Stig noticed a slim figure moving toward him and he

looked away from Edvin. "Hullo, Lydia," he said. "Come to see us off?"

In truth, Lydia had been planning to talk her way on board for the trip. She was frustrated with the lack of activity, sitting quietly by waiting for the attack to start. She wanted to be doing something, and she felt she might have a chance of convincing Stig. But the discussion she'd just overheard convinced her otherwise.

"Just came to wish you good luck," she said.

Stig smiled. "We'll be fine," he said, gesturing to the ship. "Nothing to it. Sail in, drop them off. Sail out again."

"I meant, good luck finding Hal," she said, and the smile faded as Stig thought about the night ahead of him.

"Yeah. Of course. Don't worry. We'll pick him up, all right." He felt a twinge of concern for his friend. And, oddly, he felt a slight stab of jealousy as well. Lydia hadn't been concerned about his well-being, he thought. She was worried about Hal.

Then he pushed the unworthy feeling aside. Hal was in a far more dangerous situation than he would be. Why should he feel jealous because Lydia was more concerned about him? Yet he did, and he was angry at himself for feeling that way.

"Better be going," he said abruptly, to conceal his confusion. Sensing that she had offended him somehow, Lydia made a tentative gesture toward him. But he'd already turned away and swung himself lightly up and over the ship's rail, picking his way aft through the crowded Limmatans.

Instead, she joined Edvin and Stefan to help shove the ship off. Ingvar, who had been hovering nearby, moved down the beach to help them, and the *Heron* slid backward into deeper water. Stig worked the tiller, rowing the stern around until the ship was facing the open sea.

"Starboard sail," he called, and one of the twins heaved the yard and sail up, while his brother hauled it in tight against the wind. As the ship gathered way, Stig held her in a smooth curve out from the beach. The *Heron* moved quickly into the night, a dark shadow on an equally dark sea, until the only sign of her was the occasional white flash of the waves at her bow.

Jesper flattened himself against the rough boards of the gate, scarcely daring to breathe as he heard the measured tramp of the sentry passing overhead.

Under the overhang of the gate portal as he was, there was no way he could be seen by the sentry, unless the man leaned way out, over the top of the palisade, and peered back inward. There was no reason to think the man would do so—unless Jesper made a noise.

He no longer felt the cold. Adrenaline was surging through his system, dispelling any sensation of discomfort. He waited till the footsteps receded. He knew from his observation that he had three minutes before the sentry returned. He laid the oil bladder carefully in the sand at the base of the gate, reached into his pocket for a small auger Hal had given him and stretched as high as possible to begin drilling a hole in the gate.

Hal thinks of everything, he thought. Left to his own devices, Jesper would never have thought to bring the auger and the small spike that Hal had provided. He would have gone to all the trouble and effort of making his way to the gate unseen, then realized that there was nothing from which he could hang the oil bladder.

He worked the auger round and round. It was an awkward action, reaching high above his head, and the wood was hardened with the drying effect of years of salt and wind, which had shrunk its fibers, binding them more tightly together, making them harder to penetrate. But he persisted.

The footsteps were returning and he froze once more, allowing them to pass before he continued drilling. At last, he decided that the hole was deep enough and he took the spike from his pocket and rammed it into the hole. It was a few millimeters smaller than the drill, so there was no need to hammer it in. He grinned mirthlessly. There was no way he could have hammered it in anyway, not without being heard. For that reason, he had angled the drill downward as he bored the hole. As a result, when he forced the spike into position, it sloped slightly upward. When he hung the oilskin on it, the angle would keep it firmly in the hole. He worked the spike in now as far as he could, feeling it hit solid wood as he reached the end of the hole he'd drilled.

He hung the oil bladder over the spike, arranging it so it lay flat against the wood of the gate. He released his grip carefully, making sure that the spike would hold firm. Then he stopped once more as the footsteps approached, then receded.

There was one more refinement that had occurred to him. The gate obviously hadn't been used in weeks, and a certain amount of rubbish and detritus had gathered near the foot of the wall, including several dead branches and strings of dried weed. Jesper gathered a few quickly, scuttling out from the cover of the gateway recess to retrieve them, and piled them roughly at the foot of the gate, beneath the point where the oil bladder hung. When Hal pierced it, the oil would gush down, drenching the gate. But a large amount would simply run off into the sand. This way, the oil running off the gate would soak into the dried pile of kindling he'd just collected. It would catch fire as well, and when it burned, it would help the flames spread to the hard timbers.

"Every little bit helps," Jesper muttered, eyeing his handiwork. Then he crouched as he heard the footsteps again. They passed without pausing, as they had since he'd been by the gate. Once he was sure the way was clear, he crept silently on hands and knees away from the wall. There was a deep undulation in the sand five meters away and that was his first objective. He reached it and lay facedown, unmoving in its shadow, until the footsteps passed again in the opposite direction. Then he moved off again, heading for his next stop—a tussock of rough grass to his right.

As he belly crawled across the cool sand, he sensed a change. Something was different. Something wasn't the way it had been. He reached the scant cover of the tussock and lay there, concentrating. He frowned as he sought to determine what it was that he'd sensed.

Then it came to him. The wind had dropped.

The trip to the Limmatans' drop-off point had gone without a hitch. Stig brought the *Heron* on a long, curving course into the bay, then back to the beach where the first party of troops had spent the day.

Barat had been watching for their arrival. As the bow of the ship grated gently against the sand, he waded thigh deep into the water to greet them.

"You're late," he said. "I expected you an hour ago."

Gracious as ever, Stig thought. He made a vague gesture at the night around them.

"The wind isn't as strong as last night," he said. "We couldn't manage the same speed." Then he couldn't stop himself adding, with an acid tone to his voice, "Plus we were carrying a heavier load, which nobody mentioned to us."

"Hmmmph. Well, better late than never, I suppose," Barat replied as his men began to disembark and form up in a loose circle on the beach, awaiting further orders. Ulf and Wulf stood by the bulwarks in the bow, helping any who were uncertain of their movements. Not all the Limmatans were accustomed to moving about on board ship.

Stig brought forward an armful of water skins and a few sacks of food—bread and dried meat for the most part—and handed them down to Jonas. Then he dropped over the rail to the beach.

"This should keep you going," he said. He looked at Barat. "Remember, stay out of sight tomorrow, then attack the day after, two hours after noon."

They'd added the extra day to the schedule when it was realized that Hal would probably be exhausted when they picked him up. They had set the time for the attack as mid-afternoon, which would place the sun in the eyes of the defenders as the *Heron* attacked the two towers.

Barat snorted. "Still don't know why we don't attack at dawn. That's the traditional time."

Stig took a deep breath, controlling his annoyance with an effort. This had all been discussed. But of course, Barat was choosing to conveniently forget that fact. Stig was beginning to realize that the Limmatan leader simply liked argument for its own sake. He'd fit in well with Ulf and Wulf, he thought.

"That's why we're leaving it till mid-afternoon," he answered in measured tones. "Dawn attacks are traditional, which means people expect them. That's why garrisons usually stand to just before dawn. They're on their toes. By mid-afternoon, they're more interested in sleeping off their lunch. We discussed this," he added pointedly.

Barat shook his head. "Doesn't mean I agree." Then, he gave away the reason behind his petulance, glancing up at the boat. "Is Lydia with you?"

Stig shook his head. He'd seen Lydia loitering by the ship when they were loading and guessed what she had in mind. "Couldn't fit her in. She wanted to come but we were already overloaded."

Barat regarded him uncertainly. He wasn't sure if Stig meant that Lydia had wanted to see him, Barat, or that she had wanted to accompany Stig. He hesitated, not sure what to say next.

"Stig . . . ," Wulf said quietly.

Stig turned to him, grateful for the interruption. "What is it, Ulf?"

"I'm Wulf," the twin said, aggrieved. Was it really so hard to tell him from his brother? he thought. After all, *he* had no problem with it. Stig raised a hand in apology.

"Sorry," he said, making a mental note never to use either of their names in conversation again. "What is it, Wulf?" he said, and realized he'd just broken that resolution.

"The wind. It's died," Wulf told him.

Stig swung round, looking at the trees on the top of the hills inland. They were still. Then he turned again, looking across the smooth water of the bay. There were no ripples on the surface. Wulf was right. The wind had died.

He glanced up at the stars to gauge the time. In a few minutes, the tide would begin to ebb, and Hal and Jesper would push their makeshift raft off from the beach and drift out with it, searching the ocean around them for their first sight of *Heron*.

Except *Heron* wouldn't be there. With no wind and only two crew members to row, Stig would never make it to the pickup point in time. He felt a surge of panic, forced himself to calm down and think. What could he do? What would Hal do?

The answer came to him. He stepped closer to Barat.

"I need six of your men," he said urgently. "Six men who've worked around boats."

Heron carried eight oars, although they rarely used more than four or six. With eight men rowing—Ulf and Wulf and six Limmatans—they'd make the rendezvous in time.

Barat gave a short laugh. "Maybe you do. But you're not getting them," he said. His tone was final.

Stig glanced to Jonas, who stepped forward, his hands spread out in an appeal to his commander.

"Barat, be reasonable. We can—"

But Barat cut him off with a short, chopping gesture.

"I need all the men we have!" he said. "I can't cut our force by six!"

They were speaking in low tones, and so far, the assembled Limmatans hadn't heard what they'd been saying. Stig kept his voice low now.

"You already have four extra. In effect, I'm only asking for two."

Barat was shaking his head. Stig took a deep breath, controlling the outburst of rage that wanted to flare up. He touched Barat's arm and pointed to a small clump of rocks twenty meters down the beach.

"Can we discuss this in private, please? It's not good for the men to see us arguing."

"We can discuss it as long as you like. You're not getting those men." But Barat allowed Stig to take his arm and guide him toward the outcrop of rocks. Stig jerked his head to Jonas, indicating that the second in command should join them.

The sand squeaked under their boots as they walked along the beach. Then they moved behind the rocks, out of sight.

"You realize," Stig said quietly, still forcing himself to be reasonable, "that if I'm not there to pick Hal up, he'll drift out to sea?"

Barat shrugged. "He knew the risk when he took the job," he said. "I always thought it was a harebrained idea."

"And you realize that without Hal, we won't be able to attack the towers? He's the only one who's trained to shoot the giant crossbow." At the last moment, he chose not to call it the Mangler, sensing that the name would only lead to a derisive reply. But Barat made another negative gesture.

"Do you seriously think that plan is going to work?" he said dismissively. "You lot can cruise up and down the bay shooting your oversize crossbow all you like. But it won't damage the towers. In the end, we'll have to do all the hard work and face all the danger. And for that, I'm going to need every man I've got."

Stig glanced at Jonas. He could tell from the pained expression on the man's face that he disagreed with Barat.

"What do you think?" he said.

Jonas hesitated, then seemed to firm on an opinion. "I think we could manage without—"

"It doesn't matter what he thinks!" Barat cut in sharply. "I'm in command! He's not!"

"And that's your final word?" Stig said.

Barat snorted and didn't even bother to answer.

"Well, I tried," Stig said in a mild tone to Jonas. Then he hit Barat with every ounce of his strength.

The blow was so unexpected, so out of keeping with the mild, almost disappointed tone of voice that Stig had been using, Barat never saw it coming.

It was a savage right that connected flush on the side of his jaw, lifted him off his feet, then dropped him to the sand like a sack of potatoes. Stig's left fist, cocked and ready for a follow-up, wasn't required. Barat was out like a light.

"Gorlog's breath, I've been dying to do that for days!" Stig muttered.

Jonas goggled at him. "What are you doing?" he asked, shocked at the unexpected explosion of violence.

"I'm taking six of your men and I'm going to find my friend," Stig told him very quietly, but very forcefully. "You're going to detail them to come with me."

"But . . . what about him?" Jonas asked.

Stig thought for a moment or two. "Who's your god of battles in these parts?"

"What?" Jonas asked, confused by the sudden non sequitur. Then, frowning, he answered, "Torika, I suppose."

"Good. We'll tell the men Barat stayed behind to pray to Torika for a great victory. Then you detail six men to come with me and I'll be off. Unless you have any other ideas?" He thrust his jaw forward pugnaciously.

Jonas threw his hands up. "No. Not at all. In fact, I rather wish I'd smacked that pompous idiot myself. Let's get going."

They walked down the beach and Jonas detailed six men to reboard the *Heron*. Stig nodded his thanks and they pushed off from the shore, Ulf and Wulf and the six Limmatans rattling their oars out through the oarlocks.

Stig raised a hand to Jonas.

"See you in Limmat, day after tomorrow," he called. Jonas

waved in return, then the oars bit into the water at Wulf's call and the *Heron* slid away.

Stig glanced over his shoulder at the rapidly receding beach. From behind the dark tumble of rocks, he thought he could make out a figure, staggering and waving his arms. A cry came faintly to his ears. He smiled.

"Keep calling the stroke, Wulf," he said. "Make it nice and loud."

Hal was peering around the end of the log, looking for some sign of Jesper, when he felt a hand on his leg. He started in fright, just managing to stop from leaping to his feet in shock, and snapped around. Jesper's grinning face was less than a meter from his own. His teeth looked unnaturally white in his ash-and-grease-blackened face.

"All in place," Jesper said. "Shall we leave?"

"Good grief!" Hal said, in a harsh whisper. "You frightened the innards out of me! Don't do that!"

Jesper's grin widened. His nerves had been strained as tight as a lute string for the past forty minutes. His lighthearted attitude now was due to the relief of the tension he'd been under.

"Sorry," he said. He sounded anything but. "If the sentries can't hear me move, I guess you won't either."

"How do you *do* that?" Hal asked. He had heard no sound of the thief's approach, had seen no sign of movement on the beach.

Jesper shrugged. "A lot of practice. A thief who can't move

without being seen and heard doesn't stay a thief for long. Now I'd really like to get going, if that's all right with you."

Hal gestured for him to wait and broke off a small fragment of dried wood from the log. He tossed it onto the water a meter away and watched it carefully. Slowly, the fragment began to drift toward the beach. He shook his head.

"Tide's still coming in," he said briefly. "But we may as well get ready. It'll be turning soon. Help me drag the log farther out into the water."

They found handholds on the log and heaved it backward. With two of them working at it, the log moved more easily and they soon had it floating freely. Hal watched the surface of the water around them as they held it in place, looking for the first sign that the tide had turned.

"Have you noticed that the wind has dropped?" Jesper whispered as they crouched in thigh-deep water.

Hal looked up in alarm. He'd been distracted, first by Jesper's unexpected reappearance and then by the effort of moving the log. As a result, he hadn't noticed. Now, as he gazed rapidly around, he realized that what Jesper said was true.

"That could be a problem," he said quietly.

In the next few minutes, he and Jesper would have to commit themselves to drift out with the tide. But if there was no wind, Stig would be delayed. He might not reach the rendezvous point in time. And if that happened, there was a distinct chance that Jesper and Hal and the log would continue to drift out to sea.

Hal gritted his teeth as he assessed the situation. Jesper's mind was obviously working along the same lines.

"I guess they could row," he said.

Hal glanced at him. "Four of them? I suppose so. But it'll be a long, hard pull for four people." He paused. "Maybe the wind will get up again," he added hopefully.

"Maybe," Jesper replied. He sounded a lot less hopeful about it. "I've found in the past that when you're in a jam and you really need something to happen, it usually doesn't."

"Must be great to have such a positive outlook," Hal said sarcastically.

Jesper shrugged. "So what do we do?"

Hal hesitated before answering. "Let's look at what we can't do," he said. "We can't stay here. We'll be spotted once the sun comes up."

"So we go?" Jesper asked.

Hal hesitated again, weighing the alternatives, finding there were none. He nodded.

"Stig will find a way to reach us," he said. "Maybe he'll get one or two extra rowers from Barat's men."

As they spoke, he had been watching the water around them. The small piece of wood he had tossed out earlier was slowly drifting out to sea.

"Tide's turned," he said. Jesper took a deep breath and they exchanged a long look. Both of them knew the risk they were about to take.

"Let's go then," the former thief said reluctantly, tying himself onto the log once more. But again, Hal held up a hand for him to wait.

"I'll let this out first," he said.

"This" was a bundle of ten thin wooden stakes, each about

thirty centimeters in length, wound around with twine. As Hal unrolled the bundle, Jesper could see that the twine actually tied the stakes together, with a space of five meters between each one. Each stake was rammed through a piece of cork, so that two-thirds of its length remained above the cork. A large dollop of pitch weighted down the lower end of each, while a strip of red cloth was tied to the longer end. Hal set the first stake in the water. The weight of the pitch held the stake floating upright, so that the red ribbon was above the water.

Slowly, Hal paid out the twine as it drifted away from the log. Within a few minutes, the little flags bobbed out to sea in a fifty-meter-long line, borne on the ebbing tide. In the darkness, the red ribbons were all but invisible. Once the sun rose, however, they should stand out.

"It was Edvin's idea," Hal explained. "He made it yesterday. It'll make it a lot easier for Stig to see us."

Jesper was impressed. "Suddenly," he said, "everyone's an inventor."

Hal waited till the last flag was drifting five meters from them and tied the end of the twine to one of the dead branches on the log. Then he nodded to Jesper.

"Time to go," he said quietly. He took a deep breath, knowing Jesper was doing the same. "Are you tied on?" he asked. Jesper nodded. "Then come on."

They raised their feet from the sand, letting their legs float out behind them. Slowly, the log began to drift out, away from the beach. Ahead of it, unseen in the dark, ten tiny red flags dipped and bobbed on the wavelets.

Don't let me down, Stig, Hal thought. But he kept the wish to himself.

At first, their motion was barely discernible. But as the ebb tide gathered force, they began to move with greater speed, and the beach quickly receded from sight. As they drifted out farther, they could see the torches and lanterns burning in the two watchtowers, and the ever-present halo of light that loomed over the town itself. By contrast, the sea around them looked very dark and very empty.

Lying low to the water as they were, they soon lost sight of the town. The towers dipped below the horizon and they could only be seen if the boys heaved themselves up onto the log for a better vantage point. Once the lights were out of sight, there was little sensation of movement, although Hal knew they would still be moving at a considerable speed. He tried in vain to make out the reference points he had given to Stig, but he was too low in the water to see any features of the land.

"Hope Stig gets here soon," Jesper said. His voice was tight again, from a combination of nerves and cold.

"He should turn up after dawn," Hal said. He twisted and looked to the east but so far there were no telltale streaks of light to be seen.

They drifted on. Hal's teeth were chattering and his jaw ached from trying to stop them. He was cold. His upper body wasn't too bad. The sodden sheepskin was serving its purpose. But his legs ached with the biting cold of the water. Like all the Herons, he'd grown up around boats and ships and bad weather and he was used to being wet and cold. But he'd been immersed now for some time and he hadn't expected the cold to sap his energy quite as much as it had.

He guessed Jesper was feeling the same. He glanced sideways at his companion and realized that he could make out details on the log—he could see individual branches and the waterproof packet tied firmly to their makeshift raft. He twisted to look over his shoulder and made out the tiny red flag five meters away. As they rose on a wave, he could momentarily see the next flag.

But there was no sign of the *Heron* anywhere on the horizon.

Time passed. The light strengthened, and soon the sky in the east was streaked with the red glow of the rising sun. Then that faded as the light hardened. There was no sign of the town now. No sign of land. No sign of the *Heron*.

No sign of anything but the sea.

Finally, Jesper gave voice to the fear that was growing in both of them.

"They've missed us," he said. His voice was flat, defeated.

Hal shook his head. "They'll find us," he said, trying to sound as if he believed it. "I'll give it another ten minutes or so, then I'll light the signal fire."

"How will we know when ten minutes are up?" Jesper asked dispiritedly.

Hal kicked with his legs below the surface, moving them, trying to get the blood flowing. He could barely feel them, he realized.

"We'll know because that'll be when I light the signal fire," he said.

Jesper eyed him for a few seconds. "That doesn't make sense."

Hal shrugged, still working his legs. Then a cramp hit him and he grimaced, groaning. When he recovered, he replied.

"We've chosen to drift on a log, miles from shore, hoping a ship will find us, and you want me to start making sense all of a sudden?"

Jesper grunted. "I'm thirsty," he said. "Did we bring any water?"

Hal shook his head. "One of those little details I'm famous for," he told his companion. "Stig says they always seem to involve water. I wonder why?"

"We should have thought to bring water," Jesper said.

Hal nodded. He was too tired to say anything. He realized that he was drifting away, in danger of falling asleep. He smiled to himself. That's exactly what you're doing, he thought. Drifting away on a log. He thought it might be a good idea to tie himself to the log, the way Jesper had done. But he couldn't raise the energy to do it.

"Maybe I should light the signal now," he said. "It must be ten minutes."

There was no reply. Jesper was sprawled against the log, face-down, held in place by the rope under his armpits. Hal made an attempt to heave himself up. But his weight, and the extra weight of his sodden clothing, were too much. He slid back down into the water, nearly losing his grip on the log. Now his hands were cold, as well as his legs, he thought.

In fact, he realized, his entire body was cold. His teeth began to chatter and he could do nothing to stop them.

"Where are you, Stig?" he said. At least, he tried to say it. All that came from his throat was a harsh croaking sound. He really should have brought water, he thought. He sighed. It had seemed like such a good idea. Drift in with the log, set the oil bladder in place, then drift out again.

Who would have thought that a little detail like the wind dropping could throw things into such disorder? He should have been aware of the possibility, he thought. For a moment, he was angry with himself. Then he shrugged. What did it really matter, after all? He was drifting off to sleep now and, strangely, he felt warm all of a sudden. Warm and comfortable.

But very sleepy. He'd just sleep a little while, then he'd light the signal fire. He'd be stronger after he slept. He lay his head against the rough log. He felt his grip slipping and he slid back into the water.

Should have tied myself on, like Jesper, he thought. There was a sharp end of a broken-off branch near him and he snagged his sheepskin over it to hold himself in place.

He looked sideways at Jesper. The former thief's head was lolling, just clear of the water. His breath blew occasional bubbles.

He's asleep, Hal thought. He's no fool.

The more he considered it, the more attractive the idea of sleeping became. He rested his head against the log and closed his eyes, marveling at the fact that now, after all these hours in the frigid water, he felt warm and comfortable.

I wonder if I'm dying, he thought, then decided that, even if he was, it didn't really matter. Nothing mattered.

As he drifted off, a cat's-paw of wind ruffled the water around him. Then the wind began to blow steadily.

But Hal was too far gone to notice.

A sound roused him.

It was a strange sound: Something large was moving through the water close by. His first, panicky thought was that it could be a shark. But when he forced his eyes open and looked over his shoulder, he realized that it was a heron. He could see its face. But strangely, it was carved from wood. And it seemed to be speaking to him. Even more strangely, it was speaking in Stig's voice.

"Hal! Jesper! Thank the gods we've found you."

He smiled as he saw his friend's face now, beside the wooden heron. He realized he was looking at the *Heron*'s carved figurehead, with Stig standing beside it in the bow, leaning down to grab hold of his arm.

"I had a little sleep," he said. His voice was thick and slurred and he wondered why.

Stig heaved Hal's limp form up and over the bulwark as if he were a child. Ulf and Wulf were waiting, ready. They hurried Hal astern, sat him down and stripped off his sodden clothes. They had a thick blanket ready and they wrapped him in it. Ulf began rubbing the rough wool against his skirl's near-frozen body, chafing him to bring the blood back to the surface and to warm him. Hal sprawled on the deck, groaning with cold and with the cramps that were now wracking his legs as Ulf continued to work on him.

Wulf returned to the bow, where Stig was trying to drag Jesper on board. The former thief was unconscious, too far gone to help them. Wulf held Stig's left arm while Stig leaned down, grabbing Jesper's collar and heaving on it. Something seemed to stop him moving more than a few centimeters. After several seconds, Wulf noticed the thin rope under Jesper's arms, tying him to the log. He drew his saxe knife and leaned far over the side, slashing at the rope and severing it. Once Jesper was free of the restraint, it was a simple matter for Stig to lift him over the side, depositing him on the deck like a landed fish.

Stig gestured to two of the watching Limmatans.

"Lend a hand here," he ordered. "Dry him off. Warm him up." He pointed to where Ulf was pummeling Hal with the blanket, rubbing him ferociously to ease his cramps and get his circulation going. The two townsmen nodded, understanding. One of them took the thick blanket that Stig had left handy and, together, they began to work on Jesper.

Jesper's eyes opened slowly as they rubbed and pummeled. He frowned, saw Stig and smiled in recognition.

"Stig," he said. "Thought you'd missed us."

Stig nodded somberly. "We nearly did," he said. "That log is so low in the water that it's nearly invisible. Luckily, we spotted one of Edvin's red flags, then followed the line to where you two were."

He realized that Jesper hadn't heard a word he'd said. He was lying back, eyes closed again, groaning quietly as the circulation gradually returned. Stig studied him for a moment, satisfied himself that Jesper was in no danger and turned to Wulf.

"Let's get the sail up and get back to the beach."

He moved to the tiller as Wulf began to raise the sail. Ulf, seeing what was happening, turned Hal over to two of the other Limmatans and moved to the sheets. A minute or so later, *Heron* was laid over on the starboard tack, her bow wave creaming away on either side, and heading back for the camp on the beach.

Thorn and Svengal paced restlessly along the beach, just above the line of incoming waves. Both of them were staring out to sea, looking for the first sign of the *Heron*'s return.

"They're late," Thorn said. "They should have been back by now."

Svengal looked sidelong at his old friend. "Have you ever known any plan to run to time?" he said. "Don't worry. They'll be fine."

Thorn shook his head. "I should never have let him do it," he said. "There are too many things that could go wrong."

Svengal raised an eyebrow. "I'm not sure that it was ever up to you to let him go," he said. "Hal seems to have a mind of his own."

"That's true enough." Thorn paused. "But if Stig misses them, they could be lost forever. I don't know what I'll do if that happens."

They passed the silent figure of Lydia, sitting on the sand with her knees drawn up to her chin and staring wordlessly out to sea.

"Looks like we're not the only ones worried about them," Svengal commented.

Thorn followed his gaze and grunted agreement.

"Wish she'd make up her mind which one of them she fancies," he said. He'd noticed the byplay between Lydia and the two boys since they'd first rescued the girl from the sea. "That could cause trouble between them."

"She seems to be a good type," Svengal said. "She probably doesn't know herself. And they're friends. Friends usually find a way to get round that sort of thing. They won't be the first two shipmates to be interested in the same girl."

There was something in his voice that hinted at a deeper meaning, and Thorn looked at him suspiciously.

"Anyone in particular in mind?" he said, his brows drawing together.

Svengal grinned at him. "Are you going to try to pretend that you didn't fancy Karina when you first laid eyes on her?"

Thorn opened his mouth to speak, but one look at Svengal's face told him that denial would be useless.

"How did you know?"

Svengal shrugged. "It was pretty obvious. Everyone knew. You mooned around for days, especially when you realized that Mikkel fancied her too—and that she had eyes for him."

Thorn made a dismissive gesture.

"That was a long time ago," he said. "And Mikkel was a good man."

"So were you," Svengal said. "Still are, in fact. I'm just saying, good friends seem to have a way of coping with that sort of thing. And those boys are good friends."

They paced in silence for a few more meters, then, by unspoken agreement, turned to retrace their steps along the beach.

"Ever thought of trying your luck with Karina again?" Svengal asked.

Thorn shook his head. "That ship sailed long ago."

Svengal pursed his lips thoughtfully. There was a note in Thorn's voice that indicated that particular avenue of conversation was definitely closed. He changed tack.

"He's an amazing lad, isn't he?" He shaded his eyes, looking out to sea. There was still no sign of a ship anywhere.

"Erak says we need people like Hal," he continued. "Thinkers and planners. People with ideas."

"He's got plenty of those, all right," Thorn said. He shook his head in admiration as he thought about Hal's fast-moving, fertile mind. "I mean, you know me, I've seen my share of battles. But I could never plan something like this attack. We Skandians just tend to barge in and start hitting people. But look at what he's come up with—a three-pronged attack, coordinated so that the defenders' forces will be split. And as for that huge crossbow he's mounted on the *Heron* . . . well, can you think of anyone else who could come up with an idea like that?"

Svengal nodded. "He's impressive, all right," he said. "Must be the Araluen in him."

Thorn stopped and eyed his old friend with cold eyes. "He's a Skandian," he said bluntly.

After a few seconds, a faint smile touched Svengal's bearded features. "That's what I meant."

Down the beach, Lydia suddenly came to her feet, shading her eyes with one hand as she peered out to sea.

"There she is!" she said.

• • • • •

Word spread quickly and by the time the *Heron* nosed gently into the beach, the crews of *Wolfwind* and the *Heron* were all assembled to greet her. As Stefan took the beach anchor and ran it up the beach, driving it into the sand, Stig tied off the tiller and moved to the bow, his huge grin confirming that Hal and Jesper were safe.

"We're back," he said cheerfully. "And we've got two half-frozen mackerel we hauled out of the sea on the way home."

The two blanket-wrapped figures were brought to the bow and willing hands made ready to help them down. Ingvar shoved through the press, his arms outstretched, to take Hal as Ulf and Wulf lowered him over the side. The skirl's eyes were open, although his lips were still tinged blue with the cold. Ingvar, tears threatening to mist his eyes, marched up the beach, holding Hal like a baby, to where the Skandians had built two huge fires close together.

He laid Hal down on a bedroll between the fires, where the heat from both could warm him. Thorn followed, carrying Jesper's semiconscious form, and placed him next to Hal. Lydia bustled around the two recovering boys. While they had been waiting for the *Heron* to reach shore, she had placed four large stones in the fires. She retrieved these now and wrapped them in blankets, placing them inside the bedrolls. Hal sighed as he felt the beautiful heat close to his body.

"Oh, that's so good," he said. Jesper groaned happily in agreement.

Lydia smiled at the two of them. Ingvar was hovering nearby and she knew that he'd tend to any of their needs. She left them dozing and walked back down the beach to where Stig was re-counting the events of the previous night to Thorn, Svengal and the others.

". . . I thought we were sunk when the wind dropped. But fortunately, Barat let us have six of his men so we could row back. We were a little late, but we managed to find them in time." He glanced at Edvin. "Those floats of yours were a touch of genius, Edvin. By the time we found them, Hal was too exhausted to light the signal fire he'd planned."

Edvin smiled and flushed as the others looked at him approv-ingly. Lydia nodded greetings to the six townsmen who had re-turned with the *Heron*. She knew four of them by name and the other two by sight.

She stepped forward now and said to Stig, "I'm surprised Barat let you take six of his men. That doesn't sound like him. He has some very strange ideas when it comes to cooperation between allies."

Stig spread his hands in an innocent gesture. "No. He was fine with it. He didn't say a word." He paused, then he couldn't stop a knowing grin from spreading across his face.

"Actually, now I think of it, he did say a word. He said 'Unngh!'"

"'Unngh'?" Thorn repeated, a puzzled look on his face. "When did he say that?"

"It was just before he hit the sand," Stig told him.

Lydia cocked her head curiously. "When did he hit the sand?"

Stig tried to look regretful and failed miserably.

"That would have been right after I hit him."

There was a long silence, then the meaning of what he had said began to sink in. Slowly, the listeners began to laugh. Interestingly, the six Limmatans joined in. Thorn stepped forward and laid his left hand on Stig's shoulder.

"You know, Stig," he said, "you have hidden depths, boy. Hidden depths."

al and Jesper slept for sixteen hours straight. From time to time, Lydia and Ingvar roused them to a sense of semiconsciousness to feed them hot soup. The two boys responded, without ever fully waking.

It was in the early hours of the next morning when Hal finally woke. The sky was still dark but the position of the stars told him that it must be around four o'clock. He felt deliciously warm. The two fires had burned down through the night, although Ingvar had stoked them. Now they were two massive beds of red coals, radiating a wonderful heat from either side that dispelled all memory of the near-freezing water that had so nearly claimed him.

He stretched luxuriously, groaning quietly in pleasure. Ingvar, who had been dozing nearby, wrapped in a blanket and propped against a log, was instantly alert.

"Are you all right?" he said, tossing aside his blanket and moving to kneel beside Hal.

"I'm fine." Hal smiled. "I'm warm, and I can't think of a better way to be."

Then he yawned, turned over and promptly went back to sleep for another four hours.

He and Jesper were both fit and healthy, and those factors, combined with the natural resilience of the young, left them with no ill effects the following morning. Thorn watched as Hal and Ingvar worked together, installing the Mangler in the bow of the *Heron* once more, and shook his head.

"What it is to be young," he said to Svengal. "If I'd done what he did, I wouldn't have a joint in my body that wasn't creaking and aching fit to kill me." Absentmindedly, he rubbed a hand into the small of his back, which was feeling a sympathy ache for Hal's ordeal in the cold water.

Svengal looked at him with raised eyebrows. "That's what comes of being young," he said. "And of course, he leads a clean and blameless life, which is more than I can say for you."

Thorn grunted. "You've never met anyone as blameless and clean living as I am these days," he said. Then he added, a little wistfully, "Although it's not necessarily by choice."

While Hal and Ingvar worked on the Mangler, the rest of the *Heron* crew had formed a chain and were passing the heavy ballast stones, removed for the ferrying trips, up into the ship once more, where Stig and Ulf were busy distributing them in the bottom of the hull. The floorboards had been raised and were stacked along the rowing benches. As Svengal watched, a thought struck him.

"I'd better get my men busy unloading our ballast," he said. *Wolfwind* would be passing through the shallows of the marshes, and needed to draw as little water as possible. Already, her crew had tilted her onto her beam to unstep the heavy mast. It was stacked neatly, with the yardarm and massive sail, above the high watermark on the beach. By the time they were finished, the ship would float in little more than twenty centimeters of water.

An elderly Limmatan who had escaped from the town had been detailed to act as the Skandians' guide through the swamps. He was considered too old to fight and had been delighted to be assigned to a role in the attack.

"I've been fishing and wildfowling in these swamps for forty years," he had told Svengal. "Know them like the back of my hand."

Then he had glanced down at a scar on the back of his hand and feigned shock.

"Good grief! What's that on the back of my hand?" he yelped, then bellowed in laughter as he saw Svengal's startled reaction. "Never mind, sonny, I'll get you there for the big event." He patted the sea wolf's massive shoulder. Svengal endured the joke and the patronizing gesture with surprising good grace.

A little before noon, the two parties assembled by the ships at the water's edge. Svengal, Thorn, Hal and Stig stood in a tight group. The Skandians would take the longest time to get into position, as they had to thread their way through the swamps.

The four friends shook hands all round, then Hal and Stig moved away to board the *Heron*. Lydia and the rest of the crew were already on board. Edvin and Stefan were standing by in the bow with an oar each, ready to push the ship off from shore.

Svengal and Thorn stayed behind for a few words in private— they'd been friends and shipmates for many years. *Wolfwind*'s skirl couldn't resist a grin as he shook Thorn's left hand. He'd noted that his friend was carrying the fearsome war club device that Hal had made him in a sling around his shoulder. For the moment, he continued to wear his adjustable hook on the end of his right arm. He'd change the two over when the Herons attacked the beach gate.

"I'll see you in Limmat," Svengal said to his former shipmate. "Try not to hit yourself on the head with that thing." He gestured to the club.

Thorn snorted in derision. "Try not to drop your ax on your toes," he said. "You're clumsy enough as it is."

The two friends smiled at each other.

"Wish you were coming with us, Thorn. Be like old times," Svengal said.

Thorn smiled. "I'm part of a different crew nowadays. I've got to keep an eye on them. Besides, you know I'd never take orders from you."

"But you'll take them from a sixteen-year-old boy?" Svengal asked.

Thorn nodded. "He's intelligent."

Svengal shrugged. "I suppose I walked into that one. Take care, Thorn," he said, serious all of a sudden, and he patted his friend's shoulder.

"You too. Don't take any risks."

Svengal's eyes widened. "Me? I never take risks. Risks are for them that fight me," he added, with a savage grin. Like a typical Skandian, he was relishing the coming battle.

"Thorn! Let's get going!" Hal called.

Thorn turned away from Svengal, waving a hand in acknowledgment.

"Better obey orders," he said.

Svengal grunted disdainfully. "That'll be a first. See you in Limmat."

Thorn ran down the beach and leapt up to seize the rail of the ship. Ulf and Wulf grabbed his arms and helped him over the side. As Edvin and Stefan poled the ship out from the shore, Hal rowed her stern around so that he was only a few meters from Svengal.

"I'll cruise up and down outside the harbor to get their attention," he called. "Once you're in position, flash me a signal and I'll start shooting."

"Once they see you, they'll concentrate most of their men in the towers," Svengal called.

Hal nodded. "I'm depending on it. It'll mean more targets for me to shoot at."

It'll also mean more people to shoot back, Svengal thought. But he kept it to himself. Hal knew the risk he was facing.

"Starboard sail," Hal ordered, and Stefan and Edvin heaved on the lines that sent the yardarm and sail up the mast. As the wind filled it and the twins trimmed the sail in, *Heron* swung in a smooth curve, accelerating away from the beach. Svengal watched the graceful little ship, admiring her speed and agility.

"Pretty to watch," he said. Then he turned to his own ship, grimacing as he looked at her mast-less, sail-less lines. Minus her mast, yardarm and sail, and floating high in the water, she looked more like an oversize skiff than a wolfship, he thought. But he had to admit that using her this way was practical. If the Skandians were to wade through the waist-deep water and mud of the marshes, they'd reach the western tower with their clothes saturated and heavy—and they would be half exhausted as a result.

"Let's get under way," he roared. Skandian sailing commands

were issued at full volume as a matter of course. He strode down the beach. Two of his crew reached down to help him over the bow rail and he strode aft to the tiller.

"Where's that smart-mouthed Limmatan who's planning to guide us?" he said.

The gray-haired townsman bobbed up beside the steering platform. He'd been resting on one of the rowing benches.

"Right here, sonny. Finally ready to get moving, are you?"

"Oars!" Svengal ordered. They were only using half the oars available. Once they got into the swamp itself, they'd use four of them to pole the ship along. He glanced at one of the crew who wasn't currently engaged in rowing.

"Lars! You get up here and stop me if I try to throw this Limmatan loudmouth overboard."

Lars nodded, grinning. The old guide merely sniggered.

On the far side of the town, Barat and his men crouched, concealed in the trees, barely fifty meters from the palisade.

Late the previous night, they had moved silently up the beach from their place of concealment. They had stayed inside the tree line at the foot of the escarpment behind the town, hidden from the sight of any sentry on the walls.

They could have spent the last two days here, Barat thought. Then he realized he was wrong. It was safe enough to spend a few late-night hours in sight of the wall. If they'd been here for the past two days, the chances were high that an incautious movement, the flash of light on one of their weapons or helmets, or an accidental noise would have led to their discovery.

Hal was right to insist that they move only at the last minute, he thought. His forehead creased in a frown as he thought of the Skandians. The fact that he admitted that Hal was right didn't make him any fonder of them. His teeth still ached from where Stig had hit him. There was an ugly, discolored bruise on his jaw.

He'll pay for that, he thought.

He settled down behind a lichen-covered fallen tree trunk and searched the bay for the first sign of the *Heron*. He frowned as he wondered what would happen if Stig had failed to pick up Hal. Then he shrugged fatalistically. The ship and its oversize crossbow were nothing more than an exotic sideshow, he thought. If they didn't materialize, he and his men would fight their way into the town without them.

On the other hand, if the *Heron* did appear, and her crew carried out their part of the plan, they would at least be a useful distraction. But he was under no illusions that the hard, dangerous work would be up to the men of Limmat. For perhaps the twentieth time, he scowled as he thought of the six men Stig had taken from his little force.

He'll pay for that too, when this is all over, he thought. Then he drew a deep breath. But first, let's get it over.

Hal was at the tiller, feet set wide apart to balance against the surging of the deck as *Heron* swept up and over successive waves. She was taking the waves on her starboard bow, so that the ship was performing a regular corkscrewing action. Up, roll right, down, roll left, then repeat the sequence.

"*Wolfwind*'s heading into the marshes," Thorn reported, from his position amidships, by the fin. Hal glanced over his shoulder. The long, lean wolfship was traveling fast under oars. That probably had something to do with the fact that she'd been lightened until she drew only a few centimeters of water. Less drag, more speed, he thought.

She had rounded the promontory that marked the end of the beach where they had made their camp. But whereas *Heron* was heading out to sea, *Wolfwind* was swinging to port, into the small creek that led into the marshes.

"Rather them than me," Hal said. Out here, the breeze was fresh and the air was clean and invigorating. In the swamps, he knew from previous experience, the air would be humid and still, and filled with clouds of annoying insects.

He angled the *Heron* farther to starboard, aiming to keep her out of sight of the town a little longer. He nodded approvingly as Ulf and Wulf, without any need for orders, adjusted the trim of the sail to match the new course.

"Hard to see *Wolfwind* without her mast, isn't it?" Hal remarked.

Stig, standing ready beside him, glanced at the wolfship as she angled into the creek. Her gray hull blended naturally with the gray-green of the swamp grasses and reeds. He grunted agreement.

"How long do you think she'll take?" Hal asked.

"Wallis thought just over an hour," Stig replied. Wallis was the elderly Limmatan who was guiding Svengal.

Hal nodded, thinking. "And we'll take about twenty minutes to reach the harbor mouth," he said. "We'll stay out of sight for another ten minutes, then we'll let them see us."

"That should set the cat among the pigeons," Stig said, grinning.

"Or the crossbow among the pirates," Hal said quietly.

H al tipped the thirty-minute sand glass that he used for navigation and watched as the grains began to cascade through the narrow aperture from top to bottom. He could have estimated the twenty minutes, but using the instrument appealed to his sense of accuracy. He smiled as he recalled his conversation with Jesper.

How will we know when ten minutes are up?

We'll know because that'll be when I light the signal fire.

He realized now that their minds must have been starting to wander when they had that conversation, as a result of the biting cold and the weariness that was overtaking them. Maybe that's why he wanted to be precise this morning, to prove that he was back in control of his faculties.

He realized that Stig was jogging his elbow and pointing to the graduation marks on the sand glass. Twenty minutes had passed while he'd been woolgathering. So much for his love of precision, he thought.

"We're coming about!" he called. "Time to start the party!"

They tacked smoothly, and once they were running toward the beach, he gestured for Stig to take the helm. He nodded approvingly as he saw that his friend had slung his large round shield on his left arm, so that it covered him. When they turned away from the beach, Stig would slip the shield around to cover his back. Hal checked the other shields, which were placed along the bulwarks. They were mounted higher than usual, so they provided extra cover for the crew. He caught Thorn's eye and jerked his head forward. The old sea wolf was standing in the waist of the ship, swaying easily with the ship's movement. Lydia sat close by, checking the darts in her quiver.

"Let's get ready," he said. Thorn stooped and retrieved two small, round metal shields, shaped rather like outsize bowls. He clamped his hook onto the handle of one, then slipped his left hand into the grip of the second. Lydia rose and the three of them made their way to the bow. The two Skandians moved easily, matching their stride to the ship's regular heave and pitch. Lydia was less sure-footed. From time to time, she grasped at a stay or the mast itself to steady herself.

Ingvar was standing ready by the Mangler. He'd spent the past two days making projectiles for the weapon and they were ranged now in two racks, one on either side of the bow. Hal glanced at them. There were a dozen bolts in each rack.

"Did you make the fire bolts as well?" Hal asked.

Ingvar indicated a tub set by the mast. There were half a dozen fire bolts resting in it—specially prepared projectiles with their points wrapped in oil-soaked cloth, then daubed liberally with pitch. Hal planned to use one of them to set fire to the oil-soaked beach gate when the time came. They were resting head down in the tub, which contained several centimeters of oil in the bottom to stop the soaked cloth from drying out.

The *Heron* rose on a wave and he could see the eastern tower, showing briefly above the horizon.

Hal glanced round at Edvin, who was standing ready to relay his helm orders to Stig.

"Come to port a little," he said. As the bow swung to a point midway between the towers, he raised his hands and Stig steadied on that course. Automatically, Ulf and Wulf adjusted the sail to the new direction.

"Shall I load up?" Ingvar asked eagerly. But Hal shook his head. The longer the Mangler was kept under tension, the greater the strain on its limbs, string and trigger mechanism. They wouldn't be shooting for some minutes, so there was no point in risking an accidental breakage.

"Relax," he said, his eyes narrowing as both towers came into full view. He pictured the scene on the walkway that surrounded the east tower as the lookout, lounging on the railing, eyes half closed and drowsy after a big lunch, suddenly became aware that a strange ship was approaching—and approaching fast.

There would be a moment's confusion and indecision. Then he would sound the alarm—either a bell or a horn—Hal assumed. He turned his head slightly toward the tower, testing to see if he could hear either. But the distance was too great. All he could hear was the regular hiss of the sea as the *Heron*'s sharp prow cut through it and sent it streaming down either side of the ship—that and the regular soft thump as she came down in successive troughs.

"They've seen us," Thorn said. Hal marveled at his old friend's keen eyesight. Then, as they traveled a few meters closer, he could make out the tiny dark shapes running along the harbor mole and mounting the ladder to the watchtowers. There seemed to be a lot of them, he thought, but at this distance, it was impossible to estimate their numbers. And now, he realized, he could hear the alarm, a wailing, undulating blast on a horn.

They were two hundred meters from the harbor entrance. Hal opened his mouth to call to Stig. At this stage, he didn't want to get within arrow range of the towers. But as he went to give an order, Stig swung the *Heron* smoothly to starboard. The ship raced parallel to the shore now. She was heeled a little too far and Hal turned to issue another order. But Ulf and Wulf forestalled him, easing the sheets so that she rode more upright. He glanced up and met Lydia's eye. She had noticed how Stig and the twins had anticipated his orders and she smiled tightly at him.

She's nervous, he thought.

"Looks like I'm not needed," he said, planning to steady her nerves with the joke. He was surprised to find that his voice was slightly higher pitched than normal.

I'm nervous too, he thought.

He realized he was sitting forward on the Mangler's small seat, shoulders and body tensed. He leaned back, forcing his muscles to relax. He glanced back down the ship to where the crew members crouched at their stations. None of them appeared to be as edgy as he felt. He hoped he looked as confident as they did.

Stig swung the ship back to run in the opposite direction. Stefan and Edvin attended to the changeover of sails. Hal felt the giant crossbow move smoothly under him as Ingvar tested its motion. He had a long stout pole inserted into the tail of the carriage and he could swivel the Mangler through a ninety-degree arc—forty-five degrees either side of the bow post. Hal glanced up at him and the big boy grinned.

"Just testing," he said.

Hal nodded. He didn't want to speak again in case his voice was too high-pitched.

"Anyone see any sign of Barat and his men?" Lydia asked suddenly. They were passing the spot where the Limmatan force should be hidden in the tree line.

"Well, I certainly can't," Ingvar responded, with a wide grin. Hal glanced at him again. The huge boy's nerves seemed as steady as a rock, he thought. About to go into action for the first time and here he was, coolly cracking jokes about his own short-sightedness.

"Thought I saw a movement in the trees a few seconds ago," Thorn said. "But that might just have been because I know they should be there somewhere."

"Well, if we can't see them, neither can the pirates," Hal said.

"If they're there," Ingvar said scornfully. He'd witnessed Barat's overbearing manner with Hal and he had a very low opinion of the townspeople's battle commander.

"They'll be there," Lydia said quietly.

Ingvar glanced in her direction. "Sorry, Lydia," he said. After all, he'd just insulted her countrymen. She waved the apology aside.

"Barat can be an almighty pain and a pompous idiot," she said. "But he's a good commander and a good fighter. He won't let us down."

A ragged line of splashes threw up spray twenty meters inshore of the racing ship. Arrows from the watchtower, Hal thought. They were still outside the maximum range. Just then one arrow, launched from a more powerful bow, rattled against the starboard bulwark and fell into the sea. Its energy was spent and it didn't have enough force behind it to penetrate the timber.

But it was a warning of what they would face when they went closer.

"Are you ready, Thorn?" he asked. The small shields his friend was carrying seemed a little inadequate.

"I'm ready. Don't worry about me. Just keep your mind on your shooting," was the calm reply. And suddenly, Hal's concerns were eased. Thorn knew what he was doing, he thought. The small shields might not have been Hal's choice, but Thorn knew more about this sort of thing than he ever would.

As they sailed past the first tower, approaching the second, Thorn used one of the shields to shade his eyes, peering into the tangle of reeds and low-lying islands that marked the swamp.

"I can see *Wolfwind!*" he said. "She's almost reached the starting point. There—just to the left of those two slanting trees."

Hal followed his gaze. There were two scrubby trees on a sand island close to the edge of the marsh. With so little purchase for their roots, the wind had caused both of them to lean to one side. Looking to the left, he saw a slight movement, then made out the low hull of *Wolfwind* as she passed through an open channel.

He looked back to the watchtower. They were close enough to see details now and it appeared that every eye was on the *Heron*. So far, the plan was working. Nobody on either watchtower had any idea of the threat that was creeping toward them through the marshes.

"Stig!" he called, forgetting in the heat of the moment that he had Edvin stationed to relay his orders. "Take us out to sea, then come in to attack the east tower."

With the Mangler only capable of firing in a restricted arc either side of the bow, he'd have to attack the tower head on, then turn away and head back out to sea. Then they'd turn again to carry out a similar attack on the western tower. That way, he would have less sideways correction to allow for, as he would be heading almost directly for his target. And he'd present a smaller target to the defenders, rather than the full length of the hull.

The disadvantage was that he and the others in the bow of the *Heron* would bear the brunt of the return shots from the towers. Still, he was confident that Thorn would look after that part. And Lydia, he thought. They had discussed her role several days before. If any of the archers on the tower became too accurate, it would be her task to eliminate them.

They were three hundred meters offshore now and Stig swung the ship in an arc. They'd attack the towers one after the other, repeating the attacks until they had exhausted their ammunition, or the garrisons in the towers were neutralized—whichever came first.

There was a third alternative, of course. There was always the chance that the men in the tower might just do a little neutralizing of their own. But Hal didn't care to think about that.

Peering over the sights of the crossbow, he was aware, with a detached part of his mind, of the crew hoisting and adjusting sails, then *Heron* steadied on her course.

"Load her, Ingvar," he said.

His giant friend leaned forward, seized the two cocking handles of the Mangler and drew the limbs back until the cord clicked into place over the retaining latch. Then Ingvar selected the first of the meter-long bolts and laid it in the groove on top of the weapon, ensuring that the notch at the rear end was engaged with the thick cord.

Hal was aware that Thorn had moved to a position in the bow, crouching under the bow post. When Ingvar reloaded, he would stand and provide protection with the two small shields.

Now Ingvar moved behind the crossbow, and took hold of the traversing pole. Hal peered over the sights.

"Left a little . . . left . . . left . . . back right . . ."

To avoid confusion, they had agreed that for steering orders to Edvin, he would use the terms *port* and *starboard*. Aiming directions for Ingvar would be given as *left* or *right*.

He peered down the sights of the crossbow, watching the tower rise and fall as the ship went up and over successive waves. An arrow flashed into the sea just off the port bow. They were coming into range. He heard a rapid rattling sound as three arrows struck the bow. Something hit the deck to one side of him. Not an arrow. Possibly a stone flung by a slinger.

"Everybody stay down," he called, without taking his eyes off the tower, which was looming closer and closer. His left hand turned the elevating cog smoothly, raising the bow so that the sight was centered on the pinewood railing of the tower. He wanted the first shot to be successful, so he was aiming at the largest possible target.

An arrow zipped through the *Heron*'s sail.

The tower seemed to fill his sights. He could see one of the defenders, distinctive in a bright green jacket, on the extreme left-hand end, aiming a recurve bow, drawing the arrow back. Then he released and Hal lost sight of the shaft.

A few seconds later, it thudded, quivering, into the deck beside him. They were about seventy-five meters out.

Then his sights and the target were aligned and he gently tugged on the trigger lanyard.

SLAM!

The Mangler bucked with the recoil and the bolt streaked away. A few seconds later, a section of the pine balustrade around the tower exploded in a hail of splinters as the heavy projectile smashed into it, then through it, cartwheeling among the defenders and knocking men over.

Others were hit by the flying pine splinters. They reeled away in pain and panic, wondering what had hit them.

The defenders, caught completely by surprise, dropped under the balustrade out of sight. The hail of arrows and projectiles suddenly ceased as they tried to work out what was happening.

"Ready!" shouted Ingvar. He hadn't waited to hear what happened with the first shot. He'd leapt forward to cock and load the Mangler. Lydia, seeing a way of helping, had crept forward on her knees, staying below the bulwark, and passed a fresh bolt to him.

Hal wound the elevation screw, calling aiming directions to

Ingvar. As ever, the Mangler had gone off line with the recoil of the first shot.

"Left . . . left . . . left. Steady!"

SLAM!

The range was shorter now and the bolt hit with even greater force. It caught the very top of the railing, showering more of those deadly splinters into the air, and spinning end over end through the window of the guardhouse.

"Come about!" Hal called, and as the *Heron* swung away from the eastern tower, the defenders belatedly came to life, and a hail of arrows and rocks followed her. One defender, with what seemed to Hal to be ridiculous optimism, even threw a spear after her.

But only a few struck home. The ship's speed and the rapidly widening distance left most of the missiles in her wake. Hal glanced back, leaning to one side to see past the sail. The tower's balustrade had two large, ragged gaps torn in it.

Ingvar was hopping eagerly from one foot to another.

"How did we do?" he asked. "Did it work?"

Hal had time to consider that Ingvar's short-sightedness was actually an advantage in this situation. Since he couldn't see the result of the shots, he wasn't tempted to wait and watch. Once a bolt was on its way, he was instantly ready to recock and reload the massive weapon.

"We did well," Hal told him. "Two great holes in the tower railing and probably half a dozen of the enemy hit by splinters and put out of action." He glanced at Lydia. "Good idea helping with the reloading."

She smiled at him. "Thanks. Did you notice that bowman in the green shirt? I might have to take care of him next time."

Hal nodded. "I'd be grateful if you would." He grinned at Thorn. "You didn't have much to do on that run," he said.

Thorn nodded. He didn't return the grin.

"They'll be ready for us when we come back," he said. "They'll know what's coming."

Zavac had set up his headquarters in Limmat's counting house. It was the official administration building of the town, where taxes were set and collected, public works organized, and where, in normal times, the town council met to look after ongoing business.

Zavac was using one of the larger offices to grade and separate the precious stones that were being delivered from the mine each day. The miners had struck a rich pocket of emeralds just before the pirate raid had overrun the town. In the days since, Zavac had kept them hard at work, delivering large numbers of stones each day. Now, he noticed, the daily yield was diminishing. The pocket was just about played out and soon it would be time to leave.

He was holding one of the larger specimens up to the light, admiring the way the light's rays refracted and reflected inside the stone, when the door of the room burst open. One of his men stood there, panting heavily, sweat showing on his face. He had obviously been running hard.

He hesitated as Zavac lowered the stone and glared at him.

"What?" the *Raven*'s captain demanded, his voice harsh.

The man took several deep breaths. "There's a ship," he said finally.

Zavac raised one eyebrow. "A ship?" he repeated. "A ship? You come bursting in here without knocking to tell me there's *a ship?*"

The man looked back the way he had come. With Zavac, he reflected, you could never win. If he hadn't been told about the approach of the strange ship, he would have flown into a rage, striking out at those around him.

"It's heading for the harbor mouth," he said.

Zavac spread his hands in a sarcastic gesture. "And?"

"I . . . well . . . we thought . . . you should be told."

"Is it a big ship?" Zavac asked. "A wolfship or a warship of some kind?"

"No. It's . . . small. But maybe you should take a look at it."

Zavac sighed heavily. He placed the emerald back in the tray on the table in front of him, then took the tray to a heavily reinforced wooden locker in the corner. He placed it inside, deliberately turned the key in the lock and placed it in his pocket. Then he regarded his subordinate once more.

"Very well," he said. "Let's see this ship."

He led the way out of the office, locking the door behind them. His crewman followed anxiously behind him, half trotting to keep up with Zavac's long stride.

They made their way down the broad thoroughfare to the harbor front, Zavac enjoying the way the citizens of Limmat shrank back from him as he passed. At the quay, he turned left and strode toward the boom, protected either side by the watchtowers.

He paused some fifty meters from the eastern tower. From here, on the inland side, he could see no sign of the damage the Mangler had inflicted in *Heron*'s first attack. He could hear voices shouting from the watchtower, but that was only to be expected. The members of the watch were probably yelling defiance at the interloper. Beyond, out to sea and obviously retreating, he could see a neat little ship, with a triangular sail.

He'd seen that ship before, he thought. Then he realized where. It was the ship belonging to the crew of young Skandians from under whose noses he'd stolen the priceless Andomal. His lip curled in anger.

Then he shook his head impatiently. The ship was small. She carried a crew of less than a dozen. And the harbor was protected by the two watchtowers and the massive log boom across the entrance.

He turned on his crewman, cuffing him across the head.

"You idiot!" he snarled. "They're boys, and there can't be more than ten of them! What possible harm do you think they can do us?"

The hapless pirate, who had left to alert Zavac before the *Heron* launched her attack, had no answer to the question. He cowered away from the furious captain.

"I thought—"

Zavac cut him off furiously. "Then don't think in the future! You haven't got the equipment for it!"

Turning on his heel, he stalked back toward the counting house.

"And see I'm not bothered again!" he threw back over his shoulder.

• • • • •

In the western watchtower, the commander appointed by Zavac watched with horrified fascination as what looked like a small Skandian wolfship launched her attack on his comrades across the harbor.

He wasn't sure exactly what was happening. There appeared to be some huge weapon in the bow of the ship, shooting heavy projectiles at the eastern tower. While he couldn't make out the details of the weapon—possibly a large crossbow, he thought—or the projectiles themselves, the results were all too obvious.

He heard the shattering cracks as the bolts slammed into the pine balustrade across the harbor, and saw the hail of deadly splinters as they flew among the defenders. He could also make out the bolt as it spun end over end through the crowd of men on the walkway, scything several of them down. He heard their screams. Then the ship turned away and headed out to sea.

Now she was turning back. His eyes narrowed as he saw her settle on course and realized she was heading straight for him. The western tower was obviously the next target.

His mind raced. The biggest danger, it seemed to him, was the hail of splinters that each shot sent flying in its wake. The projectile itself might hit one or two people, but the splinters could put half a dozen others out of action. A dozen or more splinters would create a deadly hail with each single shot.

He looked round, searching for something to nullify their effect, and his gaze landed on the guardhouse in the center of the platform. There were half a dozen bunks in there, where men could rest and relax while they were off duty. And bunks meant bedding.

"Get those mattresses and blankets out here!" he yelled, pointing at the guardhouse. "Drape them over the railing! And hurry, blast your eyes!"

His men, still confused by the unexpected turn of events, were staring at him as if he'd suddenly lost his senses. He shoved one of them toward the door to the guardhouse. When the man moved slowly toward it, he helped him on his way with a kick. Another gaped at him and he cuffed him across the ears, yelling and cursing at him.

"Get moving, you wall-eyed idiot! Blankets and mattresses! They'll stop the splinters flying!"

Gradually, his anger seemed to energize them and one or two of them even grasped the idea he had in mind. They moved with increasing urgency, two of them dashing inside and beginning to pass the bedding out through the open, unglazed window. The others hurried to drape the thick blankets and straw-filled mattresses over the top of the balustrade. The projectiles would go through them, the commander thought, but they'd smother that deadly hail of fragments.

Satisfied that the entire length of the balustrade was covered, he issued further orders.

"Archers! Up here. Get ready to cut them down! There's some kind of infernal weapon in the bow of that ship. Aim for the men shooting it."

Several men armed with bows moved forward to take their place at the heavily padded balustrade. Several others, having seen the fate of their comrades in the first tower, hung back. He snarled at them and shoved one of them forward. The others reluctantly followed.

"The rest of you get down!" he ordered. "Get below the railing and out of sight!"

The men were slow to obey him. They watched with fascination as the graceful little ship headed toward them. Every eye in the tower was on her. Nobody noticed the line of warriors emerging from the swamp to the west, moving quickly toward them.

On board the *Heron*, Hal watched, puzzled, as the defenders began to drape blankets and mattresses over the side of the balustrade. Thorn, crouching beside him, suddenly divined their purpose.

"They're hoping to contain the splinters!" he said. "They've seen how much damage they do!"

Hal felt a sudden surge of uncertainty. The flying splinters had proved to have a deadly effect on the defenders—far more than he had expected. Now the pirates had found a way to counteract them. And the heavy, draped cloth might even prevent the bolts from penetrating the balustrade. They'd certainly absorb some of their force. He rubbed his jaw thoughtfully, desperate for a way to counteract this unexpected tactic.

Then a grim smile spread across his face.

"Edvin, get a fire bolt ready. Ingvar, unload the bolt in the Mangler."

Originally, Hal had only planned to use the fire bolts to ignite the oil bladder on the beach gate. But now he saw an unexpected opportunity for them.

Ingvar removed the projectile that he'd loaded into the Mangler and replaced it in the ready rack. Edvin fetched one of the fire bolts from the tub by the mast. He crouched on the deck and produced a flint and steel, and a tinderbox. After half a dozen strikes, he had a small handful of tinder flaring up in the tinderbox. Carefully, he held the fire bolt's head in the flame. The oil-soaked cloth caught almost immediately, the flame quickly spreading to the pitch. Edvin closed the tinderbox, snuffing out the flames inside, and handed the burning bolt to Lydia.

"Hold this," he said briefly. Then, staying low, he moved to the bow and took up a bucket of water he'd left ready. He threw the water over the front of the Mangler, liberally soaking the wood where the burning head would be seated. This was all part of a prearranged drill Hal had devised.

The deadly rattle of arrows against the hull and deck began once more.

"Load it now, Ingvar," Hal said. He didn't want to wait any longer for Ingvar to be exposed. Lydia passed the fire bolt to Ingvar and the big boy reached up to place the smoldering bolt in position. The burning head hissed against the soaked wood, and Ingvar, staying low, scuttled back behind Hal.

"Stay down, everyone," Hal warned. "Ready, Thorn?" he called.

The one-armed sea wolf met his eye and nodded.

Hal crouched over the Mangler, slowly winding the elevation handle and watching the sights rise to line up with the balustrade. This time, he had a much larger target to aim for, so there was no need to go in as close as before.

"One shot only," he told Ingvar. He didn't want the big boy exposed while he reloaded. If the fire bolt worked, there'd be no need for a second shot.

Ingvar grunted assent. He was crouched behind the mass of the crossbow carriage, his hands on the traversing lever.

"Left . . . left . . . right a little. Steady there," Hal called.

He flinched as an arrow struck the front of the Mangler's carriage and glanced off. Then he focused his attention on the sights, trying to ignore the sound of arrows striking the hull and zipping through the sail. I'll have to patch that sail when this is over, he thought with a detached part of his mind.

The foresight lined up as the ship reached the crest of a wave, sank below the target as she swooped into the trough, then started to rise again. He eased the elevating cog to compensate, then, a second or so before the ship reached the next crest and the sight was centered on the heavily draped balustrade, he pulled the trigger lanyard. There was the usual slight delay, then . . .

SLAM!

The Mangler bucked wildly in recoil. The fire bolt streaked away, trailing a thin ribbon of gray smoke behind it. In the instant that it released, Hal knew the shot was good and he watched the thin trail of smoke as it headed straight for the center of the balustrade.

Stig was already bringing the *Heron's* bow around to head back out to sea and out of range. They heard the dull thud of the bolt striking the tower, exactly where Hal had aimed it. Staying low, he craned around to watch for the result, as the ship swung away from the target. Three more arrows rattled against the hull and the shields ranged along the starboard bulwark.

Then he saw it. A bright flash of flame shot up from the center of the balustrade. The fire bolt had impacted right in the center of a straw-filled mattress. There was a pause of a few seconds while the flames, suppressed by the wind of the projectile's flight, rekindled. Then the dry straw and canvas caught and flared wildly, the flames feeding hungrily on the perfect tinder.

"Throw it off! Get rid of it!" the watchtower commander screamed. But the flames, fanned by the sea breeze, were crackling fiercely and none of his men were willing to risk being burned. They backed away, shielding their faces from the heat.

"Curse you! Help me, you cowards!" the commander raved. He drew his sword and, holding it two-handed, tried to snag it under the mattress so that he could throw it clear. But already the flames had spread to the blankets and mattresses on either side. The flames singed his arms and eyebrows as he struggled with the heavy, burning mass of linen and straw.

He managed to tip it over the side of the railing and felt a momentary surge of triumph as it began to fall free. But his optimism was short-lived. The mattress was securely pinned to the timber by the bolt that had set the fire. It fell a meter or so, then stopped, hanging out of his reach, with flames flaring up, licking hungrily at the wood of the tower.

When Hal had planned to use a fire bolt against the beach gate, he knew he would need oil to help set the wood burning. The gate was aged, seasoned hardwood and a single fire bolt would not be enough to make it catch. But the tower was a different matter altogether. The planks and frame were pinewood—soft wood that was oozing with resin and, as a result, highly flammable. But even with this wood, a single fire source like a flaming bolt might not have been enough. It could have been quickly extinguished. The commander had made a fatal mistake when he draped the length of the balustrade with highly combustible cloth and straw. Now the flames ranged along the entire front of the balustrade, and the planks and frames were already starting to burn beneath the cloth.

To make matters worse, there was no real water supply available—just a few jugs of drinking water for the sentries. There was no way for them to extinguish the flames. The tower was doomed.

A hundred meters away from the tower, Svengal led his men out of the swamps and onto firm ground. The Skandians paused, slightly awestruck, at the sight of the flames now rapidly soaring up the sides of the balustrade and the guardhouse at the top of the tower.

The *Heron*, apparently unscathed, cruised smoothly back out to sea, turning toward the companion tower on the other side of the harbor mouth.

"By Orlog's crossed eyes, he's done it," Svengal said. He shook his head in admiration. Nobody had foreseen a result quite as dramatic as this one. He glanced around his men. They had all stopped. Several were leaning on the hafts of their axes as they watched the tower's superstructure burning. So far, the flames hadn't spread to the supporting framework, but that was only a matter of time.

"Looks like our job's done for us, chief," one of the crew said to him. Then Svengal noticed a line of men hastily stumbling down the wooden ladder that led from the watchtower. He pointed his ax toward them.

"Not quite," he said happily. "There's still a little mopping up to do."

Then he took a deep breath and bellowed the traditional Skandian command for battle.

"Let's get 'em!"

Wolfwind's crew moved forward with a roar. The scorched and bewildered pirates who had made their way down from the burning watchtower turned to see an even more dreadful sight than the flames that had nearly consumed them.

Skandians. Ready for battle.

Concealed in the tree line, Barat and his men watched the *Heron*'s attack on the first of the towers. From their position, the tower itself was mostly concealed by the palisade and the intervening buildings of the town.

They watched as the *Heron* approached the tower, heard the distant slamming sound of the Mangler releasing twice, then saw the ship pirouette neatly and head back out to sea.

Barat glanced at Jonas. "Didn't seem to accomplish much."

Jonas shrugged. "Who can tell? But the odds are they've got everyone looking their way."

"Maybe," Barat said. He fidgeted with his sword hilt as he saw the *Heron* turn once more and head back inshore, this time angling for the other tower. The details of this attack were completely obscured, but a few minutes after the ship had gone out of sight behind the eastern harbor mouth, the watching Limmatans saw a thin spiral of smoke rising above the town, from the direction of the western tower.

Before long, it had grown into a thick, gray-black banner. Something was well and truly on fire and, judging by the direction of the smoke column, it could only be the tower.

"They've done it," Jonas said.

Barat frowned. It appeared that the second attack had been successful—more successful than anyone had foreseen. He looked around. His men were poised behind him, weapons ready, faces tense. Back in the trees, they hadn't seen what had happened.

"The tower's on fire," he said to them now. "That's going to get everyone's attention, so let's go."

As one, they rose to their feet. There was a low, concerted growl from thirty-eight throats and he held up a hand in caution.

"Quiet! No war cries. No shouting. And stay close to the trees. The closer we can get before we're spotted, the better chance we'll have."

He waited, looking intently around their faces, until he was sure the message had been taken on board.

"Where are the climbers?" he asked, and four men stepped forward. Each one was carrying a bundle of short planks wrapped in rope—coiled rope ladders.

"Grapnel men?"

Two more signified their presence with raised hands. In addition to their weapons, they carried several ropes, each with a three-pronged grapnel at the end. It would be their job to throw the grapnels over the palisade and hold the ropes taut while the climbers mounted the wall and dropped the rope ladders behind them.

"The rest of you, stand ready to help out with bows, slings and spears while they're climbing," he ordered. Again, there was a mutter of assent.

"All right," he said finally. He glanced out to sea and saw the *Heron* was turning back in for another run at the eastern tower. Judging by the smoke, the western tower was now well alight.

I doubt there'll be a single eye turned our way, he thought. Then he waved his men forward.

"Right. Follow me and keep quiet!" he said, and began to jog along the fringe of the tree line. The soft sand muffled the sound of the thirty-eight pairs of feet that followed him.

There was no sign of defenders on the palisade wall ahead of them.

A s they reached the farthest extent of their run out to sea, Stig swung the *Heron* around to head back for a second attack on the eastern tower. Hal rose from his seat behind the Mangler and held up a hand.

"Heave to for a minute, Stig!" he called. Stig nodded, a slightly puzzled frown on his face, as he brought the ship's head into the wind.

"Let go the sheets," he told Ulf and Wulf. As they de-powered the sail, *Heron* slowed to a stop, rising and falling gently on the even swell. Hal gestured for Thorn to follow him and made his way aft. Lydia, not wanting to be left out, followed the two of them.

"I've had an idea," he said as they reached the steering platform. Stig was gently working the tiller back and forth, keeping the ship's head directly into the wind.

"How unusual," Stig said, grinning. He'd guessed as much when Hal had signaled for him to heave to.

"You're planning on using another fire bolt?" Thorn suggested.

Hal nodded. "Exactly. Once you get that pinewood burning, nothing will stop it."

"Except this time, the garrison aren't going to be kind enough to cover the platform with straw and dry cloth," Thorn observed.

"True. But look at the support framework, just below the platform." Hal pointed and they all peered at the distant structure. "There's a point there where three beams intersect—one vertical, one horizontal and one diagonal. It's the main support point for that side of the tower."

Slowly, the others nodded as they saw what he was pointing to.

"That junction point is a pretty big target. And even if I don't hit it exactly, there's a good chance I'll hit one of the three beams. If I can put a fire bolt in there, the wood will catch—maybe not as quickly as the watchtower with the mattresses all over it. But it'll burn eventually. And once it does, the platform on top will come down. It'll be much more effective than battering away with ordinary bolts."

Stig and Thorn exchanged a glance.

"Sounds reasonable to me," Stig said, and Thorn concurred.

"Certainly worth a try. Do you think you can hit it from a hundred meters? They'll be ready for us this time and they'll be shooting back. We've been lucky so far that nobody's been hit."

Thorn knew, although the others didn't, that their luck was unlikely to hold. Luck was notoriously fickle in a battle. If they kept getting in to close range, they would take casualties.

"I think I can hit it from outside a hundred meters," Hal said.

Stig pushed his bottom lip forward doubtfully.

"That target is barely bigger than the ones we practiced on in the bay," he said. "You needed to get in to fifty meters to hit them with any consistency."

"True. But we were moving then, and moving fast. I plan to

stop about a hundred and twenty meters out so I'm shooting from a steady platform. That'll make my job a lot easier."

"It'll make us easier to hit too," Stig said.

Hal shrugged. "We'll just have to keep our shields up and stay under cover as much as possible. Thorn, can you keep Ingvar covered? I plan to try two fire bolts, so he'll need to reload."

Thorn glanced at the distant tower, picturing in his mind's eye the hail of arrows that would be launched at them.

"Do my best," he said gruffly. "When we stop, that'll throw some of them off at first. They'll be allowing for a moving target. But then we'll be a sitting duck." He looked at Lydia. "Keep watch for that green-shirted archer. He's their best shot."

She nodded. "I'll take care of him." There was no trace of doubt in her voice and the old sea wolf grinned at her.

"You know, I do believe you will." He looked up at Stig and Hal. "Told you this one was a keeper."

Lydia flushed as the two boys smiled. "Shut up. You make sure you do your stuff with those two overgrown dinner bowls you call shields."

Thorn inclined his head. "As you say, young lady. As you say."

"If you two are quite finished," Hal said, regaining their attention, "we'll get under way again. Just give me a minute or two to brief the others."

He started back toward the bow, stopping beside Ulf and Wulf.

"We're going to stop . . . ," he began, but they both nodded.

"We heard," Ulf said. "We'll be ready. Just give us the word."

He looked at them for a second or two. They were keeping their promise, he thought. Once they were at sea, there was no sign of bickering between them. They worked together better and more instinctively than two other people might have. Possibly because of that strange mental bond many twins enjoyed.

He realized that he had been staring at them for several seconds and they were waiting expectantly, thinking he was going to say something more. He nodded curtly and turned away.

"Fine," he said.

The twins exchanged slightly puzzled looks as he made his way back to the bow. Ingvar and Edvin were waiting, sensing that there was a change of plan.

He outlined his idea to them. They both nodded their understanding. Edvin picked up the now-empty bucket, trailed it over the side on a rope and filled it, tossing the seawater onto the front of the Mangler. Then he repeated the action twice more.

"Might as well be sure it's thoroughly soaked," he said.

Hal gestured to the tub where the five remaining fire bolts were stored.

"Get two ready and lit when the time comes," he said. "Ingvar is going to have to reload fast. Once we're stopped, we'll swing up into the wind in a few minutes. When that happens, I won't be able to train the Mangler round far enough."

He paused, wondering if he'd left anything out. "Another thing, Edvin. You'll have to look after it by yourself. Lydia is going to be busy picking off the people shooting at us."

Edvin's brows knitted as he thought over the actions he would have to take. "That won't be a problem. I think I'd prefer it if she's keeping their heads down."

"All right. Places, everyone." Hal turned to call back to Stig and the twins. "Let's get moving!"

As the sail was hauled in, Stig let the *Heron* fall off from the wind. Within a few seconds, she was carving a smooth white wake through the sea again.

Barat stopped at the foot of the palisade. His breath was coming in ragged gasps, but that was the result of nervous tension, not exhaustion. Incredibly, he and his men had covered the forty meters of open space along the beach without any alarm being raised.

He turned back now and called quietly, "Grapnels! Climbers! Go!"

Four grapnels soared up over the palisade, each one trailing a snakelike length of rope behind it. He heard the four thuds as they hit in rapid succession. Then the throwers hauled back on the ropes, dragging the three-pronged hooks back across the walkway until they bit and held fast against the vertical logs that formed the three-meter-high palisade wall. One broke loose and came tumbling back down. As the handler cursed quietly and gathered it in for another throw, Barat gestured to the other three.

"Climbers! On your way! Don't wait for that one!"

The men who had thrown the grapnels now leaned their weight back against the ropes to hold them taut. Two more men moved to stand under each rope, holding a thick spear handle between them. As the first climber began to swarm up the rope, he put his foot on the spear handle and the two men heaved him upward, boosting him up so that his hands closed over the top of the palisade. Taking care not to snag himself on the sharpened ends of the upright logs, he vaulted lightly over onto the catwalk beyond. Two more climbers joined him almost immediately. They drew their swords, swung their shields around from their backs, and moved down the catwalk to form a defensive line, while their comrades swarmed up over the palisade.

Barat came up with the second wave. He glanced quickly around. The catwalk was empty on either side. There was no sign of any defenders.

We've taken them completely by surprise, he thought. Then he leapt back in alarm as the fourth grapnel soared over the palisade and clattered on the planks of the catwalk, missing him by centimeters. He kicked the grapnel over the inner edge of the catwalk so that the prongs caught on the timbers there. The rope drew tight as the unseen attacker below heaved back to set it. Then it began to vibrate as a climber mounted it.

"Alarm! Alarm! The enemy's on the wall!"

The shouting voice reached him from the town below. He looked down into one of the narrow, winding streets that ran away from the palisade toward the open plaza in the town center. Three Magyarans had just rounded a corner and seen the Limmatans gathering on the walkway above them.

The pirates started toward the palisade, then hesitated as they saw the numbers of men already on the catwalk. Realizing they were seriously outnumbered, they turned to run, shouting the alarm as they went.

"Stop them!" Barat shouted. One of his men stepped forward and hurled a spear. It took the nearest Magyaran in the upper leg and he twisted and fell to the ground, calling out for his comrades to help him. They took one more look at the crowd of armed men on the catwalk, turned and disappeared round a corner in the street, yelling the alarm as they went.

Barat hesitated a second. The palisade was undefended on this side. Hal had been right, he thought. The bulk of the Magyarans would be in the watchtowers, or in the town center itself. He gestured toward the steps with his sword.

"Down to ground level!" he yelled. "Head for the town square."

The planks of the catwalk vibrated under his feet as he led the thirty-eight men running toward the stairs.

Near the western watchtower, the Skandians had formed into a wedge shape, with Svengal at its head. They smashed into the disorganized Magyarans, axes rising and falling in a deadly rhythm. The pirates, stunned and demoralized by the sudden onset of the watchtower fire, eyes streaming from the smoke, had no chance against the charging Skandians.

The lucky ones among the enemy were those who were simply buffeted aside by the heavy wooden shields.

Some, blood streaming from their wounds, tried to crawl away from the fight, crying piteously. Others lay where they fell, ominously still. Svengal found himself facing one of the few Magyarans who seemed capable of putting up a fight. They circled each other warily. The Magyaran was armed with a heavy spear, which he held underarm, balanced at its midpoint, and a round metal and wood shield.

He jabbed the spear toward the massive Skandian. But Svengal was watching his eyes and something there told him the move was a feint. He held his ground and smiled at his enemy.

"Have to do better than that," he said. Then, seeing *Wolfwind*'s bosun, Hendrik, looming up behind his adversary with an ax, he snapped, "Leave him be!" Hendrik reluctantly moved away, seeking another foe.

In an all-out melee, it was every man for himself, and Svengal and his men would strike out at any target that presented itself. But the Magyarans were broken and defeated and this was single combat. The man was a brave and capable warrior and Svengal had no wish to see him cut down from behind.

Skandians lived for fighting—although it must be said that some of them died for it as well—and single combat, man-to-man, was the ultimate form.

The spear shot forward again. This time it was a genuine thrust and Svengal flicked it aside with the head of his ax. He saw a shadow of fear in the other man's eyes then, as his opponent saw the casual ease with which Svengal handled the heavy weapon. Most warriors wouldn't be able to match the speed and precision of Svengal's move.

The Magyaran, suddenly wary, retreated a pace. Svengal advanced, his eyes still intent on the other man's. He saw the warning of another thrust there, a fraction of a second before it began, and launched his own attack instead, forestalling the other man's lunge with a mighty overhead cut from the long-handled ax.

The Magyaran got his shield up in the nick of time and the blow slammed against the metal, cracking the wood beneath it and beating the pirate to his knees. But he sprang to his feet almost instantly and lunged again, with the strength of desperation. Svengal decided it was time to forget finesse. He caught the spear square on his massive shield, absorbing the force behind it with flexed knees, feeling the head bite deep into the wood—and jam there.

The Magyaran panicked as he tried in vain to withdraw his trapped spear. As a result, he never saw the roundhouse stroke from the massive ax that ended the fight for good.

Svengal stepped back. He looked around. Some of the Magyarans had escaped, heading back around the harbor to the town. Most of them were lying, still and silent, under the burning tower. Ash and glowing cinders drifted down on them like hot rain. Hendrik caught Svengal's eye.

"We'd better get out from under here. That whole thing could come down at any time."

Svengal stooped and tugged a cloak free from one of the bodies, wiping the blade of his ax with it, then tossing it to one side.

"Time to get across to the other tower," he said.

al sat behind the huge crossbow as the *Heron* headed toward the shore once again. He leaned back, forcing himself to relax, watching the regular rise and fall of the bow as each wave passed under the ship, attuning himself to the rhythm and timing of the movement. He estimated that they were around two hundred and fifty meters from the tower. He could see the small figures lining the balustrade, waiting until the *Heron* came in range.

Then a thought struck him.

The Mangler had a range of over three hundred meters. Of course, range was only one factor. Accuracy was another matter. On the rising and falling bow of a moving ship, Hal had found that he needed to be a hundred meters or less from his target to have any chance of hitting it. But that was a target that was a meter square. He was looking at the platform itself, a boxlike structure some six meters long and three meters high, perched on top of the wooden framework. He could hit a target that size easily from two hundred meters, he thought. The shots would be random. He wouldn't be able to place them precisely, but he'd already seen how deadly the pine splinters could be. And the sudden arrival of a meter-long bolt slamming into the woodwork would play havoc with the defenders' nerves. He turned quickly to Ingvar.

"Cock it and load a normal bolt, Ingvar. Let's give them something to think about while we're heading in."

Ingvar looked puzzled for a moment, then he nodded. He reached for the twin levers and heaved the cord back until it clacked into place. Then he positioned a bolt in the groove.

"As soon as I shoot, load again," Hal said.

Ingvar nodded, then moved to the training lever behind the crossbow.

Hal bent over the sights. "Right . . . right. Left a little. Steady." The Mangler was now trained at the middle of the balustrade.

He put the range at a little more than two hundred meters. A splash in the water ahead of the boat confirmed it. The defenders were shooting but the ship was still out of arrow range.

He let the ship come up on a wave, watching the foresight, lining it up slightly above the two-hundred-meter mark. As the bow steadied for a moment on the crest of the wave, he tugged the trigger lanyard.

SLAM!

The Mangler bucked wildly and the bolt shot away. Instantly, Ingvar leapt forward and recocked the crossbow, dropping a bolt into place. Then he was back at the training lever as Hal directed him to bring the Mangler back on line.

As he did, Hal was winding the elevating cog, so that the target point was now a little below the two-hundred-meter mark on his rear sight. As before, he waited till the ship steadied momentarily, then shot.

SLAM!

As the second bolt streaked away, he saw the first shot hit in an explosion of splinters on the balustrade, just below the top of the railing and to the right of center. The defenders scattered from the spot in panic.

Then Ingvar reloaded and was training the weapon once more as Hal wound on the elevating wheel to bring the sights down.

The bolt he had just fired hit the target at that moment and he saw another shattering strike on the balustrade. This time, a large section of the top rail tore away and went spinning.

"Right . . . left a little. Steady . . ."

SLAM!

Another shot. He checked the range and saw they'd have no time for a fourth. But the salvo of three rapid shots had done their work, causing panic and confusion on the tower. He could even see several figures hurrying down the ladder underneath the platform.

"Light those fire bolts, Edvin," he called. He hadn't seen the third bolt strike but he thought it had been a good shot. He was sure it had hit somewhere. Now the defenders were creeping back to their positions. An arrow struck the bow post, quivering. Then two more rattled against the hull. Ingvar was recocking the Mangler and an arrow only just missed him.

"Thorn!" Hal yelled. Instantly, the ragged old sea wolf leapt to his feet behind the bow post. He had the two shields ready, and as Hal watched, Thorn performed one of the most amazing feats of skill and coordination the young skirl would ever see. Years later, surrounded by his grandchildren, he would speak of it in a voice hushed with wonder.

Thorn began to use the two metal shields to block or deflect arrows as they hissed toward the boat. He ignored the shots that were going wide, concentrating on those that were on line.

Left hand. Right hand. Left. Left. Right.

The two shields moved in a blur as he caught or punched or deflected arrows in rapid succession. It was obvious now why he had elected to use the smaller shields. He could never have moved a large, heavy shield with such dexterity and precision. His hand-eye coordination was simply amazing. His vision was superb. And his reactions were like lightning. The air was filled with the clang and rattle and whir of deflected or blocked arrows. Now, seeing this, Hal began to understand how this man had won the Maktig title for three years in succession—and why nobody else had done it, before or since.

"He's incredible," Lydia said quietly, from close beside him. Occupied as he was, Thorn heard her and had time to respond.

"That green-shirted nuisance is back again. Stop gawking, girl, and take care of him."

Clang, whirr, clack, rattle. Four more arrows were deflected. Lydia, galvanized by Thorn's jibe, drew a dart from her quiver and hooked it to her atlatl. Sheltered by the mast, she watched for the green-shirted archer, seeing him appear at his old position, on the far left of the platform. He drew, aimed, shot, then stepped back around the guardhouse into cover.

Lydia began counting aloud.

"One, two, three, four."

A fraction after "four," the archer stepped back out again, raised the bow, shot again, then stepped back into cover.

"One, two," counted Lydia and on the count of "two," she stepped clear of the mast, her right arm going back, her left foot forward. As Thorn flicked the arrow into the sea with his left shield, she hurled the dart at the spot where the archer had been, in one fluid, powerful action.

". . . three, four . . ." She continued the count without missing a beat.

As she said "four," the green-shirted man reappeared, arrow nocked, bow half drawn—

And stepped straight into the plummeting dart she had just thrown.

He threw up his hands, the bow went spinning away and he reeled, then toppled over the railing, hitting the support framework several times as he fell.

"That's sensational!" Hal screamed, his voice cracking with excitement. The rest of the crew cheered. Thorn continued to deflect arrows in the bow, but he called without taking his eyes off the incoming missiles.

"Not bad. Told you she was a keeper, didn't I?"

"Just keep your mind on your own job, old man!" Lydia replied brusquely.

Thorn cackled with laughter.

Hal could hear Edvin hastily filling Ingvar in on what had happened, his words tumbling over themselves in his excitement. Ingvar finally put a hand on his shoulder.

"Tell me later. I take it she did well."

It was time. Hal turned and held up a hand to Ulf and Wulf. "Let go the sheets!"

They cast the sheets loose, letting the sail fly free. As the wind spilled from the sail, *Heron* began to slow. Ingvar and Edvin didn't need orders. Edvin had the first of the fire bolts burning and ready. He laid it in the trough on top of the Mangler, setting the notch onto the bowstring. Ingvar took control of the training lever once more.

"Get down, Thorn," Hal called. He lined the sight up, setting his aiming point between the one-hundred and the one-hundred-and-fifty marks.

"Come left. Come left. Left a little more. Steady . . ."

He could see the junction of the three beams in his sights now. *Heron* rose on a wave and he wound the elevating wheel down, keeping the foresight steady on the point where the three beams met. An arrow thudded into the deck near his foot. He made a mental note that the rate of return shots, and their accuracy, seemed to have decreased since Lydia had picked off the green-shirted archer. He guessed none of the fallen man's comrades were willing to show themselves above the railing for too long.

"Right a little," he said. Ingvar eased him to the right. The sights were on. He pulled the lanyard.

SLAM!

The moment the bolt streaked away, he knew he'd missed his target. He hadn't allowed enough for the slight delay between pulling the lanyard and the crossbow releasing. The thin gray trail of smoke sizzled through the air, passing just under the intersection of the three beams.

There was a groan of disappointment from the crew. Already,

Ingvar had leapt forward and heaved the cocking levers back, re-setting the bow for another shot. Edvin, on his knees beside the bow, reached up and placed the second fire bolt in the trough. Wisps of smoke rose from it, and steam sizzled from the wet wood of the bow.

"Missed," Hal said, for Ingvar's benefit.

The big boy grunted. "Hit it this time."

Hal leaned to the sights. He frowned. The bow was dropping off to starboard as the ship tried to turn up into the wind.

"Stig!" Hal called. "Keep her straight, for pity's sake!"

He heard Stefan repeat the order, heard Stig call an order to Wulf. There was a rattle of wood on wood as Wulf placed an oar in the rowlocks, ran it out and backed water several times. The bow swung back, away from the wind.

Hal wound the elevation wheel again, watching the sight rising past the target. He was a little off line.

"Right . . . right . . . stop!"

He took a deep breath. He reasoned that the three rapid-fire shots, aimed at a much larger target, had affected his timing. He hadn't needed the same precision. He forced himself to concentrate fiercely. The bow sank, then started to rise again.

Behind him, he heard a sharp cry of pain. Ingvar, he realized, with a sense of shock. Then the deck planks vibrated under his feet as the big boy staggered and fell.

He spun round, saw Ingvar writhing on the deck, clutching at an arrow that was protruding from his left side, close to the hip.

"Ingvar's been hit!" Hal heard Edvin's anguished cry and started to rise, then stopped as he heard Stig order Stefan to tend to the fallen giant. Hal was torn between his concern for Ingvar and the need to get the last shot away while the Mangler was still roughly on line. Without Ingvar, he wouldn't have a chance to re-load for a second shot. Deliberately, he forced the image of the wounded boy from his mind, hating himself as he did so. He yelled to Thorn.

"Thorn! Take the training lever!"

The old sea wolf nodded and leapt down from his position in the bow, moving quickly to take control of the training lever. Again the image of Ingvar's writhing body came to Hal's mind and again he pushed it away. He could hear Stefan speaking to him, and he reasoned that Ingvar must still be conscious. And that meant he was still alive—for the moment.

Thorn seemed to sense the torment in Hal's mind.

"Stefan's got him. Get on with your own job," he said harshly.

Hal nodded, realizing that his old friend was right. He bent over the sights again.

"Right . . . right . . . a little more . . . steady."

The Mangler was back on line. He watched the sights fall below the target, felt the gentle thump through the hull as the ship reached the trough between the waves.

Take your time, he thought. Don't rush. Make it count. Get it right for Ingvar's sake.

Then the bow was rising, and the sight was coming up to the target. He wound the elevator wheel down until the bead sight was a fraction below the junction of beams, then pulled the lanyard.

A brief pause, then . . . *SLAM!*

As the huge crossbow released and the fire bolt leapt away, he saw that the sight was dead on target.

He watched the thin trail of gray smoke curving across the intervening space, saw the bolt strike home into the diagonal beam, a little to the right of the junction point, and lodge there. A second later, he saw a bright flare of flame.

"Sheet home!" he yelled. "Get us out of here!"

Ulf and Wulf hauled the sail in again and the wind began to power the ship once more. Stig heaved on the tiller and the bow swung away from the tower, across the harbor mouth, and finally headed back out to sea.

A final volley of three arrows rattled off the shields along the bulwark. Then they were out of range.

On the tower platform, the commander watched the last two projectiles fly low. For a moment, he thought they'd both missed, then he felt the thud of the second striking home somewhere down on the framework.

Still, it couldn't hurt them down there, he thought. The three rapid shots that preceded them had been a different matter altogether. They'd wreaked havoc on the platform, smashing and splintering the railing and cutting down five of his men.

"Save your arrows," he called. The neat little ship had filled her sail once more, turned on her heel and headed back out to sea.

He studied the balustrade, taking in the jagged holes and long rents that had been torn in the soft wood. It had never been built to take such a pounding. When the ship turned back again, as he knew it would, he'd move his men inside the guardroom, and have most of them lie down. He'd leave a few bowmen out on the . . .

He stopped, sniffing the air. He could smell wood smoke.

With a feeling of growing concern, he leaned over the shattered balustrade, peering down at the supporting framework of timber. Ten meters below the platform, flames were beginning to lick at the timber. As the heat caused the resin to ooze out of the grain, it flared and fed the flames, so that they burned more fiercely.

He'd seen the fate of the other watchtower. They all had. The dry pine burned fiercely and they had no way to extinguish it. Now the supporting timbers below him were on fire and he knew it was only a matter of time before the guardhouse and platform would go crashing to the ground below. He turned to his men and shouted a warning.

"The tower's on fire!"

He looked around desperately, and saw movement on the opposite harbor mole. There was a large party of Skandians massing there, at the far end of the boom. As he watched, one of them lowered himself down onto the massive log and began to edge his way across, moving faster as he gained confidence.

Another followed him. Then another.

"Get out of here!" the commander yelled. "Get down before the whole thing collapses."

And, having sounded the alarm, he led the rush to the ladder.

As soon as they were out of range, Hal gave the order to heave to. Ulf and Wulf let the sheets fly while Stig brought the ship up into the wind.

Hal leapt from the Mangler's seat. A concerned group was clustered round the prone figure of Ingvar.

"Edvin!" Hal shouted. "Get the healer's kit."

"Already here," Edvin's quiet voice replied, right behind him. During brotherband training, one member from each team had been nominated to train as an emergency healer, learning about the various herbs and potions that eased pain, fought infection and facilitated healing. Edvin had been the Herons' nominee for this task.

"Give me some room," Edvin ordered, pushing through to kneel beside Ingvar. The group surrounding them shuffled back a few paces.

The arrow had hit Ingvar in the fleshy part of his body above his right hip and had passed through so that the barbed end protruded at the back. The exit wound was bleeding heavily and the deck was stained with Ingvar's blood. Stefan hadn't been sure what to do. He had eased Ingvar over onto his left side, where he lay, eyes tight closed, trying not to groan with the pain.

Edvin appraised the situation.

"Can't pull it out," he said. "I'll have to break it off and push it through."

Hal nodded. If Edvin tried to withdraw the arrow, the barbed head would catch and tear Ingvar terribly. Better to have him suffer one brief moment of pain and get it out.

"Do it," he said.

Edvin gripped the arrow shaft below the feathered end, a few inches from Ingvar's body. He took it in his right hand to prevent as much movement as possible, then quickly snapped it off with his left. He held the arrow as firmly as he could, but some movement was inevitable and Ingvar cried out with the pain, trying to sit up.

"Hold him down," Edvin said to Wulf. But Wulf grabbed Edvin's shoulder.

"You're hurting him! Stop it! You're supposed to help him!" he shouted.

Edvin looked at him, then up at Hal. Hal could see the beginnings of panic in his eyes. It was all very well to practice on mock wounds, but to work on a shipmate who was writhing in pain was a different matter altogether. And it certainly didn't help his concentration to have Wulf shouting objections to the way he was treating Ingvar.

"Shut up, Wulf," Thorn snapped, from behind Hal. "Edvin's doing what he has to. And he's doing a good job. While you're screeching and yelling, you're stopping him from helping Ingvar. Now hold Ingvar still."

The words seemed to reassure Edvin, and Hal saw the small light of panic in his eyes subside. He nodded encouragement to the healer.

Wulf dropped his eyes. "Sorry," he muttered. "Go ahead." He leaned over and put his hands on Ingvar's shoulders to keep him still.

Edvin bent close to Ingvar. "This is going to hurt," he said quietly. "I'm sorry. But I'll be as quick as I can."

Ingvar nodded, his teeth gritted and his eyes closed.

"Just do it," he said. "I'm ready."

Edvin took a deep breath, seized hold of the bloodied shaft below the head of the arrow and pulled, in one long, firm movement. He was surprised at the amount of resistance he had to overcome but the arrow shaft slid through the wound and out the other side. Ingvar let out a long, shuddering cry of pain. Then, as the arrow came free, he fell silent.

"Thanks," he said in a small voice, after a few seconds. Blood welled even more profusely out of the entry and exit holes. It was bright red, not dark in color, and Edvin hoped that signified that the arrow hadn't ripped through any of the internal organs, but now that the arrow wasn't impeding its flow, there was an awful lot of it. Edvin took a linen bandage and pressed it against the wound, trying to stem the blood flow. The bandage quickly turned red. Wulf, pale faced, released his grip on Ingvar and moved away.

Edvin bent down to speak to Ingvar again. "I've got to clean the wound out as much as I can, to stop infection setting in. I'm sorry, but I'm going to have to hurt you again."

Beads of sweat stood out on Ingvar's face. "Don't talk about it," he said. "Do it as quickly as you can."

Edvin took a thin metal probe from the healer's kit and wrapped a clean linen cloth around it. Then he doused the cloth liberally with a salve from one of the jars in the kit.

"This will clean out the wound," he said. "But I've got to work it inside the wound itself. It's no good just cleaning it at either end." He smeared more paste from another jar onto the cloth at the tip of the probe. "It's a painkiller. It'll numb the wound while I clean it out." He glanced apologetically at Ingvar. "Although not completely, I'm afraid. It's still going to hurt."

"Just get on with it!" Ingvar told him, with a flash of anger.

Hal knelt beside Ingvar and gripped his hand. "Steady, Ingvar. Edvin's doing all he can."

Ingvar looked up at him, and Hal, seeing the concern in his eyes, realized that the ordeal of waiting for the pain was probably worse than the pain itself.

"Just tell him to stop talking about it," Ingvar said.

Hal looked up at Edvin. "You might as well go ahead."

Edvin nodded. He paused, took several deep breaths, then put the fingers of his left hand on the entry wound, parting the edges while he slid the probe into the opening.

Hal felt his stomach heave and looked away hurriedly. His gaze traveled around the circle of pale, concerned faces.

"Get back to your stations! Standing around rubbernecking isn't helping," he ordered. The spectators, a trifle shamefaced, shuffled away. Hal met Ingvar's eyes once more, seeing the pain reflected in them. Ingvar's lips moved. The young skirl bent down to hear what he was trying to say.

"Sorry, Hal," Ingvar whispered, fighting back the pain that was flaring through his body. Hal's eyes misted as he took his friend's hand.

"I'm the one who should apologize," he said. "I waited too long to shoot."

Ingvar shook his head, and even that small movement caused his brow to furrow with pain.

"You had to make sure," he said. Then his eyes closed, as if the effort of speaking had been too much for him, and he slipped away—either unconscious or asleep. His breathing was short and fitful and he tossed his head from side to side, muttering incoherently. Hal gently released his hand and looked up at Edvin.

"Will he be all right?" he asked.

Edvin hesitated, looking quickly to see if Ingvar was conscious again. He didn't say anything for a few minutes. While Hal and Ingvar had been speaking, he had packed the entry and exit wounds with clean linen and was winding a bandage around Ingvar's body to hold the pads in place. When he finished, he rose and drew Hal to one side, where Ingvar wouldn't hear him.

"I just don't know, Hal. I've cleaned the wound as well as I can and I've bandaged him. That's stopped the blood flow pretty well. But he's lost an awful lot of blood and that's got to have weakened him."

"Is there anything more we can do for him?"

Edvin responded with an uncertain gesture. "I'm doing all I

can. But I don't know if it's enough. I only had a few weeks' training, you know."

The last few words were added almost defensively. Hal reached out and touched the other boy's arm. He realized the weight of responsibility that Edvin must be feeling.

"I know," he said. "You're doing fine."

He wished his voice could have carried more conviction. He became aware of another figure beside them. With the ship no longer in motion, Stig had lashed the tiller and come forward to join them. He looked down at Ingvar's prone figure, taking in the unnaturally pale face.

"Is he going to be all right?"

Hal shook his head uncertainly. "He's sleeping. The arrow went through and Edvin's got it out. He's cleaned and bandaged the wound. All we can do now is let Ingvar rest." He shrugged. "Ask us again in twelve hours."

Stig nodded. "In twelve hours, none of us might be around."

"That's true."

"So, what do we do now?" Stig asked.

Hal looked away. Truth be told, he had no idea. They still had to attack the beach gate and set the oil bladder on fire. But with Ingvar out of action, he had no idea how to go about it. None of the other crew members had the strength to load the giant crossbow. Thorn might have managed it, but it was a two-handed task and the artificial hand was a weak point. The retaining straps on his wooden hook wouldn't take the strain of heaving back on the cocking handle.

"Hal?" Stig said.

Hal rounded on him angrily. "I don't know!" he said. "Let me think for a minute!"

He moved away to the railing. Stig went to move after him, then thought better of it. Hal gripped the railing, his hands clenching and unclenching. He stared blindly out at the water around them, but he saw only Ingvar's unconscious form, lying on the deck.

He became conscious that someone had moved to stand beside him.

"Your crew are waiting for orders," Thorn said quietly. Hal continued to look out at the sea.

"My orders?" he said bitterly. "My orders may well have killed Ingvar."

"Nevertheless, standing here feeling sorry for yourself won't help him." Thorn's voice was quiet and unemotional. Hal turned to face him.

"How can you be so cold about it?" he asked. "It's Ingvar we're talking about—big, faithful Ingvar, who would do anything I asked him."

Thorn met his eyes with an unwavering gaze. "This is war, Hal. Did you seriously think you could go through a battle without somebody being hurt—or even killed?"

Hal went to speak, looked away, then said in a low voice, "I didn't think about it."

"This is not brotherband training, where you might get a few bruises or scrapes. This is the real thing. People get hurt. They die. And if you're their leader, sometimes it happens because they do what you tell them to do. You have to face that."

Hal shook his head vehemently. "I don't want to face it."

"You have to." Thorn's voice was low, but insistent. "If you simply give up now, Ingvar will have been hurt, maybe killed, for no good reason." He paused for a few seconds to let that thought sink in. Then he continued.

"You're a thinker, Hal. A planner. And sometimes in battle, a plan can go wrong. So you have to rethink and replan. We have to attack that gate and you have to rethink your plan for doing it. Now get on with it."

Hal turned then to look at him again. He saw determination in Thorn's face. And encouragement. He saw no trace of condemnation. He took a deep breath.

"All right. Give me a minute or two."

Thorn nodded, satisfied. Hal gripped the railing again, thinking through the resources he had at his disposal. No one person could load the Mangler with Ingvar injured. Stig and Thorn were the next two strongest members of the crew, but he needed Stig on the tiller and Thorn's false arm was suspect.

Ulf and Wulf, he decided and, as he had the thought, he felt a sense of renewed purpose. He turned from the railing and realized that every member of the crew was watching him, waiting for his orders.

"Gather round," he said, beckoning them into a half circle. "Change of plans. Ulf and Wulf, you're going to have to cock the Mangler, all right?"

The twins nodded and he gestured at the massive weapon.

"Let's see you do it," he said. They all moved forward and the twins took position on either side of the crossbow. He had half expected them to argue over who took which side. To his surprise, they didn't. Each of them seized a cocking handle in a two-handed grip. They looked at each other and, with an unspoken communication, both heaved back on the levers together, grunting with the strain. The bowstring clacked into place over its retaining latch.

Ulf looked at his brother, then at Ingvar's still form. "How did he manage that by himself?" he asked.

"I was just thinking the same thing," Wulf said, shrugging.

"Good work," Hal said. "I want you to sling your shields over your shoulders when you're doing it. That'll give you some protection from any archers onshore. Thorn, you'll have to take over the training lever."

Thorn nodded and Hal went on quickly.

"Jesper. You stay with raising and lowering the sails. Get one of the Limmatans to help you."

"Yes, skirl," Jesper replied.

One of the four Limmatans stepped forward and raised a hand. He was a well-built, muscular man.

"I can do that, captain," he said.

Hal nodded briefly at him, then shifted his gaze to Stefan. "Stefan, can you trim the sails?"

Stefan replied without any hesitation, "Yes, Hal."

"Get one of the Limmatans to help you as well," Hal continued. "Stig, you're on the tiller, of course."

"Right," said Stig.

"Edvin, get Ingvar as comfortable as possible. Then you'll take charge of loading the fire bolts."

"I'll pack some bedrolls and shields around Ingvar to protect him," Edvin said, and Hal nodded gratefully.

"Good idea." He hesitated, wondering if he'd forgotten anything, then found himself facing Lydia. "Lydia, with Thorn training the Mangler for me, it'll be up to you to keep any archers busy."

"That won't be a problem," she said.

Thorn let out a bark of laughter. "Shouldn't think so!" he said. "She's a regular terror with those overgrown darts of hers."

Lydia looked at him coldly. "You do your job, old man," she said. "I'll take care of my end of things."

Thorn snickered again, and she shook her head, looking away to check the remaining darts in her quiver.

Hal looked around the ship. He couldn't think of anything further to say. He glanced once more at Ingvar, hoping to see the big boy's eyes open. But he was still unconscious, breathing fitfully, shuddering from time to time as pain broke through the barrier of painkillers he'd been given.

Reluctantly, he tore his gaze away. You'll have to forget him for the time being, he thought. Then he clapped his hands together decisively.

"Right! Let's get under way. We've got a gate to burn!"

They hurried to their new stations. Stefan and one of the Limmatans hauled the sail in, so that it hardened to the wind. Stig heaved on the tiller and the *Heron* began to move once more, cutting through the water as they headed for the beach gate, swooping up and over each successive wave.

Hal took a final look at the two watchtowers. The guardhouse and platform on the western tower had collapsed in a shower of sparks and flame. The supporting framework was still pretty much intact, but now there was nothing on top of it.

On the eastern side, it was a different story. The fire had taken hold and had burned through the support structure at the point where Hal's bolt had struck it. The upper platform now leaned crazily to one side as that corner of the framework gave way. It looked as if a strong wind would send the whole thing tumbling. On the ground below, he could see men fighting, and others running along the harbor front toward the town.

Svengal and his men had crossed the boom, Hal thought. The attack was going well.

Now it was time to give them a hand.

Hal stood beside Stig as they made the short trip to the beach gate. Then he went forward to take his place behind the Mangler. He could see men on the palisade above the gate. Occasionally, the sun glinted off their weapons and armor. But there was only a handful of men visible. The greatest number of the pirates had been stationed in the watchtowers, and they were now retreating down the quay, pursued by Svengal and his Skandians. Other defenders had been drawn off by Barat's men as they had surged over the palisade and into the town. The invaders' numbers were being stretched by the multiple points of attack and there were precious few available to defend the beach gate—which had largely been forgotten in the afternoon's confusion.

Two of the defenders had bows and they began to shoot, sending arrows hissing into the water and clattering against the bow post and shields once more. They weren't very good shots, but one of them might get lucky and Hal couldn't afford any more casualties.

"Lydia?" he said. "Can you take care of them?"

She nodded as she studied the situation through narrowed eyes. The shooters weren't bothering to conceal themselves. So far, they had experienced no return shots from the ship and they were a little cocky, she thought. It occurred to her that they probably hadn't witnessed the *Heron's* attack on the watchtowers and had no idea of the danger they were in.

She selected a dart, checking to see how many she had remaining. She'd made extra for today's engagement and now she had sixteen left. She fitted the dart to the atlatl, stepped clear of the mast, sighted and threw. As soon as the dart was on its way, she slipped a second from her quiver, fitted it onto the thrower and sent it whipping after the first.

The advantage of the atlatl was that it was difficult to see what the thrower was doing. An archer was more obvious, as his bow could be clearly seen. But the thin darts and relatively small throwing handle couldn't be easily distinguished from a distance. The first the Magyarans knew about it, one of their archers went reeling back from the wooden parapet, transfixed by a razor-sharp dart that seemed to come out of nowhere. A few seconds later, his fellow archer suffered the same fate. The men around them hurriedly ducked below the parapet, out of sight.

Hal had been studying the gate and he noted with relief that the bulging oil bladder was still in position. The thought that it might have been discovered and removed had been preying on his mind all day.

"Get one of the fire bolts ready, Edvin," he said. Now that Ingvar was settled, Edvin had returned to his station by the Mangler. He busied himself with the tinderbox, and in a minute or so Hal could smell the acrid smoke from the burning fire head.

The Mangler was already cocked. Edvin soaked the front section of the bow once more, then placed the smoldering bolt in the loading groove. The flames hissed against the damp wood, sending steam wisping into the air.

Hal frowned as he stared down the sights. Although *Heron* was stationary, she was rising and falling gently on the swell. For the first time, he realized how small a target the oilskin was. It was a simple pig's bladder, filled with oil, and it was considerably smaller than the meter-square targets he had practiced on. He frowned, wondering if he could hit it.

"One way to find out," he said. He bent forward, intent on the sighting picture. Thorn stood ready with the training lever.

"Left . . . Left . . . left just a little . . . hold it . . ."

He waited for the bow to rise on the swell, taking the foresight up with them. Just before they reached the top of the rise and settled on the oilskin, he tugged the lanyard.

SLAM!

He sat back, watching the now-familiar trail of gray smoke. The shot looked good, but he was off by about half a meter to the left.

He frowned. He had only two fire bolts left. He drummed his fingers nervously on the carriage of the crossbow, thinking furiously. They'd have to go closer. But any minute, the Magyarans might find more archers to man the palisade. Lydia touched him lightly on the arm and he looked up at her.

"Well," she said, "now that we've seen you can actually hit the equivalent of a barn door with that overgrown crossbow, could I make a suggestion?"

"Please go ahead," he said. She drew another dart from her quiver and set the back end into the hook on her atlatl.

"Why don't I split the oilskin for you? The oil will gush out and all you have to do is hit the gate somewhere below it. Even you should be able to do that." She added the last with no hint of a smile.

He considered the idea. All this time, he'd been thinking that he'd have to hit the oilskin with a burning projectile. But she was right. If she punctured it and the oil flooded down the gate, a fire bolt anywhere would set it aflame. He gestured toward the distant gate.

"Go right ahead. Just wait till I give you the word," he said. She smiled briefly at him. He turned to the twins and Edvin.

"Load another fire bolt," he said.

Once more, Ulf and Wulf wrestled with the cocking levers to set the bowstring. Edvin placed another smoldering fire bolt into the groove. Then, directing Thorn on the training lever, Hal lined the Mangler up on the gate below the oilskin. He leaned back and looked up at the slim girl, standing ready with the dart in her hand.

"Now," he said. She nodded, and her arm went back, then forward. The dart sailed away. He lost sight of it against the sky and looked instead at the oil bladder hanging near the top of the gate.

He saw the dart almost immediately as it curved in and punctured the bladder. A jet of oil started coursing out down the gate. He could see the dark stain against the weathered gray timber.

"Blast. I hoped to split it wide-open," Lydia muttered, reaching for a second dart. As Hal leaned down and adjusted his sights, she prepared for a second throw.

SLAM!

The fire bolt arced away, thudding into the gate below the oil bladder, but just to one side of the stream of oil running down the timber. Lydia cast again, grunting with extra effort this time. Again, Hal lost sight of the dart as it flew and focused instead on the gate. He saw a flicker of movement as the dart smacked into the oilskin. The bladder, weakened now in two places, ruptured completely between the two points and the rest of the oil poured out in a flood, reaching the burning bolt fastened in the wood and the dry kindling below.

There was a brief pause, then a sheet of flame engulfed the gate.

Barat led his men at a steady jog through the twisting, maze-like back streets toward the town center. The half-dozen escapees who had made their way to the swamps in the past few days had reported that Zavac and his henchmen had taken over the counting house, a sprawling, two-story building that took up most of one side of the town square.

Barat and his force were in the older part of the town, where the streets were winding and haphazard, without any semblance of logic or order. Twice now they had run into resistance, at points where the Magyarans had hastily thrown barricades across the narrow street and attempted to throw their attackers back.

But the Limmatan attackers had a significant advantage over the Magyarans. They had been born and raised in this town and they knew the intricate side streets and alleys like the backs of their hands. As they came to each barricade, parties would split off to the left and right, following twisting alleys and paths so narrow that at times their shoulders brushed the walls of buildings either side. Then they would emerge behind the barricade, taking the surprised Magyarans in the rear while Barat and the rest of the force assaulted them from the front.

With each of these encounters, the pirates' numbers shrank as the defenders were scattered. Some managed to withdraw to the next defensive position but others took to their heels, abandoning the fight and searching for hiding places in the cellars and attics of the houses.

In the counting house, Zavac looked up as yet another messenger arrived, this time from the eastern gate.

"We need more men!" he shouted. "That ship has sailed around to the beach, and they've set fire to the beach gate."

Zavac uttered a curse. The strange, innocuous-looking ship, with a crew of less than a dozen men, had battered the two tower strong points into smoldering wreckage with some kind of infernal weapon mounted in its bow.

Zavac glared at the man. "Who's in command on the palisade?"

"Petrac," the messenger told him. "He says we need more men. Particularly archers—as many as you can spare. He's convinced they'll be attacking soon."

Zavac thought furiously. Reports had been coming in to the counting house over the past hour, and as he heard this latest one, he realized how seriously he had underestimated the threat to his position.

With the watchtowers reduced to smoldering wreckage, a band of Skandians had emerged from the marshes, crossed the boom and were pressing hard from the harbor side of town. A Limmatan force had stormed the eastern palisade unopposed, while he had sent men to belatedly cope with the Skandians. Now he was being squeezed between the two forces, and it seemed that a third was preparing to join the battle.

Most of those killed in the fight for the towers were from the *Stingray*'s crew. But six of his own men had been lost there as well. He'd sent a dozen back to the *Raven* to make sure she was safe. The rest of them were gathered here at the counting house, while the crews of the *Viper* and *Stingray* fought a series of delaying actions at the harbor front and in the town itself.

Finally, he appeared to come to a decision. He nodded several times, studying a map of the town, tracing the path back to the beach gate with his forefinger.

"Very well," he said firmly. "Get back to Petrac. Tell him I'm sending twenty men—and as many archers as I can get together. Just tell him to hold out until they get there."

The messenger nodded gratefully and headed for the door, breaking into a run as he reached the town square outside.

Andras stepped forward, a frown on his face.

"Are you mad?" he said. "Twenty men? That's nearly half the men we have left!"

Zavac looked around, checking that the messenger had gone, and shook his head. "I'm sending nobody," he told his second in command. "But if Petrac knows that, he'll fold like an empty coat. Get the men together. But do it quietly. We're heading back to the *Raven* and getting out of here."

In truth, there was no reason for him to stay any longer. They hadn't conquered Limmat in order to occupy it permanently. They were staying here for as long as it took to bleed the maximum amount of treasure out of the emerald mine. Now it was time to take the considerable amount they had already and fade away.

And if that meant leaving their allies from *Stingray* and *Viper* to cover their backs while he made his escape, so be it.

Andras left the inner room Zavac was using as an office. He went to one of the larger central halls in the counting house, where the *Raven's* men were awaiting orders. The room was virtually bare of furniture. In normal times, it was used for assemblies, ceremonies and public audiences. On the far side of the room, ten men from *Stingray* were gathered together, including the ship's first mate, Rikard. He was in command of the *Stingray* now. Her captain had been in the east watchtower when it burned and collapsed. The two pirate crews might be working in collaboration, Andras thought, but there was little love lost between them.

Rikard looked up now and strolled across the hall as Andras began to gather his men together.

"What's happening?" he asked. Andras jerked a thumb in the general direction of the beach gate.

"Message from Petrac. There's an attack massing at the east gate and he's asked for reinforcements. We're going to sort things out. Care to join us?"

He had no doubt that Rikard would refuse the suggestion.

"Might be better if we kept an eye on things here," Rikard said evasively. "Just in case we're needed."

Andras pretended to consider this point, then nodded. "Maybe that's best," he said eventually. "We'll see you later."

Rikard nodded. Once Andras and the *Raven's* crew members

left, he thought, he'd give them time to get clear. Then he and his men would head for the *Stingray*, moored against the quay in the inner harbor. Let *Raven*'s crew do the fighting, he thought. They could keep the enemy occupied while *Stingray* slipped away. His only regret was that his missing captain had never told him where he was hiding *Stingray*'s share of the emeralds. Still, they'd taken plenty of other booty when they captured the town. It would be enough to escape with that—and his skin.

Rikard waved in farewell as the other crew trooped out behind Andras.

Zavac, who had left by a back exit, was waiting for his men in a side alley that led toward the quay. He had a heavy sack slung over his shoulder. Andras pointed to it.

"Is that what I think it is?" he asked.

Zavac smiled fiercely. "Emeralds," he said. "We'll keep them safe for the others."

Andras nodded. "Of course. Good thinking. Be a shame to let the Limmatans get them back."

Both of them knew that the crews of the *Viper* and the *Stingray* had no chance of seeing any share of the precious stones. They could keep the attacking Skandians and Limmatans at bay while Zavac and his crew escaped in the *Raven*. Zavac studied the faces of his men for a few seconds, then selected one who had been with him for several raiding seasons. He was a man who had proved to be dependable on several occasions in the past.

"Zoltan," he said, "make your way through the alleys to the mole and cut the cable on the boom. And burn the *Viper*," he added, as an afterthought. No sense in leaving a ship behind for his enemies. "Go south initially and you'll avoid the Skandians. Then cut back west. We'll pick you up as we head out. Stay on the mole and wait for us."

The man nodded. "Aye aye, Zavac," he said. He hitched his sword belt up, turned away and ran south, into the maze of alleys and cross streets that led off the square.

"The rest of you follow me," Zavac said.

There were several relatively broad thoroughfares leading from the square to the harbor but he chose to ignore them. Any minute now, a horde of Skandians could come yelling down one of them. Instead, he led his men through the back alleys, his innate sense of direction keeping them heading toward the harbor, no matter how the streets twisted and turned.

They eventually emerged onto the quay a few meters from where *Stingray* was moored. Zavac peered out cautiously. There were several Skandians in sight, but the nearest was forty meters away. Others, seeing the quay was now swept clear of enemies—who had either died or withdrawn—had plunged into the network of streets and headed for the town center.

There were three men left on board *Stingray* to keep an eye on things. Zavac jerked his thumb at them and spoke quietly to Andras.

"Kill them. Then burn the ship."

The flames, which had burned so fiercely, were finally dying down on the gate. A thick column of greasy smoke hung in the sky. Above the blackened gate, the defenders clustered, looking down anxiously to gauge the extent of the damage.

Heron still rode the waves some hundred meters off the beach. Hal had called a council of war and his crew had moved forward and crouched round him.

"Ulf, Wulf," Hal said quietly. "Have you got the battering ram?"

The previous day, Ingvar had found a driftwood log on the beach and fashioned a ram from it, fitting rope handles so he could swing it into the burned timbers of the gate. Now the twins would be wielding it in his place.

"It's ready, Hal," Ulf told him.

Hal looked at them. "There's bound to be a locking bar of some kind on the gate. The fire won't have burned through it completely, but it will have weakened it. A few good thumps with the ram should finish the job."

Ulf and Wulf exchanged a glance and both nodded at the same moment. Hal turned his attention back to the gate.

So far, there had been no sign of archers on the palisade. But that could change at any minute. Hal glanced round and caught Lydia's eye.

"Stay back and cover us while we head up the beach. Once we're there, we'll probably have their full attention, so you can join us."

She nodded, licking her lips nervously, then glanced up and saw Thorn grinning at her. She scowled. She didn't want him thinking she was afraid.

Hal was speaking to the twins once more.

"Once you've broken through, move to either side. Thorn will be leading the attack through the gate. Stig and I will be with him. You two come after us. Lydia, find a vantage point once we've broken through and pick off any of the enemy who seem to be causing trouble."

Lydia pretended to examine the sharpened iron point on one of her darts. She had been concerned that Hal would try to keep her out of the battle. His plan made sense. She had no pretensions about her ability to take on any of the pirates in hand-to-hand combat. They were stronger than she was, and more skilled in close-quarter fighting. This plan made the best use of her principal skill—her uncanny accuracy with the atlatl and its darts.

"What about Ingvar?" Ulf asked. "Are we just going to leave him?"

"I'll stay with him," Edvin said immediately. But Hal shook his head. Thorn had often impressed on him the fact that speedy treatment of battle injuries gave the injured man a better chance of survival.

"I want you with us in case someone's injured. Stefan, you can stay behind and keep an eye on Ingvar."

It was a good compromise. Aside from Edvin, Stefan was the least skillful with weapons. He was the one they could best spare from the coming fight. As he realized that he'd be two men short, Hal breathed a sigh of thanks for the presence of the Limmatan warriors. That would help even the odds against them.

"I'll keep shooting as we go in. That should keep their heads down." He looked at Ulf, Wulf and Edvin. "Keep loading as fast as you can. Thorn," he said, and the burly one-armed man looked up at him. He was occupied changing his false arm—replacing the grasping hook with the massive, studded war club. "Once we're on the beach, you lead. You're the battle commander."

He looked round the circle of faces, some anxious, some eager to fight.

"Do you all hear that? Thorn's in charge once we're off the ship. Follow him. Do as he commands. All right?"

There was a mutter of acknowledgment.

Thorn pulled the restraining strap tight across his forearm and looked around at his troops.

"When the twins have knocked the gate down—or what's left of it—we move fast. I'll lead, Hal on my left and Stig on my right. We'll form a wedge. The rest of you, get behind us and widen it out as we drive through the enemy. Remember what I've taught you about not over-hitting. Odds are the ground underfoot will be tricky, so stay in balance."

He paused expectantly. After a brief interval, there was an affirmative growl from the assembled crew. They were all watching him intently, wondering if they'd forgotten something vital, wondering how they would acquit themselves in this, their first battle.

Thorn sensed their uncertainty and smiled at them.

"You'll do fine," he said. "Just remember what I've taught you. I've done this hundreds of times. There's nothing to it. Just keep your head, and follow my lead."

He looked around, saw a measure of confidence returning to their faces and grinned reassuringly.

"Any time you're ready, skirl," he said to Hal.

They're coming!"

Petrac, the Magyaran commander at the beach gate, yelled the warning. Not that there was any real need to do so. Every eye on the palisade was fixed on the little ship lying off the beach. She had been hove to and drifting for some minutes, presumably while her crew conferred. Now he saw the sail hauled in and she gathered speed and swung toward them.

Where are those archers Zavac promised, he thought bitterly. But in his heart, he already knew. They weren't coming. There were no archers. Zavac had tricked him and abandoned him.

A man he'd sent down to inspect the damage to the gate scrambled back onto the catwalk now.

"It's not good," he said in answer to Petrac's unspoken question. "The gate's badly burned. The timbers were dry and some were even rotten. Worst of all, the locking beam is pretty badly burned in the middle."

The locking beam was a solid timber bar that sat in brackets on either side of the gate to hold it closed. The oil and flames had spilled through the gap between the two halves of the gate and done serious damage to it. Petrac's face set in a worried frown.

"Maybe we should get down to the gate and get ready to hold them out," one of his men suggested. But Petrac shook his head.

"We're better up here for the moment. We'll try to keep them back—throw anything we've got. Spears, rocks, axes. When they get close, we'll get down to the—"

He was about to say "gate" but he was violently interrupted.

Something large and heavy smashed into the upright pine poles that formed the palisade. Splinters flew and the missile, whatever it was, cartwheeled end over end over the top of the wall, hitting one of his men and hurling him backward off the catwalk to the street below.

"Down! Down!" Petrac yelled, and threw himself flat on the planks of the catwalk. His men followed suit as another projectile smashed into the wall, a few meters to the left of the first. This one hit the small gap between two of the upright poles and penetrated for twenty centimeters before coming to rest. It sent more splinters flying, which wounded another man. Its sharpened point was reinforced with iron strips, Petrac saw.

He had little time to think about this any further as a third projectile hit the top of the palisade, smashing and splintering more poles, then cartwheeling high into the air before dropping to the ground below. This one caused no injuries, but the sound and the violence of the impact caused Petrac and his men to hug the ground even closer.

Now some semblance of reason returned to him. The projectiles were coming at intervals of about fifteen seconds. He signaled to one of his men.

"After the next one hits, get up and see where they are. You'll have about ten seconds before they can shoot again."

The man shook his head emphatically, refusing to meet Petrac's eyes.

"I'm not poking my head up to have it knocked off," he muttered. But the commander grabbed his sleeve and jerked on it, forcing the man to look at him.

"Do as I tell you," he snarled. "There's a gap between shots while they're reloading. You'll be perfectly safe."

Yet another bolt glanced off the wall and cartwheeled up and over with an eerie, whimpering sound.

"Now!" Petrac yelled, and the man, galvanized by fear of his leader, suddenly leapt to his feet to see how close the ship was.

"They're almost—" he began, then immediately reeled back, a sixty-centimeter-long dart buried in his chest. His eyes looked at Petrac, accusing him, for a second. Then he toppled off the catwalk and thudded to the street below. Shocked, Petrac hugged the ground a little closer. Having seen that, none of his men would be willing to show their faces above the palisade, he thought. He came to an abrupt decision.

"Down to the gate!" he yelled. "We'll stop them as they try to break through!"

Hal felt the *Heron*'s bow grate gently onto the sand of the beach.

"On your way!" he yelled. Already the crew members were spilling over the bulwarks and into the shallow water, running up the beach toward the gate. Thorn was one of the first to go.

"Fan out!" he ordered. "Don't group together!"

Ulf and Wulf carried the massive ram between them, stumbling in the soft sand under its weight. Lydia went over the rail half a second behind them, landing catlike on her feet and beginning to run for the gate almost immediately.

Hal had a final bolt loaded in the Mangler. He spread his feet either side of the carriage and traversed it by "walking" the weapon from side to side.

Thorn and the others were almost up to the gate now. Still there was no sign of anyone peering over the top of the palisade. Hal's hand clutched the trigger lanyard, ready to release the heavy bolt the moment he saw someone.

But there was nobody. Finally, seeing the twins and Lydia were nearly at the gate, he aimed at a random section of the palisade above the gate and released. The bolt streaked out. There was the usual splintering sound of wood and a cloud of sharp-edged fragments flew. Then, grabbing his shield, he slipped over the edge and dropped to the sand.

The soft sand grabbed at his ankles, hampering him, making him a perfect, slow-moving target for any archer who might be lurking on the catwalk. But there were none and he reached the relative safety of the gate overhang, puffing and panting, partly from the effort, but also from nervous tension.

"Glad you could join us," Thorn said. "Are you ready?"

Hal held up a hand, regaining his breath.

"Just . . . a . . . moment," he gasped. Then, after several deep breaths, he straightened and nodded.

"Ready," he said. His shoulders still heaved, but he was almost recovered. By the time Ulf and Wulf smashed in the gate, he'd be fine. Hal gestured at the gate.

"I imagine they're waiting for us," he said. "There's nobody on the wall now."

"I imagine you're right," Thorn replied. "And that'll be just too bad for them." He gestured to the twins, then to the gate. "All right, boys, away you go!"

Holding the ram by the looped rope handles on either side, the twins set their feet and began swinging it back and forth, gradually building momentum.

Thorn stepped lightly forward and pointed to the small gap between the gates, at a point about a meter and a half from the ground.

"Hit it about there," he said. Ulf and Wulf nodded, their brows furrowed with concentration. They gave one last backswing, then smashed the ram forward into the gate.

CRASH! The gate shuddered under the impact. But it held.

"Again," Thorn ordered calmly.

Once more, the twins swung the log back on the rope loops. This time they took three preparatory swings, then they smashed it forward, throwing all their weight behind it.

CRASH!

This time, the gap between the two gates widened visibly, and they heard a splintering sound from the far side.

"Again," Thorn said. The twins began their back-and-forth preparation. A surge of anticipation ran through the Herons and they involuntarily moved forward a pace.

"Steady," Thorn growled. "Hold your positions."

Hal, standing to his left and a little behind him, glanced up at him. The old warrior's face was calm and unexcited. He sensed

Hal's gaze on him, turned to meet the boy's eye, then winked slowly.

"Let 'em have it, boys," he ordered.

Ulf and Wulf hurled the ram forward in one last, lunging strike. There was a splintering, splitting sound from the other side, then the left-hand gate spun off its hinges, breaking free where the fire had charred it and weakened the wood. The ram smashed through the gate's locking at its midpoint. The two halves spun away. The right-hand gate gave as well, sagging on its hinges.

The twins, who had stumbled with the force of that final thrust, recovered and stepped to either side as Thorn advanced.

"Let's get 'em!" the grizzled sea wolf bellowed. The Herons cheered and followed him, stepping up onto the shattered pieces of timber and into the breach.

The Magyarans surged forward to stop them. Petrac was in the lead, sword drawn back, shield raised. He found himself facing a massively built Skandian, gray bearded and with shaggy hair caught up under a horned helmet. He had time to notice that the other attackers all seemed remarkably young, then noticed the massive studded club that had replaced the Skandian's right forearm and hand.

Thorn smashed the huge club down onto the Magyaran leader's shield, splintering it and splitting several of the pieces of wood that comprised it. The pirate staggered, then Thorn slammed the small metal shield into his unprotected midriff and he gasped and doubled over. A rib-cracking jab from the club finished him, sending him sprawling.

At Thorn's side, Hal caught a defender's spear thrust on his shield, slanting it so that the spear glanced off and the spearman, expecting to meet firmer resistance, stumbled forward, momentarily off balance.

Remembering Thorn's admonition—*a few inches of point can be just as deadly as the entire edge*—Hal jabbed quickly forward and saw the shock on the man's face as the sword penetrated his defense and slid between his ribs. Then Hal withdrew his sword and shoved the badly wounded man aside with his shield, stepping over him and forcing his way farther into the gap.

Behind him, Ulf shoved forward too, now armed with his ax and ready for battle. He was grim faced and determined, searching for a Magyaran defender. One of the pirates caught his eye and leapt forward, sword back for a violent slash. Ulf caught the blade on his shield, then swung his ax sideways. The hours of practice and instruction under Thorn's eagle eye stood him in good stead. The ax took the man in the ribs. He fell, with a strange, sobbing cry. Ulf, still in balance, withdrew his weapon and used it instantly to parry another Magyaran's sword. The pirate, hoping for an easy victory, blanched at the cold fury in the young Skandian's eyes. He stepped back, impeding one of his companions, who shoved him forward again. Off balance, he never saw Hal's lightning thrust coming at him from the side until it was too late.

On Thorn's right, Stig was a terrifying sight. The speed and power of his ax strokes sent the defenders reeling—much to Thorn's chagrin, as he'd marked down several of those who retreated as potential opponents. Stig's ax was a blinding circle of light as he wielded it. Thorn actually stopped for a moment to admire his young student's strength and dexterity. Stig hammered down one man's shield, then dispatched him with a whirling back-handed cut. Then he jabbed forward with the head of the ax, sending another lurching back.

"Not bad. Not bad at all," Thorn muttered, admiring the improvisation. Then he snarled as he saw movement out of the corner of his eye, casually deflected a Magyaran's cutlass with his small shield, then slammed the studded club-hand into the man's helmet.

Behind the advancing wedge, Lydia scrambled onto a pile of masonry that had torn loose with the gate. Her eyes scanned the struggling knot of men before her. At the rear of the pirates, she saw one man screaming orders and shoving others forward into the battle.

"No, you don't," she said quietly. She fitted a dart, drew back and cast. The would-be commander was on the point of shoving another pirate forward to face the whirling axes and jabbing swords of the attackers. The heavy dart hit him in the chest, slicing easily through his hardened leather breastplate, the force of its impact driving him backward before he fell.

Those around him saw him fall. Suddenly, they felt exposed. Then another dart took one of them in the upper arm and he whirled away, falling to his knees with the unexpected pain. His closest companion turned panicked eyes to where the slim girl stood at the rear of the attackers. They made eye contact and he saw her drawing another of those cruel darts from her quiver. And all the time she did so, her eyes were fixed intently on him.

It was more than he could bear. He turned and ran for the shelter of a nearby alley. Another man, seeing him run, went after him. Then a third and a fourth did likewise.

Hal, cutting and stabbing at a particularly persistent opponent, saw them going.

"They're running! They're breaking!" he shouted.

The man he was engaged with couldn't help his automatic reaction. Fearing that he was being left to face these grim attackers by himself, he glanced quickly over his shoulder. He saw that his comrades were breaking away, just as Hal's sword sank into his thigh and his leg gave out under him, sending him sprawling helplessly onto the broken timber and rocks underfoot.

The fear of those at the rear of the defending force was contagious. Petrac, their leader, was dead. So was Agrav, the man who had briefly attempted to take his place. The diminishing number of men facing the Skandian attack were now stricken by the fear that they would be left unsupported.

They, too, broke and ran.

The cheering, triumphant Herons started after them, but Thorn's huge voice stopped them in their tracks.

"Stop!" he roared. "Stop now!"

If they went streaming off into the narrow streets now, without formation or any real thought of where they were going or what they were doing, he could lose half of them. Better to let the Magyarans escape and run, and keep his young fighters in a tight-knit group.

But not all the Magyarans escaped. Before they reached the haven of a narrow alleyway behind them, another of Lydia's darts found its target and sent a pirate sprawling facedown on the cobbles.

Gradually, the battle madness went out of the Herons' eyes as they took stock. A few of them were slightly wounded. At their feet, half a dozen Magyarans were sprawled, some dead, all of them out of action.

All in all, Thorn thought, they'd handled themselves pretty well. He smiled at Hal.

"You did well," he said. "You and Stig and all of them. Very well indeed."

Hal nodded wearily. Now that it was all over, a shudder of fear ran through him. In his mind's eye, he could see that first spear thrust again. Only this time, it slipped past his shield and into his body. He closed his eyes for a second or two, dispelling the image. Then he opened them and looked at Thorn, hefting his Gallican shield higher on his left arm as he did so.

"Let's find Zavac," he said.

Thorn assessed his troops. They'd done well so far but he was conscious of the fact that they were a small group and any Magyaran band they met would probably outnumber them. There was no way of knowing what lay ahead, he thought warily, or what weapons the Magyarans might have waiting for them. It would be necessary to keep discipline tight. They'd have to move as a cohesive unit, not straggle through the town.

He beckoned to one of the Limmatans. "Which is the quickest way to the waterfront?"

The battle was obviously going against the invaders. The small number of men at the beach gate, and the lack of reinforcements, tended to point that way. If Zavac was like most seamen, he'd be heading back to his ship. That was where he'd feel most secure as things turned against him. Thorn, a veteran of countless raids, knew that feeling all too well.

The townsman paused, gathered his thoughts, then pointed to an alley on the left.

"That'll take us to the town square," he said. "The main street to the harbor runs off the square."

Thorn gestured toward the alley with his club-hand.

"Then lead on. Stig, go with him. Stay ten meters ahead of us but don't get out of sight. Stop at every corner or twist in the road until we're up with you. The rest of you, two files, either side of the street. Three meters between each man. Don't bunch up and make an easy target."

As it turned out, their progress to the town square was anticlimactic. Whatever Magyaran forces were left in Limmat were fully occupied by the Skandians and Barat's men, advancing on them in a pincer movement. The Herons encountered only a few scattered groups of two or three pirates, who, seeing the disciplined formation of armed men approaching, took to their heels.

The more immediate problem became the townspeople of Limmat themselves. As they realized the invaders were fleeing, they began to pour out onto the streets to welcome and embrace their liberators. Thorn, in the lead, shoved his way through the well-wishers, the Herons following in his wake.

The first large party of armed men they encountered was in the town square itself. Stig and the Limmatan guide reached the end of a narrow cross street that led to the square and stepped out into the open ground. Stig stopped, shield coming up, ax going back. Behind him, seeing the warning posture, Thorn urged the rest of the small force to close up.

There were more than thirty armed men on the opposite side of the square, emerging from a similar side street. Seeing Stig, the first of them also fell into a combat-ready pose. Then both sides relaxed.

"They're Barat's men," the townsman with Stig said. He advanced across the square, laughing and calling greetings to his countrymen. At the sight of him, they lowered their weapons and moved forward, embracing him and laughing in their turn. Stig waited till the rest of the party had joined him, then they moved out into the square together, meeting their allies halfway across.

The two groups mingled together for a few minutes, exchanging jokes and accounts of the battle so far.

Jonas, the Limmatan second in command, moved to where Hal stood and shook his hand gratefully.

"That was great work!" he said enthusiastically. "You drew their forces completely away from the east wall. We simply climbed over with nobody to stop us. Any Magyarans we've seen since then ran like rabbits."

Inside the counting house, Rikard and his small band peered fearfully out at the sight of their enemies laughing and joking together. Rikard cursed his luck. He had waited too long to escape to the ship, unsure where Zavac and his men had gone and suspecting that they might return at any minute. Now, it was too late. The enemy were outside.

"Must be forty or fifty of them," Rikard muttered.

One of his crew, who was not renowned for fast thinking— or, indeed, any sort of thinking—fingered the edge of his heavy cutlass.

"Will we attack, chief?" the man said. He was used to attacking unarmed and helpless civilians and, as a result, expected any enemy he faced to turn and run.

Rikard looked at him with disdain.

"Attack? Are you insane, or just stupid? They're all armed men out there. They outnumber us four to one and they're looking for revenge. We need to find a back way out of here. We're getting away to the ship. And keep the noise down!" he added, in a savage whisper.

Quietly, the remaining men of *Stingray's* crew made their way to the rear of the counting house. By chance, they used the same back exit Zavac had chosen. Then, stealthily, they headed down the alley toward the quay, continually glancing back over their shoulders to where they could catch brief glimpses of the townspeople and Herons mingling together.

In the square, Barat pushed his way through the laughing jam of warriors. He could see Stig's tall form, standing head and shoulders above those around him as he talked with Jonas. The Limmatan commander shoved through to them, coming to a halt with his chest thrust out, a few centimeters from Stig's.

The *Heron's* first mate held out his hand in greeting.

"Barat," he said. "Good to see you."

Barat slapped the friendly hand aside. His face grew dark as he looked at the young, smiling face.

"You and I have a score to settle," he said. The men around them stepped back uncertainly. The Herons who had heard his words looked angry. His own men looked uncomfortable at his ungracious and threatening words.

Stig eyed him carefully. With a great effort, he held his own temper in check. Thorn, watching closely, marveled at how Stig had matured. A few months ago, Barat's action would have provoked an unthinking, aggressive response from Stig. The boy was growing up fast, he thought. Maybe it was something to do with the added responsibility he had shouldered as Hal's first mate, and as *Heron's* helmsman when she went into battle. But there was a limit to how much his barely restrained temper would bear.

"Settle down, Barat," Stig said in a calm voice. "We've just had a victory here. It's no time to start fighting among ourselves."

Barat let out a short bray of laughter. "I'm sure you don't want to start fighting now. Not when I'm ready for you! That's not your way, is it, you coward?"

Stig's face began to flush red. The Limmatans around them muttered uncomfortably at Barat's insult. Jonas stepped forward and laid a restraining hand on the battle commander's forearm.

"Barat, this is wrong. These Skandian boys have done us a great service today."

"Have they? They left the greater part of the fighting to us! Nice of them to turn up when it's all over!"

Jonas shook his head, perplexed.

"We were virtually unopposed!" he pointed out. "There were no defenders on the walls because Hal and his men drew them off. We've had minor injuries to two of our men. Do you call that *leaving the greater part of the fighting to us?*"

His comrades began to close in, voicing their agreement with Jonas's words with increasing force. But still Barat would not be placated. He jabbed his forefinger into Stig's chest.

"No matter what you say, Jonas, I have a score to settle!"

A deep voice interrupted him. "Then you'll settle it with me."

Thorn pushed his way through the crowd to confront Barat.

His left hand jabbed forward and he shoved the Limmatan back with surprising force. Barat recoiled several paces before he recovered. When he did, he found that Thorn had followed him, stepping close to him, thrusting his face into the Limmatan's.

"You preening idiot," Thorn continued. "I've just watched these boys fighting for your precious town. And nobody fought harder or better than Stig. Now, we don't have time to waste with you at the moment. We're after Zavac. But once we've got him in the bag, I'll be delighted to come back and split your skull for you. Just wait right here for me."

He brandished the massive studded club-hand under Barat's nose. Thorn's hair might have been gray and his clothes shabby, but he was a big man, massively built by Limmatan standards. The heavy club, and the ease with which he wielded it, was a daunting sight. Barat blanched. He opened his mouth to reply, then closed it.

Thorn turned away contemptuously. "Herons! Let's go! We've wasted enough time here and the job's not done yet!" He looked around, saw the Limmatan who had acted as their guide. "You! Which way to the quay?"

The man pointed to a broad street on the western side of the square.

"That'll take you straight to it," he said. "Do you want me to show you?"

Thorn studied the long, straight street. "I think we can find it," he said. Then, signaling for the crew to follow him, he strode purposefully across the square.

As they neared the harbor, Thorn heard the unmistakable

sounds of fighting ahead. Axes hammered onto shields, swords rang against each other. And over all, there were the sudden high-pitched cries of the wounded. He quickened his pace, settling into a steady jog, with the Herons behind him in two loose files.

With the collapse of the watchtowers, Magyaran resistance had largely collapsed as well. Svengal and his men had crossed the harbor, using the boom as a makeshift bridge, and climbed onto the eastern quay.

The survivors from that tower's garrison had seen them coming and fled before them, breaking into small groups and disappearing into the winding, narrow streets of the town. Svengal paused, then split his men into three squads to pursue the scattered Magyarans. Two of these, he sent off into the town itself. The third, he led down the quay. He could see the *Raven* moored deep inside the harbor. *Stingray*, the green ship, was moored alongside the quay only a hundred meters away. As he watched, a tongue of flame leapt up her mast. He could see several figures running away from the ship, heading down the quay toward *Raven*.

"Come on!" he yelled, and led the charge after them.

And that was the moment when Rikard and his ten men chose to emerge onto the quay in front of them.

It was ten against ten. So, as Svengal later recounted, it was no contest. He had the enemy outnumbered three to one.

The fight was short and sharp and vicious. Rikard saw the massive Skandian leader bearing down on him and shoved one of his own men between himself and Svengal, backing away in fright. The Magyarans were not prime fighting men. They were more accustomed to attacking relatively small crews of unarmed ships or making sneak attacks on an unprepared town like Limmat.

Faced with professional, and thoroughly eager, warriors like the Skandians, they had little chance. Svengal simply bowled over the man Rikard had tried to use as a shield, then cut down Rikard himself. Some of the pirates tried to stand against the wild northmen. They were either struck down by the flailing axes, or simply shoved off the edge of the quay into the harbor.

By the time Thorn and the Herons arrived at the harbor front, there were only three of the Magyarans left. They were on their knees, pleading for mercy. The Skandians, who had never been cold-blooded killers, granted it reluctantly. Some of them urged the Magyarans to pick up their weapons and try their luck once more. The pirates might have been cowardly, but they weren't stupid. They declined the invitation. The Skandians consoled themselves by delivering hearty kicks to their enemies' backsides, sending them sprawling.

Behind him, the *Stingray* was now fully aflame. It was too late to save her. The fire ran up her tarred rigging and spread along her hull, feeding off the tar-soaked wool that caulked the gaps between her planks.

Svengal spun round warily as he heard running feet approaching. Then he relaxed as he recognized Thorn, Hal and the others.

"You're late," he boomed.

"Seems as if you've got things under control," Thorn said. "Except for that, of course." He gestured to the *Stingray*. For a moment, the spectacle of the burning ship held them all, with a kind of horror. It was a sight no seaman could ever enjoy, even if the ship had belonged to an enemy.

Thorn glanced around at the bodies and the cowering survivors. "Is this all that's left?"

Svengal gestured toward the streets behind them. "The others have scattered through the town. I've sent men to winkle them out." He glanced to Hal and Stig. "Your boys did well," he said quietly. "Especially young Hal."

"They did," Thorn agreed. Then he looked around the quay. "Did you come across Zavac at all?"

Svengal shook his head. "Haven't seen him," he replied. "He'll turn up eventually. I'm looking forward to that."

"I think you might be disappointed," said Lydia, pointing down harbor. Unlike the others, she didn't have the same emotional reaction to the burning ship and she'd been looking around the harbor for signs of damage to her hometown.

Thorn and Svengal followed the direction of her pointing finger. At the bottom of the harbor, thirty meters from the shore, the *Raven* was hauling in her anchor. As they watched, a bank of oars appeared on either side of the black hull, as if by magic. They began their rhythmic rise and fall, and a small ripple of a bow wave formed at her prow.

"She'll never get out," Svengal said with satisfaction. "The boom is closed."

But Thorn was already looking in that direction and he could see the massive logs drifting in toward the western mole with the incoming tide.

"I think someone's just opened it," he said.

C urse him!" Svengal snarled. "That boom was our way back to *Wolfwind!*"

He looked around frantically, seeking another route to the far side of the harbor. The boom had obviously been cut loose and there was no way they could close it again and use it as a makeshift bridge.

"We can use the *Sea Lion!*" Stig shouted, pointing to the small ship Zavac had used as a decoy in his attack on the town. It was still moored alongside the mole, just inside the harbor mouth. But even as they began to run toward it, flames shot up its mast and rigging and spread rapidly along the hull.

Hal looked back down the harbor. Zavac's ship was moving slowly as he picked his way through the moored fishing boats and barges that filled the inner harbor.

"We've got to get back to the *Heron*," he said.

Thorn looked at him for a brief moment, then nodded. He glanced at Svengal.

"Are you coming with us?"

But the skirl shook his head. "We'll go round the bottom of the bay and back along the other side to *Wolfwind*. We may just make it in time."

He and his men started to run, spreading out in a line along the quay as the faster ones among them pulled away. The *Heron* crew hesitated, then Hal looked at the *Raven* again and felt hope surge in his heart.

"She's aground!" he yelled, pointing. As Zavac's own first mate had feared some days before, Zavac's lack of skill as a helmsman had come back to haunt him. He had misjudged a turn in the narrow channel and the *Raven* had run straight onto a mud bank. The mud had been exposed at low tide but the incoming flood had covered it with a few centimeters of water—enough to let the pirate ship run onto the bank for several meters before it stuck fast. They could see the evil shape of *Raven*'s ram above the surface—a heavy, iron-shod beam that projected from her bow—as she ran aground, and saw the mast tilt unnaturally as she fell off to one side on her keel.

Men were running frantically on her decks as they tried to free her. Some tried to reverse their oar strokes and row her off. But she was too deeply fixed in the mud. Others took oars and tried to pole off the bank with them. But the mud was too soft and they could gain no purchase as they tried to shove her free—the oar blades simply sank into the stinking, semiliquid ooze.

"She's trapped!" Stig said delightedly. "We've got her cornered."

"Not for long," Thorn told him. "The tide's coming in. She'll float free in ten minutes or so. But it does give us time to get to the *Heron*."

They turned and ran back down the wide thoroughfare that led to the town square. Behind them, the three surviving members of Rikard's crew looked at one another, not believing their luck. Furtively, they retrieved their weapons and scuttled into one of the narrow streets running off the quay. Somehow, they felt safer in the dark, narrow alleys than they would on the broad main streets.

But it was a false sense of security. They hadn't gone twenty meters when they rounded a corner and found themselves facing a large crowd of angry townspeople, all armed with makeshift weapons—clubs, knives, cleavers and even kitchen stools.

They were searching for Magyaran stragglers and they had several days of cruel mistreatment and brutality to avenge. After a few brief, violent moments, the townspeople moved on, leaving the broken, battered bodies of the pirates sprawled on the cobbles.

Hal's sword in its scabbard banged awkwardly against his side with each stride. His left arm was still encumbered with his shield, so he tugged his sword belt around until he could hold the scabbard steady with his right hand.

Not ideal conditions for running, he thought grimly. But they pounded down the broad main street, gradually stringing out as they went, the thudding of their feet on the cobbles echoing back from the faces of the buildings.

Stig was in the lead, with Jesper close behind him. Hal and Thorn were next, with Lydia easily keeping pace beside them.

They erupted into the square, drawing startled looks from the townspeople and warriors still gathered there. But there was no time to explain. Hal saw Stig hesitate, not sure which side street led back to the gate.

"Second left," Lydia called, pointing. Stig nodded and increased his pace again, Jesper on his heels.

It was late afternoon by now and the alleys and side streets were all deep in shadow. The sound of their running feet and the rattle of their equipment bounced back with increased volume from the close-set walls and houses. Stig glanced back at Jesper and grinned.

"Knew I should have run that race against Tursgud," he said. During their training period, Hal had selected Jesper ahead of Stig for a footrace. It had rankled Stig and, although he had acceded to Hal's decision, he had always believed his friend had made a mistake.

Jesper glared at him. "Is that so?" he said, and clapped on the pace, drawing level with Stig, then ahead of him. Stig accelerated as well, but Jesper continued to pull away, widening the gap between them. Watching Jesper's back draw farther away, Stig muttered to himself.

"Or not."

The smell of burned wood reached them before they came in sight of the shattered gate. But then they rounded a final corner and there it was. Through the gap, they could see the trim shape of the *Heron* drawn up on the beach. The incoming tide had crept up past her bow and she was beginning to lift and stir restlessly on the wavelets as they ran in. Stefan, who had been left behind to tend to Ingvar, had put out a beach anchor in their absence.

The crew poured through the gate onto the beach in a ragged

procession. Jesper paused halfway down the beach to retrieve the anchor, hefting it with him as he grinned triumphantly at Stig, several meters behind.

"You were saying about Tursgud?" he said.

Stig contrived to shrug, then reached for the anchor. "Let me have that. You're too delicate for such a load."

They shared the weight between them. As he reached the ship, Hal assessed the rapidly rising water around the ship's prow. Thankfully, they wouldn't need Ingvar's massive strength to shove off.

"Get aboard!" he yelled. "Stig, Jesper, shove us off!"

He ran aft to the tiller. The *Heron* slid smoothly into deeper water as Stig and Jesper shoved against the bow. As she began to move freely, they leapt for the bulwark. Willing hands heaved them aboard.

"Stig! Stefan! Starboard sail up!" Hal ordered.

The ropes shrieked through the wooden blocks as Stig and Stefan heaved, sending the starboard yardarm and sail soaring up the mast, to fall into place with a dull clunk. The ship began to turn head into the wind and Hal let it go for a few seconds, then worked the tiller back and forth to bring her farther around.

As Ulf and Wulf brought the sail in, the wind caught it and *Heron* turned faster. Thorn, without being told, leaned on the fin and shoved it down. Hal felt the positive response as the ship held course more firmly. He brought the *Heron* round until the wind was astern. Ulf and Wulf let the sail right out to run before the wind and *Heron* began to move faster and faster. The chuckle of waves against her bow and down her hull grew louder and more rapid.

Then she was cutting a white wake through the water as she headed for the harbor mouth to intercept *Raven*.

Thorn joined Hal at the steering platform. They cast anxious gazes ahead, looking for the first sight of *Raven* or *Wolfwind*.

"D'you think we're in time?" Hal asked. There was a note of desperation in his voice. They had been so close to catching Zavac. So close to retrieving the Andomal. So close to being able to return home.

Thorn shrugged. One thing he had learned over the years was not to prejudge a situation. If they were in time, so be it. If not, they'd have a long chase after the *Raven*.

The setting sun was dropping close to the horizon now, and they peered ahead into its glare, shading their eyes. So far, they could see nothing.

Svengal and his crew had rounded the bottom end of the harbor and were halfway back along the western quay before the *Raven*, raised by the incoming tide, finally drifted free of the mud bank.

As they ran past her, several of his men had yelled abuse and threats.

"Save your breath," Svengal told his crew. "You'll need it for running."

Now he glanced back over his shoulder as he saw the *Raven* begin to move again. *Wolfwind* was only a hundred meters away. If *Raven* had a clear run out of the harbor, they would have no chance of intercepting her. But she had to pick her way carefully through the moored fishing boats and punts, and after his mistake with the mud bank, Zavac wasn't taking any further chances. He was moving slowly and deliberately.

Then the Skandians were clambering aboard *Wolfwind* and there was an urgent rattle of oars as the crew ran them out through the oarlocks. Svengal had only ten men with him—the rest of his crew were still chasing down stray Magyarans in Limmat's back streets. But ten should be enough. They could hold Zavac and his men until Thorn and the Herons arrived to help.

They'd still be outnumbered by the pirates, he thought. But then a savage grin lit his face. Being outnumbered didn't worry him. They were Skandians, after all.

He heaved on the tiller as the men began to row, five oars a side. There was a narrow creek through the marshes where they'd left *Wolfwind*, leading to the open sea. Glancing toward the harbor, he could see *Raven's* tall mast, seeming to glide over the intervening sand and mud banks of the marshes. She was picking up speed as she came to the clearer waters of the harbor, but they had a lead over her.

It was going to be close, he thought. No time for fancy maneuvering—just cut her off, run alongside and board her. They'd have one chance. Once *Raven* reached the open sea, she'd outdistance them easily.

But *Wolfwind*, lightened as she was for her passage through the marshes, was responding more willingly than he'd expected. The men bent to their oars without any need for him to urge them, and the hull, drawing only twenty or thirty centimeters of water, flew down the creek and out into the open sea.

He glanced over his shoulder again. *Raven* was almost to the harbor mouth now and she'd hit full speed as well. The relative positions of the two ships remained constant and he realized they were holding their own with her. But his men would be the first to tire in this race, he knew.

Hurry up, Thorn, Svengal thought. We're going to need you.

As the *Raven* cleared the harbor mouth, Zavac pounded the tiller triumphantly. They were clear!

Then he felt a start of surprise as he saw another ship emerging from the marshes. He hadn't noticed it because, without its tall mast, *Wolfwind* was almost indistinguishable among the sand islands and scrubby trees of the marshes.

But now she was in clear water, a white bow wave at her prow. She looked like an overgrown rowing skiff, he thought. But she was moving fast through the water, and he could see the horned helmets of her crew.

Skandians.

His eyes narrowed as he studied her more closely and his spirits began to lift after the initial shock of seeing her. He counted the oars—five a side. So she had only ten men aboard her, while he had more than forty.

He could fight her, of course. But there was no need. And he had no wish to tangle with Skandians, even ten of them. Instead, he would bear away to port and leave her in his wake. The Skandian ship could never maintain the killing pace *Raven* was setting at the moment, not with only ten men rowing. He glanced at the sun, where it seemed to balance on the rim of the horizon, huge and red. In half an hour it would be full dark and he could make his escape. He leaned against the tiller, preparing to angle the ship to port, away from the speeding wolfship. The longer he could evade her, the more he could drag the race out, and the more tired the Skandian oarsmen would become.

And the farther behind the Skandian ship would fall. A smile began to spread over his face.

"Sail! Sail on the port bow."

Zavac's smile vanished in a flash. He swung round to where his lookout was pointing. It was that cursed ship with the strange triangular sail. She was running before the wind, spray sheeting up to either side as her bow cut through the water. She was farther out to sea and moving faster than he was. He could see that she would easily cut him off if he held to this course.

There was only one course open to him. Head back to starboard, back toward the wolfship.

And ram her.

Svengal saw the black ship turn back toward him. He'd felt a moment of triumph as *Heron* had appeared round the headland, speeding to cut the pirates off. Now it faded as he saw what Zavac had in mind. *Wolfwind* was the only obstacle between the *Raven* and freedom and he could see the pace of her oar strokes increasing as she headed straight for him.

"Pull!" he yelled at his crew. "Pull for your lives!"

If he turned away, the *Raven* would easily overtake *Wolfwind* and run her down. His only chance was to wait until the last moment, then cut across the *Raven's* bow. If he could evade that first attempt at ramming, they'd survive. Zavac wouldn't turn back for a second run, not with *Heron* speeding down on her. His men strained and heaved, gasping with the effort. Svengal leaned forward, frowning as he measured angles, speeds and distance, and saw they were going to pass clear. They would avoid that deadly ram by a few meters.

But that was enough. They'd won!

Then he realized that the *Raven* had increased her pace.

"There they are!"

It was Stig who screamed out the first sighting of the two ships. Hal craned down to peer under the sail and saw them.

Raven was heading away from *Wolfwind*, her oars whipping the water to foam down her flanks. But as they saw her, she obviously sighted them, and after a few seconds, she swung away, heading back to starboard.

Now *Raven* and *Wolfwind* were on a collision course as Svengal tried desperately to cut across *Raven's* bow. Thorn was beside Hal at the steering platform and they watched anxiously as the two ships drew closer and closer.

"She's going to make it!" Hal screamed. But Thorn's long experience told him otherwise.

"*Raven* is foxing," he said quietly. Hal's triumph turned to horror as he saw that Thorn was right. *Raven* had begun to move faster and her ram was heading like an arrow toward *Wolfwind's* fragile side.

• • • • •

At the last moment, seeing the collision was inevitable, Svengal played his final, desperate card.

As the *Raven's* bow bore down on them, he screamed an order to his men.

"Everyone to port! To port! Now!"

It seemed an insane order. The black ship was bearing down on their port side and every instinct was to escape to starboard. But Svengal knew if they did that, the hull would heel, exposing its lower reaches to the ram.

This way, the weight of the crew moving to port heeled the ship toward the *Raven*, so that when the ram smashed and splintered into their ship, it did so much higher on the hull.

The terrible, smashing impact threw Svengal from his feet and he sprawled on the deck, staring at the massive rent that the ram had torn in his ship. Vaguely, he could hear the triumphant shouts of the pirate crew, and the cries of several of his men who had been injured in the collision. But he regained his feet and yelled orders at his uninjured men.

"Fend her off! Get oars and fend her off!"

Seawater was pouring into the ship around the edges of the ram. It was an iron-shod beam that projected two meters ahead of the *Raven's* bow below the waterline, and it had punched a thirty-centimeter-square hole in *Wolfwind's* side. For the moment, it was still firmly embedded in the wolfship and, to a large extent, was plugging the hole. But when the *Raven's* crew backed water and withdrew, the sea would gush in and Svengal and his men would have only minutes to save their ship.

Four of his men had oars now and they were trying to shove

Wolfwind free of the ram. But the ships were jammed tight together and their efforts were having little effect. Then Svengal heard an order from the stern of the *Raven*, and her crew began to back water, withdrawing and leaving the *Wolfwind* to wallow with a huge gap in her bulwarks and hull. Now the sea rushed in in earnest and Svengal heard Zavac's mocking laughter as the *Raven* turned away and headed west.

Even as Svengal grabbed a bucket and yelled for his men to start bailing, he knew it was hopeless. He didn't have enough men to stem the flow of water into the stricken ship. Without help, she was doomed.

And he knew that losing *Wolfwind* like this would break Erak's heart. His old friend would never forgive him.

The crew of the *Heron* heard the crunching impact of the two ships across the intervening water. Someone groaned, probably without even realizing it, reflecting *Wolfwind*'s agony as the cruel ram savaged her sleek hull.

They saw Svengal's last-minute attempt to minimize the damage. But as the *Raven* backed slowly away, they could see that the rent in *Wolfwind*'s hull was too big for her reduced crew to handle.

Raven pulled away from *Wolfwind*, leaving her listing in the water. She would have sunk already, had it not been for the fact that, without mast and ballast stones, she was riding high in the water. But they could all see that she was critically hurt and it was only a matter of time before she went under.

"*Raven*'s turning toward us!" Edvin called from the bow.

Hal had thought that *Raven* would try to escape downwind.

Now he watched her shape foreshorten as the black ship swung to point at the *Heron*. It seemed that Zavac, having dealt with *Wolfwind*, was now seeking to make sure there was no ship left to pursue him. The oars began their steady beat, and a white bow wave formed at the pirate ship's waterline. As she rose on successive waves, the huge ram could be seen clearly.

Heron was angled to pass in front of the other ship. Hal crouched at the tiller, peering forward, using the forestay as a reference point. The angle to *Raven* was changing slowly, which indicated that the two ships were not on a collision course. If both ships maintained their current courses and speeds, the *Raven* would pass safely astern of the *Heron*. It would be close, but *Heron* would be safe.

Which was exactly what Svengal had thought, he realized. He narrowed his eyes, watching the rhythm of *Raven*'s oars. Her crew were rowing fast, but he thought they probably had a little in reserve.

Thorn had come aft and was standing close by him.

"Be careful," he warned.

Hal nodded. "I know." His gaze was still riveted on *Raven*, watching for the inevitable increase in pace. He glanced quickly forward, to where the inert form of Ingvar lay, wrapped in blankets on the deck by the mast. If only they had thought to reload the Mangler, he thought, he could give Zavac a nasty surprise as the ships drew closer. But then he dismissed the idea. In a tight situation like this, he knew he'd never hand the tiller over to Stig.

There! The oars had increased their rate, almost imperceptibly. But because he was looking for it, he saw it, saw the white bow wave grow a little higher. He crouched, using the forestay as a reference once more. Now the bearing to the *Raven* remained constant. They were on a collision course and the huge ram was aimed implacably at *Heron*'s heart.

Thorn saw his movement and realized, a few seconds after Hal had done, that the *Raven* had increased speed.

"He's—"

"I saw it."

The two ships swept on. Hal's forehead was creased in concentration and he was aware that every eye in the *Heron* was now on him. If he turned too soon, *Raven* could spin quickly after him and, in these conditions, under oars, catch him before he could gather speed and ram him from astern. To escape, he had to wait till the last moment, letting the other skipper believe he hadn't noticed the increase in speed, then slip past to safety so they were heading on diverging courses. Zavac would make one attempt, he thought. If Hal could keep his speed up and slip past, it would take too long for the pirate to go about and follow after him. Zavac would like to sink them, but his prime concern was to escape into the gathering darkness.

Raven was awfully close now. She loomed larger and larger in his vision, rising and falling on successive waves, revealing that awful ram like a huge fang. Thorn shifted nervously beside him. There wasn't a sound from the *Heron*'s crew.

For one terrible moment, Hal thought he had misjudged the distance. He pushed the sudden panic aside. He was about to cross *Raven*'s bow. He saw Zavac alter course slightly to port, then he shoved the tiller far out, yelling to Ulf and Wulf as he did so.

"Ease the sheets! Now!"

Heron had been sailing with the port sail hauled in tight. Now, as her head swung to port, the twins cast off the sheets and let the sail right out, with the wind behind it. They surged back the way they had been coming, too late for Zavac to counter their radical change of course. Silently, Hal gave thanks for the fin, and the extra speed and turning ability it gave the *Heron*.

Thorn was right, he thought. Speed and agility are our best weapons.

Zavac tried to match the *Heron*'s turn, hauling on the tiller to bring the bow round at them, but he was too late and the *Raven*'s response was too slow. The two ships slid past each other, *Raven*'s bow actually cutting through the disturbed water of their wake. The crew of the *Heron* cheered wildly as they saw the enraged pirates slipping past them.

At the *Raven*'s tiller, Zavac shook his fist, his face dark with rage. Then Hal saw a sudden panic sweep over the pirate as he ducked hurriedly beneath the bulwark, releasing the tiller as he did so, so that the *Raven* yawed wildly off course, angling still farther away from the *Heron*. A second after Zavac ducked, one of Lydia's darts hissed viciously through the space he'd occupied, to thud, quivering, into the stern post.

"Missed!" she said in disgust. Then the two ships were past each other and the gap between them was widening.

"*Raven*'s setting sail!" That was Edvin, in the bow. They all looked and saw the vast square sail falling from her crossyard, filling with the wind as her crew sheeted home. She began to gather speed.

Hal watched her, measuring wind and sea conditions. With the wind over her quarter like this, she was on her best point of sailing. But in these conditions, *Heron* was probably a little faster. All he had to do was turn after her.

"We could be up with her in two or three hours," he said.

Thorn nodded. But he said nothing. Hal was the skirl. The decision was his.

Hal watched in a frenzy of indecision. *Heron* was set on a course midway between *Raven* and *Wolfwind*. He had to choose. His gaze darted from the *Raven* back to *Wolfwind*, seeing the wolfship lying lower in the water with each minute. If he did nothing, she would sink and her crew would drown—within sight of land.

But the *Raven* was escaping. The *Raven*, and Zavac, with the Andomal, Skandia's greatest treasure.

She was escaping, and the only chance Hal and his friends had of redeeming themselves, of living a normal life in their home country, lay in going after her. If they didn't get the Andomal back, they would remain outcasts and pariahs, with no country, no future, no honor. With each minute, the *Raven* was pulling away. Soon it would be dark and he'd lose sight of her. She'd be gone.

And so would any hope for his future happiness. He had to decide. And he had to decide now.

He took a deep breath as he realized there was no decision to make. There was only one course he could follow. No matter what the future held, he would have to live with himself.

"Stand by to come about," he called. "We're going to help *Wolfwind*."

They came about in a smooth curve and began to accelerate toward the stricken wolfship.

"Get buckets and bailers!" Hal shouted. "Anything that'll hold water! Once we come alongside, get on board *Wolfwind* and start bailing!"

Lydia approached him. "Is there anything I can do?"

He nodded curtly. "Like the rest of them. Get hold of a bucket and bail the water out of her. We have to lighten her or she'll go down."

"Is there any way we can plug the hole?" she asked. But her voice was doubtful. They'd all seen the size of the ram on the front of the *Raven*. The hole it smashed in the hull could be anything up to half a meter wide. Hal glanced forward to where Ulf and Wulf were standing by, ready to trim the sheets.

"I'm working on that," he said. He glanced forward again. They had the port-side sail raised and he could see they would reach *Wolfwind* without needing to tack. Then he raised his voice. "Ulf! Wulf! Cut the starboard sail loose from the yardarm. Bring it with you when we board."

The twins nodded and reacted as one. Drawing their saxes, they began to cut through the two dozen small loops of rope that attached the sail to the slender yardarm. They bundled the heavy canvas up, ready to take it with them.

They were almost up to the wallowing wolfship now. Hal judged that the moment was right and called for the twins to let the sail fly loose. They coasted on, slowing gradually, until their bow was level with the wolfship's stern post. Stig was standing in the bow, ready with a length of rope. Hal nodded to himself in approval and gratitude. Stig was the ideal first mate. He didn't need to be told to do the obvious. As the two ships bumped gently together, he whipped the rope around *Wolfwind*'s stern post and made it fast, tying the two ships together, bow to stern.

We'll need to cut that in a hurry if *Wolfwind* goes down, Hal thought. Then he tied the tiller off and followed the rest of the crew as they rushed to board *Wolfwind*, buckets and bailers ready in hand. Ulf and Wulf waited for him by the mast, carrying the bundled starboard-side sail between them. Their expressions told him they had no idea what he had in mind, but they were ready to follow his orders instantly.

"Get aboard and go forward!" he ordered, and they followed him as he leapt across the narrow gap between the ships.

Immediately as his feet touched the wolfship's deck, he could feel how heavy she was with the water she'd taken on board. Whereas *Heron* rose and fell like a seabird on the waves, *Wolfwind* rode sluggishly, feeling as if she were more part of the ocean than riding on it.

He led the way past the frantically bailing members of the two crews. With extra hands to help, water was going over the side at an increased rate.

Svengal turned to him, a puzzled frown on his face as he saw the sail the twins were carrying.

"Nice of you to come," he said. "But we don't have a mast for that."

Hal pointed forward. "We'll slip it over the bow, then drag it aft under the hull until it covers the hole," he said. "It'll slow the water down."

Svengal's eyes widened in understanding.

"Good idea," he said. He turned and led the way toward the bow, threading his way through the mixed group of Herons and *Wolfwind* crew members, all busy hurling silver showers of water over the side.

They rapidly unfolded the sail, slipping it round the bow post, then let it slide down over the rounded bow until it was set under the hull. Ulf and Wulf took the starboard side. Hal and Svengal took the port side and they dragged the sail back along the hull until they reached the point where the *Raven's* ram had savaged the *Wolfwind's* planks.

"Just a moment," Hal said. He'd seen a discarded shield close to hand. He picked it up and shoved it down between the sailcloth and the hull, positioning it over the jagged hole. Then they hauled the sail tight until it was over the hole, holding the shield firmly in place as a plug. The inrush of water forced the sailcloth into the gaps around the shield.

"Haul it tight!" Hal called, and Svengal and the twins responded, heaving on the lines attached to either end of the sail. The canvas, heavy, closely woven and impregnated with oil, wasn't completely waterproof. But, combined with the shield, it served to seal off most of the water.

The torrent flooding into *Wolfwind* slowed to a trickle as they tied off the ends of the sail.

A few of *Wolfwind's* crew had turned to watch them as they put the sail in place. Svengal roared angrily at them.

"Get back to work!" he bellowed. "We're not out of the woods yet!"

Startled, they began to shower water over the side again. For a few minutes, there was no appreciable difference. Then, with eighteen people at work, bailing furiously, Hal felt the wolfship begin to lighten. He let out a deep breath of relief. While they'd been working to save the ship, he'd had a niggling worry that their efforts might be in vain and the *Wolfwind* would go under, dragging *Heron* with it. If that happened there would be enough debris and wreckage in the water for people to hold on to and stay afloat, he knew. But the unconscious Ingvar, laid out behind the *Heron's* mast, would almost certainly drown before anyone could reach him.

Now that the immediate threat was past, he stepped up onto the rail and turned to look after the rapidly disappearing form of the *Raven*.

Night was almost upon them and he only caught a brief glimpse of her sail in the distance before she faded into the gloom.

Svengal muttered a curse. "He's slipped away again," he said. "He has the luck of the devil, that one."

Thorn had approached while they were watching the pirate sail away. He nodded agreement.

"That's not surprising. I've heard the devil looks after his own," he said.

Hal shook his head, the taste of failure bitter in his mouth. They had come so close, he thought. Somehow, he couldn't think of a curse sufficiently vehement to match the moment. His shoulders sagged.

Thorn saw the movement and dropped his left hand onto his young friend's shoulder.

"Bear up," he said. "The day isn't a total loss. You've attacked a town, driven out or captured over a hundred bloodthirsty pirates, and you've saved *Wolfwind* and Svengal in the bargain."

"Erak might not care about me," Svengal added, with a grin. "But he'll be grateful that you saved *Wolfwind*."

Hal let his gaze switch between the two of them. "It won't make up for the Andomal, though, will it?"

The two old comrades exchanged a glance. Svengal shrugged. But Thorn answered.

"We'll worry about the Andomal later," he said. "For now, let's get this ship to the beach."

The light of a hundred torches flared and flickered around the square, shining on the faces of the towns-people celebrating their deliverance.

Whole sheep and pigs turned on spits in the center of the plaza, the fat dripping down from them and spluttering onto the red-hot beds of coals beneath them. The men turning the spits had their energy and enthusiasm maintained by tankards of ale from several casks that had been broached for the occasion. Off to the side, a stack of further casks waited to replace those being rapidly emptied.

It was a festive occasion and the crews of the *Heron* and *Wolfwind* were happy to join in. When the party died down, Hal planned to depart, sailing with the evening tide in pursuit of the *Raven*.

Although exactly where that pursuit would take him, he had no idea.

For the moment, however, they could enjoy the bustle and noise of the party, and the thanks of the townspeople who approached them.

Svengal grabbed a flagon of ale from a passing tray and clapped

Hal on the shoulder. "Wish we could come with you," Svengal was saying, shouting to make his voice carry over the hubbub of laughter and singing that filled the square.

Hal shrugged. "You need to get *Wolfwind* seaworthy again," he said. "That'll keep you busy for at least a month."

Once they'd beached the wolfship, Hal and Svengal had assessed the damage that *Raven*'s ram had done. Several frames were smashed and would need to be replaced, along with two of the main stringers that ran the length of the ship. Of course, there were shattered planks to be torn out and replaced as well. Hal's experience in Anders's shipyard told him that the ship needed major repairs. A quick patch-up job wouldn't serve.

Svengal nodded morosely. "That's true," he said. "I need to get her in shape before I take her back to Erak."

Hal grinned sympathetically. The Oberjarl's fondness for his ship, and his protective instincts about her, were well-known in Hallasholm. They stood in companionable silence for a while, watching Stig's slightly overwhelmed, but thoroughly delighted, reaction as a succession of attractive young girls from the town claimed him as a dance partner. Then a thought struck Svengal and he turned, looking round the packed square.

"Where's Thorn?" he said. "Not like him to miss a party."

Hal pursed his lips. It had occurred to him that Thorn might not care to be surrounded by the temptation of open ale barrels and flasks of brandy.

"I'm not sure," he said. "He was here earlier, then he grabbed Stefan by the arm and spirited him away. I don't know where they went."

"Hmmm," Svengal said thoughtfully. "I'll warrant he's up to something."

The Limmat jail was a squat, solid building of brick and timber, built over a deep cellar, where the cells were concentrated. Like most jails, it was dimly lit, with only the central room that accommodated the warders having more than basic lighting.

A single torch was mounted on the wall above the massive metal-bound oak doorway. Its flame cast a flickering circle of yellow light on the cobbles beneath it. Two figures emerged from a side street and approached the door. The faint sounds of the party in the town square carried to them.

One of the men was a Skandian. His massive frame and horned helmet were unmistakable. The other was smaller and slighter in build, and wrapped in a heavy cloak.

"Ready, Stefan?" Thorn asked. His companion held up a hand.

"Just a minute," he said. Then, he gathered his thoughts and squared his shoulders, letting the hood of his cloak fall forward to further shade his features.

"All right, I think I'm ready now," he said. But the voice was no longer Stefan's. It was a perfect rendition of Barat's voice.

Thorn shook his head admiringly. "I don't know how you do it."

Then, as Stefan nodded, Thorn rapped on the door with his wooden hook. There was a long pause, then they heard slow footsteps dragging toward the door from the inside. There was a rattle of a key in the lock, and the door was dragged half open, its bottom edge scraping on the flagstone floor.

"Yes?" The jailer was the night guard. He peered around the half-open door at them, his body blocking the way in. He was overweight and had a heavy limp, which accounted for the slow footsteps. He was also in a less-than-amiable mood, having been roused from his post-dinner nap by the peremptory hammering on the door. People didn't come to the jail often. And they rarely came at night.

"I'm Barat Tumansky," Stefan snapped. "I need to question the prisoner Rikard. It's urgent."

The jailer remained blocking the doorway. He glanced back over his shoulder into the dark corridors behind him.

"It's late," he said grumpily. Thorn opened his mouth to speak, but Stefan beat him to it, drawing himself up and replying angrily.

"I know it's late!" he snapped. "I said this is urgent! I need to question him now. Hurry, you idiot! I'm late for the festivities as it is!"

He jerked a thumb in the general direction of the sounds of revelry coming from the square. The jailer wavered, but remained standing fast. Stefan's voice cracked out in an unmistakable tone of command.

"Let me pass! Do you know who I am?"

The jailer, cowed, moved to one side, bowing his head slightly. He dragged the door open and admitted the two men. Stefan snapped his fingers impatiently.

"Right! Where is he? Get moving, you fool! I don't have all night!"

Slowly, the jailer led the way to a stone staircase leading down to the cells below ground level. He wheezed his way down, Stefan close behind him and Thorn following. They emerged at the bottom of the stairs into a long, low corridor, lit at irregular intervals by torches. There was more shadow than light down here, Stefan thought.

The jailer indicated one of the cell doors, halfway along the corridor.

"He's in there," he said. Stefan's barely controlled anger exploded.

"D'you expect me to whisper to him through the keyhole? Open it, you blockhead!"

Mumbling to himself, the jailer dragged his way to the door, fumbled with a ring of keys on his belt, then opened the door. The hinges squealed as he did so.

"I'll have to stay while you talk to him," he said. His tone said that he wasn't sure Stefan would agree to that. And he was right.

"The blazes you will! Get back upstairs at once. I'm not having you spying on what I'm doing and saying! Get out of here!"

"But . . . the prisoner—" the jailer began uncertainly.

Stefan cut him off briskly. "My man here will make sure he doesn't get away." He indicated the massive form of Thorn, looming in the dim light beside him. "Now, get back to your post!"

Grumbling to himself, the night guard shambled away, mounting the stairs with several backward glances. Thorn was fascinated to see how the assumption of authority could cow such a subservient figure so quickly. Pretend you have the authority, he thought, and most people will give it to you.

As the jailer reached the top step, Thorn gestured to the open door.

"Come on," he said, pausing to add, "Great work, by the way."

Rikard looked up incuriously as the two figures entered his cell. He was one of the few surviving pirates to have been captured. Many had fled into the surrounding countryside. More than half had been killed in the battle, and the others had escaped on the *Raven*.

Rikard had been involved in a brief fight with Svengal and his men on the quayside. He had unwisely singled out Svengal as his opponent and had suffered a blow from the Skandian's ax as a result.

But for once, Svengal had been slightly off target and the blow had glanced off the pirate's helmet. It had been enough, however, to leave him lying stunned, as if dead, by the quayside. Hours after the battle was over, he had regained consciousness, and was quickly taken prisoner as he staggered, dazed and giddy, through the streets.

Now that the jailer was gone, it was Thorn who took over the role of leader. He sat opposite Rikard, who was seated on a bench at a plain wooden table.

"I want information," he said, getting straight to the point.

Rikard sneered at him. "Why should I give it to you?"

"Because I can get you out of here," Thorn said. He noticed a quickening of interest in the other man's eyes and continued. "You know what'll happen to you if I don't?"

"They plan to hang me," Rikard said. His voice caught on the word *hang*.

Thorn nodded. "That's right. That's what happens to pirates. People hang them. Not a nice way to go, either."

"Did you come here to torment me?" Rikard demanded, but Thorn shook his head.

"Not at all. I came to give you a chance to get away. Just as long as you tell me what I want to know."

But Rikard was watching him suspiciously. "Why would you want to help me?"

"I don't," Thorn replied. "As far as I'm concerned, they can hang you as high as last week's washing. Or not. I don't care either way. What I do care about is where Zavac is headed. And I think you can tell me."

He was watching the man's eyes closely and even in the dim light of the candle he saw a spark there. Rikard knew where Zavac was heading. Thorn was sure of it.

"Tell me what I want to know and I'll get you out of here," he said.

Rikard lowered his head, peering warily up at Thorn from under his eyebrows. "How can I trust you? If I tell you, you could just as easily leave me here."

The massive Skandian shrugged his shoulders. "That's true. But I wasn't planning on turning you loose once you told me. You could be lying to me. I plan to take you along with us until we know you're telling the truth. Then I'll set you free."

He waited while Rikard digested that information, then added in a softer voice, "Or, if I decide you've been lying to me, I will simply drop you overboard."

There was a long pause. Then Thorn spoke again. "Your choice. But we're running out of time."

Rikard glanced at the open door. "What about the guard?"

Thorn let out a short bark of laughter. "Do you think that sack of lard could stop me?"

Rikard shook his head slowly, considering.

"All right," he said finally. "But I'm not telling you until we're at sea."

Barat moved to a podium set to one side of the square, in front of the counting house. He held up his hands for silence and gradually the hubbub of noise and chatter died away. A few people called out his name, and added exclamations of praise. He smiled graciously in their direction, nodding to each one.

"Thank you, friends," he said, when the voices finally died away and there was an expectant hush. He smiled then, looking around the sea of faces before him.

"My friends, it's been a terrible time we've been through. We've all lost friends and relatives, and we'll mourn for them in days to come."

There was a mumble of agreement from the crowd. Then Barat raised his voice in a positive note.

"But tonight, let's celebrate! Let's celebrate that we've thrown off the yoke the invaders tried to put on us. We've faced them and fought them and defeated them!"

A spontaneous cheer rang around the square. Or was it spontaneous, Hal thought. He could see several of Barat's troops leading the cheering nearby.

"I want to say how proud I am of my men. My fellow Limmatans who stormed the wall with me and drove the invaders out!"

Again, cheering interrupted him. He held up his hands for

silence. "And in particular, I want to give praise to a young lady who fought as bravely as any man in the battle." He looked around the square. "Lydia? Where are you? Join me here."

He knew she was standing a few meters from the podium, where she had been talking to several old friends and neighbors. He pointed at her now and gestured for her to join him. Annoyed, she shook her head. But the crowd began to chant her name.

"Lydia! Lydia! Lydia!"

Realizing there was no way out of it, she pushed her way through and stepped up onto the podium, ignoring Barat's outstretched hand. Her face was flushed red. He quickly drew her to him, one arm around her.

Reluctantly, she resisted the temptation to pull away.

"Here she is, my friends. No braver girl ever graced this town, and I'm proud to tell you, she's going to be my wife!"

"What?" Stig said aloud. Then he saw Lydia's reaction, saw her head shaking as she spoke angrily to Barat. But the crowd had gone wild with the idea, and Barat merely smiled at her as they cheered. Crowds love a good romance, after all, and Barat was aware of the fact.

He held up his hand for silence again. When the noise died down, he spoke in a serious tone.

"As I said, we've all lost friends this past week or two. But we didn't give in when things looked blackest. We kept fighting!"

"You ran off into the marshes, more like," said Edvin angrily. The other Heron crew members muttered agreement as Barat continued.

"We came up with a plan for our counterattack, a counterattack that I led in person. And we won through!"

"Funny," Stefan said, following Edvin's lead, "I could have sworn that *Hal* came up with that plan. Don't remember Barat did much but object."

"Shut up," Hal said, through set teeth.

Barat glanced over the heads of the crowd then to where he could see the small knot of Skandians.

"And I'd like to thank our allies for providing the diversion that helped us prevail." He led a gracious round of applause then, while the Herons seethed.

Jesper turned to Hal, who was watching, stony faced. "You knocked down the watchtowers. You transported Barat and his men to the east wall. You beat back the defenders at the beach gate. You sent Zavac and his men packing! What did he do? He climbed a wall!"

"Let it go," Hal said. "Can't you see he's running for office? He's planning to get himself elected mayor."

The former mayor of Limmat had been one of the pirates' first targets. He had been killed in the early days. Now, Hal realized, Barat was using the respect he'd gained as leader of the Limmatan forces, and the positive emotion of his public proposal to Lydia, to cement his own position as the new leader of the town. As he had the thought, Hal realized that Lydia was no longer on the podium. In the past few minutes, she had slipped away somewhere.

"So, my friends," Barat was concluding, "let me say to you all, if there is any way I can serve you or our town in the coming weeks, then I humbly make myself available."

There was a ripple of applause and appreciation through the crowd. He smiled, then raised his hands to them all.

"But tonight let's celebrate our victory. Tomorrow, we can start picking up the pieces and making this town great again."

The crowd cheered and he held up both hands to them. He glanced around, aware that Lydia was no longer beside him. A quick frown crossed his face, then he covered it with a smile, bowing and waving to the crowd.

"Come on," Hal said to his crew. "Let's get out of here before I'm ill."

Svengal and some of *Wolfwind*'s crew accompanied them to the harbor, where the *Heron* was moored alongside the quay. Ingvar was sleeping amidships on a sheepskin, covered with blankets. Edvin went to check him, saw that he was sleeping peacefully and nodded reassurance to Hal. They had discussed whether it might be better to leave Ingvar to recover in Limmat, but once he had regained consciousness, the big boy had vetoed that idea with great vigor.

"I'm a Heron," he said decisively. "I'm coming with you." And since he seemed to be recovering from his wound quite well, Hal had agreed. It wouldn't be the same without Ingvar, he thought.

Thorn and Stefan were waiting at the ship when they arrived, and once he had seen that Ingvar was comfortable, Hal eyed them curiously.

"What have you two been up to?"

Stefan's grin almost split his face apart. "We broke Rikard out of jail," he said. He gestured to a tarpaulin piled untidily in the forward rowing benches. "He's under there."

Hal said nothing for several minutes. Then he looked Thorn straight in the eye.

"All right," he said. "Why?"

"He knows where Zavac is heading," Thorn told him. "I made a deal with him. He tells us and we help him get away."

"Exactly how did you break him out?" Hal asked.

Thorn hesitated but Stefan was ready with the answer.

"Thorn thumped the jailer. Knocked him cold. Then we just walked out."

"You . . . thumped . . . the jailer. Did he recognize you?" Hal asked.

Thorn shrugged. "Not a chance. He'll probably confuse me with some other one-armed Skandian."

"And what if Rikard is lying?"

"We'll hold on to him until we know one way or the other. If he is lying, I'll toss him overboard."

Hal screwed up his lips while he thought about it. "Fair enough," he said. "But let's get going before the jailer wakes up and raises the alarm."

They clambered down into the *Heron*. Svengal and two of his crewmen made ready to cast off the bow and stern lines as the crew settled into the rowing benches.

"I'll send a man along to open the boom," Svengal said.

Hal nodded his thanks. "Fair winds, Svengal," he said.

"Fair winds, Hal. We'll see you again in Hallasholm."

"With the Andomal," Hal said firmly. He glanced around, making sure the way was clear. He was about to signal Svengal's men to cast off when a slim figure darted out of the shadows.

"Hold it a moment," Hal said to the line handlers. "Lydia? Is that you?"

The girl had paused at the edge of the pier. She looked down into the *Heron*, looking at the faces turned up to her. She saw several smiles of welcome.

"I want to come with you," she said.

Hal went to speak, stopped, not sure what to say. So she continued.

"You heard him, didn't you? I couldn't stand to stay here with that pompous, overbearing prat of a man. How dare he announce that I would marry him? How dare he?"

Still Hal said nothing, lost for words. She went on desperately.

"If I stay here, I'll stick one of my darts in him before the month is out. Besides, I still have a score to settle with Zavac. His men killed my grandfather."

"Let her come, Hal," Stig said, and the rest of the crew chorused their agreement. Hal threw his hands in the air in a gesture of defeat.

"Why not? Who am I to refuse? Anyone else want to come? How about you, Svengal?"

The wolfship skirl grinned. "I'd love to, as a matter of fact. But I'd better get *Wolfwind* repaired."

Lydia had her bedroll, a rucksack and her weapons fastened in a bundle and she tossed them down to Wulf, who caught them easily. Then as she prepared to climb down into the ship, Stig stepped forward, grinning, his arms out to help her down.

She eyed him disdainfully.

"Back off, Skandian," she said. "Just because I don't fancy Barat doesn't mean I do fancy you."

She dropped easily down into the boat as Stig backed away, turning his gesture into a courtly bow.

Thorn cast his eyes to the sky as the *Heron* pulled away from the quay.

"Oh, it's going to be *such* an interesting voyage," he said.